TALES OF THE METRIC SYSTEM

MODERN
African Writing
from Ohio University Press
Ghirmai Negash, General Editor
Laura Murphy, Series Editor

This series brings the best African writing to an international audience. These groundbreaking novels, memoirs, and other literary works showcase the most talented writers of the African continent. The series also features works of significant historical and literary value translated into English for the first time. Moderately priced, the books chosen for the series are well crafted, original, and ideally suited for African studies classes, world literature classes, or any reader looking for compelling voices of diverse African perspectives.

Books in the series are published with support from the Ohio University National Resource Center for African Studies.

TALES OF THE METRIC SYSTEM

A NOVEL

IMRAAN COOVADIA

OHIO UNIVERSITY PRESS　ATHENS

Tales of the Metric System © 2014 Imraan Coovadia
By Agreement with Pontas Literary & Film Agency

Published in the United States by
Ohio University Press, Athens, Ohio 45701
ohioswallow.com

Printed in the United States of America
Ohio University Press books are printed on acid-free paper ⊗ ™

First published in 2014 by Umuzi
an imprint of Random House Struik (Pty) Ltd
Company Reg No 1966/003153/07
Estuaries No 4, Oxbow Crescent, Century Avenue, Century City,
7441, South Africa
PO Box 1144, Cape Town, 8000, South Africa
umuzi@randomstruik.co.za • www.randomstruik.co.za

Cover design and illustrations by Joey Hi-Fi
Author photograph by Victor Dlamini

26 25 24 23 22 21 20 19 18 17 16   5 4 3 2 1

ISBNS:
978-0-8214-2225-0 (hardcover)
978-0-8214-2226-7 (paperback)
978-0-8214-4564-8 (electronic)

'I set forth how I viewed the history of my people in the light of God's Word. I began by addressing my hearers: "People of the Lord, you old people of the country, you foreigners, you newcomers, yes, even you thieves and murderers!"'

– Paul Kruger, *Memoirs*

CONTENTS

1970
SCHOOL TIME

The Jaguar wouldn't start. Ann sat behind the leather steering wheel and watched the ruby-red light fade in the dashboard. Neil's late mother had donated the car to them at a time when she had been lying in a hospital and writing letters to parliament in fountain pen despite a catheter in the neck. It was difficult to refuse her mother-in-law's gifts. Sometimes the old woman seemed to have crockery in her face.

Ann spied her neighbour on the porch. She got out of the car and tried to attract his attention. Mackenzie was her shot. He liked to help her. When the mains tripped Mackenzie had his man bring the step ladder and climbed up to the panel. He would reset the stiff green switches, one by one, until he found the broken fuse. In July the Security Branch had arrived while Neil was away. Mackenzie had sat in the lounge for moral support. He had read his own magazines on the couch—*Scope*, for men, and *Creamer's Illustrated News*, an engineering gazette—while the policemen had examined Neil's desk, checked the numbers circled in the directory, and searched the cupboards.

Mackenzie brought his servant, a muscular old man who must have been in his sixties and who sat perfectly upright in the back of the Hillman Avenger when accompanying his employer.

For a moment Ann thought Mackenzie was going to put his hand on her shoulder. Instead he placed it on the bonnet of the car.

—It's the salt in the air. The same engine that runs for five years in London may only survive eighteen months out here. But your husband must see to the maintenance.

—I'll tell him.

—Get in and release the handbrake. This fellow will push you to the top and you can start the engine. Coming back you should be fine. The battery will charge on the motorway.

Mackenzie's man, as old as he was, started to push, the thick brown veins standing out on his dark arms. He began to perspire immediately, his body shining, and allowed the car to stop at the top of the road. The engine caught on the downhill. By the time she went past the Caltex garage the car was moving fast.

To see Mackenzie's servant in the mirror, standing exhausted in the road, reminded Ann that she had never learned the man's name. She wasn't sure of her own. From her first husband she was Ann Rabie. She had once been Ann Bowen, whose father, commodore in the Royal Navy, met her mother at a ball during shore leave in Durban. For some reason which lay between herself and Neil she had never completed the switch to Ann Hunter.

In town, she parked near Greenacres. The shop assistants were dressing the plaster-of-Paris mannequins in the window, holding pins in their mouths as they went over the clothes. Something to do with the wirework and the gluey brush strokes on the dummies' arms disturbed Ann. They would hex the car. After her conversation with Lavigne, she would have to wait in their papier-mâché company until the truck arrived from the Automobile Association.

She hurried. Her son Paul had been caught with alcohol on the school grounds. Curzon College was strict. The penalty could be as severe as a suspension for the whole of Michaelmas term. Lavigne represented the school board. In his first letter home, Paul said Lavigne defined College as a place where punctuality came second to godliness. She couldn't afford to be twenty minutes late.

She went past the telephone booths occupied by white men and women. The newsagent was setting out the overseas newspapers, his blue shirt rolled up above the elbow. The shops sold signs and flags claiming the province of Natal as the last outpost of the British Empire. Curzon College was a school of the same empire, attracting the sons of factory owners and Midlands farmers, members of the United Party who proposed extending the franchise to educated Bantus, Durban lawyers and bank managers.

Ann found Lavigne at the entrance of the Royal Hotel. He was compact in the shoulders, wearing a gold-buttoned blazer, grey trousers, and black shoes, which she imagined him brushing as fiercely as his teeth. Every Curzon College man, new boy or prefect, housemaster or headmaster, shone his own shoes.

Lavigne stood in his perfectly buffed shoes between the doormen, looking straight onto the road as the tram came clattering along, and didn't see her until she was at his side.

—Mr Lavigne, Edward, I apologise for being late. My car refused to start. Every red light I was petrified it would stall.

—It's of no consequence, Mrs Rabie. I must remind you, however, that my next appointment is set for 1 p.m. across town. These few days I spend in town are booked end to end. I reserved a table in the tea room.

Ann went past the doormen, noting their long white leather gloves and high red hats.

—Are you staying here?

—College has an arrangement for a reduced rate.

—I wasn't objecting.

—The chairman of the hotel company is an Old Boy. It is the express wish of the board that the school maintain a certain standard. It should be this way to the tea room.

Ann went past wallpapered rooms and a procession of fronded plants in big brass pots. There was a long brass-framed mirror beside the lift in which she caught sight of herself while a clerk in a waistcoat pushed a cart in the opposite direction. The staff were lying in wait, looking for any reason to approach a visitor. Since returning from Paris, she had started to resent the omnipresence of servants and clerks over here.

The tea room was cordoned off by a rope looped through the eyes of four gleaming brass stands. She and Lavigne sat across from one another at a table beside the wall. The waiter, an Indian man with the pitted skin of a smallpox victim, wore a turban in addition to the stiff red tunic prescribed by the hotel. He spoke through his long moustache as he distributed the items for tea, placing them on the clean linen as if setting up his side of a chessboard, and then retired to his post to stand and watch.

Neil was right. To be a so-called European, here where you were supposed to be top of the heap, was a predicament. You were under surveillance, first of all by other Europeans, and second by the natives, who might have something to gain or to lose, and by Indian waiters beneath their turbans. European women were the most severe on women like Ann. She couldn't escape the suspicion that, beneath his unshakeable business manners, Lavigne was acting to punish her on behalf of the general opinion.

—Mrs Rabie.

—Call me Ann.

—Ann, then. I have followed Paul since he entered the school in standard seven. I believe he won a scholarship at that time, a minor exhibition. Subsequently I acted as his housemaster, not to say his Geography teacher. I am delegated to take care of our best young scholars, the ones who might proceed to Cambridge. After the last rugby match, I invited Paul, along with three other promising young men, to dine at the Balfour Hotel.

—I know you have a good relationship, Edward. Whatever has happened has never altered my son's loyalty to the school.

—Loyalty is a virtue the school endeavours to inculcate. Allow me to do the honours.

Lavigne poured the tea through the strainer, offering her the first cup without turning his face. He added a sugar cube to his own cup and then two drops of milk as carefully as if he were using an eye-dropper. He sat up straight and drank, his blue blazer with its heavy gold buttons done up and his long hands almost disappearing into the sleeves. She saw that he was wearing cufflinks and remembered Neil's pair, inherited from his father, which had been borrowed and never returned by Sartre.

—I regret you and your husband have been unable to attend any of the important matches that make up our calendar.

—My husband is busy, Edward. He has taken a big part at the university since we came back from Paris. Sometimes it means that other things go undone.

—There's no obligation whatsoever. Some of the boys travel from homes in Johannesburg or London. Others come from remote farms located in Rhodesia. We understand that parents have different circumstances. Nevertheless, it is a shame that our first real conversation should be under these circumstances.

—I agree.

—Then we understand each other. You understand the situation. A prefect brought his suspicions to me. Naturally it fell to me to investigate and to search Paul's locker. That's when I found the spirits.

—Should you be encouraging the boys to spy on each other?

—Spying is not a term I would use. The prefects have a duty to keep good order in the houses. The same system is in effect at leading schools in the United Kingdom, so there can be no question of our fairness in this matter. I found two bottles of Klipdrift, cheap brandy. Paul has refused to explain their provenance, which has only worsened his situation. Did he bring the brandy from home? Some students have been known to raid their fathers' liquor cabinets in an attempt to win popularity.

—That doesn't sound like Paul. But Neil doesn't touch spirits. There is usually some wine in the house. I sometimes have a glass in the evening.

—And that's no sin.

Lavigne and his dry laugh acted on her nerves. There was some intimacy in their conversation which Ann disliked, as if the housemaster wanted to show that he was in on her secrets. She thought that he didn't mind offending her. She watched him more closely. Even in Neil's utopia there would be a Lavigne.

—Paul probably went to an Indian shop, Mrs Rabie. They operate just beyond the limits of the Curzon estate. By law, they cannot obtain freehold in the area. So who rents them the land? At the board's request, I am investigating the proprietors who allow these traders to operate. When we discover the names of the culprits we will take action. They must conform, or their tenants will have their licences revoked.

—It sounds severe, Edward.

—Severity is called for. I am not a racialist, believe you me, but I know that there will never be a peaceful settlement in the country until we have brought everyone up to a certain standard. I take an interest in the university. In which department does your husband work?

—Neil's in Philosophy. We came back early from Paris so he could take up the position. I would have stayed in France longer if I could have. I married early, the first time, and never had a year to wander around Europe.

Ann wasn't sure why she was saying more than she had to. She tried to be on good terms with other people. She wanted to help Paul.

—I had three years on the continent, Mrs Rabie, at Oxford. It convinced me that my place was here, because this is where our civilisation is being put to the test.

Lavigne excused himself for the toilet. Ann watched his solid figure striding down the corridor, confident that this life and the next belonged to him. In his Anglican afterlife he would shake hands with the boys whose backsides he had deliciously caned in the privacy of his study. They would thank him for putting them on the right track.

Ann was born Catholic, the product of Irish grandparents. She had been confirmed, but did nothing more than light a candle when she entered a chapel. She was divorced, moreover, and did not fit in the same category as the other parents. It occurred to her that the private schools resembled the church. They shared the assumption of universal rule. Edward Lavigne could have been a bishop.

Ten years ago Ann would have been impressed. But she had enjoyed the years in Paris, living on the Boulevard Saint-Michel, visiting the houses of Lévi-Strauss and de Beauvoir. She didn't mistake a Natal private school for the height of civilisation. She simply didn't want Paul to lose a year. He had adapted to Curzon College, arriving on the bus at the end of term in black blazer and tie, eager to relate to her the great schoolboy debates about motorcycles, batsmen, and bowlers, and the rumours about the border that filtered down from older brothers.

Neil had been Dux at a similar institution. The table of punishments hadn't changed since his time. Boys could be beaten with a cricket bat or cane, privately in the housemaster's study, or in a line in the gymnasium in the case of a group offence. A boy could be forced to run cross-country miles, denied the privilege of going home on a long weekend, or made to reproduce tables of Latin conjugations.

It was a prodigious schedule of human sacrifice. Between her and the mother of an Aztec there was not so much difference as the historian supposed.

By the time Lavigne returned Ann had resolved to ignore the subtle current of his mockery. He had combed his sandy-blond hair so severely across his head that his grey scalp was exposed to her. When he spoke he set his head at an angle as if he were deliberately revealing a part of his nakedness. He wanted Ann to see the thinning top of his head.

His vanity offended her. The same quality had been harmless in Parisian men and women, playwrights and university philosophers, pianists and surgeons, who were so fierce talking about themselves and their doctrines. It reminded her that Edward Lavigne was the unusual man with a French surname and an English accent.

Lavigne wanted to complete his piece of business.

—At this stage of the term, we cannot refund Paul's fees. That is the view of the school board, having taken legal advice on the matter. We will allow you to remove Paul from the school at your own initiative. I am willing to make a favourable call to my good friend, the headmaster of Kearsney, or, if you prefer, send a letter to an excellent public facility like the Durban High School, assuring them of his character. Many boys who have been asked to leave College go on to become substantial personages in the world.

It was as bad as if Lavigne had reached over the table and slapped her with one of his finely shaped hands.

—We haven't established that Paul needs to be taken out. Other boys misbehave. They haven't been asked to leave.

—Mrs Rabie, I simply cannot compare one boy's treatment with another. The facts change with the individual case. Permit me to be frank. So far you haven't given me any reason to consider Paul's case in a new light. Therefore, so far as I am concerned, the headmaster's decision stands.

They waited for the bill. On the borders there were new guerrilla armies. The rouble and the dollar had replaced the pound sterling. The kilometre and the kilogram and the litre were new ways of measuring miles and imperial pounds and fluid ounces. In Zaire, Patrice Lumumba had been murdered on the instruction of the White House. They wanted to expel her son for possessing two bottles of brandy. The measurements made by Curzon College were as outdated as yards and inches. They didn't know what counted.

Without arranging it, Ann found that she was walking Edward Lavigne to his car. He had parked on a parallel street, behind the City Hall where they hadn't installed meters, and accepted her company.

Ann thought that they had come to an impasse. She wanted to make him aware that Gert, Paul's father, had a close connection with the old families of the National Party. Gert's own father had been Transvaal Minister of Education. The private schools remembered that their subsidies came from the government. They never crossed a sponsor, whether it meant removing *Lady Chatterley's Lover* from the library, excluding non-whites, or accepting the son of an expatriate Japanese businessman as an honorary European. The Special Branch might well have advised the school against enrolling Neil Hunter's stepson.

Lavigne's car stood in front of the post office. Paul had told her that his Geography master drove a Bugatti, the Italian sports car noted for its attractive lines. Lavigne was a bachelor, usually splendid in a bow-tie, and was sighted tooling around the town of Curzon, the seaside resort of Margate, and hotels in the Drakensberg around Champagne Castle. Who he visited was a mystery. Could it be another man? Ann considered the possibility that he was a homosexual as Lavigne took his car keys from the striped silk lining of his blazer. It explained his style and his exactness with a phrase, his way of holding himself as well as his sentences, and his uncomplicated sadism. She should blackmail him back. Fair was fair.

—If you don't mind, Edward, before you leave. You run a school for young men, not a convent. Boys get up to high jinx. So I have to ask you, does this turn of events have anything to do with my husband? As it happens, Paul is not Neil's son. Paul is the son of Gert Rabie. I understand the school is politically sensitive but you cannot punish Paul for my husband's beliefs. That is not fair play.

Lavigne unlocked the car door, then put his hand on the green bonnet and looked, for the first time, as if he was confused about what to say next. Through the windscreen Ann saw a pair of men's gloves on the dashboard. They were cream-coloured, heavily stitched around the fingers, and latched together by a string and two beads. They were driving gloves, popular among automobile-club members, who drove for the pleasure of being on the road. She imagined Lavigne fitting them onto his hands in preparation for a particular piece of work. She was his item of business.

—Mrs Rabie, if you ask for my own opinion, then, privately, yes, I will tell you that Paul is not being treated leniently. But then you must come so far as to comprehend our position.

—I fail to understand how it serves Curzon College to push my son out.

Lavigne bent down and took the gloves out of the car. He held them without putting them on, as if he were testing their weight. They must have been too hot from sitting on the dashboard to put straight on.

—Let me offer you two insights into the thinking of the school board. It's not merely a question of drinking. Paul circulated a petition against cadet training. He didn't tell you? Mrs Rabie, political agitation is something we cannot have at our school. You may confer with your husband how far it is proper to impress his own ideas on the mind of your son. I can tell you that James Nicholson does not change his mind easily. He makes an assessment based on the relevant facts. Nevertheless, it is not impossible to change the facts. For example, Curzon College is currently raising money for a new music building.

Ann's family, on her mother's side, had been bakers, ships' chandlers, naval accountants, and clerks in Southampton before moving to what was then the South African Republic, a country without a port to call its own, in the second half of the nineteenth century.

The Rabies, a family Ann hadn't managed to leave despite the divorce, produced teachers, priests ministering to congregations in the Boland, a mining engineer who served in the command of Jan Smuts before being elected to parliament, and Gert Rabie, who ran a surgical practice between Dundee and Newcastle in the Natal interior, tending to agricultural towns and isolated households and farms in the high country. As a houseman, Gert was already noted for the delicacy of his hands. When a birth cord needed to be disentangled, or an infant heart needed its ventricle repaired, they summoned him. He was younger than her by a fortnight. When they met, at university, he had been interested only in rugby and medicine. They had been twenty on their wedding day. He talked about her as an old woman.

Gert had a loner's temperament and would book a trunk call with his son once a month. The other Rabies stayed in closer contact. They visited Paul at Curzon College, driving hours to watch Saturday rugby, to talk with the captains of the opposing teams, consider the performance of the fly half and the flanker, and unpack their hampers in the stands. Paul stayed with them during the July holidays. The Rabies continued to invite Ann along whenever they took Paul. She had the sense they didn't see her as an individual, therefore didn't hold her accountable for the separation. They didn't seem to mind that she never accepted an invitation.

Then there were the Hunters. They turned out redheads and great eccentrics. Neil's mother ran the family farm for twenty years. His aunt had been the first anthropologist to live in a Fingoland village and record the traditions. Neil's great-uncle played the piano on a cruise liner, wrote detective novels, had been a friend of Randolph Churchill, and disembarked in Durban from time to time to arrange séances.

Neil himself was not entirely handsome. He had a flat face, bony arms, and legs that made him six feet and two inches. He always had a project. When they met, he had been constructing an alternative system of English spelling with the potential to reduce illiteracy. He was the only person who had prepared for the adoption of the metric system by trying to use metres and litres and kilograms in his head before the conversion started in the shops.

Neil didn't have to be the model for her son. Paul might never come to believe, like his stepfather, that the Bantu were wiser and more honest than Europeans. Paul was interested in school. He didn't listen to any and every passing Indian like her husband did, sitting on the patio, his lovely leathery red-freckled hands spread out on his thighbones, attending to the wizened Tamil electrician Chunu's small-minded opinions, his lectures on Ayurvedic diet, marvelling at the fenugreek seeds Chunu spread out on his palm. Neil admired Chris Padayachee, an advocate who associated himself with Gandhi's remaining relatives in Natal and the cause of the Phoenix settlement he had founded. The very dark-eyed lawyer, with his detailed knowledge of Nehru and Jinnah, was as pompous as a professor. Neil wouldn't have listened for a minute if he had been raised in the province.

On Ann's return Mackenzie and his man were in the yard, stringing chicken wire above the concrete fence. They communicated with grunts as they paid out the thin knotty wire from a spool. In front of them were the hadedahs tipping and rising, dredging the grass with intelligent beaks. They weren't aggressive but neither did they move aside as Mackenzie's assistant edged a wheelbarrow past loaded with scraps of wire and uprooted poles. He made no sign of noticing her.

She came in through the kitchen. The radio was on in Neil's study. She hadn't expected him to be back. He often returned after dark with a stack of mimeographed articles that had to be read by the next morning. After years of marriage Ann still felt a tightening at the heart when she expected to see her husband. She went up to complain about Lavigne.

Instead she discovered Nadia Paulson, one of her husband's graduate students, sitting cross-legged in a short dress surrounded by books and open dictionaries and encyclopaedias. At first Nadia didn't budge. She continued to take notes. Then she turned the radio down, and moved her dyed hair to the other side of her face. She still didn't get up, but she smiled.

Each time they met it took half a minute before Ann wanted to slap the girl. It wasn't jealousy. The girl intended to cause aggravation.

—I thought it was Neil here.

—There was a demonstration. The police closed the library. Neil gave me the key so I could concentrate on checking the footnotes. We're finishing that article for the *Labour Bulletin*, you know, the one about Pixley Seme, Clements Kadalie, and the difference between national rights and workers' rights.

—I'll leave you to get on with it. I want to get something in the oven.

The kitchen was Ann's favourite room. Everything was useful. There were big windows and a Dutch half-door opening onto the yard, wooden shelves on which were set a bowl of glazed fruit and a stack of gold-rimmed plates. Pans hung on nails. In the glass-door cabinet, she kept an array of pewter mugs and spoons, and the collection of Paul's engraved school trophies.

In the lowest drawers, which she opened no more than once in a year, were streamers and box kites, thimbles, egg-timers, and other fossil footprints. They instructed Ann that life was in progress, distributing junk, and that any strange sensation in her heart today was inconsequential. It reassured her to run her hand along the chipped blue tiles on the kitchen counter and think that they were almost cold on the hottest day. She believed, as she did it, that her life with Neil was as solid as the tiles.

Nadia was her husband's most assiduous graduate student. She was from Cape Town, but had some family connection to Mauritius, where she had spent a year and picked up French. She did rough translations for Neil from Merleau-Ponty, Fanon, and Alexandre Kojève, and kept the minutes for the Free University, writing them in secretarial shorthand. Her looks impressed, her light-brown skin and her large, slow, and nearly stupid almond-shaped eyes. In Durban, where Group Areas kept people to their own locations and the buses and drive-ins and restaurants were segregated, Nadia had few options for adventure. Naturally she wanted to belong to Neil's sphere. And it turned out you couldn't keep somebody out when they wanted to come in.

When Nadia came down, her satchel loaded with books, Ann found that she was pleased at the intrusion. After Lavigne, anybody was a relief.

—You're going?

—I reckon the library must be open again. The police go in and find anybody who was protesting and then they leave.

—I can drive you to the university once I manage to get this cake out of the oven. I am trying a recipe from *Fair Lady*. If it's successful I'll make it again for my son.

Nadia put her satchel on the table.

—Paul was in Neil's office last term. He was waiting to go to a lecture in Botany. Something about ferns. He is the mirror image of you.

Ann was already putting out forks and plates for the cake, and set the kettle on the stove. She cut two thin slices for her companion, one on top of the other, and another for herself, rejoicing in the texture. It was light and aerated. She was good at baking. It was rare that something refused to rise for her.

—Paul knows everything there is to know about ferns. He is really a Rabie, his father's son. He trusts authority.

Although here you can see through the pretence. I was just meeting with his Geography teacher who wanted me to contribute to their music building to help Paul. They're brazen about it.

—Neil said something was going on at the school with Paul. I'm not surprised. My first boyfriend went to Kearsney. We had to keep our relationship a secret from his family. It taught me about their way of doing things. They insist there are rules that have to be followed, but then, when they want, the rules suddenly don't apply.

Ann poured two cups of tea and brought the milk from the fridge.

—What did Neil tell you about Paul?

—He just said there was trouble and he wasn't surprised and didn't want it to interfere with Paul's schooling. You know that, for Neil, everything comes down to education, how you liberate your mind. He won't allow us to get involved in demonstrations at Howard College like today. He knows how quick they are to expel a non-European.

It took some time for Ann to see the cause of her feelings. Nadia dressed tightly, in her thin dress and blue cotton blouse, so that when she was across the table you could not but be aware of her body living and breathing beside you. Before coming downstairs she had repaired her lipstick. You became conscious of her mouth. It was strong and beautiful and nevertheless insinuating. It said to Ann that she would soon be obsolete, that before long her skin would be cracked by sunshine, that her sinews and thighs would dry in the heat, that her body would never again breathe and love and blush and burn as it had with Gert, and that no man would ever run his hand with so much pleasure along her side. It said that her second marriage, this dream of connection to the Hunters, was also finished, and instructed Ann not to resist the alteration.

Ann was impatient when dealing with a foregone conclusion. She turned to the end of a book before she made it halfway. If a problem put her in suspense, she would do almost anything to bring it to an end. It was for this reason that she had made the decision to marry so rapidly when she met Gert, and, after that, Neil. Now, for a minute, she found she was looking forward to the end of her marriage.

On the way out she didn't say anything more to her companion. The car started without further difficulty. She drove to Howard College. The wind was searching through the trees and along the ground among the flower beds in front of the bookshop and the red-brick tea room and the dormitories. There was no sign of police. Two men were pushing a roller over the tennis courts at Golf Road, the cylinder moving ponderously across the clay. The new library building had bronze windows.

—Thanks for driving me, Ann.

—You're welcome. We'll see you.

Nadia got out. Then she put her head back into the car.

—Isn't the Free University meeting at your house tonight? I might have to take the minutes.

—Neil doesn't give me a word of warning. I turn around and the house is full of people wearing disguises. Do they really think it will stop them being picked up? Last time one of them left his false beard next to the sink. I couldn't make head or tail of it until Paul put it on.

—I would expect visitors tonight. They also closed down the hall at Howard College, where the workers' councils were meeting. They used teargas. Some of those people are friends with Neil. They need somewhere to go.

—I didn't realise it was so bad. Why didn't you tell me before?

—I thought Neil had warned you. He was worried that they were going to come to his office next. Just in case, he was moving some of his books to the department tea room.

—They may come to the house as well. I should clear up.

Ann called Neil from the telephone outside the library but the switchboard couldn't connect her to his office. On their home telephone she sometimes heard the clicking of the recording machine when she picked up the receiver. She drove back home, locked the gate onto the street, and began to collect the books and pamphlets in the lounge. Neil tried to keep them on one shelf: Marx, Kropotkin, and the red-starred workerist journals, silkscreened in the Art Department, which had not been banned because nobody knew about their existence.

It was a routine. You heard from somebody that a raid was imminent. You put the chain on the door. If it was late and Paul was home from school, you called a friend to collect him. You checked the passports, drivers' licences, the level of petrol in the car, and the spare money in the glove box, although you couldn't imagine skipping the country. You made sure there was nothing that could be read on the typewriter ribbon and tore up the blue-and-gold sheets of carbon paper under the Olivetti. You couldn't remember where you last left the cheque book with the column of subtractions along the side.

If there was time you called your sister in Schweizer-Reneke to give her advance notice to fetch Paul in case there was trouble, and then the other sister in Graaff-Reinet, the one who was married to a captain in the navy. You hadn't heard her voice for so long that you wondered if she would recognise you. Your heart was in your mouth until she said your name and it was as if nothing had ever come between you.

You listened for the rapping on the door, which might come in the early hours of the morning, and tried to think if there was anything you had missed. You went upstairs again and checked the shelves and made sure that any entries in the telephone book had been scratched out. It was impossible to live without creating clues. Suddenly, as if a knife was buried in you up to the hilt, you yearned for life in an ordinary country, ordinary happiness and unhappiness.

Ann packed the material in one box and moved it into the kitchen. She sat down at the table and realised she had no idea what to do next. Neil usually took charge. Sometimes they heard an hour beforehand there was the chance of a raid. He would put the box of books in the trunk of his Valiant and take it to a friend's garage, where it sheltered under a warped table-tennis table. Otherwise he would leave the car parked across from the gaudily lit hamburger restaurant and walk the ten minutes back down Essenwood Road, past the old-age homes, in full view of the racecourse. He would be in time to receive any policemen who did arrive.

For all the energy invested in the problem of their books, multiple visitations from the Security Branch had produced no great interest in the contents of Neil's library. The major in charge might confiscate a volume or two, if it was prohibited, but it wasn't his real concern. He wanted to know whether Neil had a certain individual's current address, whether he had been in touch with any of the persons on a list that he read aloud, whether Neil had advance notice of the student council's plans and could remember the members of a particular union or branch of the Black Sash, whether either of them knew the whereabouts of the son of the woman who did the neighbour's laundry. It was only in a place like Paris where knowing the books someone loved, whether they followed Lévi-Strauss or Sartre, was the yard-stick by which to measure them.

Ann was still thinking about what to do with the box when the telephone rang. She rushed to get it, picking up the black receiver, which was as cold as a hammer.

—Neil, I tried to call you at the department.

—You heard about the library? I had to go to the bank to make bail arrangements for some of the students. It's been a tough day.

She wanted to tell him that the day could only improve. It might even turn into a day like the one, five years before in a jeweller's shop in Rome, on a holiday subsidised by her mother-in-law, when Neil settled an off-white pearl necklace around her neck, running his fingers around her collarbone until Ann believed she would faint.

—Nadia was here when I came back. She told me about the demonstration. She thought that we were about to get a visit here from our friends. Before that I was busy with Edward Lavigne. Now I am trying to think of what to do about some of the books. Why didn't you let me know, Neil?

Ann remembered, a minute too late, that the call was likely to be recorded. It was an impossible situation. She couldn't live her entire life in code. They didn't care about the books.

—You know everything I know.

—Then why do I hear it from Nadia?

—Ann, how could I predict any of this?

—You couldn't.

Nothing could be foreseen. Unpredictability was a force to be reckoned with. It was no less relentless than the Special Branch. There was no place in Durban for extravagant jewellery or listening to music. Ann felt that the veneer furniture they bought at Joshua Doore, on a hire-purchase plan, and the lines of brown-brick warehouses along Umbilo Road proved something dismal about their own state. It would be an offence to try to live better. What had been attractive in Paris was twice as expensive here, not at all beautiful, in this context, but repulsive. A gullwing Mercedes was ravishing on a street in Rome but abhorrent over here.

On occasion Ann thought that she would die at the hands of her thousand worries. There was hardly the space to be taken up with one when another was knocking and then another and another. They were soon hammering out any other idea that might have been in her head. Neil was more efficient. He put out of his mind anything that could not be mitigated.

—You're making a fuss out of nothing, Ann. I sent Nadia to the house to complete some work. If you want, I will ask her to return the key tomorrow. Does that suit you?

—And come home now, please.

—I want to hear about Edward Lavigne.

—When you get here.

Despite the suspicion that it was a false alarm Ann took the box of books out of the house. In a section of the outside wall, adjoining the Mackenzie place, was a garden cupboard. She opened it to reveal the neat heaps of tools, stiffening green coils of the hose, a jam jar filled with a gravy of snail poison, and a shovel.

She put the box under the hosepipe, which was heavy to lift. It would do nothing to keep the books away from the Special Branch. If they wanted to confiscate Neil's contraband they would be sure to look outside and in the trunk of the car and at the bottom of their suitcases. And where would they put everything they had confiscated? One day, under the new government, which was coming as surely as the day, people would use this library of everything that had once been forbidden.

The house was old by Durban standards. Over time it had developed a sound and structure of its own. It had a good position at the top of the Berea. It had been put up by a sugar baron for the use of his manager, a man who promptly contracted yellow fever on the ship from Lourenço Marques. The place closest to it, in Ann's opinion, was the house in Amiens, in the French countryside, to which they had been invited by Neil's cousin, a baronet expatriated from the United Kingdom.

The baronet drove at reckless speed along the flower-lined roads, kept the two of them in residence for a fortnight when Neil wanted to return to his dissertation in Paris, and subsisted on pigs' knuckles and luckless rabbits which tasted of gunpowder, litres of red wine, and, most memorably, the Atlantic lobsters, whose speckled green brains he grimly but proudly beat into a sauce. The Amiens house had been calm, undecorated, and filled with lengths of sunshine.

Ann wanted to hear Paul's voice. However, they wouldn't connect her to Newnham House if she called at this hour. You could telephone your son at school between eight and nine in the evening on a week night, or between three and six on a Saturday afternoon when the sports teams had finished their matches.

Ann didn't know which person she would have to battle next. She went on with dinner. The leg of lamb came out of the refrigerator. It was hardly colder than when she bought it yesterday, and still so perfectly pink that she believed the butcher's boast that the animal had been playing in the Midlands on Sunday. The meat reminded her of a polony. In Paris their butcher and his apprentice had been professionals, as impeccable in their aprons and unswerving in their opinions as doctors and lawyers. They didn't say too much. Whereas you could rely on a Durban butcher, with his smudged red hands, to patter on, never noticing that the customer across the plywood counter wasn't smiling.

Ann put on the oven to heat. She washed the lamb under the tap, turning it around to clean the entire leg. Then it was dried with a paper towel, stretched out on the cutting board to be hammered flat, and rubbed with salt and rosemary she took from the kitchen window. She waited for the oven to reach two hundred. The cleaned scent of the meat and the clatter of the water in the sink, the branches of rosemary, the dogs finding each other's ears in the evening, the children being called indoors, servants standing on the road for the Indian bus, and the rising heat of the oven against the remaining heat of the day made her aware of her own happiness. This happiness was like the sea wind when the temperature of the water and land reversed and everything was free in new darkness.

She put the radio on. It was Radio Port Natal, playing translated copies of American pop music, a programme that commenced when the English service ended for the day. The voice of the announcer was as thick as gravel. It was odd that she could be happy when she had been married twice to two such different men, odder still that she had cried to leave Gert although she had made the decision to get a divorce. Ann saw that she wouldn't cry for a minute if she and Neil should separate, and yet she was closer to him than she had been to Gert by a factor of a thousand. That was her contradiction.

The contradiction was Neil's all-purpose explanation. This country was in a state of contradiction, starting with an economy which made many rich and far too many poor. The individual was also in contradiction between his heart and his mind, his angel and his demon. Anywhere there was life, there was contradiction.

It was a contradiction in which Ann found herself, settling the lamb into the roasting pan, trying not to burn her hands, while wishing for the end of her marriage. She would rather see her second divorce decree on the luxury paper the solicitors employed than find Nadia in the house again. She would give her husband to Nadia in gift-wrap to keep from having to look into her long mouth for one minute longer.

Did she have anything to worry about? The students at Howard College, along with the members of the Free University, idealised her husband. In his thirties, he was the local equivalent of a Sartre, a king of the revolution. There were no queens. While there were women overseas who smoked in mini-skirts, spoke openly about abortions, bombed aeroplanes, it was also true that heroic men like Sartre and Che Guevara assumed the same rights over women as kings and millionaires.

One afternoon in Paris, for example, Jean-Paul Sartre had made a pass at her while she was slicing a ham on the dining table, using the other hand to keep it in place. Neil had just run down the stairs to find a tin of mustard. Sartre had been examining Neil's poor student library, holding the volumes

35

of Kojève and Heidegger in his hands and making comments about individual passages which he read out to her in excited French. He found his way closer to the table, set the books on the edge, advised her on the best cutting procedure, and, without moving his wall eye from the direction of the ham, established his astonishingly strong, bony, and discoloured hand on Ann's thigh. Yet it seemed to interest him less than the texture and fineness of each slice she carved. Ann removed the philosopher's hand, once she understood what was happening, set his plate on the opposite side of the table, and allowed him to continue examining the bookshelves, where, after a minute of displeasure with her, he was pleased to find several editions of his own books.

Ann kept her distance from Neil's supervisor for the remainder of their time in France. He treated her as if she had let him down. He looked disappointedly in her direction at gatherings, although his mistress and his wife were present as well, and then, as if to punish her, monopolised her husband's attention. She could still summon the memory of Sartre's touch, too hot and yet too cold at the same time.

It had taken Ann a fortnight to tell Neil. He hadn't been nearly as exercised by her story as she expected. She didn't want him to fight with Sartre and lose the work he had done on his dissertation. He never took up the matter with his professor. It wasn't something that mattered to him. Neil had the strength of his convictions. It made him inhuman in certain respects. Gert would have hit the man.

The lamb had begun to sizzle. Ann opened the door and admired it, watching the creepers of flame rise and fall at the back of the oven, and the burned brown crust appearing along the sides. The kitchen was warm with the smell of the meat. She rinsed a handful of mint leaves, tore them up, and mixed them into a pat of Crown butter. Outside it rained out of a clear sky, pouring for ten minutes, chattering on the roof.

She stood at the window to watch the dark rain, which disappeared to reveal lines of white and blue stars across the heavens. On the far side of the harbour, where the seaside lights hadn't yet been turned on, she thought she saw the flash of a shooting star. You didn't often see them so close to sea level.

The lamb was done long before Neil returned, along with an amount of potatoes, carrots, and turnips, which Ann placed out on the table under upturned dishes where the entering members of the Free University came to admire them.

Every two or three minutes somebody rang the bell and she would go and escort them to the sitting room, where they waited for the session to begin, talking quietly among themselves or coming to ask her if they could use the telephone for some emergency. She didn't mind the telephone bills, although she didn't show them to Neil either. He would have been shocked, but then, like many people who were old-fashioned at heart, he couldn't adjust to changes in the value of money. The rand was not as stable as the pound. It was a harbinger of the metric system.

The Free University was open to anybody who wanted to expand his understanding, from government workers and municipal clerks to students from the Philosophy Department and others from Black Consciousness groups.

No register was taken. Often, several Anglican clergymen arrived, both black and white. They had asked the permission of their bishop to attend. There were some young photographers who had started to document the townships, taking pictures of the magistrates' courts and the municipal beer halls, as well as following the Black Marias in their patrols around the giant locations of Umlazi and KwaMashu. There was a young man, Lelo, who worked as a security guard at the petrol refinery on the Bluff and made it to their house by taking three different buses, and John Mantis, who wrote poetry and drew cartoons for the newspapers and collected books and pamphlets concerning freemasonry and demonology.

Communists and liberals refused to participate. Nevertheless, Neil had recruited a number of workers and strike leaders from the councils that had appeared on the Durban docks and in the textiles factories.

Some participants in the Free University had become friends. Archie Msimang, in his late fifties, had manners as impeccable as any of the Hunters'. Employed as a machinist in a workshop in Pinetown, Archie was the product of a former mission school, a barrel of a man coming to her shoulder, almost purple on his large and expressive countenance. His way of speaking, his way of halting halfway through a sentence to survey it to the end, reminded her of the priest who officiated over her wedding to Neil.

The friendship went in both directions. Archie came to consult with Neil on a matter that had nothing to do with the Free University, some issue to do with his pass book or opening a savings account, but ended up sitting in the kitchen with Ann and talking, slowly and courteously, about his dilemmas until the afternoon vanished from the windows. She knew about the wife who had died suddenly on Boxing Day, his brother who left the country after Sharpeville and had never been heard of again, the woman he had begun to court who worked behind the counter of the BP garage.

Ann was pleased when Archie came to see her. He was wearing a white shirt that bulged over his belt, and polyester suit trousers that must have been bought second-hand from his employer. Many of the small-business owners around Durban weren't rich, having come with nothing from places like Edinburgh and Belfast to join in the boom. They brought their frugal habits, supplementing their income by selling their old clothes to their workers.

Archie stood in the corridor, waiting for her to invite him inside.

—Comrade Ann, good afternoon. Or I see it is already good evening.

—Hello, Archie.

He smiled at her and sniffed the air ostentatiously. She saw that the heel of his shoe was bound with Sellotape. He must be the same size as her son. She had bought extra pairs of shoes in Paris for Paul and was keeping them in boxes until he wore out the others.

—I have been sent by the other comrades to inform you that, while we are waiting for Neil, you have truly awakened our appetites.

—It's a leg of lamb, Archie. It's done and I am still waiting for my husband to pitch up. You think I should make everyone a plate?

—I believe it would be appreciated.

Archie came inside and took his usual chair at the table. He helped her to carve the lamb and put it on plates. She thought that Archie didn't seem to have distinct political views. He seemed to be listening and trying to make up his mind. He was unusual by the standards of the Free University, which ran the gamut from outspoken communists to Christian socialists, pan-Africanists, black nationalists, revolutionary Muslims.

There were the more practical members of the Free University who believed in a non-racial future, but pursued their business in the interim. That meant Royal Saloojee, the dentist who also had a stake in an insurance brokerage. Roy had latched onto Neil when he sold them life cover. Now he was selling insurance for fire and water damage, for illness and death benefits, to comrades, not to say doing their teeth on the side. He had put a bridge in for her.

Archie helped Ann take the plates to the living room. He gave everybody a serviette, knife and fork, and then sat down to eat in front of the telephone. Nadia arrived and made herself at home. She sat beside Roy the dentist. He had brought some forms for her to sign dealing with the annual renewal of her policy. She tried to read through them while keeping half an ear on the proceedings. The discussion, which had been scheduled on Fanon, began without Neil.

Ann watched without wanting to take part. She didn't have any ideas of her own. There was some other principle in her heart today. She saw that, in each hour of this day, she had been unwilling to concede any defeat, whether to Lavigne or the Jaguar. Not to the Rabies nor to Curzon College, not to Neil, not to her son Paul, who needed to drink at sixteen and had landed them all in hot water. It was only at the spectacle of Nadia that her heart had turned over. She was sure that she had lost even before she started to resist. Her husband wouldn't leave her in the lurch. At the same time he was capable of making her leave him.

What was there to do? Her adversaries had the upper hand. Curzon College was as secure in its mentality as the Vatican. They made her ashamed to use the same language.

The degeneration was there in the schools, in the misery of offices where they fingerprinted native men and where young white men scolded older men like Archie, and in the drumhead courts, and the racial signs posted along the beaches and in the bus stops, enforced by the Black Marias, which carried a dozen men in their cages.

Neil appeared as the members of the Free University had begun to drift away. Archie had already left in Roy's car. Lelo, Nadia, and John Mantis were at the door, where Neil talked to them for a few minutes and walked them to the end of the driveway. Then he came into the kitchen, looking surprised as if he had heard something unexpected, and unbuttoned his jacket to put it over the back of a chair. He sat down.

In his shirt Neil was thinner and younger than the image fixed in her memory, his beard scarcely speckled with grey. He was again the man she had married in an Arniston church. In London or Paris, at thirty-five, Neil would count as a young man. Here he had Methuselah's responsibilities.

—I'm sorry, Ann. I should have warned you when the day went to pieces.

—You should be sorry.

She forgave him at once.

—I really didn't have time to get to a telephone. There was the issue of bail money. I had to go to the bank to get a draft. Some of the students had to be ferried between the police station and their homes. One lived far into Springfield, next to the power station. He says all the youngsters have asthma. He wanted me to write a petition for them. But forget about all of that. Tell me what happened with Lavigne.

—He had a new complaint about Paul's objection to

military cadets. In any case he had nothing to offer. Unless we come up with a donation to the music building he's planning to put Paul on the bus at mid-term, with all his belongings.

Neil settled into his chair before he looked back at her.

—He's blackmailing us over a bottle of brandy?

—Two bottles. And the petition Paul started.

—This country is full of surprises, Ann, but I have never heard of a school blackmailing the parents before.

—Given what crooks they are behind the scenes, Paul might be better off at DHS. For a government school, it gets good results. Didn't Sartre want them to shut down every French private school?

—I'm not defending the existence of these schools, Ann. You and Gert wanted to send him there. It wasn't my choice. But now Paul is well established. I suppose if we have to pay Lavigne, we can pay him with the money left over from my mother's estate. I have never had to draw on that capital before.

It sounded as if Neil, who was without emotion under most circumstances, was growling at her. He was in the grip of some unfamiliar emotion. Ann wasn't sure that her husband was adapted to real frustrations. He wished for a world in which fair play was the norm and believed, following Sartre's example, that injustice must be strenuously opposed in each detail. And yet politics, even in this country, was one grey thing opposing another. She couldn't teach him this, didn't necessarily want him to submit to this fact, and therefore had the sensation of being far away from Neil. He had said nothing to push her away and yet the prick of it was as real as when her hand found a safety pin in her purse.

Neil had some news of his own.

—You won't believe what I heard today. I worked out why Edward Lavigne's name sounded familiar. It turns out his older brother Percy is the deputy dean. He may be the acting dean next year.

—I don't believe you.

—I have no idea why nobody said anything to me either. I just never put two and two together. And it's an unusual last name. They must be quite a pair. I've had dealings with this Percy character and he's every bit as slippery as you describe Edward. Rumour has it that he feeds the Security Branch information on the lecturers. You can't take rumours for granted, of course, but it sounds as if the younger one might also have a similar understanding with the police.

—I don't believe it.

—Wait a minute and I'll tell you something else. They say a few years ago Edward was arrested in Pretoria. They dropped the homosexuality charges before the Sunday newspapers could get hold of it. You know how they'll print anything on the back page if they get the chance. But why did they drop the charges? It's not impossible that the younger Lavigne is their man in the private-school system.

—If he insists on expelling Paul, then we have to show him up, Neil. We must go public.

Neil was solemn.

—If you go to war with the system Paul will have to leave anyway. The easiest way, assuming we want him to stay, may be to give Lavigne the donation for his music building. How much harm can music do? Do you want to hear something else?

—I'm not sure that I do.

—I didn't either. Some people, who don't want to be named, suspect Archie is also working with the Special

Branch. There's no real proof, from what I understand, but people have noticed that he has more money in his wallet than they expect him to have, considering the shoes he wears. They have seen him in certain parts of town when there was no reason for him to be there. Now there may be nothing to it at all. Nevertheless, once it gets started, something like that can take on a momentum of its own. But I can make neither head nor tail of it.

1973

THE PASS

At five in the morning, the Edendale bus paused at the entrance. The engine was loud. Victor didn't open his eyes. He put his hand into the inner pocket of his Crombie coat lying beside him, the former property of a sugar millionaire whose name was spelled beneath the collar in blue thread, and felt for the pass book. There was nothing. It was impossible to accept. Victor went back to sleep, to dream about his coming good fortune. He had all the luck, all the friends, a sponsor in the caretaker, another sponsor who was going to be famous around the world.

In his dream he could almost touch the soft brown face of his father, a beacon of friendship, and see the freckles spaced evenly from his forehead to his chin. The old man had been deft. With a fingernail he had lifted the black-and-white photograph from the pass book, which belonged to a Mozambican miner returning to his country, and replaced it with Victor's own photograph, taken by the Indian assistant from Crown Portrait Studios. Since then the endorsements at the back, stamped and indecipherably signed and dated in a table of purple ink, had been checked a hundred times by policemen, court administrators, and government clerks. No word had come from his father.

Either the pass book was in his pocket, where his blind hand couldn't find it, or it lay somewhere beside the mattress. Victor checked under the coat and around it. Without opening his eyes he searched along the mattress.

Suddenly he was wide awake. He heard the clopping of a horse on the road, as if it were coming towards him, and stood up. Through the window he saw the tall animal between the arms of a cart, pulling the trussed bundles on the back to the side of the road. Its eyes were rigged with severe black blinkers, joined by a strut over its head. The driver, wearing a corduroy cap, stopped it outside the tea room, where it continued to switch its tail as the man went into the shop.

Victor saw the horse was no longer young. Its high grey chest, brushed with dark hair at the top and bottom, was muscled like the bodybuilders who tested their weights at the back of the hostel. He kept looking at the horse underneath the awning of the tea room and tried to ignore the discomfort rising in his chest. He didn't know if he would be as lucky today as in his dreams.

He tidied up first so he could find it quicker. He folded the blanket under his arm and stored it under the mattress. There was nothing when he turned the bed on its side. Nothing in his shoes apart from the smell of polish. Nothing in his shirt buttoned on the hanger. Nothing to be found in the back pockets of his trousers nor in the overalls that he wore to the print shop. He felt he was trying to answer an impossible riddle.

The room was the riddle. It was hard to survey the entire area, which, besides being his bedroom, was used as a storage closet. Two mops stood in buckets beside pungent cleaning supplies. Some boxes contained broken light bulbs. They were kept, like eggs in a carton, in case one fine day they should flicker into light. The caretaker of the Caledonian Christian Men's Hostel, his friend Mr Samuel Shabangu, hated throwing things away. So there was a roll of knotted chicken wire, tins of Dulux with spattered lids, lengths of catgut, and, on a separate blanket, various tools, spanners and screwdrivers and a spirit level, necessary for the kinds of repairs that the caretaker did on a daily basis.

Only a spell, forbidden to a Christian like Mr Shabangu, could have moved the reference book out of his pocket and across the room. Nevertheless, Victor began to check under the tins. He moved aside the heavy roll of wire to see what it might be hiding. Nothing. He had become a criminal overnight.

Victor had skirted the law to stay in town. His father had a permit when he worked at Natal Command, the barracks across from Durban North Beach, bringing oats in hot pails for the brown horses in the cavalry yard, and washing down the boots of the riders. As a boy Victor had helped with the work. They settled blankets on the backs of the horses when the regiment returned from exercise, inspected the shod feet of the animals, combed out their manes as the horses knelt in front of the barracks.

He and his father had slept side by side in a stall of their own. At midnight, he woke to hear the pleased sounds of the horses urinating, the scuffling of hooves against the stall doors, and the soft conversation with which the animals engaged each other, horses and dogs. The rough-tongued German shepherds slept nose to nose, and trotted suspiciously five metres behind the horses. Each befriended a particular horse and rider. They were liable to snarl when they were displeased, strong enough to rise on their back legs and pin

49

Victor against the wall, powerful enough in the shoulders to hold him there as he turned his head away from the pouring out of salty dog's breath until some expression on his face satisfied them. But they almost never bit.

Three years ago a certain individual sought to take his father's job. That man told tales to the European staff sergeant, accusing his father of mistreating the dogs and trading their feed items to an Indian market-gardener. The accusation hung in the atmosphere despite the lack of evidence. His father's cough had worsened while he worried about being put in jail on suspicion of theft or having the right to have his son with him in the barracks taken away. He hadn't been able to sleep, and had lost the desire to talk to his many friends among the European riders. The pressure soon proved too much to bear. His father resigned from his position, bought the permit for his son to stay in the province so that they didn't lose the foothold, left him in Pietermaritzburg, and returned to their native area, near Lesotho, in sight of the mountains. He promised Victor to return when rumours about the supposed theft cooled down. Since then, no message had come.

For three years, asleep or awake, Victor had never been out of reach of his reference book. The fever rose in his head while he searched again in the coat and turned it inside out. He moved the paint tins one by one and set them down in the other corner, pulled the drying rack from the wall, and, finally, opened the door to the outside. There was no lock on it. Light from the corridor came into the room and gave no clue to the whereabouts of the piece of missing property. His head spun.

The building was silent. The naked bulb above the staircase shone pale and yellow into the morning without producing any light. Victor looked past the staircase into the yard. At this hour the inhabitants were invisible, a hundred and eighty grown and grizzled, restless and fearless men, who argued from their beds and the rows of open toilets, who borrowed rapaciously and tried never to return what had been loaned except to Mr Shabangu.

The men were exhausted. The day before, in place of church, they had practised dancing on the cement. They drank jars of illegal fizzing orange beer before sharpening their knives for the fights that developed on the way back from the beer hall. They treated Victor as an extension of Mr Shabangu, sending him with messages, warnings, requests, notifications of disputes, and other announcements that were meant to go first to the caretaker and, through him, to the council of supervisors, five Europeans drawn from the church hierarchy and the police. Their lordly messages, however, were received and then ignored by Mr Shabangu.

Victor looked for his friend. He should be around. The custodian didn't seem to sleep. At any hour he might be prowling the hallway, inspecting the burglar bars for spots of rust, taking the council members on a tour, leading a policeman to an interview with one of the men about a theft or an assault, standing and thumbing the passages in a Gideons Bible, which shone in an oiled black leather cover.

Mr Shabangu, after all, was the person to ask if you had lost something or were looking for someone. There were no obvious limits to his knowledge. Sometimes he even seemed to know the future, who might find a position with the machinist shops, a fitter and turner and a large tool and die maker on Rissik Square, which of the residents might wind up in the district hospital, and which one might be arrested in connection with the burglary of a certain premises. Mr

Shabangu stood for a system, fixed in place, in which you knew how to measure who and what was important.

Down the corridor, the door to Shabangu's room was closed. Victor considered knocking. The caretaker hated any disappearances in the building, whether it concerned a man or a woman or an item of property, because it reflected poorly on him. He had seen the worst that a man could do, many times over, and liked to remind you of the lessons he had learned while drinking straight from a carton of very sour Juba in which the alcohol was as piercing as a European woman's perfume.

Many identified Victor as something of a son to Mr Shabangu. They were wrong. Sometimes there was no connection with the older man. The caretaker had to struggle, on certain occasions, to recall Victor's name. His large face would go blank while he was trying to fix on the letters, as if someone had relaxed the string holding his eyes and mouth in harness. He was unable to set his jaws. It was frightening. You feared that the man had been overcome by a fit and that he might choke. After a minute or two, Mr Shabangu recovered his self-possession, completed his sentence, retreated his tongue, and again seemed to recognise the other person. Afterwards he didn't refer back to these incidents.

The people Mr Shabangu truly remembered, for whom his face tightened on the string, were the ones to whom he had loaned money. On Fridays he set up at the desk in the entrance, behind the frosted-glass door, and doled out new two-rand notes in exchange for their signatures. Over Christmas he made longer-term loans, which the residents took to the rural areas to pay for a new roof, or a coffin, or a daughter's or sister's dowry, or the celebrations to mark a boy's circumcision. He took down their pass numbers as part of his security. Looking over the top of plastic glasses, he copied the details into the end pages of the Gideons Bible. When you repaid your loan, a line went through your name with the help of a Parker pen and a ruler.

The outstanding accounts belonged to men who vanished. Some chose not to return to the urban area because of the pressure. Others died after a short illness and were buried in a potter's field. Several had left the country to join Umkhonto, in which case the disappearance was not mentioned. Their names were nevertheless kept in the book and transcribed into a new Gideons when more space was required. They might come back into the country someday. Mr Shabangu repeated the numbers under his breath, updating the principal to allow for each month of interest, when he went through his records column by column. He was the only man who could do such calculations in his head. He was as good as an Indian.

Victor knocked on the door and listened. There was no movement. He waited and put his ear to the door. Sometimes in the passage he heard the caretaker talk to himself on his long trestle bed after he had stored his mops and buckets. His stern lips recalled the names of the debtors and the amounts outstanding in a voice so low you had to stand beside the door to make out the words and numbers. You almost believed you had caught Mr Shabangu casting a spell.

Victor went back down the hall and into his room, remembering the feeling of bad magic about the custodian. It was common knowledge, when somebody fell behind on his loan, that misfortune was sure to follow. Shabangu sent Victor to remind the person when a payment was due. Victor brought back promises, excuses, and other stories, and the knowledge that the payment would be made. Nobody defied Shabangu for fear of what he could do at a distance.

When he wanted to celebrate a sizeable repayment, the custodian came into the store room with a dish of sugared and startlingly orange baked beans, or a bowl of saltless bone-white pap from which rose the merest scent of water. On a long holiday, when certain longstanding accounts had been closed, he might bring an unlabelled tin of golden syrup. He ate slowly and delightedly without, however, offering Victor so much as a spoonful. Nobody knew Shabangu's people. Victor was clearly his favourite at the hostel and perhaps in his life. Yet he didn't get a spoon.

Towards others in the hostel the caretaker was obscure and even unfriendly. If Mr Shabangu wasn't much liked, he was respected on account of his longevity. He was understood to be the oldest man in the building, snow having settled thick on his eyebrows and in the stiff hair around his black mouth. He walked up and down the staircase while hitching one of his legs. He sat down on a chair with a noticeable degree of discomfort and could only find peace in certain positions. Nevertheless, Mr Shabangu was not yet out of his forties.

Victor went to look again in the store room. He couldn't rely on his friend to save him.

Mr Shabangu didn't knock. He simply arrived by right, putting his broad hands around the door and hauling himself inside the store room, where everything had been turned upside down and moved away from the wall.

—And how are you this morning, Victor? Is everything going to your satisfaction?

—I have no complaints, Mr Shabangu.

The pass book was nowhere. Victor could cry out loud. The past was gone. There wasn't anything you could do to return lost objects to their positions. Nor could a person trace his steps so exactly that he would discover at which point he and his possession had parted.

—Everything is out of its place in here, I see. I can also see that you have moved my supplies from their usual locations. I prefer this room to be ship-shape, as you know.

—I understand. I will put it all back in the right place.

The caretaker put his hands out to make a sign.

—Everything must fit together like a tea set.

—I promise to put it back as it was. I misplaced something.

—Nothing too important, I hope. I know you have extra work thanks to the recent invaders. That gentleman Polk is to blame, I believe. He has put an extra strain on you.

—He gave me a chance to work on the play.

—Nevertheless, it takes a toll. I understand completely. When you are distracted it is only natural to lose track of your property.

Mr Shabangu smiled broadly. It seemed to be the product of some dislocation at the jaw. Mr Shabangu had moods which were monotonous for months at a time, strung the one on the other like beads in a necklace. He got through Christmas and Boxing Day without the slightest trace of good cheer, singing hymns in the front row of the choir with a face as clouded as a Scotsman's, and afterwards drinking the red fruit juice from the punchbowl with no more joy than if it were medicine.

In the same instant Victor understood that it was his landlord who had taken the reference book. He had come to the store room to gloat, declaring there was nothing that could be done.

Victor saw he was as lost as his permit. Shabangu had been at the top of his list, the first of his patrons. Victor tried to be friends with everyone who could help him. Now, for no reason he could understand, the custodian had taken the permit. There was no sense in it. He was bare in front of Mr Shabangu. He staggered. He wanted to sit down on the floor. He had never had such a flux of hot and cold sensations.

The intruder came further into the room, looking around at the items displaced by the search and the thin mattress, which stood on its side against the wall. There was one window in the store room, barred, although you would have needed a long ladder to reach it from the road. Through it, the cornmeal-coloured sunlight suddenly poured. It gave Mr Shabangu's face an unexpected golden aspect, a King Midas who had brought his hands to his head.

Victor understood, for the first time, that it wasn't a trustworthy countenance. Mr Shabangu was lean elsewhere, in his hands and chest, yet his neck and chin resembled a lizard's collar. He was pleased by the knowledge of other men's frailties and superstitions, information he relayed to Victor, by the discovery he made every day that nobody in the building was better than him. There was no African to beat him.

How had Victor borne it for three years? How had he survived the weight of the caretaker leaning on him, for three full years, and stealing the breath out of his chest? How bad was his luck that, in a single month three years ago, he had lost his father and gained a succubus to drain his life energies? He couldn't measure his misfortune. This Shabangu would sit on him until he died.

The caretaker settled on the bottom of the mattress.

—For you, Victor, life can be delightful forever, provided you have the rent for me. Yes, it is true that I came to remind you of that unlucky day of the month. Not that I wish to be the messenger of bad news only. This evening, I am buying meat from Clover butchery. I have ordered mutton chops. You can join me if that suits you.

—I have the rent money right now. Only I cannot eat with you, Mr Shabangu. Mr Polk wants me from the afternoon. Tonight the play opens downstairs. They didn't inform you? It is supposed to go until quite late.

—Indeed that is what they have warned us to expect.

—So I don't think I will be free.

—Well, that is a pity then. Good chops.

Victor was surprised to find the notes where he had left them in his trousers. He counted out the four rands and twenty cents to the caretaker. They were accepted in the good grace that had struck Mr Shabangu like a ray of moonshine. Victor remembered that the caretaker was the only person in the building who knew the secret of the reference book. Before he left town his father had taken the caretaker into confidence, consulting with him as to the proper price to pay. Shabangu had protected Victor for three years. In this fatal week when Polk's play was about to open, the caretaker had been unable to prevent himself taking advantage of his knowledge. He wanted to profit on both sides.

They went downstairs together where Mr Shabangu had to start opening the doors and running after the kitchen staff. Victor tried to understand the caretaker's complete change of mood. Shabangu was the riddle. Why would he do it? Why would it make him happy? The police were useless. If he was correct about what had happened, and the caretaker's smile shone into his soul as the proof, then it was up to Victor to search the money-lender's heart, not to say Shabangu's room, and rescue his permit.

In the meantime he couldn't afford to alert the other man. He couldn't let the pass book leave the building. Then he would be finished.

They stood for a minute in the canteen, where the preparations for the play were almost complete.

—You won't come to see the performance, Mr Shabangu? The tickets are for free, of course, because you have assisted the production. You can also stand on the stairs over there and watch through the window. Mr Polk doesn't mind.

—Then he is a very unusual European. I have never heard of such a man. Not to worry about the tickets! But I have seen enough to agree with you that, with Mr Peter Polk, what we have is a different kettle of fish. In any case, Victor, my religion does not believe in plays.

The older man's lips were twitching, as if he were unwilling to erase his victorious feeling and become unhappy again at the changes in his kingdom. He looked around the large room.

—I don't know why there has been such a fuss about Mr Polk's play. For weeks they have turned our lives upside down. For a piece of make-believe!

In this regard Mr Shabangu was quite correct. Despite the way Polk had presented his plan to the supervisors, the preparations for the play had come to interfere with the routine operations of the hostel. The canteen, where there were usually churning pots on the stove holding shining Maizena porridge alongside piles of hairy corn cobs bedraggled from boiling water, had been converted into a theatre. The benches had been shifted from their usual place. Black drapes had been nailed over the makeshift stage. In the evenings, when the men remained on the steps to talk or to practise their dancing, there had been the sounds of rehearsals behind the locked doors and the beguiling voice of a woman. Late into the evening there had been the outbursts of Polk the director, as likely to come to the boil and spill over as one of the pots on the stove.

They were also skirting the law. There were certain ordinances that prevented black and white actors performing professionally, for money, on the same stage. Polk thought he had found a loophole, by changing the method of payment, and had chosen four Caledonian residents to work alongside his two principal actors, Roland Adams and Janet Gilfillan. Victor had become as interested in the actor and actress as in Polk himself. They seemed to fly from thought to thought, feeling to feeling, like acrobats. Polk's company seemed to work outside the law, beyond what could easily be measured or defined, and yet, as you overheard in their conversation, they had their own strong sense of what counted. They chose the individual over the system and their own ways of doing things above everything else and everybody else's expectations. The two of them stayed on the same floor of the whites-only hotel despite Roland's complexion.

There was a chance Polk and his actors would understand Victor's predicament. Polk could try to help. If Victor complained about Shabangu to any of the hostel residents, however, they would laugh at him. After all, he had told a Christian his secret and exposed himself.

—I can come to your room afterwards then, Mr Shabangu. I will see if you are still awake. Maybe we can still celebrate together.

—I will see you then. Enjoy your play.

Victor waited until the caretaker had gone into the passage and then closed the door. He was shivering. It would be this evening or never that he had the reference book back in his hands. When there was unrest the laws were enforced more strictly. If it was found that the endorsement in your pass book had expired, you would be put in a lorry to the native reserves.

Victor wanted to travel in a Mercedes and in an aeroplane, attend the double feature at the European drive-in, buy more meat from the Clover butchery than a man could consume in a sitting, walk the streets without fear of interception, and kiss the reluctant women in town. To do any of it he needed to recover his permit from Mr Shabangu before it was gone forever.

He wouldn't be able to do anything during the play. The caretaker would most likely stay in his room during the performance, as agitated as if he had to prevent demons entering from downstairs. It was a unique occasion. Since Victor had arrived at the hostel, Polk was the first person to give Mr Shabangu pause under the roof of his kingdom.

The world changed with the units of measurement. There were no more inches and yards, no more distances in miles on the road signs, no more pound notes fetched from the drawers of the cash register, no more pints and gallons as defined by the Imperial System. Instead, there were metric units, which simplified division and multiplication and therefore exposed any confusions in existing arrangements.

At the Shell garage they had converted a row of pumps to sell petrol per rand per litre. When the oil supply was interrupted in the Middle East, a queue of Chevrolets,

Cortinas, and Hillman Avengers stood bumper to bumper. Next door was Galaxy Tea Room where the men bought provisions, and which had started to stock white sugar in fly-bothered half-kilogram packets, along with milk in half-litre glass bottles, while, behind the counter, the proprietor, Tarun Naicker, announced that now he was doing things by halves.

You weren't familiar with litres, not to say centimetres, kilograms, and electricity sold in bundles of kilowatt hours. The terms had the ring of the space age, the vocabulary of astronauts and cosmonauts. You had heard about the success of George Foreman, studied the indistinct portrait of the world heavyweight champion in the same newspaper where you read that the Vietnam war had ended. Two beauty queens travelled to London on the same Jumbo jet to compete for Miss World, a Miss South Africa who was fair-skinned, blue-eyed, and long-legged, plus a Miss Africa South who was a long-legged coloured. Skylab 2 was launched to survey a planet where the star of a hundred kung-fu movies, Bruce Lee, found sudden death. On September 11th, General Pinochet levelled the Presidential Palace in Santiago.

And it was opening night at the Caledonian Christian Men's Hostel. It was the only drama the building had seen apart from the Nativity plays put on by visiting evangelists. Polk was calmer than ever. He sat behind the wheel of his Datsun, instructing the workers through the open window as they brought in cartons from the back of the van. He was not far into his forties yet he seemed as heavy as an old man when you considered him sunk into his seat.

—Have you seen Roland? He was meant to be here by now.

—I haven't seen him, Mr Polk. Must I go and look for him?

—You can go and look, but I don't think you'll find anything, my boy. On opening day Roland is bound to act up. You go inside. I don't want to have your Mr Sobukwe giving me the evil eye.

—Mr Shabangu.

—Mr Shabangu who has this place in his toils. I don't envy you being under his thumb.

Victor didn't mind flying back in search of Roland. The actors would be gone by the weekend. He wanted to memorise each unlikely minute of their appearance, to drink in the picture of Janet in her satin blouse with raised red roses on the pocket. She was already standing on the stage, repeating her lines from a card, red hair pinned tightly to her bone-white scalp. He could have spied on her all day from his vantage point in the passage. She had the strange immeasurable beauty of a witch. He wouldn't be able to get her out of his eyes.

At the same time Victor didn't want to be caught in the act of looking. Only some people had the right to look at others. Even with Polk and his stars, who were unlike any other Europeans he had encountered, Victor had the instinct to flinch when they tried to talk to him directly.

He went back out and put his head through the window of the van.

—Roland never arrived. Janet is there.

—Get in on the other side. We can go and find a Castle Lager.

Victor got in and sat on the other side of the van, which had no seatbelts, and a rusting panel where the radio had been. Polk was wearing his standard uniform consisting of a short-sleeved safari shirt, belted light-brown pants and brown dress shoes. He looked like a farmer. He showed a certain pleasure in the bulk of his body. You could see it in the way he steered the bakkie.

—You don't want to check on Roland first?

—When we come back from the bottle store, then we will see if he is here or not. If he still hasn't arrived we will go after him. Then he's had his chips.

Polk talked like a farmer, turning the sentences around in his mouth, descending to an accent so gravelly and so sincere that it was no longer believable. You could only speak like that if you lived in the heart of the country, never listened to an LP or to a radio drama, if you still counted your produce in terms of pounds and gallons and fluid ounces rather than litres and kilograms. But Polk wasn't a farmer. He had been around the world and he had already begun to undermine the system of Mr Shabangu.

On the main road there were Bedford trucks on their way to the vast harbour under construction at Richards Bay. The canvas rose under the ropes at the rear to reveal stacks of pine planks and canisters of diesel gas. In between them were smaller vans used by employers to transport their workers to building sites, shoeless men in shorts sitting on the back of the vehicle holding hoes and rakes.

Polk parked outside the bottle store and waited for Victor to bring his order. Then they sat on the side of the main road and drank beer from an ice-filled packet. It wasn't the first time they had done it. Each evening, once rehearsal was done, Polk emptied a string of Castles, one after the other. He drank in the front seat of his Datsun until his face was red in the atmosphere of the car light. When one bottle was finished he staggered out of the car and opened the trunk to find the next. He had told Victor about the nineteen months he spent on a merchant ship after failing out of university, sailing across the Persian Gulf with cargoes of soy beans and car parts, and about his first play performed in a one-room schoolhouse in King William's Town, and about the open spaces of the country which subdued and exalted the heart.

Victor liked to listen to Polk. He would have listened to him, and drunk with him, for another few hours today. But he didn't want the director to tire himself out so early on the day of the opening performance. He suspected Polk would fall asleep if he consumed another bottle, his thick legs wedged unnaturally on the safety brake.

When Polk opened the door to piss in the parking lot and looked fondly at the bottle-store window, it was time to remind him to go back to the hostel and see about Roland. Polk could hardly understand the question. He looked bewildered. Victor couldn't think where, in such a sodden man, the power of imagination was located.

Polk soon recovered, however. He sent Victor to get a very hot cup of coffee with Cremora from the adjoining tea room. He drank it without being scalded, and drove back carefully on the other side of the street, leaning towards the windscreen to get a closer look at the road. Every morning, after all, it was as if the previous evening and the previous bottle never happened. Already Polk couldn't remember being angry at Roland. The guy would have a second portion of chips.

At noon, however, Roland hadn't arrived and couldn't be raised on the hotel telephone. Polk concentrated on Janet and made some adjustments to her movements around the other actors. He drew a map for her in red ink, where she would stand and where she would be looking during each major speech, and made her memorise her itinerary around the stage before he tore it up. He showed no further ill effect from the alcohol. During rehearsal, as he sent Victor along with messages, he was far more awake than the actors. He rolled cigarettes with one hand, tightening the tobacco inside the wrapper as if coaxing a screw, and watched the scenario through the brown smoke.

As Victor heard how he dealt with his actors and explained the correct gestures and expressions and the way to occupy a certain volume of space, how to react to the other person, how to pause on or speed over the phrases in each sentence, he felt that the director had a wisdom that was, after all, as certain as any farmer's.

When the rehearsal was over Polk came up to him.

—We should probably find Roland now. Are you coming?

—Of course I am coming. I will do anything, Sir.

—Anything is not required. You only need to catch sight of him.

—I'll find him, Sir.

—You have to be like a bloodhound. I gather he and Janet had something of a showdown. It's not the first time. In my opinion, the responsibility is on both of them. He keeps after her. For her part, Janet can act like a bitch on heat. So this is our drama. He's in love with her. She's in love with me. I am in love with myself. We have a merry triangle going.

—I didn't notice, Mr Polk.

—You notice everything, Victor. Let's see if we can find the van before the metre maid has her way with it.

—The metre maids don't come over here.

—So we have the metres and not the maids. The best of possible worlds.

They were in luck. Polk continued to talk as he drove through town. It was busy. From Friday noon, lasting until Sunday evening, the factory workers had money to spend on alcohol, brown bread, tinned vegetables. The farmers came from the interior of the province, the bachelor in his bakkie and the married man in the family Mercedes, to buy supplies, meet their friends at the new hamburger restaurants, pick up magazine subscriptions at the Christian bookshop, check the catalogues of agricultural machinery, and, perhaps, attend performances of the Natal Philharmonic, which courted controversy by programming Russian symphonies.

At the next intersection a cement mixer was stuck. Polk put the car in neutral.

—What is it, Victor? Is it a woman? Is it Janet also?

—Sorry, Sir?

—Something's wrong with you today. You're usually as cheerful as a starfish. I will work it out eventually if you don't confess.

—It's okay, Mr Polk.

—It's okay. It's not okay. Sometimes you are as difficult to piece together as your friend Shabangu. You can tell me your troubles if you want, but I won't force anything out of you. Now do you suppose they will ever move this truck?

The robot went from red to green while the mixer continued to sit in the middle of the road, its massive green cylinder sputtering and the exhaust pipe breathing clouds of unhealthy white smoke, while the driver studied the engine hopelessly. Other men got out of their cars to advise him.

A Black Maria clambered onto the pavement, two men in the compartment whose arms were handcuffed to the railing above their heads. They looked out at Victor as if to remind him about his permit book. But he was luckier than them.

Polk continued.

—In any event, you can't be worse off than Roland. His father was white. His mother, on the other hand, was a certain coloured lady, Yolanda Adams, and so he was brought up in a coloured area and went to coloured schools and so on. Roland has suffered from a broken heart since he met Janet. The three of us met at the same time, donkey's years now, when I was putting on my first production. Since then Roland has good days and some bad days when nothing can get his chin off the floor.

—I can see that, Mr Polk.

—Ah, but what you don't know is that all this time, Roland has been quietly married to a very nice lady who is a secondary-school teacher. I have met her and she has nothing to do with any sort of drama. He has a son in class two, plus a daughter in standard three. He is as happy as a clam in the heart of his family, but none of it can protect him from the negative influence of Janet's existence. That's love for you. Roland resents me because he sees Janet is in love with me. In my opinion Janet is in love with the idea of love. She has never been committed to the physical side of it.

—I think it's too complicated, Sir.

—We get most of our energy from complications. If you were to ask me, right now, where I get half my ideas from, it is from the two of them, Roland and Janet. But there is also a cost to it. Sometimes I feel that I have to carry around Master Roland on my back, and all his moods and his grievances. I never get the opportunity to put him down.

When he was drunk, Polk was as sad as the night was long. When he was back to sober, there was a good feeling that came off him, as if you were sitting around a fire and having your hands and face warmed by his confidence. The same was true for the others in the production. If the sun was up, then Polk would continue to pull at your unhappiness until it unravelled.

The mixer was pushed to the side of the road and they could be on their way again. Victor wanted to tell Polk about his situation with the reference book. Yet there was nothing obvious the director could accomplish. You had to be a good judge of what people could and couldn't do for you. Many of the Caledonian residents had the idea that they could take their problems to a European and they would be sorted out. Victor thought it was wishful thinking. If Polk made a noise about the disappearance of the permit, then the people in the hostel would know about his plight. One of them would report him to the other, and the magistrate would be forced to apply the rules that were his professional existence. Victor would be arrested by the end of the day.

They went through the old section of town, where there was a line of fruit-and-vegetable shops shuttered for Friday prayers, and then an international hotel, the library, and post office. Victor read the signs in the shops and the sandwich boards announcing the rugby results.

Polk had based the play, which focused on the idea of a false accusation, on a story that Neil Hunter had passed on to him. He had tried to explain the connection between the story and the play but Victor couldn't see it for himself.

—I invited Neil again although he says one visit to the set is enough. I don't think he will come.

—Why not, Sir? As you said, you put some of his ideas in your play. You wrote about him and his life. I would love to see a version of myself in a play.

—That way you would live forever. But Neil doesn't really like plays and novels. He prefers abstract concepts instead of life itself. Neil sees the world in a straight line. Maybe you saw that when he came to see the rehearsals. Neil does not understand why we tell stories instead of conveying the facts as they happened. For example, he wants me to say what I think out loud and take the consequences for it. What do you think the police would have to say? Out of the two of us, he is the naïve one. What he is doing, with the Free University, is too much in the open. Because they can see it, they will find a way to stop it. What we are doing is hardly even visible.

—You think it's better to be invisible?

—Making plays to be invisible? You can't insist on scientific logic if you want to live in this world. As you see, Victor, I can't rely on the actors to turn up, for the electricity to stay on. I make do with whatever arrives. So I have to learn the trick of making something appear out of nothing. But sometimes, I can promise you, it's better to make nothing out of something.

Polk sent him inside to find Roland. The out-of-town actors, soloists, and studio musicians who came for shows or to record parts in a radio drama went to the bar at the end of a shopping arcade, past the women toting their bags on the escalator, convenient to the hotel and the main station. There were three ladies with coloured curlers in their hair sitting underneath the hood dryers in the salon, their handbags laid on the leather chairs behind them.

Victor realised he was hungry. The sharp smells interested him, burning coffee and sausage rolls in tin foil in the tea room where the court reporters and the advocates went. However, he had to go in quickly, careful not to attract attention in case a policeman or shopkeeper came to question him. Up until today he hadn't minded, because there was some strange pleasure in giving his pass over and having it found to be in order.

Roland was at the back of the room, stirring his sour spirits at a table. The bar was decorated with signed photographs of sportsmen in blazers, standing in black-and-white cricket pavilions, alongside portraits of Natal prime ministers and a painting that depicted, in heavy brush strokes, King Shaka bending his legs behind a cowhide shield.

Besides the actor there were only Europeans, a bartender in a short-sleeved white shirt, and several older men sitting at the counter. Roland passed for white in their eyes, although he had never claimed to be a European in Victor's earshot. The sunshine revealed his golden-brown skin. Yet he appeared to enjoy the freedom of entering a bar or hotel, a restaurant or the beach, without worrying about being caught on account of the idle syllables in his voice which sounded nothing like a European. He seemed to settle back into his skin when unobserved.

Victor approached, hoping that nobody would stop him from entering the room, and saw that on the stained wooden table, covered in burn marks, was a thin-necked bottle, Mainstay rum, and an extra glass with ice. Roland's attention was at the bottom of the bottle. But then he put down the drink and seemed to straighten out his expression.

Victor sounded ruder than he felt.

—Mr Polk sent me to fetch you, Mr Adams. You must come now.

—Is Peter waiting in his car? He comes to fetch me and can't be bothered to come in. Let him wait until I have decided what to do with the rest of this bottle. He's not the policeman of me.

—The whole cast is waiting.

—I can't pretend and put on a performance. I told Peter to leave me behind for this one. I told him I cannot work with Janet. What can you know about it? With your name, at your age, you can only expect to win. Whereas I am the master of losing.

Victor didn't sit down. He was dizzy, and didn't know if it was still from happiness. He needed Roland to come. Otherwise he would never dislodge Mr Shabangu from his roost and take his pass book back. He would never be safe.

—I can see that you are unhappier when you are separated from Janet. So I don't think Mr Polk is to blame.

—On every production Peter has to have a favourite, apart from Janet. Do you know that I used to be his favourite when I was a few years older than you are right now? Today you happen to be the favourite. Although you are only a helper on the set. He has plans for you.

—Your life is still good.

—It only looks like that from the outside. Inside I am still as desperate as when I was your age.

Victor wasn't sure how to reply this time. He had heard it before. There was so much feeling in the man. When Roland had sent Victor on a mission at any point in the past few weeks—to take money to a jockey at the turf club who might send back information on the condition of the horses, to take a receipt to the Tattersalls, to make an appointment with Janet—he spoke from his throat.

—I will come after I've finished my bottle. In the meantime, I can tell you something you haven't noticed. Do you want to hear it, Victor?

—Please.

—That caretaker, Samuel, is jealous of you and Peter.

—Don't worry. Just come. So long as the play starts on time, I can handle Mr Shabangu.

—He is trying to be a father over you. Even Peter would be better than that.

In the car Roland continued to talk to him in the back seat. He ignored Polk. To Victor's surprise he was more interested in what was happening in sports than in anything to do with the play. It wasn't just the luck of horses and jockeys that Roland depended on, but cricket and rugby teams, Arsenal and Manchester United, and the Cape Town league games. He was someone, like Polk, you could learn from.

Roland fell silent when they went past a building site in the centre of town. The crane was crowned with a line of red lights and protected by a security gate. Two soldiers sat at the boom. They were armed with long rifles that lay in their laps.

You heard the occasional gunshot, then distant sirens, yet no report came on the radio or in the newspapers. After an incident, the police were surly, interrogating Bantus, checking the details on their endorsements, listening gravely to military radios at the roadblocks that sprang up, and hauling anyone for any reason into a Black Maria. Every Bantu was in trouble. If you were caught so much as smiling at a European it would go badly. Nonetheless, directly after an attack, Victor sometimes found that he was looking a policeman straight in the face and wondering if he was going to be hit with the man's truncheon. He knew that his gaze was too direct.

Roland continued talking.

—Look at what people read about, Peter. They want to know about the war in Biafra, to justify how they keep the Bantus down, and what the service is like on the Concorde, and the lifestyle of Aristotle Onassis. That's what your plays want to take away from them. So they're not interested. They care about what gratifies them. However, there is someone who does pay close attention. I have it on good authority that the Security Branch will be in attendance tonight.

—You're telling stories again. You have the disease of telling stories, Roland.

—I have it on good authority, Peter. For now, that is all I am permitted to say.

Polk was annoyed.

—Considering the state of the border, I hope the National Party has a better sense of priorities. If they have nothing better to do than listen to every word of my poor play, then we are truly lost.

The evening proved Polk wrong. The strike at the Clover factory, and the collaboration between some theatre groups and the trade-union movement had aroused the government. On the other side there were rumours about a new Mandela plan, a Mandela day on which freedom would be created at a single stroke.

Most of the men staying in the hostel came to see Polk's play. They were tough, did stick-fighting in the road, worked as security guards or assistants to plumbers and electricians. The Christians among them wore their church clothing, Jewish shirts and pants on credit, while others wore hand-me-down jackets and re-soled Bata shoes. Victor was helping

73

Janet with her costume. She released him after twenty minutes.

When the play was about to begin, the main light was switched off. Victor found a place sitting cross-legged at the side of the room. The hum of the electric fan rose as the men in the audience stopped their conversations.

In the dusk he was aware of the breathing ranks of people, their washing-powder smell, and the proximity of their legs and arms. There was a young woman, no older than he was but more confident, whose hand was close enough he could hold it. She wore beaded blue and red bracelets on her arms. She was intent on the stage. He ached to look her properly in the face. She was good enough to hypnotise Mr Shabangu.

Roland and Janet were standing, folding and unfolding their bodies like dancers, to indicate the start of the performance while the curtain was unfurled in front of them. Someone put on the eight-track cassette that had Polk's carefully chosen music on it, songs by Duke Ellington and Dollar Brand. After some time the curtain came down. It was rolled up like a carpet by a stagehand, and transported behind the stage. Victor thought he had never been so happy at such a moment of danger. He couldn't understand his own feelings.

It was the first time he had the chance to see the play from beginning to end. The setting was a private Christian school near Cradock, in the eastern Cape, where Janet was a teacher, head of the History Department, and Roland was the guard on the property. You first saw Roland alone, nailing a blackboard to the wall to the tune of a wireless radio, and complaining to himself about the wrongs in his life. He was unexpectedly large in the middle of the canteen.

Victor was surprised to see Roland on stage. He became

a different person. Even his arms were more muscular. Roland spoke too much in real life, a sing-song man, but on stage he talked in a stripped-down dialect, using only flat sentences and questions, language as bare as the stage, which held only three chairs and a hat rack, and the blackboard with corrections on it, and with as few elements as the tools in his hand. Polk was noted for the spareness of his script and stage. He would only admit a word, or an action, into a play when it satisfied some internal ruler. He made sure everything counted.

Janet's husband was the principal of the school. Nevertheless she had fallen in love with Roland. She kept an eye on him as she marked the class essays, her red pen held at an odd angle in her strong hand. Through the window, on the sports ground, the students were doing hurdles. She would get up and watch them when she could no longer concentrate while Roland painted the ceiling from a step-ladder.

They talked when he came down to clean the rollers. In the play it was an unequal relationship. Roland's character was handsome; he was far more certain in his skin than Janet. He had five children who never appeared on stage. She taught him to play the piano, which stood on the right-hand corner of the stage and sounded much louder than you expected when they played together.

At one point her husband came in. He was played by the husband of the nurse who came to the hostel to administer certain injections. The principal didn't acknowledge his wife's presence as he gave Roland a set of detailed instructions about the geyser. The principal had a soldier's posture and harsh voice. Victor didn't understand how the character could have been based on Polk's friend Professor Hunter. They had nothing in common apart from a patch on the elbow of the tweed jacket that Polk had borrowed from his friend for the duration of the play.

The second act brought trouble and reminded Victor that his permit book was somewhere in the very same building. One of the students stole from Janet's purse. She counted it, and decided that the guard had taken her property. Victor stirred in his seat and wondered if he should try to sneak out of the performance. It was too early. As he had suspected there was no sign of the custodian on the staircase, listening intently to the antics on stage. Mr Shabangu preferred to steer clear of what he could not control.

Janet called Roland to her classroom and tried to persuade him to confess. She told him that she didn't want to report him to her husband on account of his five children. She made him empty out his pockets in front of her and then give her the key to his locker. Victor wished he could do the same thing with Mr Shabangu. His world was full of accusations. Roland refused to admit to Janet that he was guilty. He thought it was because she had fallen in love with him that she was willing to go to such lengths. He had never stolen a thing. He wished that he had never listened to her stories in the first place. It was worse for him because she had told him about her husband and family, the school board, and the operation that had left her unable to bear a child. She slapped him. He pushed her away.

Around him Victor sensed the audience becoming more excited by the different predicaments, as if some secret, usually lost in the spaces between people, had become visible. He was distracted by the nearby girl and then by the question of what to do about Mr Shabangu.

When he came back to the play not much had changed except the progress of their feelings. Anger crackled between the main characters with all their unsatisfied and disappointed love. Victor saw that he was also angry at Polk, at Roland, who had delayed him, and at Davidson the printer, who employed him to set the government gazette and then pretended not to remember his name the next time he went to ask for a job.

At the beginning of the final act the guard picked his hammer out of the toolbox and never put it down again. He kept it behind his back, hidden from his companion but visible to the audience, the head going up and down as the tension between the actors varied. What was said between Janet and Roland didn't matter. The hammer mattered. When she accused Roland to her husband it listened and drew its own conclusions.

It was only in the final minutes of the play that the hammer revealed itself between the two principals. The guard was supposed to be collecting his possessions when she went into his room on the back of the property. Janet couldn't take her eyes off the hammer when she saw it in his hands. The tension was unbearable in the canteen, hardly relieved when Roland hit her twice on the back of the head, just as if he were testing the soundness of the hammer against bone.

His victim didn't have a chance to protect herself. She collapsed as the curtain was rolled down and lay stretched out on the stage, her feet trembling more slowly, for a few minutes before getting up again. The audience began to clap although you couldn't say what they were clapping for. Perhaps it was for her resurrection. Janet, Roland, and the principal stood in the front of the canteen and bowed.

Victor also clapped but he didn't believe in Polk's story. It was too neat. It was told from the wrong side. In his experience, it was the one who was safe, who had money in his pocket, who told stories, who also had the hammer in his hand and would stand over your body shedding tears to prove his humanity. Mr Shabangu, for example, had the hammer. Janet, or her husband, would have had the hammer.

He was sure his good luck had returned at the end of the day. Everybody's secrets had come out on stage. It was as if he had been drinking a secret liquor all day, watering a seed in his breast which had blossomed into happiness. He saw Polk, who stopped Victor to talk. He was as exhilarated as Victor. His shirt was open to the navel.

—You think it worked, after all?

—I didn't expect the men to understand. But it looks like they did.

—When it comes to a play I don't think understanding means much. Chekhov acts on your heart, on your breathing. Like Shakespeare. Next year I am going to put on *Macbeth* in Zulu. I hope you will come and assist me.

—I will be happy to come.

The girl Victor noticed before had vanished. He didn't mind. Polk, with his rusted white beard and wine on his lips, looked like a hero. Nobody else in the building mattered.

—Everything will be different now, Victor. We proved something here.

Victor wasn't sure what Polk meant. The audience was breaking up and the volunteers were folding chairs and putting them against the wall. He had to hurry.

—So your Mr Shabangu didn't come after all. I expected him to fix his evil eye on us for taking over his canteen. He couldn't forgive the intrusion. Steer clear of that man, Victor.

—I will try. But I have to go and see him now. I believe that he has taken my reference book.

Polk didn't appear to hear. He had turned away and was already talking to Janet. Victor couldn't expect any help from him. The building was almost empty and the men were already in their beds. When Victor went upstairs, avoiding the last members of the audience and Roland, who had come out with his face scrubbed, he found he was alone in the hallway.

To Victor's despair, the light was already on in the caretaker's room. He knelt and looked through the keyhole to establish the situation.

Mr Shabangu was nowhere to be seen. Instead there was a European sitting at the desk on which the caretaker checked his calculations and did his accounts. The pad of carbon paper had been replaced with a complicated machine, a motor bearing two spindles through which was passing a section of thick brown tape.

The caretaker was sure to have arranged it ahead of time. Victor couldn't imagine the machine being set up in a single evening. He was surprised that Mr Shabangu hadn't warned him to stay away from the top floor after the performance. It was as if he wanted to get caught in the act, wanted to show off his European friend.

Crouching in front of the door, Victor noted the man's reddish-brown, big-buttoned leather jacket on the back of the chair and the short trimmed hair on his rectangular head. He had earphones over his ears and was adjusting the dials on the machine.

At some point the caretaker would reappear. He never slept in any other place, never travelled for the holidays, never spent a night in the hospital. So there would be no other chance of looking in his room. Victor's opportunities were diminishing by the hour. Last night Mr Shabangu had eaten him. This evening a new man with a recorder had appeared to guard what had been taken.

Victor was sure that the man was a Special Branch. An SB wore civilian clothing, a leather jacket in place of a blue uniform. He had the reputation of being more intelligent than the average policeman. They were soft-spoken, possessing an individual potency that was feared throughout the country. You could disappear forever in the company of an SB. He could invalidate your employer's endorsement on the spot and tear up your pass book. If you were a European, he could confiscate your passport, put you on an aeroplane to another country, place you in detention, or recommend you to the Minister for house arrest. If he caught you, then you had your chips.

Victor was just standing up when he found that he had been picked up by the neck and was being forced through the door into Mr Shabangu's room. The man behind him, efficient and strong, forced his arms behind his back and didn't allow him to turn around. The man in front of him stood with his face suddenly red, removing the earphones and turning the recording machine off.

—I found a friend outside. Seen him before?

—He's working with Polk. Isn't that so, my friend?

A thrill passed through Victor's body, from his feet all the way to his head. The world was a performance. He and his father and Samuel Shabangu were players without a name, people who didn't count in the grand scheme. He couldn't say a word out loud to the Special Branch. But he defied them. He didn't mind being tongue-tied in front of them. He was even luckier than he had ever been before. His name would be a legend.

The man behind him held his ear and spoke.

—We are like the bioscope for you? You think you can watch us like this, my friend? What are you even doing on this floor?

—I sleep in the next room, where the mattress is. I was just passing by to see Mr Shabangu.

—Your Shabangu is not here to save you. Where's your pass?

—I am Victor Moloi. Mr Shabangu will tell you. He took my permit today. It's somewhere here in this room.

—You are full of beans, my boy. I must tell you that you are full of beans today.

Victor was held to the man's head. He stood on his toes, hardly recognising the pain, and watched the other man start to pack up and put on his jacket. It was a relief to be held, to be located, and commanded, and forced to confess. He had been on the run for three years. Now he could be clear of it all. He could go back to his father.

—Well, you will have to stay with us for a while, my friend. In any case we can't let you go and tell stories now to Polk and his brilliant parade of actors and actresses. We don't want to trouble his beautiful redhead. Tomorrow we will begin to clear up what happened here. We will begin to have some conversations with those involved. In the meantime you have come in the middle of an entire operation.

The man in the back released Victor and pushed him onto the bed. The two policemen, now both wearing their leather jackets, sat in front of the recorder, trying to remove the two spools without breaking the tape. He thought they were even more helpless than he was. Their system of pass books and police forces, prisons and tape recorders, this system which they carried in their hearts and treated as their gospel, was a childish invention. It had fatal effects, and yet its reasons were no more serious than a child's logic.

—My reference book is here, in this room, because Mr Shabangu sold it to me in the first place. Everybody knows. When you give him enough money he will go to the department and come back with a reference book for you.

—You're making a serious accusation. Mr Shabangu has been a friend to our department for many years. I don't believe he is trading pass books.

—Let me look around the room. I can find it and I will show you.

They didn't allow him. The other man went to fetch the caretaker. He came back, after a few minutes, with a smile that stayed on his face. There was no pleasantness in it.

—Our Shabangu must have heard something. He is gone like a shot.

1979

BOXING DAY

The arrival of the machines had destroyed the holidays. On the electric piano it was Neil Diamond. Boney M had released a Christmas album which used a drum machine at the bottom of the harps. The new Yamaha synthesizer took a star turn at the request of bands like the Carpenters and the Bee Gees, but it made the sound of a silicon chip. It didn't count as real music.

From Christmas Eve to New Year's Day, Yash was in pain. He couldn't close his ears to ten thousand radios in Phoenix township. Someone in his wife's family was sure to bring a radio-cassette player, neglect to ask permission, and set it up on the parapet, whereupon the old and the young, the toothless aunt and her thirteen-year-old niece, the grandfather in his sleeves and waistcoat, and the grandson in short pants, nodded along. It hurt him that his relatives didn't ask to put on their Lata Mangeshkar or Carpenters tapes. They wouldn't dream of listening to his recommendations. Yash was surrounded by the Naidoos and the Naickers, people who would sooner walk on burning coals than ask his permission. But that wasn't the reason he wanted to die.

This Christmas there was a swan boat at Blue Lagoon that you could pedal around the basin. The funfair offered bumper cars on electric rails, operated by his cousin Logan. Non-Europeans couldn't drive. For those who didn't own a television there were replays of *Taxi* starring Red Kowalski on Radio Port Natal. Logan had cousins Australia side who had private copies of the entire history of *Star Trek* on Betamax cassettes. But you could never trust a cassette in terms of quality.

In the window of the record shop in Commercial Arcade, Yash had registered the presence of the new album by the Shadows. That one group didn't need computers to make good music. If he wanted to possess their new record before the end of the year, he would have to face the annoyance of Kastoori and, no doubt, her mother and her father. But he couldn't borrow any more from her parents. They were involved in everyone else's money matters, particularly those of their daughter Kastoori and her husband, who had gone too deep into debt to be excused for his expensive record collection. They were just looking for a chance to make him sell it back to the shop at a steep discount.

The Naidoos were as stern with him as they would have been with another person's difficult child. Yash was a performer. They looked at his existence as a kid's performance. He played the guitar, read British music magazines on special order, associated with that Logan and his troublemaking friends, followed the adventures of Captain Kirk and certain comic books, and, in general, caused them nothing but pain and perplexity by his way of life. They saw it as the ultimate cheek.

For his part, Yash welcomed being caught out. He accepted that he was in the wrong from society's point of view. Modern music itself was in the wrong. The Dutch Reformed Church wanted to prevent rock-and-rollers, like the Beatles, from entering the country.

The parade of visitors on Boxing Day would be worse than Diwali. They needed to be prepared. First of all Yash had to get Sanjay cleaned. It was still early.

Left to his own devices, the boy refused to bathe. He feared water like a cat. But he liked it when Yash scrubbed him and rubbed him dry, keeping his head in the towel like the women in the salon who sat under the perm machines. Sanjay enjoyed the close attention from his father. While his hair was dried, he would close his eyes and smile like a prince. On occasion, Sanjay would throw back his head, hold up his arms, and keep laughing until he had been buttoned into his good set of clothes, consisting of cream trousers and a tasselled top. The green flash of his eyes drew your attention to the unusual length of the boy's eyelashes.

Yash went outside to get ready. He ran hot water into the plastic tub while through the open window Kastoori started to wring out and flay the sheets and curtains in the big basin, her elbows flying this way and that. They didn't speak. She had started the preparations late.

He took no pleasure being out and about. There was no sunshine on the day after Christmas, only a layer of cloud and the feeling of warmth remaining in the ground. The ranks of green- and red-walled houses, tin roofs dull despite the morning, were arrayed on eroded hillsides. The vast Indian township, set behind two lines of hills from the ocean, could have been a hundred kilometres inland for all that you could dream of the water. But there was mother-of-pearl light painted on the shell of the sky. There was only a cement truck moving on the road. Its green funnel with yellow stripes rotated lazily, almost as if a child's hand were turning around a toy.

Yash put the tap on, waited for the bath to fill, and heard, over the running water, the sounds of the houses around them starting to wake up. The firm voices of women were addressed to their African maids and then, alternately soft and scolding, to their children. The din of kettles and frying pans and outdoor taps and household dogs shaking themselves into rapid life and joyfully barking came over the cement walls.

At first there were no men to be heard. But by the time the bath was slopping, Yash saw the usual procession of older men moving along the sanded road below the property in the direction of Govindsamy's private bus. They were familiar, although he didn't know their names. Some wore black waistcoats and hats, bound for service in Umbilo car dealerships and the bookkeeping sections of Pinetown factories and the manifold departments of the Durban Corporation.

It wasn't exceptional for an Indian to rise to the clerical level, to manage books or inventory, although an African was beyond the pale. Yash was ineligible for advancement because, at the age of fifteen, he had failed his standard-grade mathematics paper, a fact his wife and her family held against him and would continue to do so until they returned from having him cremated. Then they would take turns accusing his ashes.

He had brought bad luck on them after all. He didn't defend himself. Yash had been preceded in Kastoori's affections by a boy whose family had a share in a petrol station. The boy in question had been ill with asthma, had dropped out of government school for the year, and thereafter out of Kastoori's affections. But he remained in her heart as a possibility whenever they passed the Shell garage, and maybe any garage. As her husband, Yash didn't grudge Kastoori her dissatisfactions. There was something impersonal in her numerous complaints. They happened to be against him. They could have been against anyone. These dissatisfactions filled her soul, occupying her passing attention like so many motes moving in a column of sunshine.

He found Kastoori again in the bedroom. She was noiselessly and angrily washing her face, making her wiry black hair into a bun, and pinning back the clean pair of nylon curtains to let in the air. It wasn't unusual for Kastoori to ignore him for twenty-four hours if she had consented to intercourse the night before. In the dark, she wound her cold bony legs around him and talked her nonsensical heart into his ears. She turned her narrow back to him so that he felt the curve of her side and the pulse in her arm. After ten minutes she withdrew and continued to behave as if Yash had injured her dignity. He couldn't help thinking that it injured her and the other Naidoos that a man without money should penetrate Kastoori.

You got used to certain facts about a person if she happened to be your wife, just as you became accustomed to a flat, collected, never altogether beautiful face, and a small, stocky, chocolate-brown body which was tense with pride. He had never seen her moved by any piece of music except for Christmas pop. She didn't subside, didn't relax her hold, and therefore occupied more space in the room than size suggested. To others Kastoori was imperceptible, a slip of a thing who was exhausted by her roles as mother and wife and daughter, sister and sister-in-law, cousin and aunt, pious burner of incense in the temple. There was nobody else who could believe that, in Kastoori's shape, there was something dangerous to his life.

—What you wasting time for, Yash? I thought Sanjay would be finished with the bath already. I must do the next load of washing in the bath. The sink is full up.

—I am about to get him out of bed.

—You can go straight ahead. Go straight ahead.

Nevertheless, he stood there, unwilling to move at Kastoori's instruction. Having opened the house to the outside she retreated to the counters in the kitchen, where she was in the middle of sifting brown rice into a blue-and-white Dutch biscuit tin. She emptied the sieve after each cup of rice, straining her eyes with the effort of watching for tiny insects.

Yash was excited by his wife's nearness to him, by her indifference. Something from the previous night had carried over into the morning, some kind of current that flowed between them. It didn't matter that she repudiated him at any opportunity and that her heart was like a corporation air-conditioner. She was plain. Yet, in this minute, Kastoori exerted the same power as a beautiful woman.

—Electricity does not come for free. By the time you finish standing there, the water will already be cold, Yash. Any minute your family might turn up at the door. Since you don't have shame about the state of the house, why should I? Let them see how things really are.

—We have the whole day.

—Don't you have to pay a visit to your European friends?

—Yes, as you know, I have to collect the money saved for a number of performances. They promised it to me from before Christmas.

—I know that you can put on a performance for your European friends. You should put on a show for your son. He wants you to take him to Logan's house to watch *Star Trek* on the video, assuming that Logan didn't already record over it.

—*Star Trek* is not for children, Kastoori.

They weren't arguing, only pretending, as if neither wanted to touch the shadow of the other person. If Kastoori suddenly forgot about the bath and the brown rice and the Hong-Kong-factory curtains pushed strictly to the side of the window, and sat between the two speakers that Logan had organised for him to listen to his Pink Floyd records properly, then, Yash reckoned, his life could be made worthwhile. But she didn't make the effort.

So Kastoori closed her ears. Yash enjoyed a measure of freedom. He hadn't ever sold a record, had never worked a day in his life in the back room of a petrol station, refused to act the dogsbody for one of the richer Naidoos or Naickers, who preferred to hire a family member rather than plucking somebody out of the phonebook. Yash hadn't gone into business with Ashok, Kastoori's brother, the one person in her family who could stick him. Ashok was already driving a Mercedes and had taken Sanjay and the other children in the family on expeditions to Stanger and further afield. But Ashok would never be able to impress you with his knowledge of music.

It was also true that Kastoori could wait ten years before disclosing her views on any particular topic. She held her breath, preserved the grievance. The fact disconcerted many stronger persons. Much older women and men, grandmothers and great-aunts and other luminaries, stood in a tentative relation to her. On the one hand she was insignificant, nobody you would look at. On the other hand her insignificance allowed her to burrow further into life and under their feet.

Today, in turn, Yash was underneath the feet of Kastoori. He had burrowed beneath her. He was prepared to die, therefore he was in the stronger position. She was ironing the previous night's linen so furiously as he continued to stand in the kitchen that the sheets would never again be crooked and the pillow cases would never rise and yet he felt excitement. He wanted to kiss his wife's puckered peppermint mouth and take her breath. But he would never do it. It was something illegal.

Yash entered the bedroom and stood above the unvarnished wooden-legged child's bed. It was hot in here as well, still heated from the blaze of the previous day when, for Christmas, the sun had made the earth burn in its joy like a woman in a bed.

Sanjay pretended to be asleep. He had moved both his arms above his head and was trying to stop his hands trembling with joy. When persuaded to start being awake he would be deliriously happy, running into the cupboards and in and out of the small house.

Yash bent over to speak in the boy's ear.

—It's Boxing Day, Sanjay. This is a day to enjoy properly, one more day of holiday. The weather report promises the full day's worth of sunshine. Maybe we can make it to the beach once my work is finished. Get up now. Otherwise your mother will be cross with me.

There was no reply, although Sanjay drew the sheet tighter over his shoulders. At ten years old the boy was more of a slip than his mother. You could imagine one of the rough, tough, backhanded and black-faced women in Kastoori's family shaking out the pitch-pine bed and throwing Sanjay onto the floor without noticing.

—I will be late for my appointment with Mr Robertson. He is the most important booking agent in this whole town here. Enjoy your bath while the water is hot.

Still no answer. He was talking to himself. For Yash, the summer's sunshine, an endless tide of gold-white light, was darker than night. He couldn't stand another such burning hour, whereas once Sanjay started on his feet no force on earth could stop him declaring himself like a rooster. It wasn't clear where such a tremendous quantity of joy originated. The Naidoos, and even the Naickers on his side, were fatalists, pessimists, cynics who distrusted other people and would slander and betray them. The only answer was that Sanjay came from the void whence the greatest tunes came.

Finally Yash picked him out of the cot. He held the boy close to his shoulder and felt that Sanjay wanted to escape from pretending. His heart strained at its line, one of the space-age balloons sold at the beachfront and filled with helium until it snapped into the air. In a township dominated by such Naidoos and Naickers, by the million-armed Govenders and the incense-burning Govindsamys who knew everybody's business and the Singhs who controlled a fleet of trucks, it was only the hot and soft touch of his son's nape that produced this sensation in Yash's soul. He had been surrounded and crowded, nagged and harassed to the point of exhaustion, until he wanted to kill himself in protest.

Yash carried his son out of the house and put him down beside the tub. Sanjay unbuttoned his top. He left it on the cement steps and washed his face in hot water without opening his eyes. He submerged himself in the tub, blew out bubbles, came up to rest on his elbows, stayed up and examined his skin.

If you let him stay there, Sanjay would look at his thin chicken-brown body for fifteen minutes at a stretch, show it off on one side and then the other, display his body to his mother with the utmost confidence. His girlish looks weren't the same as either of his parents'. The boy was a foundling. It occurred to Yash that his son had the manners of an imperiously beautiful woman, one drawn in the lavish colour of a Hindi film poster.

The routine asserted itself. While Sanjay balanced in the tub, Yash swiftly dried him from head to toe.

—You promised we could sleep late today.

—Did I say that?

—You promised.

—I might have. Sometimes a promise is what you hope will happen.

Yash hung the towel on the side of the tub. He pulled the shirt over his son's head in stages. He held up the trousers for Sanjay to put his legs into, and buckled the rhinestone-speckled white vinyl belt which had been his Christmas present.

—Your mother changed the plan. She needs to prepare for tonight. Do you know all who are coming? Your grandparents will be here, your cousins, and Verachia, who should live right next door before he emigrated to Australia. We are going to be in town so long. Don't forget how lucky you are.

—I'm not lucky. Last year I was the only one in school to have chickenpox.

—That's not enough to take away from your good fortune.

Sanjay had been kept out of school for fear that the other children would contract chickenpox and had lost the year. Since then the boy had started to complain that he had been left out of something important. He thought that something could happen when he wasn't around to enjoy it. Whereas, for Yash, nothing in Durban promised genuine adventure, neither the swan boat nor the bumper cars, hardly the *Star Trek* on Betamax which people brought through customs. He had guitar heroes, like Yngwie Malmsteen and Keith Richards, but they were far away. Their pale imitators played in Durban's surf-and-turf restaurants, policeman pubs, and motorcycle steakhouses. And Yash was even beneath the imitators.

Sanjay was his last true pleasure. Sometimes Yash thought that there was a piece of dry ice in his chest, smoking in its own coldness beneath the layers of flesh and blood. He wanted to tear it out, see it smoking in front of him. He needed to go and see Christiaan Barnard, the international heart surgeon.

Yash had been planning to kill himself for almost a year. He dated the decision to the Diwali before last, soon after the start of television, when his cousin Logan bought a dozen boxes of fireworks from Singapore Retailers. They had orange fuses and flaking green paper sides, smelled of the bitter black pepper of gunpowder when you held them in your hand, and shone with an alien light in the sky above that Logan's uncle's house. There had been a Catherine wheel turning back and forth like a hosepipe full of sparks and yet its brilliant white revolutions struck him as unendurably sad. Yash had been unable to stop his eyes filling with tears.

On the same evening, the Pioneer sound system had been stolen out of Logan's car while the guests were in the yard. Although Logan's uncle had immediately identified the thief, who lived across the road and subsequently played his own music on the stolen speakers, it was impossible to have his cousin's property returned because the miscreant was the nineteen-year-old, ne'er-do-well son of a sergeant in the police force. He and his father could make life difficult for Logan and his uncle, teachers in the same government school, if they went to lay a complaint.

Logan wasn't the type to forget an injury. Under the proper conditions he was prepared to take action. When the school boycotts came here to Phoenix, Logan had promised to march up to the sergeant's door, ring the buzzer until they were forced to let him in, and take back his speakers and graphic equaliser.

Yash thought that he wouldn't live to see the day this Logan put his speakers back in the sockets in the doors of his car. In the meantime, they remained empty to remind Logan of the theft, also because he couldn't afford to replace the system on his junior teacher's salary. Yash had an idea that Logan was one person who was capable of bringing about a revolution.

In a way none of them were good for him. Logan and Sanjay and even this Kastoori made claims on life far stronger than his own. Could they know that this difference in their intensities, the sum of their wills to survive subtracted from his own, reduced him to thoughts of suicide? He was at less than zero.

Kastoori waited to talk to him until Sanjay had eaten and gone to the neighbour's boy. She was unsympathetic to the change in his fortunes and his state of mind. Nevertheless, she was careful concerning certain points of etiquette. In public, for example, she didn't instigate.

—Yashwin, did I hear you correctly? Didn't you play last week this time with your European friends when we stayed for the night by Sea Cow Lake? Was it that Richard and Jeff I hear so much about? I am not starting with you, but I want to know which one still has to pay you out.

—You have it wrong. Colin collects the money. Peter is the leader of the band. Jeff is his brother. Sometimes, like last week, Jeff comes with the bass guitar and also a vibra-harp. It sounds a lot like a xylophone. People are going mad for it.

—Can you get in touch with Colin then, put through a trunk call if necessary, and make it clear that you are relying on him to give you the money for today? That man will never pay you out if he has a choice. The holiday is too expensive by now to survive on my salary alone. I cannot go to the café and spend a fortune on Sparletta and chips for the children, and then put it on account. That Govender will skin us alive for the interest alone.

—You can ask your father to give the money this evening. I will pay him back. I am going to visit Colin.

—Meanwhile, you have spent the rest of the money on more records. When will you have enough records?

—There isn't a limit. That's not how it works.

—In that case, I don't know how it works. My father is not a bank, you know, to cover up for you. My brother Ashok has said that unfortunately he cannot bail you out right now. My family can also have difficulties with cash flow. That one cousin of yours, I don't know if his last name is also Naicker, has said he will take you on at the petrol station. At the moment he has only an African there. In these past few years we have endured enough, Yashwin.

—I don't deny it.

There was nothing to be denied. It was only unusual for his wife to persist, reminding him they had reached rock bottom this holiday. Yash noticed when his full name was put into use and had come to resent it, just as if Kastoori was intent on placing the bit between his teeth. The Naidoos and Naickers used his name to move him around, to point him in the required direction, and, finally, to put him at rest. He wanted to be shorn of it.

His European acquaintances called him Yogi during rehearsals, sometimes Gandhi, Freddie for Freddie Mercury, born Farrokh Bulsara in Zanzibar. Never plain Yash. That would be letting him off scot-free.

—Be firm. You must get your money. That Colin at the bar thinks it is fair to exploit you because of the colour of your skin. How many times have you performed for him only for him to pay you out last and come short on the money?

—Colin is not a mere racialist, Kastoori. How often must I tell you? I have seen the receipts. The cover charge hardly makes up for the cost of hiring the equipment.

Kastoori could never accept his accounting arguments. She knew too much about the way figures were fiddled.

—I can promise you that he is walking away with big profits. Big profits. You accept nonsense from him on account of his complexion. If it's European, therefore it must be good. On their side they will be delighted to exploit you until your dying day. Meantime, you want to play music for them. You play their music for them.

It was Kastoori's formula, which she brought out like a bishop in chess, the piece that centred her attack on the society and also on her husband's musical interests. She didn't use English to develop it. For some reason, you almost never heard pure Hindi or Urdu or Tamil or Gujarati spoken in public anymore. Nevertheless, there were certain attitudes his wife didn't express in English. They were the things that were most important.

—You are quite correct, Kastoori. There I cannot argue with you.

—Then you must argue with Colin. You must give him a piece of your mind.

Kastoori went back to her ironing. They might not exchange another word in the course of the day. It was no better than a stalemate between him and her, which was no better than the stalemate between Yash and the world. For the first time in years Yash noticed his wife's small strong brown hands, almost white on the palm and bent around the hissing iron, the knuckles so hard in them that they might have the weight of bricks. They seemed to have no other wish than to flatten, batter, and beat.

Yet it was by the same hand of Kastoori's that their lunchboxes were assembled on a normal day, a blue Tupperware for him and a smaller box for the child containing a slice of brown bread, a hard-boiled egg, and a sloshing vinegary salad of grated carrots and raisins in factory-made Miracle dressing. The plastic containers were the gift of a cousin who organised Tupperware parties in Chatsworth. Kastoori's same hand had pressed his temple with no sign of impatience on the rare occasions that Yash couldn't sleep in the evening or when he lay on the trestle bed unable to play records because of an unexpected power cut.

Kastoori had given him a shot. It made it worse that she had trusted him and that he had failed. She expected him to take up a line of work and yet, up to today, he had no career to speak of. Meantime, certain families had begun to enrich themselves despite the legal disadvantages imposed by the government. The Singhs, who had once been market gardeners, serviced and operated trucks around Zululand. The Gujaratis and Muslims were moving on from tea rooms to becoming doctors and accountants, accumulating properties and shares on the Johannesburg Stock Exchange and quantities of gold jewellery at the back of their women's cupboards and Krugerrands in their shop safes. In this way they spread unease among those who felt themselves to be left behind.

Yash could have told Kastoori that he wasn't content with his lot. He wanted to do better and improve the situation. One day soon he would make a record so great and so unsuspected, so tightly arranged and so original in its deployment of trumpets and half-tones and slurring rhythms and the kettledrum and tabla, that it would go gold. Weren't pipe dreams right for pipers? His music would astonish the country. Rock and roll had no restrictions on it, as Freddie Mercury had proved. They would discard their prejudices, play it on LM Radio, and sell his records in the front rack of the Central News Agency, where today they were interested solely in European performers. Of course his hopes were only another form of excuse. Kastoori wasn't interested in his excuses.

It was entirely without desire, at first, that Yash noted his wife's strong haunches beneath her apron. There was the presence of a girl in her. It interested him. He put his hand on her back. Kastoori didn't move away, didn't turn off the iron, didn't look at him, neither encouraging nor discouraging him. She had never done much in the way of encouraging him since their days in school, when she had been vigorous defending her honour. She was still defending her honour although, in the meantime, she had borne a child and the schools had seen an uprising.

He pulled Kastoori towards him and put his hand into the front of her dress. She looked up at him, but stony-faced, as if nothing he did could touch her innermost parts. This aroused Yash more. He pulled her small head along his neck. He ran his mouth from Kastoori's shoulder to her ear, which was flecked with tiny and very sharp black-brown hairs. There was nothing in the world to move his wife beyond herself. She was an object, as cold in the mouth as a stone from the road, and could never be dislocated by his desire.

If he leaned down to kiss her, he would lose his breath forever. At the same time Yash knew there was nothing inhuman about his wife, nothing exceptional and nothing untoward in her soul that would not be found in a billion others. At the bottom of it there was nothing more to his desire than what made the dog spasm and the long green-and-yellow crickets sing from the gutter when the rain was pouring around them.

The instant he was inside Kastoori he regretted his movement towards her. They were interlocked in such a way that she looked up and brought her legs around him so that he had to hold himself upright against the table. She opened her eyes for an instant to reveal dark-brown beauty in the pupils. It struck him as a promise of uncountable luxury, some ravishing fact in her uncertain, ink-dot pupils. Yash had opened himself in the same act and had allowed his wife to take more than she should out of his skin.

He wanted to weep and to go straight under the tap in order to clean himself. Instead he closed her eyes with one hand, ending the connection between them, and pushed into her hips. He couldn't hear her breathing.

While Kastoori was dressing, she recovered her self-possession. The iron had burned a brown oval into the board. As a result she seemed to dislike him again.

—Take Sanjay with you. If he's here, he will have to be the centre of attention.

—He stays by himself outside for hours, Kastoori. You criticise the poor boy for faults he doesn't have.

—You can explain to me when you come back. Meantime I must make the house ship-shape.

On his way to collect his guitar from under the bed, Yash caught sight of himself in the tall mirror on the hooked inside door of the pine dressing cupboard, left open because Kastoori had stopped in the middle of her ablutions. The mirror told you just enough truth to catch you, like the witches in his setwork. Yash had a wide head, shoebrush hair that couldn't be parted, and a broad smile on an occasion like today which he didn't necessarily feel, brightened by a slender gold cap where he had lost part of a tooth in an accident with Logan.

There was no sign of the musician. Yash saw that he was an average man who might be found in the township of Chatsworth as much as Phoenix, in Verulam, Sydenham, Stanger, or Port Shepstone, wherever their grandfathers had settled to cut sugarcane and subsequently opened shops, temples, and petrol stations. He was nothing special precisely because he was one of a kind. There were Europeans with mullets and others in crossboned leather jackets playing metal in Hillbrow, Africans in white lounge suits in Soweto with their trumpets, but there was nobody looking like Yashwin Naicker, with his long brown head and fine-as-insects eyelashes. He was the first man to be born in Phoenix who wished to be reborn out of the ashes of rock and roll.

They boarded Govindsamy's green bus on the main road. It staggered through the sets of traffic lights, picked up new passengers at the intersections who stood on the stairs and paid the driver behind the high gearbox who put the change in a Salvation Army tin, and hardly picked up speed on the straight part.

As the road descended, getting closer to the European centre of town, the bus got quicker and quicker until it was rattling around the curves faster than the cars. At each turning you thought it was about to plummet right down the hill and held on to the bench while you watched the driver wrestle this way and that with the massive steering wheel. You imagined the bus burning down to its steel ribs.

Yash pointed Sanjay out the window. The hills were tattered in the direction of Asherville, red ground showing in their eroding sides, electricity masts floating along their backs, tightly strung telephone poles leaning in the direction of the slope, and closely adjoining wooden houses with porches and vegetable gardens installed behind their cement walls. On the other side you saw the quarry. Trucks came down from the exposed face bearing heaps of stone.

Next the bus went past the new mosque and religious school, bricks and other building materials remaining on pallets inside the gate. The facade was nail-polish pink and reminded Yash of an over-decorated woman, who might have been Kastoori's aunt, whose dry powder smell nudged you when you came close to her at the back. The mere memory of the sensation produced a headache in him.

They went down past the golf course, which had been designed by Gary Player. Logan had introduced Yash to Papwa Sewgolum, the caddie who learned to be a champion, beat the Europeans at their own game, and who had seen his passport withdrawn by the government to prevent another such embarrassment.

—Papa. Are you okay?

—I am hoping we survive the trip on Govindsamy's bus. This driver has really picked up the pace. I believe he is the son-in-law of that one Sydenham Govindsamy. So, as usual, there is no point in lodging a complaint. That family only knows how to stick together.

—You looked different.

—It was just something in my face. We are almost by Colin. If he is quick we can make it to the beach in time to meet with Uncle Logan.

Sanjay had his head on Yash's shoulder and was half asleep, his eyes closing despite his best efforts. The houses along the interior side of the ridge gave way to rusting railway lines and a coal depot, the pastel walls and link fences of workshops and petrol garages, and the factories along the highway sitting silent for Christmas beneath their unsmoking chimneys. Near to the beach was a shopping centre for Europeans, its walls tiled in blue and green squares like the bottom of a swimming pool, on the ground floor the dark corner of a bottle store and a surf shop with a dozen boards standing outside. Yash pulled the line for the bell and Govindsamy's bus deposited them at the corner.

Colin's place was separated by a distance from the shopping centre. You went past some palm trees and electricity pylons, observed the abandoned cartons of sour milk and radiant brown beer bottles, and then the hurried water in the nearby ocean and the cruise ships with their long decks settled out to sea and the radio hiss of the tide. A heavy-chested Japanese motorcycle leaned on its kickstand beside the trellis door to the kitchen.

Through the door you heard the Staple Singers playing and remembered, as if someone had touched a bell pull in your neck, hearing them for the first time almost ten years ago when Logan's friend brought the album from overseas. Music was the king of the soul.

—I see you brought your son, Gandhi. I assume it's your boy.

—His mother tells me so. Do we look alike?

—Like two peas in a pod. Tell him to wait outside. I will be with you now.

Sanjay was settled on a chair outside. Yash watched Colin operating on one of the big, smoky-voiced and porous-faced amplifiers that had started to arrive from Taiwan. They were temperamental. Colin was silent in order to concentrate. He had opened the front and was intent on adjusting some piece belonging to the innards of the machine. The coloured wires were clipped to the side of the amp with a clothes peg, curved for the hand like a chess piece. Yash watched, wincing for Colin, who was soldering the copper-orange buds of the electrical contacts, made sure the unit was taking power, and replaced the panel. Yash felt that the atmosphere in Colin's otherwise ordinary restaurant was charged with copper and electricity, with spilled liquor and Stuyvesants, women's lipstick and knickers, chips and vinegar and glazed boats of monkeygland sauce, and, in general, a thousand secret nights of rock. What did history know?

It had been Richard Stephenson, the manager, then Colin who had given him the opportunity to play guitar with a band. The group had been started in Durban for the purpose of imitating the new approaches in foreign places, from Tangiers to the Beatles, Del Rey Rock Festival, heavy metal. If Yash never joined a recording session, then he was still better off than being strangled in Phoenix. He only didn't see how to convert his son to the right approach. Sanjay didn't respond when Logan put *Sergeant Pepper* over the hi-fi. It was strange to Yash that the same child who reflected each passing sensation like a pond with its face turned to the sky should be deaf to a beat.

Sanjay was standing just outside the door. Colin pointed to him.

—Your boy has been so quiet, I think he needs an amplifier.

—He won't talk around anybody new.

—You shouldn't have brought him then.

—I want him to know what it's like, Colin, to have all the opportunities. I didn't even hear good music until I was fifteen, twenty years of age, when my cousin Logan began to introduce me. And to this day I cannot say to you that I have real knowledge, like a collector. Whereas Sanjay will have LM Radio, overseas concerts on television. The records I have collected will one day be his property. And in addition he will hear things we have never dreamed of. He will know what is truly important in music.

—Make him go back outside while I get my account book. We can settle it here and now.

Colin opened the heavy green account book and began to check for Yash's name, adding and subtracting in the margins. He had solid arms in short sleeves, much more muscular than you expected, and tattoos running to the shoulder.

Unlike the rich Natalians who ran the companies and country clubs, who got rich off sugar and ran the boarding schools, Colin was rougher and tougher. You knew the minute he opened his mouth to speak. He might have managed a block of flats or worked as a builder's foreman or an electrician. Despite Kastoori's theories, men in Colin's class weren't high and mighty. They weren't necessarily racialists. They simply maintained a pugilistic mood. They had the bearing of boxers and would push you off the European side of the pavement without waiting for the police's help. They lived in their bodies, were more comfortable in their skins than anyone in Phoenix was. They were used to colliding with other bodies.

Whereas Yash had his Christmas feeling, Boxing Day feeling, which instructed him to be at peace with the world. He didn't want to push anybody out of the way, not even Kastoori, not even his Naidoos and Naickers. He saw that his good sensation could not be distinguished from fearfulness. This desire to settle on good terms was the product of his situation. The more he tried to escape Phoenix the more it pulled him back with the snap of a rubber band.

—Colin, I am hoping to teach Sanjay the basic chords this holiday. I must only convince his mother, Kastoori. She does not want him starting to be a musician. I cannot blame her entirely, considering the trouble I have put her through.

—You're a super guitarist, Yash. I'll never deny you that.

—You are too generous. I wish you could have accepted my invitation to dinner last year. My wife would have been extremely pleased to meet you. In fact I consider that you would both have liked each other.

—Some time I will come.

—I will wait for the right occasion to ask again.

Kastoori was not entirely mistaken. Around Colin today, you spoke in an accent you couldn't recognise as your own. You held in and flattened the syllables, avoiding the up and down speech that reminded you unpleasantly of all the Naidoos and Naickers, the Govenders and Govindsamys. You would have said you were at ease with Colin.

But today you saw that Colin's intimacy had been withdrawn. It could happen with Europeans. A trapdoor opened and you fell through the floor. No explanation would ever be given. He owed you too much money to give an explanation.

Somewhere between Christmas Eve and today, and perhaps for many years, your relationships had taken a wrong turning. It had only just become clear. For the second time on Boxing Day, this day which had lodged in your heart, someone treated you with coldness enough to make it winter. You could hardly take another breath when Colin began to count rands onto the table. The Dutchman in his oval portrait on the note looked affronted at the simplicity with which he was meant to circulate from brown hand to black hand.

Colin pushed the blue-lined account book over. He put the notes on the table.

—I can't pay you more than the other musicians, you understand.

—I understand. All on the same level.

Colin underlined the figures with a pencil as he counted up the numbers in each column.

—All on the same level. No special treatment. You get the same amount per hour, minus the charges for transport, food, beverage. And when you work it out on paper, as I have done right here, it doesn't leave very much. I admit it.

It's not a big figure but I wanted to pay you out before the end of the year. The band has been losing money for some time now. Here is my suggestion. I pay you fifteen rand today, Gandhi, which is more than I promised you, and you can walk out of the door with your dignity intact. Then our business is finished. You have more dignity than I know what to do with.

—You said forty rands for four times, Colin. And I am not asking for special treatment. You paid the others before me. I have been counting on this amount for three weeks.

It had been more than three weeks, three months, and even three years since Yash had been free of the need for money. Money pursued him into his dreams and daydreams, spoke to him in a silk-purse voice, and then put a hook in his chest. He imagined dying there at Colin's feet and eluding its soft and hard embraces. Only the sight of Sanjay prevented him. The boy was impatient and had come soundlessly to the door. He was the last thread binding Yash to the wheel of life and its fiery lash of money.

—You can take it or leave it. I don't care which. You have seen the accounts with your own eyes. The book doesn't lie.

—What has happened to the other twenty-five? Did you pocket it?

—Your problem is that you have a suspicious attitude. Not everyone is trying to cheat you.

Yash regretted bringing Sanjay along. It was Kastoori's bad idea. Sanjay was as innocent about the facts of the world as he was about the way African servants slept in cement rooms behind the Indian houses in Phoenix and were spoken to as if they were idiots. For this reason, he took the money from the table. He thought that books could lie more easily than people.

Colin had another item to discuss.

—One last thing. I had a visit from the Durban North police station. They wanted to know what excuse I have to let you play in a white restaurant.

—You said music was the most important thing to you. You said I can play up to the proper standards. Why should we stop because of politics?

—It's not a political issue. Which group do you belong to? Play for them. Bring them up to the level you want. Instead you constantly want to take from us and hang around with us. I can't make enough money from the people who love Africans.

—I don't care if they love Africans.

—Don't make your problems into my problems, man. You have the money. Now go. Otherwise I can call the police.

Yash stood there. He couldn't understand the change in Colin. Colin couldn't understand the need in him to be able to perform. For there was nowhere to go. He would be a laughing stock if he had to go home and tell them that the Europeans had sent him away. Nobody in Phoenix ever appreciated his ability. Nobody had anything to give him for it. Their music was sickly sweet like drinking cough syrup. Not even his cousin Logan heard what Colin could hear. Not even Logan knew, as Colin did, that there was something you told the guitar that could never be disclosed by any other instrument. So Yash was more insistent than he should have been. He was used to losing every argument. He was trying to win an argument for his life.

—You can call the police, Colin. Well and good. I will be so good as to inform them that, because of you, I am money short. They will read your book and see how the accounts stand between us.

Suddenly he was facing Colin on the same side of the table. Yash was surprised that he was ready and that he had time to wave Sanjay to turn around. He was alert to the red sideburns on Colin's head, his very thin red eyebrows, and the red knuckles in his heavy hands. Colin's fists looked like shotput in a bag. If it came to blows, they had an undeniable cruelty to them and yet they would be as cruel moving along the side of a woman's body. They might finish you at a stroke. Yet there was nothing to fear. He had surrendered his life on the stroke of Christmas Eve. He was prepared for a fight.

Before he had the chance to change his mind, Yash found that he was lying on the tiled floor and could see Sanjay's bare, knob-kneed legs through the door and that his son's hair and eyes were the most luscious shade of black approaching blue. Yash's head was ringing, a bell whose sides had been struck as rigorously as you dared and yet from which you didn't sense any hint of a sound, no more pain than if you had turned your neck at the wrong angle to look.

According to the Durban by-laws, the best beaches along the Golden Mile were restricted to Europeans. Next to the discount hotels, not far from Natal Command, was the fenced-in Indian and coloured section. Logan had taken the trouble to read the municipal ordinances and discovered that the sand was open. The segregation rule applied to the ocean and not to the land. You could step on the sand, be you Indian or African, Chinese or Mexican, without a policeman being able to ticket you. Only if you put a foot into the swirling green water, sliding sideways along the beach and then disappearing into the undertow, could you be apprehended and taken to the charge office. This was the letter of the law.

It would be stupid to rely on a technicality. But if you were as clever as Logan, you might use the top of the Indian beach, across from the inexpensive counter at Tong Lok restaurant, to meet people it wasn't safe to see under your own roof. Logan, after all, was the kind of person who gave Indians a reputation for being intelligent.

The beach had different dangers to the city and different possibilities. Yash couldn't persuade Kastoori to set foot on it because it would ruin her complexion. His head continued to ring, from time to time, where Colin had hit him. Yash didn't have a chance to hit him back. Nobody was going to hit Yash on the beach. The worst was you might get stung.

It was a bad day for jellyfish. They were buried everywhere in the sand. You could be stung by a bluebottle and have to be taken to the first-aid table that had been set up on the embankment. Under an awning the nurses in their boat hats and uniforms dispensed purple stripes of calamine lotion and no-nonsense cortisone shots to the reddened arms and legs of the afflicted. In seaside suffering, for once, there was no preference paid to colour. Black, white, and brown stood in the same line for treatment, commiserating in their stung hands and legs amid the fierce salt wash of the wind.

Yash got a stick and pointed out the ready black stinger connected to the transparent bladder by a line of ink like a Bic pen. He warned Sanjay to watch where he put his big feet, something that the boy would never do, and rolled up his trousers for him. He watched Sanjay run down to the water and back in search of Logan, along the wall which met the esplanade and past the lifeguard on his wicker throne until he reached the line of fishermen, who placed their catch in a common cooler box.

Yash worried that Sanjay would suddenly jump up at a bluebottle's touch and have to stand in line for the nurse's tent. He couldn't afford to get the boy stung on top of what had already happened today. He wouldn't have the strength to go back and explain a crying child to Kastoori. His head had already been stung. He imagined that the people around him on the beach and in the water could see the outlines of the man's fingers on his face. If they looked closely, they would also find the shadow of Kastoori's fingers.

He went down to look for Logan where two men had brought a rope net full of sardines from the water and were selling them fresh, five fish for a rand, on the edge of the tide. The fish had gleaming silver scales and green eyes and continued to flap their tails, their gills shuddering in and out, until their heads were sliced into a bucket. On the flat blue ocean were the white-decked passenger ships and oil tankers, yachts tacking back to the harbour under straining sails, and flurries of seagulls which rose here and there and disappeared, only to reform on new points in the water.

Sanjay abandoned the search for Logan. He clambered on the sand round and around the net, investigating the slabs of fish, which one of the men was skinning and chopping before parcelling them in a newspaper. The same man gave Sanjay the chance to hold the sand-encrusted fish in his hand before he prepared it to be sold.

Yash looked forward to seeing his cousin. Out of the whole family, Logan, a bodybuilder who shaved and oiled his chest and worked as a maths teacher at Riverside Secondary, was the one who could lift the weight off your shoulders rather than put it back on. Day-to-day difficulties meant next to nothing to Logan, who put his faith in the future. It was the present he distrusted. He saw the injustices, the unfairness of the courts, the immunity from prosecution under the Internal Security Act, which allowed the police to detain and murder Ahmed Timol at John Vorster Square, Dr Hoosen Haffejee in Brighton Beach police station, and Steve Biko in the back of a van. Logan was certain it would be different in the future.

Yash knew the rumours that the Special Branch had started a file on his cousin since the start of the school boycotts. They had already kept him in detention for six months, releasing him only because of the publicity around Neil Hunter's murder and Logan's connection to the case. They would be ready to pick him up again if they knew who he was in the habit of meeting at the beach and what the titles were of the books he gave and received under the auspices of the weightlifting society in Sea Cow Lake. Logan was strong overall. He could pick up a table with one hand, holding his spectacles on with the other or folding the ends of his brown-black sergeant-major's moustache, and had arms as hard as a dumbbell. He was a small man of steel.

However, Yash knew that somebody like Logan, idolised at home by his mother and four sisters, with whom he played endless rounds of tunny, a hero to his secondary-school students, might not come out of the jail in the same good shape on the second occasion. When you went into detention the newspapers were forbidden to print the news. When you were lucky enough to come out, whether or not you had talked, sometimes you didn't want to say anything else. Many people didn't recover. Logan's sisters and mother were unusual in the latitude they allowed their hero. Among the rest of the Naidoos and Naickers, it was generally believed that you got what you deserved if you meddled in politics. Even a white man, like the respected Professor Hunter, could be shot to death in his house. There was no space for an Indian to misbehave.

Being put in detention, however, was the one thing Logan didn't want to talk about. It was as if he wanted to look over Brighton Beach and John Vorster Square to the new future, just around the corner, when there would be no unemployment and no police, no inflation, and no reason to go to the beachfront to talk politics. His cousin was only careful, Yash thought, because he would be dismissed if he was suspected of instigating a boycott. He enjoyed the admiration of the matric students too much to be parted from them.

The one thing you could criticise was that, beyond the Beatles, Logan had no real interest in music. If there was a radio playing, that was enough. In the company of his card-playing sisters Logan would even listen to Hindi movie music without complaining. He had ordered records from overseas on the recommendation of others, but he ended up leaving them with Yash. Logan would never concede that music was better than politics. In the ideal world, according to Yash, everybody would play music. In an ideal world, who would play politics?

On the beach Logan called to him. He was sitting on the wall next to the promenade, a holy man of the sun almost naked on his towel except for a pair of rubber sandals and the black Speedo he favoured and the thin gold chain that hung around his neck. His short tough brown arms glistened. You were immediately aware of the existence of his body. Later you saw that Logan was as distant from his physical body as you were, somehow removed from the armour of his own muscles, and the suggestion of fenugreek Yash associated with his cousin.

Next to him on the wall, Logan had a friend who stood up and introduced himself. He had a cloud of curly black hair on his head.

—I am Satyadev. Logan has been telling me about you, Yash, man, for years now. He says you are a heavy thinker. Delighted to make your acquaintance.

—Now which Satya are you? Who's your family? Are you from the Chatsworth Moodleys by any chance? There was one Moodley there who should run a shop for second-hand records on Brickfield Road. There was a Satyadev in that family if I remember correctly. You can't be his brother?

—We can keep to first names. Is this your boy? Come over here, my young brother. Is he stubborn?

Yash considered the question. He watched his son through the new and unaccustomed eyes of Satya Moodley, whose brother had sold a jumble of good and bad records. The boy, his boy, was slender, clever, with his helmet of pitch-black hair. Sanjay had found another boy with a plastic bucket and spade and was making his sandcastle with no awareness of the grownups. Pleasure started in Yash's heart, some strange pleasure at the five metres of separation between him and his son.

Nobody, however, could see his inner workings. He didn't want to explain the fight today either. Not even Logan could understand his situation as a musician. To think that, far in the future, when records would be out of date, Sanjay might find his father's profile on the plastic shell of an eight-track cassette, meant that his prospects were better than Logan's. The Yash Band would play music as secret as King Crimson and Captain Beefheart, to be circulated from hand to hand behind closed doors like the pamphlets for which Logan was risking his life.

—No, I don't think he's particularly stubborn. He wants to keep building his sandcastle.

—Let him build, man. So long you and me and Logan can talk. In fact Logan says you and I are both heavy thinkers and so is he. The three of us should have something in common then.

Was he a heavy thinker? Who would suppose it? Across the ocean, life had moved far beyond politics into new music, new unbounded seas of thought, amid free and beautiful women. It made their conversation on the beach painful to Yash's ears. Even his cousin sounded off-kilter. They were competing to prove something to Yash.

—According to Satya over here we shouldn't use the excuse of being Indians, Yash. He believes that we are truly African. He says we mustn't distinguish between comrades. We can't even call ourselves Indians.

—Your cousin is so clever he is dangerous. I knew Biko when he was in medical school here. Even when he was working for the Black People's Convention, some years ago, we kept in touch. And I can tell you that the only man who compares to Biko, in terms of pure intellect, is your cousin here. The truth is the truth.

—You don't need to flatter me, Satya.

—The last thing I will do is to flatter you, Logan, my brother. It is not a matter of the colour of your skin. The European can also be an African while the African can fall victim to the European of his own volition. If a black individual can use hair straighteners and make his hair to fall out, if a black woman can buy these skin-lightening creams, which the whites are all too happy to sell us, and destroy her own skin, then how African can she be? Why is it you won't see a single Indian woman on the beach here unless she is covering her whole body? They send their children for English tuition, only for English tuition, and forget their own languages. Where do you still hear Gujarati and Tamil and Hindi? Why do they dress like an imitation of a European gentleman? They keep their own food and music and give up everything else.

—You can't say ahead of time which music is going to catch you.

—I grant you that, my friend. But let's make no mention of how we treat the blacks in our homes. That is the one time we speak in Tamil or Urdu, to put them down in front of them. How many names do we have to call an African? We pretend they cannot understand as if there is someone who is too stupid to hear when he is being called a name. Then we go running to the European, pretending not to hear the names that he has for us. Why must they accept us now when we hate ourselves? Biko teaches us that the real revolution comes in consciousness. First, we free our minds. For that we can use the best of thinking from around the world. Second, we must know the history. Then we have the possibility of freeing the country.

Satya spoke as if he were highlighting each word with a pen. Yash knew before from Logan that his friend Satyadev was considered to be as dangerous as a communist by the provincial authorities, not to say the Special Branch. In Biko's absence Satya had become the leading speaker for Black Consciousness at the age of twenty-nine. He had been detained, had shots fired at his house, and continued to produce numerous pamphlets and opinion pieces on a printing press loaned by an Anglican minister.

Yash sat down on the wall next to Logan, and admired his cousin's bare legs and muscles more than anything his friend had to say. Nothing ran in families. He wasn't properly Indian. He would never be truly African. There was a length of sadness, exacerbated by the greenness of the ocean and the blueness of the water and the sky, between himself and his cousin. They were close and yet this distance stood between them. Happiness had all the languages on its side while unhappiness would be restless to take any fixed form of words.

Satya continued to talk.

—Before he died, Biko went with me to visit Neil Hunter. You heard of the late Professor Hunter? Ah, I should like him very much. At the same time he should always tell us how well we were doing even when we weren't doing well. He made a point of bowing down in front of us, which I could not understand. If blacks are not disposed to imitate white people, he said, that is a sign of their good taste. He believed in objective truth. I would tell him that it matters out of whose mouth the sentence is coming. That if a true sentence comes out of the wrong mouth, it cannot help but be false. It's the inevitable result of a society like this one, this world we have come into where whites have the history, the culture, the technology. For them, a sense of superiority is only logical. It took someone as dedicated as Professor Hunter to try to escape from that prison and still he didn't succeed.

—You don't think so?

—In the end he wasn't dedicated enough. I could never understand why he left his wife in the middle of his saga. People must learn that their personal desires don't always come first.

—I agree.

—And do you truly think, Yash, they will ever find his killers when the same people who are looking for the culprits are also the guilty parties?

He didn't. But Yash didn't understand men who divorced. There was something flagrant about it. He couldn't bear to part with any other person consciously, not even Kastoori. He could hardly tolerate having to leave Colin behind. Only he didn't like to offer his judgements in company, especially around Logan's crowd. He couldn't trust his very names for good and bad. His records, his fear of separations, his fight outside the restaurant paled beside their matters of life and death, their philosophy and their love of black skin.

Satya had pulled out a bottle of cold drink and poured from it into three plastic cups. His hair, in the bulk of its majesty, was unsteady around his head. It trembled like Kastoori's type of jelly.

—You need to speak for yourself. Otherwise people will speak for you. That was my only objection to this same Free University before the police closed it down. Biko would say it's an institutional disease for white people in this country. They want to speak on behalf of others. Even when they are with you, they want to speak in your place. The moment we start to speak for ourselves, this government will be over. That's what I have been telling your cousin Logan here.

—You don't need to lecture, Satya. You are also at the mercy of your own voice, chief. Let Yash here learn for himself, man.

To Yash it didn't sound like a real quarrel. The two men seemed to be good friends, on good terms, so this might be something of a performance for his benefit more than a discussion when people's opinions could move.

For a minute he resented them, even Logan, for using him as an audience. Then they went on, ignoring him and also Sanjay, who was running around the beach. They talked about politics, using the first names of people Yash didn't know. They spoke to each other as if they were both involved in the same game, an exciting one, but also a game which was much more real than the people on the beach around them, the concrete piers that stood on their grey legs leading into the ocean, and the buses that nudged the pavement, the drivers standing outside, talking to each other and nursing the burning lengths of their bidis while their passengers fumed inside.

Satya turned back to Yash after a while.

—Your cousin will tell you that I am no longer part of the working class since I went to University College, which was designed just for Indians. Do you know that they used to have it on Salisbury Island in the Durban harbour in order to keep the Indians away from the proper university? But I have learned something there to bring back. What we are looking for has to be a new form of life, a new way of thinking altogether, otherwise, at the very best, blacks and whites will only change places. Today's oppressed will be tomorrow's oppressor. To have blacks as the oppressor … what a change that would be! Yash, Logan here has been very active recently. We want you to do something also. We want you to carry messages for us, because nobody will suspect a musician.

Yash thought for a while before answering. Someone like Logan wanted the government to listen to reason and wasn't prepared to listen to reason himself. It was all in what you listened to. The Shadows could never lead you astray. He wasn't sure he was supposed to have an opinion. Logan, Satya Moodley, even Neil Hunter, who had become a legend since his assassination, were not so very much older than he was, but they had the energy and width of grand figures. They had a sense that the spotlight of something—

of history, of force, of people in their millions—lay upon them, whereas he wanted to avoid the attention. He wanted to perform but he didn't want to be in the spotlight. It was better to live in the crevices.

Yash couldn't reply to Satya. He was tongue-tied. Instead he was abandoned to his memories, from Kastoori's body in the clinic when it had become an object in thrall, to the women who had immediately oiled the baby from head to toe, shaved his head in a bowl of warm water, and combined milk, ginger, and honey to feed him. Yash had stood in the corridor, dressed in white leather trousers and a rhinestone shirt which nobody had noticed, and had then gone to play a session in a new surf 'n' turf restaurant in Umhlanga Rocks, the kind of place where they placed tiny white umbrellas in the patrons' drinks on each Formica table, where Yash had known that his fingers could search out any chord like a Chinaman on an abacus, where the conversation swirled around the tables, where the multi-coloured lights glowed on antlers stuck in the walls, while Valiants and Ford Cortinas stopped proudly outside, and where the Europeans were sophisticated enough not to mind that the backing musician was an Indian in a fringed yellow jacket.

The arrival of the machines had destroyed the holiday.

1985

SOVIET EMBASSY

President Tambo was in town. The train schedules in this part of London hadn't been restored since the long strike. Someone had called in a bomb threat, claiming the authority of the IRA. In addition, the pipes had burst at Queensway. The station was being cleared by a stern, orange-jacketed engineering team.

The city wanted to delay her but Ann was weightless. She ran past, conscious of her heels, along the side of the park in the direction of the embassy. She was supposed to meet Sebastian. She checked to make sure she wasn't in love. Her heart was as weightless as the rest of her body. Several pigeons high on the railings scolded her between their curled feet. Their voices were flat in the increasingly dark afternoon. One rose into the air and was lost amid the larger hiss of rain and the cabs smoking through the water on the roads.

The rain doubled, pouring like black syrup from the sky. You could hardly see to the embassy's long white building. There was no sign of Sebastian's tough yellow raincoat and boots, no promise of his steady face, which was so easy to conjure up. Sebastian might be considered handsome, by a sympathetic observer, despite the plum-pudding eyes vanishing into his head. When talking to him you suspected that his tongue had also vanished and that he was talking to you from a faraway point in his being.

Ann found that she was smiling. In sympathy with her expression, the man himself appeared at the next traffic light, his tall and thin figure moving steadily along the queue of taxis and vans. The rain had no power to hurry him.

Sebastian caught up with her and removed his hood. His raincoat was shining with water. The sparse salt-and-pepper hair was plastered to his scalp. She noticed that, because of it, his nose was more prominent in his face and his eyes had almost entirely disappeared. He tapped his watch.

—I'm late. You have my apologies. The French publisher went on. I had to sign a dozen contracts one after the other, initial every page. The moment you can make money for people, you're at their mercy. And how are you?

—I'm well.

—I can see that. I'm very sorry, Ann, to hold you up.

—I've been standing here for a grand total of one minute. The Russians can wait.

He was joyful. She couldn't say whether it was because he had escaped the rain or because he had endured it, whether it was because he had found her in a corner surrounded by curtains of water or because three days had gone by since they had last seen each other.

At the thought, Ann wanted to reach out and brush him beneath the ear where she saw the silver-grey start of a beard. It was unusual for Sebastian to neglect to shave. She hadn't imagined that someone could count for her again in the way that Neil had. His character was as tangible as a piece of marble sculpture. He was fixed in place while her mood this afternoon was as light as a balloon. Ann couldn't remember when she had been taken by such feelings. It had been years.

—You're not planning to wait outside?

—Farhad is supposed to meet us. He's late because Oliver Tambo's plane was delayed. You can never trust a Tupolev. They won't let us into the Soviet Embassy on our own cognisances.

—Before we catch our death of pneumonia, why don't we ask? I've found the Russians to be very reasonable about protocol. And I can drop Sasha Konisky's name. He was the political officer here before being recalled. I don't think you ever met him, but he helped me with a number of details.

—I haven't met him.

—At the time I suspected that he got in trouble for helping me with the plot of my book. The Soviets read every word I write, apparently.

They worked their way around the building to discover an entrance, a pair of heavy doors bearing a brass faceplate engraved with Cyrillic characters with the address stated in English in the right-hand column. It was sheltered from the rain.

In the space of five minutes, a procession of men and women in dark coats rang the bell, coughed their names and Russian explanations into the grille, and were admitted. They had Plasticine faces. Nobody gave Ann or Sebastian a second look as they came in from the rain. Despite her experience at the Defence and Aid Fund, it remained strange to Ann that an outpost of the Cold War should be exposed on an ordinary street in London, in earshot of the Round Pond in Kensington Gardens, with only a brass plate and an intercom to mark it off from the Western World.

In another minute, to her surprise, they were inside the embassy's double doors. Sebastian was engaged in Russian with a guard and then with an official over the telephone. She hadn't known he was so fluent. Considering the progress of her feelings, considering the half-clandestine nature of her work at Defence and Aid, she didn't know Sebastian nearly as well as she should. What if he was also a spy? Her feelings shouldn't be so flexible. Like the other exiles, she had a conservative heart. They drank to the bottom of the bottle and smoked gold-banded cigars provided by the Cuban mission and they were serious at heart. They had nothing in common with the young men and women who lived on the dole and went to demonstrations, dyed their hair purple, smoked Benson & Hedges resentfully on the top of double-decker buses, and moved their possessions into and out of squats as dictated by their squabbles and love affairs.

Ann watched the guard while Sebastian continued to argue. He was a very young man, hardly older than Paul. He was impassive, an open countenance that Ann identified as Asiatic rather than Russian. His white uniform bore gold piping along the shoulder. He held a long rifle standing almost to his own height, the heavy wooden stock polished to the clarity of a mirror. It had the frightening weight of a club. She imagined the young man suddenly turning and using it to bash in her brains.

Instead he insisted that Sebastian step back from the telephone box, held the rifle off to the side, and consulted the voice on the receiver. Then he returned and stood in front of them. Sebastian turned from him in annoyance.

—He wants to see the invitation. No wonder the Soviets are losing the Cold War if they can't keep a proper guestlist.

—Farhad should be here at any minute with O.R. This is a reception for the president, after all. Isn't it more interesting to be out here with me? That would be the gallant thing to say.

—Of course, Ann. I don't need to be inside the Soviet Embassy. But there's a principle involved. Once you allow them to get away with something like this, you will then be at their mercy. The Russians have to know where they stand.

—It's their embassy.

—Nevertheless. People have to know where they stand.

And Sebastian went back to the guard and to speak into the heavy black telephone receiver. The Soviet Union wasn't the lone offender. It wasn't clear to Ann which of the great powers caused Sebastian the most resentment. Nor was it clear where Sebastian's adversaries should be standing when they included everyone from the Soviets to the diplomatic corps, reviewers in the London newspapers, the various standing establishments from mailmen to Oxford dons, academic cliques and certain London clubs, meter maids, switchboard operators, branch managers at the district bank, and waiters. Sebastian waged an insurgency against authority in each and every one of its manifestations.

There was nothing bad-tempered about it. When he was insisting that the woman behind the cash register ring up each item on the bill again, his perfect manners and good humour were like standing in the sunshine. He refused to admit what he was doing. For Sebastian each was an individual case, a particular deficiency and vice—the mailman, who had gone to seed, the lazy bank manager, the small-souled reviewer for the newspaper. He didn't see himself as the common thread that linked his disagreements. Ann liked him for the fact that he scarcely took up space in his own view of life.

And he was usually more successful than you expected. After ten minutes of back and forth on the intercom, a new official unlocked a side door, presented himself to them, and began speaking in Russian. He held himself upright as if he were a shirt on a hanger, and had a dried-out, peapod face which made you think he was reserving his true feelings. Sebastian went to put the umbrellas outside.

The Russian looked at Ann's soaked socks and shoes, nodded fiercely to himself, and then extended his hand.

—Vadim Gerasimov, information officer for the embassy of the Soviet Union. I was on the telephone myself with our mutual friends and have verified your position at the Defence and Aid Fund. You are Ann Rabie, Farhad's right-hand woman, and your guest is Sebastian Gilliam, who is well known to me for the quality of his novels. Not, however, for his sympathetic views on the Warsaw Pact.

—I don't know if Sebastian has a political bone in his body.

—I am not here to judge. As a member of the diplomatic service I am bound to understand. Actually, as a reader, I appreciate your friend's writing. Very tight plots. One thing leads to the next, and not a piece of information is wasted. I will tell you the secret that I have never liked the endless tomes of Russian literature. Sebastian's writing is much closer to what I admire in a book. If we get the chance I would like to discuss certain points about his books with him.

—I have not managed to get anything out of him about his books. Nobody can, apparently. It's like something he does without thinking.

—That I cannot believe.

—Well, it's my experience, Vadim. On the other hand, we don't know each other very well yet.

Gerasimov paused for half a minute and then put out his hand to her, as if he had to convey a matter of some delicacy.

—President Oliver Tambo has been delayed. Farhad has been held up along with him. It gives us some additional time. Will you allow me to show you around the embassy before we make our way to the reception area? It offers features of considerable interest to the architectural historian.

Ann waved.

—Show us what you want.

—That would take the whole day. I studied architecture in Leningrad before joining the corps of diplomatists. Just have a look at this staircase. At the top, on the right-hand side, you will find the gallery. The endowment for the building and the art collection was originally provided by Czar Nicholas, who wanted to preserve the correct image in his dealings with the fellow imperialist powers.

Sebastian returned. They followed Gerasimov up the staircase and past a hall filled with unoccupied desks on which sat new typewriters. At the top of the building, the gallery was long and narrow. In their ribbed gold frames the oil paintings were brighter than the bay window.

While Gerasimov was talking about the collection, Ann was more interested in the scene outside. The rain had relented above the bone-white roofs adjoining the park. There were panels of sunshine. There was a fire engine parked on the road beside a telephone box, the bright red metal identical from the one to the other. She wondered why Gerasimov hadn't offered her a towel. He was too intent on questioning

Sebastian about his novels and hadn't noticed that her hair was still wet. She turned back to the window.

In the vision of the city, different to Paris, was something to stop Ann's heart. She saw the infinity of bridges and motorways, squares and churches, more solid than the plain houses she had left behind in South Africa. This infinity told her that Neil had died at the edge of what was meaningful and could be recorded. She was no better than a spectre in the system of what could be defined, counted, and exchanged. She was only grateful that Paul was better situated. Ann listened to the fading hiss of the rain and thought that the new lightness in her heart had nothing to do with the appearance of Sebastian. It made her want to pick up the telephone and talk to her son.

There was something else. To this day she considered herself a Catholic, attended mass at the chapel around the corner from her place, and took communion. She had never been a perfect believer though. Since Neil's death, however, she had entirely lost the sense that something was watching her, registering her good and bad deeds and the actions and reactions of feelings on her soul. Her inner motions were now no more substantial than the crackling of the bubbles in a glass of Coke. They came and they went and they made no difference. And because of this very lightness, she was more likely than not to fall in love with Sebastian. Whether it would happen today or tomorrow or at some indefinite point in the future was more than she could tell.

She wanted to tell Sebastian, to explain the lightness in her heart and the laughter which took hold of her, but she saw that he was being instructed on the important points of the largest painting in the gallery. Gerasimov didn't ask questions. His facts were announced from behind a hedge of very small, unruly, tobacco-stained teeth, Soviet teeth which had nothing to do with certain types of questions.

The Soviet Union might be at the end of its rope, as Sebastian believed, but its gradual decline was not giving it any clearer perspective or greater scope of imagination. The Russians were not altogether different from the Americans. They had the sense that certain serious questions had been settled by the existence of the Soviet Union. They couldn't imagine that other places might be on their way to different futures.

Gerasimov turned his attention to her. He was sombre, as if he had to pass on another piece of difficult news. He adjusted the sleeves of his blazer, put his hand on her back, and steered her further around the corridor as Sebastian finished studying one of the landscape miniatures. The diplomat was suddenly smiling. She thought he must be mad.

—Ann, you know the plots of your friend's novels?

—I've never read them, you know. In time I will.

—You must. When I was reading, I told myself that here is a man who has the grasp of what it is to do intelligence work. He does not exaggerate. That, in my experience, is very unusual in a writer of fiction. So I congratulate you. I congratulate both of you. What do you put it down to?

—I don't know. Sebastian's observant. Ask him yourself. Here he comes again.

—I believe, Sebastian, that novels are more important than ever. They are more important than video recorders and record players and television because they enable us to exercise our minds. They allow us to step back and see where the history is taking us. I also believe that the 1980s are the crucial decade since the end of the war. What was fixed then has now begun to flow. Do you not agree?

—I agree perfectly.

—Good. I am quoting almost word for word from one of your books. By the end of this decade, then, many outstanding questions will be resolved. I am not only referring to the situation in Afghanistan. Speaking as a Russian, this is when the value that is contained in literature truly begins to count for the enlightenment of mankind. Leo Tolstoy would say that literature is a disease that we can catch from books and that this disease can cure us. Not that I can bear to read him.

She was relieved that Sebastian was entertained by Gerasimov's explanations. He had been ready to accept her invitation to the embassy, after all, having learned Russian on a Berlitz course as a young man to get the conversations right in his second novel. He hadn't used the language as much subsequently, because his books had been set in places like Rio de Janeiro, Florence, Dar es Salaam, and Bulawayo. Sebastian detested the critics in the newspapers and the radio interviewers who asked him questions about his political and social opinions and his relationship with his famous brothers and cousins. But he seemed to like Gerasimov.

—Is this the official thinking we're hearing from you?

—In the Soviet Union today, nobody knows what is the official policy. The capitalist system itself is changing with the introduction of computers, satellite television, youth culture in general and the tendency to question authority. Some of these trends favour our position. Others, realistically, do not. And so I say, prove it to me that these changes work in the interests of humanity and I will follow. I don't need to tell you about the double standards of the West protecting its favourite son in Pretoria. What is their loss is our gain. Working in the embassy we not only have Farhad's wife, Parveen, but, thanks to Parveen, we now have Tanith. As we speak, she is moving our accounts onto the computer. I suspect that almost half the staff here and at the various peace groups are South African. It's not surprising, by the way, because in your country you can see the bare face of capitalism. You see the true rules of the system exposed.

—Do you like working with so many of us?

—Oh, you make excellent employees. Although it is not the universal opinion, Ann. Sometimes you are seen as wild and unpredictable. For me, this is not necessarily a bad thing. Each of you knows by heart what we have to learn in the Soviet Union, each one by himself.

—What is that?

—That it is not necessary to follow the rules too closely. Rules are there for the benefit of the people, not for their own sake. That there is a certain wildness which is indistinguishable from freedom, something which the English and the Americans have lost because they are too used to being under mutual observation. But I should be asking questions about Sebastian's novels. I have several prepared.

From her experience, Ann knew that Gerasimov wasn't speaking out of turn. It was the time of Yuri Andropov as General Secretary. The empire was in decline. Individual Soviets let you know that they were not entirely in agreement with the system. They practised a certain kind of irony that you might hear from the person on the top as well as the one on the bottom. Even this sophistication was encouraged by the system.

Sebastian was interested.

—What did I get wrong?

—No, in general I was impressed. However, I will tell you, there is an extremely romantic conception of the Yugoslavs from one novel to the next. The characters coming from Zagreb and Sarajevo are usually portrayed as free spirits, no different than you would find in a certain kind of French film. I saw the sympathy for Tito and his attempt to manoeuvre between the great powers. In my opinion, this is a typical British mistake. In reality, the Yugoslavs are not underdogs at all. It is simply the case that their great crimes as a society, the ones in which each and every Yugoslav is implicated, are smaller in size than it would be for you or for me. There is nothing innocent about the Yugoslav. Have you had a chance to go there? We can arrange for you to go there and see for yourself.

—I visited Zagreb in 1976.

—Then you know what I mean. You already know. Why am I lecturing you? Now I must take you to the reception. Parveen will be looking for you. She sent me out to you in the first place. In my opinion, by the way, in case we don't get a chance to talk again, Farhad is not the real asset to your organisation; Parveen is the real asset. She is the one people fear.

Gerasimov took them down two floors into a large receiving area. People were already milling around, trimming and smoking cigars in one corner, drinking spirits from square-bottom and dimpled glasses, stretched along the cracking red leather benches or standing next to the wood-lined walls and conversing in a pleasant mixture of unexcited Russian and English. He escorted them to a bench, where he poured drinks from one of the decanters standing on a leather-covered table and filled with dark-yellow spirits that seemed to glow in the smoky light. Gerasimov excused himself abruptly and went out of the front entrance, rubbing his hands on heavy blue trousers as he walked.

Ann wondered about him. He had been so happy on encountering Sebastian and having the chance to talk about Sebastian's spy novels. But by the time he left, he was morose again. It wasn't only the Russians. Today her own heart could move up and down around Sebastian as it hadn't done since her matric dance. She had been thinking about Sebastian and his long and friendly face and hands since he had put his arm around her shoulder the week before in the lift up to the Defence and Aid Fund offices. His hand, lying next to her neck, had been as cool as plaster.

It was amazing that the temperature of a man's hand could have so much of an effect on her feelings after a week. In her heart, despite the hardening effect of her history, there was no proportion between the cause and the length of the effect.

The spirits went straight to her head. They blended together the profusion of glass chiming on the tables and low yellow light from the chandeliers and noise of the rain into a new cocktail. Her arms and her chest became hot. She was sure she would remember this time, on this particular day on the second floor of the Soviet Embassy, for the remainder of her life. She could tell about Sebastian that, one day, she would fall in love with him.

She stood nearer to him, almost pressing against him and steadying her glass, aware that the flush in her chest showed above the collar of her blouse. It went from her breasts all the way into her neck and face, an oval of heat that sometimes formed on her front. Ordinarily, Ann would button her shirt and turn away from any company, roll a scarf around herself until it subsided, but she wasn't embarrassed by it today. There was pleasure in being opened.

If Sebastian reached out to her in the middle of the sparkling room, which was suddenly lit by champagne light, and were he to touch her on the cheek with his long, thin, and astringent hands, then she would hardly push him away. There was no more intense a wish she could recall. It could only be compared to her desire to see the outlines of Neil's face just one more time on the platform as the underground came into a station and her need to have Paul stand beside her with the puzzled expression that a mother could bring out in her son.

But they were absent. Paul was studying in Boston, acting in plays in his spare time, and writing her aerogrammes twice a month. He had an Ethiopian girlfriend. Neil had been buried in the same farm grave as his mother in a procession attended by a thousand men and women, white and black and brown, in a dry churchyard covered on the day of the burial with blue and red flowers that drank no water. Sebastian was right beside her in the embassy hall, although she couldn't understand what he was saying and didn't know where she had stopped following his conversation. It was as if she had lost her place in time. She looked into her glass, remembered the sweet-and-sour spirit on her breath, and thought that no drink had affected her in this way for twenty years.

Meanwhile the party had closed in on them. There were more faces from the sympathetic churches, friends and supporters of the Defence and Aid Fund, and the six cheerful, red-faced Scotsmen who staffed the dockworkers' union and could be depended on to turn out for Soviet and Cuban functions. Then there were a number of reporters and British officials, who acknowledged her from a distance while Sebastian was speaking merry Russian with the men and women around them. You could take Sebastian into any room in raining London, from a Whitehall bureau to a private school club to a trade-union hall or a mechanics institute or Turkish bath house. More likely than not he would know somebody and have the common ground to talk to almost anybody. Not even Neil had been so good with different people.

Despite his Conservative connections Sebastian had an affinity for revolutionaries. He was close to Farhad and on good terms with the people you met in Farhad's company, from those in the African National Congress and Communist Party to men banished from Guinea-Bissau, Nablus, Beirut, Burundi, Rwanda. They inhabited cold-water flats, drawing stipends from their Chinese and Russian sponsors, while they dreamed of being buried in their tropical homes. Secret money kept everybody in business. The Defence and Aid Fund channelled Scandinavian funds into the country to assist captured operatives. It went to support their families or to their advocates when they were allowed to mount a legal defence. Others were turned by the Security Branch, became askaris, and perpetrated the severest atrocities against their former comrades.

In the reception room Ann bumped into people she knew from work. She had to make polite conversation with them. It took some time to find her way back to Sebastian's side and another five minutes before there was a gap in the conversation. She had seen Farhad's wife come in. She had another woman in tow.

—I've been dreading Parveen's arrival. Don't look over, Sebastian. She's untamed without Farhad.

—Why does she work here?

—It was the Soviet strategy to keep Farhad close to them, to keep closer tabs on Defence and Aid. Little did they know they were getting someone to rule their lives.

—Like the story of the frogs who asked God for a king. They begged and begged, and eventually he sent them a stork. Then the stork began to eat them.

Ann sat down in a chair, looking away from Parveen. Sebastian sat in the opposite corner. They were still close enough to talk without being overheard.

—I feel that Farhad is one of my closest friends in London and yet he didn't say a word to me about getting married. He never lets out any unnecessary information. You won't know he has a wife until you meet her in the flesh. I suppose he's a good communist.

—If there is such a thing, Ann.

Was there a good communist? Sebastian was careful about committing to an opinion. Since they met he had hardly said a word about his own profession. Ann had the idea that his writing dictated a basic feature of his disposition. He was friendly but also watchful, paradoxically polite while capable of striking other people as rude, confident in his beliefs but careful to listen to anybody and everybody.

—The funny thing is, despite the fact that Parveen works here and terrorises the commissars, she's the opposite to a communist. If it wasn't for the limits on Farhad's salary she would only shop at Harrods and buy the right brands.

She had said too much. Farhad had indeed made a non-revolutionary marriage. Nobody had anticipated it from the reddest Leninist in the London contingent, who was as serious about revolutionary scholarship as he had been about memorising the Quran at the age of eighteen. Certainly Farhad made a strange doctrinaire. The more you were opposed to him, the more inflexibly friendly and charming Farhad became, until you wondered how anyone resisted the man.

His friendliness went as far down as his secrecy. Farhad was a confirmed bachelor when Ann started working for him, married to the movement and hardly on speaking terms with his own family, who were scattered from London to Leeds to Fordsburg. When somebody raised the possibility of companionship, he smiled and was impregnably evasive on the topic. Even the formidable combination of Tambo and Slovo, central players on the National Executive Council, had been unable to persuade Farhad to take a wife, although Slovo had drawn up a list of candidates. Nevertheless, Farhad had arrived one Tuesday as a husband, smiling no more than he usually did.

Farhad's marriage had placed a perceptible strain on his other friendships and relationships because, despite being a new arrival, Parveen treated certain of his connections with a slight but unremitting hostility, as if there was some knowledge of her husband it was her duty to eradicate.

So Parveen's presence was enough. Ann's champagne mood began to tremble, as if to signal its imminent disappearance. The unhappiness of her body began to return, the pinch at her waist and the uncomfortable mass of herself along with the cold sensation that had accompanied her since the inquest into Neil's murder. Parveen was a spectacle. Across the great reception chamber you could see her talking intently, her jaws working away like a mill grinding flour.

Somehow it reminded Ann of her unhappiness, as did Parveen's heavy arms, the dark hair on them visible when you stood next to her in the short-sleeved dresses she liked to wear, which had something to say about any woman's condition and her stubborn unbeautiful flesh. In the rain and cold, which had penetrated the reception room in the embassy, Parveen's arms would be covered in goose bumps. She moved them around rapidly when she wanted to charm the other person. As the wife of a diplomat, which was how she saw Farhad, it was Parveen's job to make you like her. She did it with a determination that came across as ill humour. And it was Ann's job, and even more her duty as Farhad's good friend, to go and talk to her.

Before she could approach Parveen, however, Gerasimov returned. He had in tow a journalist from one of the conservative newspapers who wanted to meet Sebastian. The reporter had dressed for the occasion in a double-breasted suit and solid brass cufflinks which weighed down his hands at the wrist. Gerasimov put his hands on Ann's arm. She thought they were too hot to be healthy.

—I am back as I promised. I was just on the telephone with Farhad, who is at the airport with the president. They are going to Farhad's house directly. Ramalho is also on the way. The embassy car will take you and Parveen there in fifteen minutes. I trust you have enjoyed the hospitality of the Soviet Embassy. Ann and Sebastian, you will allow me to follow up in the near future with a second invitation. If I may, I would like to strengthen your connection with the embassy.

Gerasimov hung there truculently, anticipating a contradiction. None came. Nothing would have made a difference. It was no easier to advance against his settled nature than against the Red Army. He found a pair of rectangular spectacles in an inside pocket, placed them on his nose as if they had to be balanced to stay in place, and looked back at them. There was nothing to say. His eyes blurred under the fat milky lenses and his posture was unsteady. On his breath there was the heavy perfume of spirits.

Ann realised that he had been completely drunk from the minute he'd met them at the entrance. He hadn't explained, but he hadn't tried to conceal it either. Soviet men and women, Ann thought, had no organ to produce shame. In the same way Parveen had no shame in her thick body. Nor did the Rabies. The system was as complete in its effects at home as in any Soviet Socialist Republic. It was difficult to listen to Gerasimov because he spoke in the smoker's way, effortfully changing breath into words. You saw the collarbone moving in his open-necked white shirt, which was made of ostentatiously poor Soviet material, and you began to feel out of breath yourself.

Ann decided that the visit to the embassy had been a kind of practical joke. Gerasimov had been play-acting, although for what audience she couldn't say. She disliked jokes, especially such humourless experiments. During the many months of the inquest into Neil's death, she had developed a fear of jokes. It was the Security Branch that played jokes on detainees, allowing a young man to slip from a tenth-floor window in John Vorster Square or to hang himself with a rope that he had never possessed. There was a certain sense in the fact that the men in her life weren't inclined to humour.

Parveen made them wait at the back entrance for the embassy car while she made a trunk call upstairs. Tanith, Parveen's new friend, stood with them although she didn't say anything at first. Tanith wrinkled her nose.

—Do you want to keep standing here in the rain? I can't bear it.

Ann stayed where she was.

—It'll be a minute for Parveen. Didn't you come in with her?

—We didn't have far to go. We both work here, if you can believe it. They pay surprisingly well.

Ann thought she wasn't unfriendly. She was simply a strange young woman to discover in the corridors of the Soviet Embassy. She had a cattish face, as bright and brown in complexion as if it had been varnished by the many people who had looked at it, green-grey eyes that didn't look right in the afternoon atmosphere, a small body and straight shiny black hair that reminded Ann of a Chinese woman. Tanith was dressed for the occasion to outshine Parveen and, indeed, the Soviet ladies, who had turned out to be dowdier than the men.

Tanith had a fortune on her person. She wore a heavy gold piece around her neck, a watch with a thin gold band on her wrist, earrings, and bangles to her elbow. She held a tiny square handbag covered in glass tiles in her painted hand, and had applied a metallic-gold blush above her eyes, which was unexpected on her skin. She didn't look at Ann but seemed to be interested in Sebastian. Ann returned the dislike.

Tanith produced her car keys.

—We don't have to all wait for the embassy car, you know. I have my own car. But it only has two seats.

—Parveen asked us to wait, Tanith. I don't know what to do now.

—I'll drive around and pick her up in front. If she comes out here you can tell her that's where I've gone. Then you and Sebastian come with the Russian car. We will see you at the house.

—See you there.

Tanith hesitated before she went.

—People have said the president will be present. There

are rumours flying around about his health. You must see him quite a lot in the offices.

—We don't. Farhad is one of his favourites but that means we get left alone. O.R. trusts him to get on with the work. Even if Farhad is godless he works very well with priests.

—I understand that, Ann. Farhad and Parveen are my close friends.

—I'm glad to hear it. Go and get your car then. We'll tell Parveen.

On some occasions, when you overheard your own voice talking about Oliver Tambo and the Soviet Union and the manoeuvrings at the Central Committee level and you saw yourself in this annoying golden young woman's eyes, when you spent the day in the company of the rueful Soviets, when there was a space in your long narrow bed and a saffron-threaded bulb burning on the staircase you shared with a medical student from Bangladesh and an Argentine playwright, when you signed for automatic weapons bound from Czechoslovakia to the frontline states, then you thought that some other mad life had grown inside your own.

Not five minutes had passed before Tanith reappeared. She was driving a two-seater Mercedes-Benz with a white top and silver-blue trim. The car's bonnet was bulbous and muscular. The flanges indicated the strength of the engine. Although the windows were up in this cold spring weather, you could hear the pop music loud on the radio.

Tanith didn't look at them as she went around the corner. Sebastian didn't notice until Ann pointed her out.

—Parveen has a friend.

—What do you make of her?

—They make a good match. Did you see that car? How does a young woman from Pretoria afford a car like that in London?

—I don't know, Ann. I'm not an expert on your country. Maybe she has a gentleman friend. Or her family has money somewhere. You can never be certain where money is coming from. It's as mysterious as blood.

—That's ridiculous, Sebastian. Money is a fact.

—On the contrary. In your country, from what I do know, money is the great equaliser. It's the one thing that puts a black and a white on the same level. In future, as the system is forced to change, it will be even more central. You can see in Parveen, for example, that she can't stick herself. I would say, like communism, there is something inherent to that system which degrades people in their own eyes. But when you have money, you can admire yourself again. Despite all this talk of socialism and communism, you might end up as the most capitalistic country in the world.

—I think we will have our own way of doing things.

—You already have that, Ann.

—You don't know how South Africa works.

—I told you I was speaking in ignorance.

There was no easy way to respond. Sebastian spoke, as he always did, as if he simply stood back a foot and considered the situation. There was often some unexpectedness in his mental life, in the things he said and believed. And what was surprising at first became logical after a minute.

Ann wanted to put her hand against him, to touch him on the stomach, to find herself bent into the turn of his neck and his long gravedigger's chest, to survive in the spotlight of his face that seemed to have lengthened with the years. His forehead reminded her of a good headmaster, as did his

146

grey-blue eyes held in reserve behind his nose. Around him was the icy scent of cologne. He had come into her life from nowhere. They had met in the course of Ann's duties at the Defence and Aid Fund. She had been raising money from one of the local congregations.

Ann collected the names and fax numbers of anybody who might help the organisation in the future. They would be asked to provide a bed for a visiting dignitary, to distribute posters in their church and university groups, to allow a trunk call to be booked to a number inside South Africa from their house, to write a letter on behalf of a prisoner, or to attend a protest against a touring South African side. Sebastian's name had been given to Farhad. He, in turn, asked Ann to follow up after meeting Sebastian himself and liking the man. It seemed that a writer could be useful in a number of ways although nobody could quite specify them. Farhad was careful about formal recruitments, though. They couldn't afford to take a South African agent into the local structures.

London in 1985 was more difficult than Paris in the 1960s. The organisation was riddled with spies. There had been murders at what were supposed to be safehouses while many of the operatives who were sent back into the country from the United Kingdom were detained at the airport. Many of the rest were discovered, guns and code books and radios in the trunks of their cars, at roadblocks set up like magic at the right time. Each time it happened, Farhad would say nothing. He continued to smile, and then made three times as many telephone calls from his cubicle as on an ordinary day. He wrote out and received three times the number of faxes, which he fed into and took out of the machine with his back turned. But there was no sufficient number of telephone calls to reveal the identity of a double agent.

The embassy car arrived with its unsmiling driver. It was a limousine with a velvet bench in the back and a massive car telephone behind the gear lever. Despite the driver sunk beneath his tartan cap, it was exhilarating to be out in London next to Sebastian. The street lights began to turn on and hang in the afternoon glow in their own papery light. The car went so fast that, through the wet windows, the streaming sources of light resembled a certain kind of movie and brought Ann the sensation that the day was a recollection.

The rain had vanished and the evening promised to be clear. Sebastian was fully in a discussion with the driver, using his Russian, holding her by the elbow as they sat next to each other, leaving Ann alone with her thoughts. The last time they had met he took her along to a bookshop in Piccadilly Circus, where he agreeably signed stacks of his novels at a desk. Ann couldn't decide whether he had the habit of entering any bookshop and offering to sign his works. He had telephoned her the next evening and invited himself along to the Soviet Embassy. There was something brazen in Sebastian which pleased Ann in the same way it pleased her to be Paul's mother.

You couldn't resist Sebastian. If she told the switchboard operator she was unavailable, he would turn up at the office and she would be completely unable to deal with him. You couldn't win against him if you had any amount of imagination. Everything that happened to Sebastian turned out to be interesting. He cultivated a curiosity in everything under the sun, from the foibles of politicians to the cultivation of Spanish oranges in greenhouses, Parsi burial customs, and piano concertos. He had told her about his travels in Afghanistan, where he met the old king, and the monsoon month he spent in Varanasi when bull elephants could hardly keep their heads above the brown water and the silvered burning bodies were tipped from the concrete landings along the Ganges. He had travelled alone to write his novels and then, more often, with his sons after his wife's death. His eldest son, Bruno, was at Harrow while Bruno's younger brother was spending the year with relatives in Rouen. Neither had met Ann. Sebastian had been a widower for three years. His wife had been diagnosed with breast cancer and had gone through rounds of radiation treatment which had reduced her to a burn victim. She couldn't hold his hand at the end because her skin was sensitive to any pressure.

Before they came to Farhad's house, to Ann's surprise, the telephone in the middle of the car rang. The driver picked it up. He had a short conversation, holding the heavy receiver close to his head, and brought the car to the side of the road, motioning to them to open the door. Sebastian waited until the man put the telephone down. The driver put his head between the seats.

—You must get out here. It's not far to walk. Go down here and then it is left on Gillespie Boulevard. Get out now.

—We're not getting out. If you want you can take us right back to the embassy and we can help you with the emergency. What does it have to do with Gerasimov? I heard them speak his name.

—You must get out.

—Take us to the corner, behind Farhad's house, and we'll get out. Comrade.

—

They went from one set of comrades to another. The house Farhad shared with Parveen and their numerous visitors had found its way into history thanks to a sympathetic local council which maintained links with the Sandinistas as well as the African National Congress. It stood in the midst of identical red-brick residences which had brass lettering on their post boxes and tall windows on their second and third storeys. You could see a middle-aged man in the nearest house lifting weights, bringing an enormous dumbbell up to the level of the window and then pushing it above his head, his wide black moustache hardly pinned to his straining red head, while on the floor above him, at the top of the house, a woman was patiently winding a clock with a long key.

Ann knew the neighbourhood. There was nothing outwardly to differentiate Farhad's house from those of plumbers and taxi drivers, teachers and union corporals. Tonight, however, it was lit up and the air had been cleared by rain. You could see through the entire house from front to back with supernatural clarity. You could hear with the same clearness, as if the day had been cleared of unnecessary noise. People were standing and talking in every room. You heard South African jazz playing, the trumpet of Hugh Masekela, the sly piano of Dollar Brand and the voice of Miriam Makeba, records that had been given to Farhad over the years by the very musicians who found their way to Shepherd's Bush.

They stood on the steps unnoticed. Just as Sebastian was about to ring the doorbell, he turned around, put his hands to Ann's face as if he wanted to turn her head in another direction, and kissed her. It came as a relief and then a comparison between the cold in the evening and the warmth of his forehead. Sebastian put his arm around her shoulder for a minute and then released her to press the bell. It was characteristic of him.

She felt a flood of affection. He was so beautiful in his nature. He pursed his lips while someone came down the hall. Ann blushed to her shoulders. She was grateful that it was dark outside. She would have preferred not to have to go into the light inside the house. It was hard to believe, on an unremarkable London street which bore a red telephone box, that she was in love and in the middle of a faraway war. She was pleased again, for no reason she could identify, that Sebastian hadn't liked Parveen. It mattered as much as the fact that he had touched her.

Then Farhad was in the doorway and they were inside. While they were still in the corridor, Farhad had already involved them in his questions.

—I am very sorry we were delayed. However, the president is right here. You'll find him in the kitchen with Parveen, his favourite. I told him already he can have her if he decides to take a second wife. He can have her. Why should I hold her back? She has her friend Tanith in there also. You can go through and talk to them. You know that I am not suitable company for my own wife. She has greater expectations than a mere diplomat.

—For us you are right at the top, Farhad.

—Then you must tell my wife. If she truly believes it, she won't have to socialise with the president. I tell you, that man can't help making eyes at her. If I was truly in love with my wife, I would have to take it up directly with O.R. and I would lose my job.

It was as difficult to divert Farhad in mid-conversation as it was to dislike him. The man had spent part of his childhood in Fordsburg, in Johannesburg, and the other part in London, where his mother had immigrated. He wasn't much more than fifty years old, as tall as Sebastian, and yet he had developed a mad scientist's demeanour with a ring of forlorn white hair on top of his head, bottomless reserves of conversational energy, an unhealthy pallor and the readiness to tease and engage and question each person he came across, whether a child or an adult, to the precise point of resistance. Ann thought he would have been a natural professor. Because of his work, Farhad didn't have time to go to the cinema or to read books, beyond the political pamphlets and briefing documents that came his way at the office, but he was good at prying out your opinions about the latest films and novels and comparing them with those he had collected from other people. He always wanted to know what mattered.

—It's been a day of high drama, do you know? Parveen was already on the telephone with the Soviet Embassy. Did you talk to a man called Vadim Gerasimov? He is the information officer there.

—He was the one who came to the door and then took us around the building. What happened, Farhad?

—Apparently the security discovered that Gerasimov was planning to defect. They searched his desk while he was busy at the reception. He must have been busy with you in fact. Then they took him back to his room and put him under arrest. The next thing that happened, according to Parveen's informant, was they came back and found him hanging. All in a matter of minutes.

—But we were just talking to him. He showed no sign of wanting to escape. If anything, quite the opposite. I thought he was quite drunk at the time. That's shocking.

There was some strange expression in Farhad's face. It was so unusual to see his eyebrows raised a fraction and his nose set to the side that it took Ann a minute to identify the sentiment. Farhad was embarrassed. In another minute he laughed, as he would laugh away any question about his own period in detention, and was now prepared to laugh despite the colder image of Gerasimov swinging from a curtain rail. There was something in the Gerasimov situation which you should be treating at arm's length. You had to look at it sideways, in the form of a silhouette, to keep it in the right proportion.

At the same time Ann's own heart was racing at the news. She wanted to go into the kitchen and sit down.

—Parveen is very hurt. At one time her office was next to this Gerasimov character's. They often had lunch together at her desk. I suppose, in a case like this, you don't know what to think.

—I'll go and talk to her.

—Do that, Ann. She has always liked you.

—Do you mean that?

Farhad stopped for a minute, and looked at her passively through his bifocals.

—Yes, I mean that. She will need another friend. The Soviets will be turning everything upside down for the next six months, examining every telephone call and letter and telegram they can get their hands on to see if they lost anything. As for our operations, I don't think we're exposed. Gerasimov didn't know anything about us. Times like these I thank our lucky stars that we set up our operations independently. If we were more closely aligned, then a single defector could take across the real names and addresses of everybody who helps us in the United Kingdom. Sometimes

I think it's better not to keep files in the first place. What's up here, in your head, can never be stolen. They have to take the whole person to get at the information.

She understood. She remembered Archie Msimang and Neil, Biko and Neil Aggett. Later Ann found herself at the record player. She heard Sebastian and Farhad's voices settle into the sound of people who had business to finish. She smiled at the idea of their conversation, the writer who had been born to a Scottish administrator under the Raj, and Farhad, whose hard-line views contradicted his welcoming manner. Their hearts and their minds were in different places. They were God's spies on the planet. You could trust a man like Sebastian or Farhad on account of his inner divisions and contradictions. They would hear you out, bear with you until the bitter end, because there was always a part of them that agreed with you.

Whereas Parveen didn't have the sense to listen to anybody. She was standing in the kitchen with the president, talking to him at full speed while simultaneously reading a recipe from one of her note cards, which had been copied in her schoolgirl writing from various women's magazines. She gestured with one hand to Ann to come into the kitchen and join them, but Ann stayed in the doorway and listened.

Oh, Parveen! Even if she was fat and ungainly, even if her thighs looked as thick as trees in her comfortable elastic pants, even if she had a birthmark the scarlet fingers of which reached to her neck, there was some unexpected lightness to her being, which came out in her voice. She was part flesh, part vibration. So it wasn't surprising that she depended on her voice and used it to fill the room around her.

Strangest of all was that the president was charmed by Parveen's performance. He was happy to stand there and listen, holding the counter with one stiff hand, as if to remind you that recently his health hadn't been good. People talked about it. They also talked about his liking for Parveen. President Tambo could be in negotiations during the day with non-aligned politicians, bureaucrats from the European community, representatives of the Reagan administration who refused to have any formal contact and insisted on lecturing him from briefing papers. He could be red-eyed and hardly able to stand as an effect of confinement to meeting rooms and offices and the barracks seating of Soviet aircraft, and having to deal with army raids in Swaziland, and yet, on the same evening, he would listen to Parveen speak the purest nonsense for two hours.

If he had been a younger man and any less serious, you might have said that he was infatuated. But the president was as fond of Farhad as of Parveen. There was something else in the relationship. Parveen had the talent to lighten the president's spirits. Maybe that explained most of what happened between men and women. You took someone's troubles away from them, even for fifteen minutes at a time, and you were more interesting than a movie star.

Then there was the fact that Parveen could cook. She fed the visiting corps of diplomats, fund-raisers, propagandists, and militants who came to London. She was doing it again. Parveen continued talking at high speed to the president about the greatness of her friend Tanith, about the verruca on her foot, about her mother's kidney disease, about the parking tickets she paid on behalf of the embassy diplomats, about Gerasimov and the strange comments he had made to her in recent months, while she scraped together ginger and garlic on the chopping board and pushed it into the hot frying pan.

The smell came up into the room, fresh and sudden. Ann was hungry for the first time in a week. The thought of Sebastian had kept her from eating. Now she was stirred. She wanted to live. She wanted Paul to come to London and live with her. She wanted to have the warm weight of Sebastian's head on her chest.

The president was called away to the telephone. Parveen had no audience and stopped talking. She cleaned a chicken under the tap, her stubby fingers adept as she rubbed the skin under the water as if she were washing a piece of clothing. She splayed it on the cutting board, salted it, and rubbed the pink flesh with red pepper.

Ann admired her from the door. Even a dunce like Parveen could be an ace in the kitchen. There was nothing she was as good at handling as this chicken, and certainly not Farhad, who was so careful not to show any pain or embarrassment at the conversation of his wife. He would joke but he would never say anything serious against her. You began to suspect that Farhad planned it. His friends were convinced that Parveen mortified her husband yet could never get him to admit it. He wouldn't even show it by a sign or gesture. Neither did he try to convince them that the opposite was true. He let others judge her.

Ann felt unfair towards Parveen and her new gold-wearing friend, who had come from shopkeepers' childhoods in the capitals of Pretoria and Pietermaritzburg, far narrower than the Rabies and the Hunters and the Bowens, and had adapted to an entirely different milieu. Someone like Parveen would have been in her element driving her husband's Mercedes around an inland Natal town, shopping for bolts of fabric and reading borrowed photo romances and *Fair Lady*. Instead she was the president's favourite cook and conversationalist, a scheduler at the Soviet Embassy, den mother to two hundred militants, and the wife of a man who was generally beloved, ironical, secretive, and therefore not the simplest of partners. If you went to watch Parveen in her kitchen, you thought that she had been born to this revolutionary life.

Sebastian came to rescue her. She knew that he agreed with her about Parveen. Ann was grateful. She shouldn't dislike the woman who was married to her boss. However many secrets and hiding places and double bottoms Farhad built into his life, he was her good friend. It was to his credit that Sebastian saw the good and bad of the situation without needing an explanation.

Because of the Gerasimov situation the president had to leave, along with his bodyguard, before dinner. The doorbell rang soon afterwards to announce the arrival of Tony Ramalho, an apparently young man who brought a pipe out of his jacket and, underneath a cloud of smoke, with a glass of whisky at his elbow, entertained the entire table when it was time to sit down. He had a short beard and was the kind of man you recognised as handsome without any physical implication. He was too contained in himself to attract a certain kind of woman.

Despite the fact that he looked no more than forty, Tony had been exiled since 1961 when the killings at Sharpeville showed that the government was not ready to tolerate peaceful resistance. The Ramalhos had been involved in the movement since the turn of the century. They were dedicated to political intrigue. Tony was Farhad's closest friend, more reliant on Farhad and Parveen even than the president, although he could convince you that you were closest to his heart in a matter of minutes. He talked to Ann that way, cared for Parveen as a sister, for Farhad as a brother, was so struck by Tanith's beauty that he put down his pipe to admire her, and was only uninterested in Sebastian.

Tony didn't speak loudly, but he was confident that the table was listening to him.

—My Labour Party friends tell me that, because of the economy, they have an excellent shot to win the next election. Still, I think we may be going home before they have the chance to go back into government. In that case, we will invite all our British friends to Pretoria. We are going to be the first proper socialist country because we are benefitting from all the failures around the world.

There was only one question that people wanted to ask. It seemed that they all asked together.

—You think we'll go home in our lifetime, Tony?

—It may only be a matter of months. Why are you so pessimistic, comrades? Are we in a worse position than Mao during the Long March?

Ann took the lead.

—We don't have any certainty that the government is planning to negotiate. They could be planting rumours as usual. We know this by now, how they operate. It's part of their strategy to fool the Americans and keep the world from interfering. Look at the Maseru raid. More than thirty people died. Most were women and children. Victor, Victor Moloi, was almost blown to bits. If they were hoping to negotiate, is this what they would be doing?

—Only a fool will tell all his secrets, Ann, isn't that so? But I am going to Maseru next and I will personally take charge of Victor's case. We are paying for a Swiss surgeon to go and take care of him. We hope that he will be coming home with us, back into the country.

Farhad and Ramalho both kept their secrets. The difference was that Tony Ramalho gave the impression of being entirely open. You heard him and, against all the evidence, you believed that one day soon you would put a foot on the flight to Johannesburg. Nobody else said it out loud. From day to day they lived in London, Luanda, Lusaka and made friends and married, bought cars on instalments, sent their children, if they had any, to a safe school. Every year Ann continued to renew her passport at the embassy in Trafalgar Square, where each time a woman staff member administered a questionnaire on her intentions, treating her firmly but politely, making no mention of the facts that lay between them.

It had been impossible for Ann to stay in the country after the inquest into Neil's murder. Yet she had never been formally banished. Unlike Farhad or Tony or any colleague at the Defence and Aid Fund, she could enter South Africa without the certainty of being imprisoned and tortured. She and Neil's second wife, Nadia, had both ended up in London. For the most part Nadia had severed her ties with the political groups and had started work as a hypnotist and astrologer, an expert in the migration of souls. So she had left her former situation behind and moved to a different level of significant action.

For Ann as well, the possibility of returning home was no more substantial than starlight. Her life with Neil was twice buried. Nevertheless, there were minutes in which she couldn't look at Sebastian because Neil's image was so brightly revived in her. Anything that moved her inside, even Sebastian's hand, redoubled the intensity of her memories.

Before tea came, the party had dispersed around the house. Tony had attracted Farhad and Sebastian to the lounge, where he folded away the cloth draped over the colour television and turned on the news. Parveen was busy in the kitchen, boiling the kettle, talking to herself, and laying out gilt-edged tea cups on a tray.

The bathroom door was closed and Ann went upstairs to the one on the top floor. The house was high and narrow, set throughout with dimpled plastic runners laid over the carpet, and lined with bookshelves on which Farhad had set out his books like game pieces—Wallerstein, Gordimer, Aldous Huxley and John Reed. In Durban the same books would have had to be stored in a suitcase so that they could be hidden. Here you could put them out in your house and nobody would notice.

Farhad's books were forlorn. They had been abandoned by their owner, who never had time to open their covers. But they had once been potent. In Johannesburg Farhad had worked as a pharmacist and had been led away from syrups and potions by what he found in history books and books of politics and sociology. They had come with him into exile, first across the border to Swaziland and then to the camps, to the German Democratic Republic, where he continued his training, and right now to Shepherd's Bush, where his mother had lived.

Ann went to the top of the staircase, conscious of the lights and conversation on the ground floor, trying to imagine where each of Farhad's books had been bought, from which bookstore had come this alteration in the direction of his existence from a Durban pharmacist to the mastermind of a guerrilla movement. She couldn't remember seeing him with a book in his hands apart from the school register in which he kept the unofficial accounts for the Defence and Aid Fund.

She walked silently. At the top there was a small window looking onto the red-brick backyards and washing lines behind the houses. Ann could also see Tanith on the floor of the main bedroom, quickly copying information from Farhad's telephone book into a journal.

When she turned around after a few minutes Tanith looked at Ann without any obvious reaction. She didn't get to her feet. Ann thought that, one way or another, Tanith would hide for the remainder of her golden life. She would create a serpent of a life and she would hide herself in her own golden coils.

—Tanith, you seem very busy.

—Let me clear up here. I upset a pile of these books.

Ann came into the room and took the telephone book from Tanith's hands. She remembered Archie Msimang and thought that history took the true heart and left the false one sitting on the floor of the attic with gold earrings and a convertible car.

—Leave your journal on the floor, Tanith. In fact, take everything out of your handbag and leave it on the floor. Then you can run out of the door. I'll give you a chance to get into your car before I inform Farhad.

—Why do you want me to run?

—If they catch you, they will have to keep you here until they find out what you've done. But there is no legal power for them to do it. Who knows where it will end? I would rather keep them safe from their own worst instincts.

—They'll blame you for letting me go.

—I think they will trust me for keeping them out of a bad situation. Later tonight Farhad will figure out what information you have taken. This is the best way to protect us. So run, Tanith.

Ann stood alone in the room at the top of the house until she heard the front door closing two floors below. Down there was Sebastian's voice, as deep as a cello, and, once she had the journal in her hands, she went gratefully down the stairs to meet it.

1990
THE NECKLACE

God doesn't love a young thief. Mandela wouldn't release him from prison. Nor did anybody in Tembisa think to run to the police station, behind two lines of electric wire, on his behalf. He was thirty kilometres from the centre of Johannesburg but he might as well have been a thousand metres underground.

The boy, Shabelo, arrived at the locked door of Mr Shabangu. He was shouting for his life. He went around the house trying to get in, knocking on the window, begging the occupant to allow him to enter. He tried to scramble onto the roof. His pursuers were catching up and he took off down the street, hoping to get in somewhere further down. The tin-and-cardboard shacks were set here and there, no rhyme or reason to their placement, as far as the eye could see. There were deep pools of muddy water between them.

Mr Shabangu counted to a hundred. Then he unlocked the door and tried to work out what was happening. He didn't like the commotion, at his age, so early in the day, nor the fact that the boy had drawn attention to his house. Why today of all days? And what did the boy have to gain? He didn't stand a chance of escaping from his punishment. There were already a number of men in front of him, warned by the people behind not to let him pass. Shabelo seemed to be running into their arms as much as escaping from his pursuers.

As Shabangu watched, the boy realised he was surrounded. He stopped in the middle of the street, poised to run further, until one of the men pushed him to the ground. From there nobody was sure how to proceed. A ring of people formed around him, but, as long as he continued to sit there, no one approached him. The hum of conversation rose between the men. Shabangu compared it to the sound of a turbine.

Shabelo must have been caught red-handed to have half the township after him like this. Mr Shabangu had often imagined himself in the same predicament. You had to be supernaturally careful to avoid being caught if you made a career out of stealing in the location. Nobody was going to come and lay a charge against you at the police station. They were more likely to take matters into their own hands.

Since Mandela walked out of prison, in any case, the police had been remarkably passive. They refused to intervene in disputes, sullen behind their fence or in their armoured cars. They wouldn't enter many sections of the township. In their absence there had been a spate of vigilante attacks when a man wouldn't repay a debt, when he injured another man and didn't pay compensation, when he carelessly caused a fire, or hurt his girlfriend beyond a reasonable point. The punishments usually amounted to no more than a kicking and a beating by the concerned parties. The community imposed limits. No bones should be broken.

Shabelo was in worse trouble. Even the old women came into the road and called out encouragement to his captors.

Mr Shabangu went inside and washed his face and arms,

looking into the brick-coloured water at the bottom of the bucket. In it there was no premonition of what the future held. He went back to the door, hoping against hope that the fifteen-year-old boy had found a mysterious way to escape.

The day was clear, shedding pleasant light on thousands of tin shacks, so close in places that their roofs were touching, on red clay roads leading nowhere, and pylons on the far side of the highway. Nearby was the undercarriage of a burned-out van from the month before, a mass of shocked white ash beneath the axles which for some reason hadn't dispersed. The men were marching Shabelo by the arm around the carcass of the van.

It was something you wanted to keep tabs on. Shabangu put on his coat and then put his Bible in the pocket. His grandfather, a converted Christian, had been the first to own a Gideons Bible, which had a magnifying glass tied on a string to decipher the tiny print. If Shabangu hadn't set up in Tembisa as a locksmith, and had continued to rely purely on his old methods, there was no doubt he would have been caught by now, the same as Shabelo, and would have been burned as a sorcerer. People lived too close together, ten thousand to a square kilometre of shackland, and developed suspicion. He was an old man, in the middle of it, who kept to himself and stayed awake late into the night and had the power to open any door or lock. He had to keep his eye on any disturbance in the vicinity, making sure it didn't come back to him later.

The scene had assembled not fifty metres away from his house. Shabangu could identify several of the figures involved. There was the retired bus driver, a man with a withered arm from whom he had taken a laminated road atlas. That man, who had taught himself to steer with one arm, had been out of work since an act of arson destroyed the buses. There was the fellow who worked in the bioscope, selling Rowntree chocolates. He had acquired extensive knowledge of American movies from which he quoted long sections of dialogue. Behind him was a woman in a long wig from whom Mr Shabangu had once taken a tortoiseshell comb.

Not to be caught Shabangu took extreme precautions. He had dug a space underneath his bed, sealed by two planks, to keep an item secret until it could be safely carried to the pawn shop. By prising out a few nails he could examine his takings in the early hours, when even the shebeen was silent and the cats had settled their disputes. He should have been entirely at ease, yet Shabangu often found that his heart was beating too fast for comfort when he opened the floor. He didn't know where it would end. And where could it end? He had white lines for eyebrows, suffered from vitiligo in most of his face, and arthritis in the knees that no amount of Grand-Pa headache powder could fix. He urinated with severe pain. He was hoarding the remainder of his days. But to what purpose? He had forgotten how to measure his own life.

The case of the boy was not unknown to him. Shabelo was an orphan. He collected the deposits on glass bottles, sold stolen hubcaps on the roadside, burgled houses when their owners were at work, and was even suspected of selling information to the police. Nothing about Mr Shabangu could be known to the boy, but he had noted the similarity in their names with trepidation.

Shabelo had been the subject of bad gossip. Now his bad end had arrived. It would have taken the slightest shift for Shabangu to be there in front of the people, his old man's body prodded with a rake. He had given some thought to what he would say to his neighbours if it came to pass. He would admit that he was worse than they were. That he had no explanation. That he harboured certain wishes and pursued them to their logical conclusion. That he had hurt the poorest of the poor and turned them against each other. That he had sowed unnatural suspicion. That he neither hated nor loved himself as he appeared to the eye of God. That he was simply the thing that he was. That no man was better than him.

He listened to the discussion outside while padlocking the door. Shabelo's voice was not much more than a child's while his accusers' were serious. They had been scolded by parents and employers and policemen. They were returning the favour on Shabelo. Everybody passed it along.

There were other cries and yells, some from inside the houses, others from as far away as the tarmac from which a young woman was shouting at a group of men who had brought spades. She could have been shouting to her boyfriend. Her face was lit with joy.

After leaving the hostel, Mr Shabangu had worked as an orderly in the outpatients of a hospital. He remembered the same happy tone from the young nurses talking to their suitors under the awning while around them men were disposed on stretchers, wheezing blood. He had often been alone with the patient in the loading bay and used the opportunity to ransack the pockets. It was important to get in first. Once inside, the patient would be searched, first by the junior nurses who contributed a share to the senior sister, then by the stretcher bearers, and finally by a certain registrar who rifled through the possessions of anyone under anaesthetic.

A hospital, like a hostel, was a good place to accumulate property. Whereas the community was unpredictable in Tembisa. It burned to take revenge for its memories. A career in the shadows, in the deepest of these shadows, was unreliable. You could borrow a hundred men blind, then run into Victor Moloi, who had given him the fright of his life twenty years ago. Now there was news Victor had turned up again, like a bad spirit coming home to roost. Shabangu could have sent the information to the authorities, and provided them with the guns to prove it, but he didn't like to have any more dealings with them than was necessary. He didn't have a long spoon to sup with the devil.

Shabangu worked his way past the people on the street, many of whom were keeping an eye out in case the police intervened. The man who had taken charge was not yet thirty, wearing a clean shirt and epaulettes. Made redundant from a timber depot, his face had been burned on one side. This man would sit at the bus stop, factory bread in his hands and on occasion a tin of golden syrup, refusing to meet anybody's eye. Later you found him beside the church, hands folded over his chest, a felt hat tipped over the burned side of the face, a poisonous bottle of spirits and a hunk of bread at his side. You would have taken the hat if nobody had been around.

Today that same unemployed man was in command. He leaned on a length of pipe, listing the allegations. Shabelo had been a long-time nuisance. Although he had never been caught red-handed until today, he was suspected of opening handbags on the bus, taking change from the cash register at the bottle store, removing the hubcaps of the doctor's car in broad daylight, then stealing the electric fan from the clinic so that, in the end, the Indian doctor refused to come back.

Nobody had hit the boy yet, except to drive him down the street and keep him on the ground, but now the labourer began to kick Shabelo in the back and legs between accusations. Then he retreated and removed his sandals while he consulted with the other men.

—And what do you have to say about it, Mr Shabangu? Finally, he has been caught red-handed.

—What is my opinion?

—You are the expert, isn't it, Mr Shabangu? We must hear your opinion before we make a decision.

—No, you have it wrong. I am not the expert on anything.

The man leaned on the nearby wall and brought his foot up with his hand. Shabangu looked away at first. When he turned back he saw the obscene purple flesh of the man's foot, exposed to the general view, and felt a bolt of sympathy for both sides. Your heart was on both sides. It was only in this place, on this burning occasion, that a barefoot stevedore would find himself at the head of the community. The man wasn't suited to the occasion. His blood was in his feet, not in his head.

—According to people, you have been living here longer than anybody. In fact, you are the oldest man in Tembisa.

—Why are you putting the responsibility on me now?

—Because you have the history. You, more than anyone, know what we should do with this boy who has stolen from everybody. You can tell us what the punishment must be.

—You must do what you believe is correct. There is no other option now.

—You are the wisest man, Mr Shabangu. I have relied on your advice in the past. It has never put me wrong.

Shabangu could not recall any such advice passing between them, no more than he could imagine himself as the oldest and wisest man in the vicinity. Did everybody older than him die? How did you measure the right punishment? What were the right units to balance the crime and the penalty? His interlocutor didn't help him come up with the answer. The burned portion of the other man's face seemed to block the expression of any feeling. This was a man of wood and stone, wood and stone rattling in his voice box. He was no more excited by the proceedings than if he were loading pine planks into the back of a Datsun. Today was merely a piece of business.

The man went around the corner, limping on the pipe, and came back with a present. He was carrying a tyre that he now placed over Shabelo's shoulders. There had been many killings in Tembisa, most by the police, but there had also been rough treatment for councillors or railway policemen who refused to resign and anyone who didn't honour the boycotts.

The tyre was a gate to a different condition. You saw it and believed that you had entered the severest hour of your dream. At the same time, there was nothing fantastical in the sight of Shabelo sitting on the ground, awkward because of the tyre, which confined his arms. He was moving in every direction to avoid the blows that had started to come from other men as well. They began to stun him. He was quieter as it went along, as if a boy who lived by stealing hubcaps accepted dying in a tyre. He took the fault on himself.

Shabelo had brought his trouble on himself by being conspicuous. Indeed, there was something unlikeable about him. His demands for money and bread and attention meant that not even the older men and women, for whom he carried shopping bags from the bus terminal to their doorstep, talked to him with affection. Nor did he get on with the other boys. They carried knives and chased guns and young women, drank beer in the mornings, played cat and mouse with the police, and stoned cars on the highway. They were rated normal.

—Are you satisfied?

—What do you mean?

—This is your doing, Mr Shabangu. You made the judgement. I am simply prepared to carry it out. Are you satisfied?

—I am satisfied.

The labourer turned his attention back to the boy. Shabangu couldn't help moving closer and closer as well, pushed by the hands behind him, listening for the sound of a siren, and at the same time searching for a feeling in the boy's countenance. Shabelo tried to stand up again, only to be pushed down.

Other men joined in. They took turns hitting the boy on the head while another man was clapping him on the back with a sandal. That man put his hand into the tyre before turning the boy around while he reached forward and slapped him again. Shabangu thought that Shabelo was too young to be murdered in the open. It was too much like sports.

The very distance he felt moved Mr Shabangu to the front of the proceeding. He wasn't stopping to look and was pushed forward as a result. He was close enough to Shabelo to revile him and kick him, to handle him by the tyre, to sense the heat and sweat of the boy's body as sweet as a golden syrup. He was expected to join in. While he did nothing, he was as good as confessing his guilt. He had pilfered from their pockets and shopping bags, taken from cash registers and shop counters, from shelves and cupboards in unattended houses. He had opened half the doors in Tembisa. His neighbours hired him when they misplaced their keys or broke their locks. His collection of skeleton keys, in fact, was a matter of public knowledge. So far nobody had thought to connect him with any robberies. He was protected only by the direction of their thoughts. They would sooner blame Shabelo. Many of the deeds that had been ascribed to the boy, no doubt, were the acts of Mr Shabangu. His guilt exceeded Shabelo's as a drop was exceeded by the ocean. If he admitted it, they would both die.

Shabelo stopped moving. The men and women were no longer hitting him hard, as if to consider the threshold at which they had arrived. Rather than striking him again, they were pressing him on his wounded head and back, encouraging him to sit. He rocked back and forth in the tyre. Somebody at the back received a box of matches and passed it forward. It was given to Shabangu, who felt the sandpaper sides on his palms. Without making any motion of his own, he in turn had the matchbox taken out of his hands. He turned round to see who had given it to him.

As if in a dream he saw a woman in a red blouse carrying a petrol tin past him. She poured glittering petrol over the tyre, the liquid shining in the sun as its penetrating scent spread. Shabelo put his hands up to the tyre. He made an effort to raise it from his shoulders, but the woman placed her hand gently on the rim to prevent it. She kept her hand on the tyre while Shabangu heard the matches struck by an unknown hand, one after the other, and applied to the rubber. It started to smoke, poured out its concentrated brown perfume, and began to crackle healthily around the boy's shoulders.

You thought, if you listened closely, that underneath the delighted conversation, you could hear Shabelo talking softly but determinedly to his assailants. You heard him explain his plans, reminding them that he had never stolen anything more than a bag of white sugar to make caramel. You heard him distinguish between the man who stole as a luxury, as a way of testing his relationship to God, and the boy who was hungry enough to sell false information and who might have done nothing more than call up the talking clock to find out the time. He muttered that accusation wasn't the same thing as proof.

A circle of fire sprang up. It was orange and fierce, so terrible it was impossible to see Shabelo's shoulders and head. The fire had a fresh hot sensation, blaring into the atmosphere. It subsided and turned metallic, producing a trail of chemical smoke. Shabangu allowed himself to be overtaken by the men behind him. More people were coming out of their houses while, for no obvious reason, at the back of the crowd, one man with a brick in his hand was methodically breaking the windows in a house on the other side.

The fire was rising over the roofs. It would be visible from the highway. The police station would send a patrol. There would be no proportion in the response. The day might end in barricades and petrol bombs, the entry of armoured vans, the hiss of teargas, and the pop of rubber bullets. The security forces would search every house for contraband.

The men in front fell back. Mr Shabangu also moved. He was giddy and thought he might fall down. To steady himself, he put his hand on the back of the individual beside him. He recognised the man as Alfred Koroleng, a clerk at a mining house in the city centre. Koroleng had formed a connection with Mr Shabangu because he was just as serious about keeping his books straight. They had been on friendly terms many years ago. But it was impossible for a thief to maintain too close a friendship. Shabangu couldn't trust himself to take anything from the Koroleng household and risk discovery. It created too much pressure, having to hold back from his instincts. So the two men had fallen out of the habit of conversation although they greeted each other.

It was perhaps no great loss. Alfred Koroleng had only one subject in life. He was the father of four daughters ranging in age from a sixteen-year-old, who was still in school, to a much older nursing sister. They lived in the same house as their father. Not one of Koroleng's daughters had borne children of her own. None had received a good marriage proposal so far. He had no sons nor any grandchildren, no cattle to call his own and to add weight to his existence.

For this reason he was considered a figure of misfortune. Yet Koroleng didn't identify himself as such. He praised his four daughters at any opportunity, revelled in their achievements, and was unable to hear the strangeness in what he said. There was something offensive, something childish and repugnant, in this love for something so near to oneself, some unnatural and milk-blind desire working its will, which provoked one to action.

If Shabangu could have stolen a daughter, he would have done so. That would have made it possible to continue as friends. But you couldn't put a man's daughter in your pocket.

—My friend Alfred Koroleng, what are you doing here? I believe you are even older than I am. Go home. The police can arrive at any minute. You should be at the house with your daughters.

—But my daughters are out here, Mr Shabangu. They are in front of us now. There is Esther, wearing red, and Grace is standing there. Perhaps you don't recognise Esther.

In the past year, in such a short space of time, she has become a full-grown woman.

—Is this something for them to see?

—Mr Shabangu, my daughters are the ones who brought me. The day before Christmas this boy ran away with Esther's handbag. He went all the way to the power station before they caught up with him. Today, however, they are determined to put him straight. People warned him. Apart from that, he was seen on a number of occasions using the telephone. He was doing it again today when they pulled him out. Now you can inform me, Mr Shabangu. What purpose can a boy who is fifteen have to use a telephone? It had to be brought to an end.

The payphone was situated in sight of the police station. It was regarded with suspicion as encouraging people to report information to the security forces. In the city centre there were often lines waiting to use the booths while, in Tembisa, the call box was deserted. Anybody in it made himself conspicuous.

It was more dangerous to create suspicion than to be guilty. Mr Shabangu was watchful in case he should run across someone from his caretaker days. In the train he moved to a different carriage if there was a face under a cloth cap that had a familiar feeling to it. He needed to be four times more careful than an ordinary man in order to achieve a ripe old age. He should be at home, making sure that nobody broke in and looked under the bed, instead of watching a boy burn. Yet the excitement had been unavoidable. He hadn't felt so much alive in years, so certain in the continuance of an immortal part.

—Alfred, you should take your daughters safely away from here. My advice to you is to leave the location and go back to your village for a week. The police may not have interfered but tomorrow they will tell everybody to come for questions. Somebody will be punished.

—Their time to ask questions is over, Mr Shabangu. Mandela will stop them.

—Mandela can't be here and there and over the hill. We depend on ourselves for the time being.

—This boy, Shabelo, couldn't continue like this. He was not ashamed when they saw him with Esther's handbag. He took all the coins out of it and left the paper notes. If Mandela comes we will inform him.

It was impossible to convey the need for safety because the other man was involved in a dream. In this dream, which had become visible to Mr Shabangu, Alfred's eldest daughter Esther, arrayed in a red dress, was laughing as she turned over a box of Lion matches, lit them one after the other so that her nails seemed to catch sudden scarlet fire, and tossed them onto the small log of Shabelo. The boys burst into fire throughout the Witwatersrand. There was electrical fire in the mining shafts, fire in the workers' hostels and train stations, infinite tides of fire to make the world honest. In this dream Mandela was at the front, his face shadowed by the flames. And half in this same dream, half in the world beyond it, one heard the siren on a red-beaded ambulance calling from the highway.

As if she had heard their conversation Esther came to join them. She wore neat black shoes and churchy stockings under her dress. Shabangu wouldn't have recognised her except for her flat expression, which hadn't changed. She had prominent teeth which made up the front of her face. On her lip there was a flash of perspiration to remind you that a boy had burned very quickly on a pyre of black flames.

Shadrach, Meshach, and Abednego had been sent into the furnace. They had come out of the flames with cold skin.

The fire had almost died down. The smoke had vanished. Some of the remaining men surrounded Shabelo's body and beat it idly until its blackened limbs seemed to move. Mr Shabangu wanted to lie on the gravel next to him.

Behind them, on the main road before the bus rank, a police truck had appeared. Some of the men went to hide in the direction of the shebeen, which boasted plastic tables and a limited supply of beer. Others went to the bus stop, where no bus or taxi would come until the unrest had subsided.

The universe resisted the simple application of the gospels. Two thieves had been crucified at the sides of Jesus Christ. One had been condemned and the other had been forgiven.

Mr Shabangu was ill with the sweet and sour scents of the burning around him and thought that he would collapse. He leaned on Esther and then fell in front of them. The ground was rough on his legs. There was blood in his mouth. He wondered if he had broken a tooth. Esther helped him to stand up again. He put one arm around her back and another around her father's.

—Come with us, Mr Shabangu. If they find you here the police are going to go into all of our business. And I know that you are keen on privacy.

There was no more solid reason, when he tried to find it in himself, that Shabangu had cooled towards the five Korolengs, apart from his unwillingness to take something from them as a souvenir. It could only have been the father's faith in his daughters which proved offensive.

Shabangu had never wanted to divide his possessions with a wife. He would say about himself that his character had not developed in a straight line as befitted a husband. It had its own roots and crooked branches, its own system of loads and balances which would have been broken by marriage and would therefore have prevented him from being in Tembisa to tell the tale. He had managed to survive and could tell Victor about it.

He had sacrificed the better part of life to an aspect of his character. Good life went after bad. It lay beyond explanation. Such restlessness came into his hands at the chance of taking possession of some piece of property. It was even a compliment to the man who owned that thing. Mr Shabangu had been in the prime of his life at the hostel. He had been in his element, comfortable with every man. Women hadn't been allowed in. They were not his natural targets. Shabangu disliked their tins of skin-lightening cream, the vegetable smell of their bundled hair, and had no urge to rob them.

In the case of Victor, the young man had been universally beloved in the dormitory and had by turns taken away all his joy in his own existence. If it hadn't been for Victor, Shabangu would never have had to depart so suddenly in the middle of the night. Victor was the hidden cause of his existence, the same boy whose face he had longed to view and whose story he wished to hear completed in exchange for his own. He had never been in love until he encountered Victor. The memory of it was still strong in him.

So Shabangu didn't want to run for his life. He would have been relieved to act the part of the thief alongside Shabelo. He would wait until the crowd entered his house, took him onto the road, and hung a tyre around his neck. He would wait out the scarlet flames until he saw himself from the outside, a body on its way to be buried in a brick field. His bones would wait until the spaza-shop operator took the money in his account and paid on his behalf for a plot of land and the mahogany coffin Shabangu had already selected. He had admired the garlanded silver handles along the side, as ornate as an old-fashioned kettle.

He could rest with the dead. There would be no possessions. Meanwhile his treasure weighed on his spirits. Mr Shabangu wished that he could disgorge each piece of personal property he had ever taken and return it to its owner. It would weigh down that man instead. He would leave instructions. People believed that thieves enjoyed the easiest life. Although their fingers were light, nevertheless their hearts were heavy. Compared to Mr Shabangu, Shabelo had died with a light heart.

Mr Shabangu could not have explained how he went from the road outside his house into the Koroleng household and found himself sitting on a hire-purchase armchair with heavy arms and antimacassar. Someone put a cushion behind his neck and took the teapot, which had been parked on a doily on the short table in front of him. The teapot had a crocheted cover.

The inside of the cement house was unexpectedly dark thanks to the thick curtains. He could hear the grumbling of the police truck on the road outside as the water cannon was brought into position and policemen fanned out from the top.

In one corner of the room was a lamp. It shone suddenly into his eyes through its animal-skin lampshade. Beside it was a shelf which held a steam iron and some books leaning on one another for support. Below that were several volumes of an encyclopaedia. He was relieved. The light of the lampshade was the purest orange, the same colour as the sun through his eyelids. To one side of the room was a record player and a hi-fi cabinet filled with albums, a vase with plastic flowers, and kitchen merchandise, such things as Maizena and tins of baked beans and Zimbabwean tea. It seemed that he had fallen asleep and woken up in a different place, perhaps in Harare. He had an idea, plucked out of nowhere, that in Harare you could find the good life. There, across the border in Harare, was the opportunity for a dignified retirement.

In the next room were the noises of people moving around, then a kettle boiling. Alfred appeared carrying cups on a tray. He wore a brown-buttoned heavy blue cardigan, smarter than any outfit you would catch him in outside. Alfred, at an age when most men were unwilling to smile, had the broadest of grins. It struck Shabangu that he couldn't remember smiling himself.

The host put the tray down carefully on the table and studied his face. He was concerned for his visitor. It was unusual for Shabangu to be inspected in this way. In many years nobody had looked at him closely, and he didn't look into the tin mirror behind the door.

—Sleeping beauty has returned.

—How long was I asleep?

—Only for forty minutes. We were hoping that you could sleep for the rest of the day. You can't go home because the police have been questioning people on the street. You need some rest and tranquillity, Mr Shabangu.

He found that there was warmth stealing into his face, as if he had been caressed. It was odd that so old a creature as Alfred, straining at the very limit of his existence, could cause such a feeling. Maybe there was a purpose to old men, in the increasing stiffness of their cocoon.

—I don't remember properly what happened.

—You went out like a light the instant I went into the other room. I see from your expression, my friend, you have not been sleeping. Do you have something on your conscience?

—Everybody has something on their conscience.

—That is too true, especially after the events of today. You are too good, as I have always said. You are too good to be true. But is there nothing in particular, Mr Shabangu?

—If there is, I can't say what it is.

There was. There wasn't. There was no method to answer the greater part of the questions which could be put to a man. There was no such thing as a conscience independent of God. There was the fact that Alfred Koroleng spoke as if they were exchanging jokes with one another. Mr Shabangu hadn't thought they enjoyed such a close relationship. There was Esther, the eldest daughter, who sat down beside him on the couch and crossed her legs. There was the fact that Esther's deportment reminded him of the Pietermaritzburg church ladies, European women who ran fêtes for charity, organised bake sales in the park where they superintended tables lined with cream cakes in the shape of boaters' hats, took charge of the finances of the school's regatta, consulted regularly with the board of the Caledonian Hostel on the promotion of Christianity, yet whose tenderness was confined to dogs.

Esther must have changed her clothes. She had a soapy scent. It impressed Shabangu that she should come into the house after the events of the morning to place perfume on her neck. In the same minute he regretted that he had no such daughter to call his own. His life had been stolen away from home, hour by hour, until there was almost nothing remaining to him. He could not say whose hands had been the culprit. He had stolen from himself in never taking a wife. Victor had come in the way. It could be the bitterest minute of his existence.

—Isn't my eldest daughter the beautiful one?

—They are equally beautiful in my eyes, Alfred.

—Now you are practising your famous courtesy on us. Don't try to be polite, Mr Shabangu. We still think of you as part of the family although you tried to leave us behind. You remember that you used to come to our house every Sunday, for lunch.

—I didn't abandon you. I simply have to keep to myself.

—Don't make excuses, Mr Shabangu. Who are we to make demands on your time? We are only grateful to have you back in our bosom.

Shabangu was jealous then. He saw that Esther's eyes shone in the dark room from where you could hear the tread of men and the rumble of trucks on the road outside. She could never be stolen. Lit by his memories of Shabelo, in contrast to the day's events, her eyes were especially beautiful, the speckled brown of a certain egg that he had once turned over to encourage an unproductive hen. They stole the last amount of old man's breath in his chest.

Esther put her hand on his wrist.

—Mr Shabangu, can I check your pulse?

—What do you mean?

—I want to check your heartbeat for practice.

Alfred had been winding the clock in its cabinet. He turned to face them.

—You would not know this, Mr Shabangu, but Esther is in her second year of training to be a professional nurse. She is at the big hospital, Baragwanath, which, of course, half of Johannesburg depends on. One day, which may be far in the future, when the clinic cannot help you, they will send you to Baragwanath. In that case Esther will be your senior sister in the ward. And she is top of the class. Allow her to monitor your pulse, Mr Shabangu. It never hurts to know if there is a problem.

—We mustn't boast.

—My daughter is tops. Mr Shabangu would want to know about it.

Mr Shabangu lay back in the armchair, the clock ticking in the background, Esther's cold hand on his wrist. She counted almost under her breath while warmth continued to run into his face and chest. Not since Victor in the hostel had a young person taken an interest in his person. Nobody had put a hand in his own. At the time, the proximity of the boy had been difficult to bear. It was all a question of jealousy, a question of exposure to someone whom he had laboured to protect. Shabangu's thoughts had followed Victor and his voice around the hostel. It had made him unaccountably jealous when he discovered the young man in conversation with a young woman, a policeman, or one of the actors who had arrived so abruptly and turned the ordinary business of the hostel upside down. Victor challenged the fullness of his own condition. You couldn't tamp down the energy in the young man.

Nor was that the worst of it. In Shabangu's life only Victor Moloi could pronounce a negative verdict because only Victor had come close enough to him. Victor should have known what counted, what the value of gratitude was, what the value of the esteem of Shabangu was. In three years the custodian had cared for the boy, had sent the police in the other direction, had overlooked the matter of the false pass book, and had then been superseded by the director Polk at the drop of a hat. Why should a European gentleman take the boy? Why should Shabangu lose the boy to the first new person who wanted him? For this reason there had come into his heart the irresistible impulse to take the boy's permit when an opportunity presented itself. There had been no financial motive. He had no one lined up to buy the document, and had therefore risked keeping it. It would have been a souvenir of his affection.

For the first time Shabangu rued his independence. He wanted to put his bony, old-man's arms around Esther's young neck, hold her to his shoulder, and feel her heart ticking within his own circumference. The disused parts of him demanded to be put back in operation. He would hold Esther as closely as the tyre that had been settled over his neck and was starting to smoke. In the end, the tyre would burn through his joy until there was nothing but ash in his heart. In this way he might steal something from God.

Esther stood up before he could do anything. She brought a thermometer, shook it, and placed it under his tongue. It was as cold as the railroad track.

—Your pulse is still very high, Mr Shabangu. I am telling you so that we can take action. One day soon we must take you to the clinic. There are as many troubles in the mind as in the body. You must clear your head about what happened. That Shabelo had been running amuck in the township. He took money out of people's handbags on the taxi. Many people had spoken to him. He knew that he was coming to a bad end. Therefore he talked on the telephone.

—Was it so bad?

—We couldn't leave it for his conscience to solve.

Esther removed the thermometer. She read the number, shook it again, and replaced it in its case.

—Every man has something on his conscience.

—Except for my father, Mr Shabangu. I am sorry to inform you that you have a slight fever. For this condition we prefer paracetamol to aspirin.

On cue, Albert sat down on the sofa. His daughters arranged themselves around the room, four dark flowers who poured tea for their father and Shabangu and then for themselves. A cake was unlocked from a tin and gave off the sugared breath of almonds and apricot jam while thin slices were shaved from the side of it. They had changed and were wearing dresses and print blouses fit for church. They were as good as the English ladies, the wardens and sextons and choir masters who populated the curfewed capital of Pietermaritzburg on any given Sunday in the 1970s.

Before, he always wanted things to belong to him. Now he wished more than anything to belong to Alfred Koroleng and his daughters, in any capacity that would suit them. He would be husband or son, cousin or brother as required, friend to the Korolengs or Esther's confidant.

—Mr Shabangu, you have become quite a chatterbox, if you don't mind my telling you that.

—Nobody has ever suggested it before. That I am a chatterbox. Can it be true?

—But you have changed, my friend. I believe it. When I first had the pleasure of your acquaintance, when my daughters were still young and their mother was still alive, you were legendary for your silence. Some people did not even know which language you spoke. They said that a week went by and you would not say a word out loud. You would put the exact money on the counter and take your bread and your polonies. At one point I do believe you had warmed up to us but I may have squandered it as a result of demanding too much. I came to your door too often and made a nuisance of myself. Today, when I have four daughters to take care of my every need, you have a comment to make on everything under the sun. I hope I am not making you uncomfortable?

—I am not aware of any change you talk about, Alfred. Nevertheless, since you mentioned it, there have been many years in my life in which I did not find it important to express my opinions. I have always been able to read the gospels.

Esther put her hand on her father's shoulder.

—My father is prone to exaggerate, Mr Shabangu, as you can tell. But he is right that you have talked more today than I expected. The last time I met you, you would hesitate before you told another person what your name was. Today you are the soul of conversation.

Was he the soul of conversation? Was he the delight of the Korolengs? To Shabangu it seemed that he had watched and listened throughout his life. Was Esther also pulling his leg?

What was indisputable was Alfred Koroleng's condition. He was the happiest man on the planet. His four daughters, each coming from a single seed, were delighted with each other. Here was the music of the Korolengs. The comparison sat in Mr Shabangu's throat. The sound of his own life was the hissing of a bladder.

Even the police had disappeared. Children were out, playing and fighting, spinning hoops, blowing tin whistles, and rolling tyres between the houses. For a fortnight, since the last confrontation with the police, the adults in the township had been sour. Today's action dissipated their frustrations. At this hour life was good. It was better than it had ever been. The black pimpernel, Nelson Mandela, was free to lead all the people to freedom. Soon it would be Mandela Day.

Esther looked at him, talked to him, admired him with inquisitive eyes. She sat opposite from him on a plywood chair, her dress not quite below her knees, so that he could appreciate the strength of her legs. Mandela was coming for her. Esther had attractive shoulders with the bones as clear as struts, the smell of Omo detergent lodged in her clothes, thoughtful, ingenious hands with secret black hairs on them, and an attachment to him which was a beautiful fact. It was fitting and proper that she should pardon him for the fault of his existence. Not even a boy like Victor, who might be said to have loved him at one stage, could have known the sum of the facts concerning Samuel Shabangu and have offered him redemption.

Shabelo should have been given the same chance. Nothing about the boy had made an impression on the world besides his end. His petty thieving had already been forgotten. At the end he had been reduced to glue and bones, burned to glue and bones, for opening a handbag and for taking a red apple when hunger gnawed on him, and for talking on the public telephone. There was no more room for conscience in the best men and women in Tembisa than there was in the clock cabinet. What was there in a thief? You craned your neck to look inside and found nothing but what was displayed on the surface. And what was there in the best men and women? What if there was nobody better than a thief to hold the world together?

As he understood this Shabangu was dizzy again. The room floated around him, a merry-go-round on which his friend and four daughters were set in place like plastic horses. The children's voices outside stretched to the length of fun-fair music. He put down his cup, swaying on the couch, unwilling to admit that he was unwell. To be discovered was the solitary misfortune in the life of a thief. As a result he had been protected from many other difficulties. Yet today he had been uncovered. He felt shame burning slowly, like incense, in his blood. There was a man coming to his house in the evening. There were guns in his house along with the two heavy ridged green saucers of the landmines.

The things he loved were moving towards him. Alfred had fallen asleep in the chair. Esther collected the cups and took them to the tub.

—You will come back and see us, Mr Shabangu, for my father's sake? To meet you after such a long time has been a real treat for us. You won't wait five years to return?

—I hope to come back when there is an invitation.

—Choose a convenient time and we will welcome you properly. You are our prodigal father, Mr Shabangu, and we must celebrate your return like the prodigal son. Also, when you come back, we can talk about what happened today. You will understand that it was necessary. That boy could not have been allowed to betray the entire community for another day. He was making a fool out of us all. People could see that when they found him using the telephone.

—There are other people who have used that same telephone.

—What reason can a boy have to use a telephone? There is only one reason, Mr Shabangu. He was reporting us to the police station. Since Mandela was released, they have been twice as interested to know whether this man here or this one there has a gun. They want to keep the guns out of our hands in case they change their minds. Do you know that the man who was supposed to marry me was killed by a bullet three months ago?

—I am sorry to hear it.

—They say he was shot by accident. Everything that is wrong is an accident so that no one needs to take responsibility. I have been left a widow and I have not even had the chance to be married, Mr Shabangu.

Esther had an expression of such ugliness it surprised Shabangu. Something invisible in her beautiful face had folded over it. Yet as soon as it had appeared it also vanished. Esther took his hands and brought him to his feet. Angela, the youngest, Alfred's rose, was straightening out the beds and airing the sheets, pegging them to a washing line which ran indoors.

There was a flurry of busy hands throughout the house. Another daughter put herself to ironing shirts and blouses on a board, while the third put out a plate on which there were a few slices of white bread, thick pats of butter, and jam. Shabangu saw the dark seeds in the red jam, as plain and nevertheless mysterious as the traces attended by a fortune-teller. His mood had no bottom. Nor was it any more tangible than the bounds of his conscience.

Esther walked with him to the door, where there were children playing with a hoop on the sand. Samuel thought that this life belonged to him as a kind of miracle. He was a creature of God. Moreover, there was no clearer message from God than what was written in his own nature. He was the measure of good and evil.

—You must come back soon, Mr Shabangu. If not, you are bound to receive a visit from one or more of Alfred Koroleng's four daughters. I am not telling you which one.

Shabangu found that he was unable to reply. There were certain facts that had long stood between him and anyone with whom he might carry on a conversation. On the insistence of a man who came to his door in the name of Victor Moloi, he had concealed a package. Even before Shabelo's death, his mood had been aroused and lightened by the illegal cargo that was there.

He wasn't the only one keeping guns. Since Mandela's release nameless men and women came to Tembisa in the dead of night and cached equipment. The police would treat a man who stored the guns with utmost severity, but they would have to care enough to catch him.

Esther's perfectly inquisitive face made Shabangu pity himself again. To conceal the thing he was, it had taken the incrustations of seventy years, from the scattered orange warts beneath his chin, as finely featured as certain snails, to the surplus length of toady skin which threatened to blind him, to the whistle in his dented windpipe and the horny scales on the bottom of his feet. Underneath these warts and scars, underneath the sounds that he uttered to protect himself, the thing he was became transparent. He was a thing that breathed and stole.

He wished to burn in the circle of Esther's eyes. At her disposal he could be taken to the sandy yard between the butchery, with its tattooed carcasses, and the liquor store, where she could slide a tyre around his throat with a daughter's joyful hands. He wanted to burn in her hands. It wasn't out of the question that, like Shadrach, he too would come out refreshed from the pyre. For at the centre of the pyre today, behind Shabelo's slow speaking, Mr Shabangu had seen and heard something he never anticipated. In the flames he had heard the imperishable delight of life itself.

On the way home from the Koroleng household there was little to distract Shabangu from his discovery. He walked slowly, his body dragging behind him, through a street that had been cleared of children. It was as quiet as in the aftermath of a public holiday when the butchery and the liquor store ran out and men and women, boys and girls, slept out their dreams of plenty.

In the distance was the thud of a police helicopter, the body as insubstantial as a dragonfly against the cold light. Some policemen were laying out rolls of barbed wire around the borders of the township. Only monsters could slay monsters.

There were no cars in the vicinity, just the sound of a metal whistle, but Mr Shabangu paid no attention to it. He didn't want to be noticed. There was no time for conversation with his neighbours. His heart was still beating fast since he had come close to Esther. He supposed he had left his old skin at the scene of Shabelo's execution, the wary, familiar, stale snakeskin belonging to the thief of long standing which had worn out his nose. In his skin, moreover, was concealed his guilt. In it was reckoned his butcher's bill. Shabelo was the latest in a long list. He walked in the full quantity of his guilt.

In future Shabangu would be able to enter the Koroleng household on an entirely different footing. From there he had taken a hoop hung with keys, a flat-iron hinge intended to wind the large clock, a pewter teaspoon whose face was clouded over, and, right as he exited the house, a pair of Alfred's woollen gloves, which had been hanging on a peg. He had done what was needed to maintain the connection.

His heart was as light again as his fingers. In the items he had stolen was recorded the real history of his life. Shabangu put the gloves and keys in a shopping packet and wondered where he could put them out of sight.

Underneath his bed, buried in the clay, was a thirty-kilogram container that contained a claymore mine and revolvers. The plywood box bore curled foreign writing on the top. Although he couldn't read the letters, he imagined that it was the same alphabet in which the gospels had been written.

The carton had been brought to him by an Indian man who arrived at midnight, driving a Nissan right into the location. He had a circle of uncombed white hair on his head, and confessed to knowing numerous details about a certain Mr Shabangu the caretaker. He had been unnecessarily friendly. This strange man had come out of the blue to talk about a boy whose name he hadn't heard in many years and to remind him of a history he had left behind in Natal. Shabangu had no idea how he had been discovered. Nevertheless, he placed the carton underneath the floor. When he received a letter under the door specifying today as the time for collection, he was scarcely relieved. He had become more anxious when Shabelo ran past and promised to bring the scrutiny of the security forces down on Tembisa. His life had seemed simple to him, at each point, and yet it had been made of crooked planks. He thought for a minute about the possibility of settling down with Esther and having a child. Was Mandela a younger man than Samuel Shabangu?

—

He had fallen asleep in the evening when a van parked at the side of the house. It was almost perfectly dark inside. Shabangu had been so distracted that he had left the door ajar. In it, sketched in moonlight, appeared the young man who once paid two-rand rent to sleep at the top of the Caledonian Christian Men's Hostel. His thin face was as polished as a pebble at the bottom of a river. He wore a long shirt, one arm cut short so that you wanted to straighten him out of his lopsidedness. He hadn't changed.

There was nothing disturbing in the sight of Victor. You wanted to hold him in your arms and decide whether he was your enemy, the one whose imminent arrival you feared more than anything on earth, or the being who was dearest to your heart. If he insisted, you were ready to make your peace and leave. You would distribute your property to the neighbours and pay to slaughter a cow.

—Mr Shabangu, I hear that you have taken good care of our package. I congratulate you on that. I knew that you, of all people, would have somewhere safe to put it.

—I can't understand why you decided to come back to me after all these years. It is too late to punish me for anything. I am too old for that.

—I wanted a safe place to hide these. You wouldn't have been able to call the police, Mr Shabangu, unless you had changed your stripes. And who do we know that has ever changed his stripes?

—I should lock up behind you. I have never had a visitor before. I would have welcomed you to stay if you had come years ago.

Shabangu locked the door. He lit the wick of the paraffin lamp, feeling that his hands were shaky. The match dropped on the floor. Victor picked it up and rubbed the burned head between his two fingers. He was surprisingly dexterous with only one arm.

—In all this time, Mr Shabangu, I am your first guest? As you can see, I have lost half my arm. I had to learn to use my right hand in place of my left. In fact I had to learn to tie my shoelaces from scratch.

—I am sorry to hear it. I will make tea.

Shabangu closed the curtain. Then he put on the kettle to boil. He had some constriction in his chest which left him unable to breathe, or even to talk properly. His life was coming full circle. This was the good news he had been awaiting. He listened to Victor with his back turned while he opened a new tin of milk powder. The powder was off-white and had the scent of cheese.

—Shall I tell you the story? Are you interested in hearing it, Mr Shabangu?

—I am listening.

—Do you remember that the trouble between us started with a play? The first time I went to a play again, after so many years, was since we came back into the country under the amnesty law. Meanwhile they had assigned me to keep a watch on this area, to make sure the situation is under control. One fine day I heard that a man was living right here under the name of Mr Shabangu, as the local locksmith. It was too much of a coincidence. I thought you would have changed your name a long time ago.

—My name is what I am. The odds are against somebody recognising it. There is no telephone book to look in, for Tembisa.

—The right answer is that you were tempting fate, Mr Shabangu. You were putting your luck against the world. I have seen many other cases.

Shabangu scalded the bottom of the pot. He threw an inch of water into the sink, placed the tea bags into the pot, and scalded them.

—I will put milk powder and golden syrup, Victor. That is how you liked it.

—You are the perfect man to keep this for us, not to attract attention.

—I tried to keep away from attention. Then I became the oldest man in Tembisa. People started to come to me for advice. You must take it away. After today, it is not safe anywhere in the location.

He moved the end of the bed and pulled up the rug, exposing the planks underneath. Victor knelt beside him, brought out the planks, and opened the carton. He took one of the revolvers, produced a roll of brown tape from his pocket, and started to tape the gun securely under his shirt.

—This is our insurance policy, Mr Shabangu. We have opened insurances around the country. I don't know why you didn't get an insurance for yourself. Somebody in the Bantu Administration would have sold you a new identity document for peanuts.

—I was waiting for you to find me. Now I have paid my debt. Back then both of us got caught because of me.

—Then we have found each other at last. I also have regrets. Some of them are very recent.

—How is that?

—I am responsible for this region, for keeping the feelings of people in check. If I had given better instructions, that boy from today, that Shabelo, would still be alive. In the last few months he has given me a lot of useful information. I used to thank goodness for that telephone. But now they have killed that boy over nothing.

1995

KING MIDAS

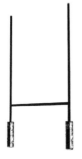

June 24th. Uncle Ashok was taking Sanjay and his girl-friend Ursula to the Rugby World Cup.

King Midas remained behind the panes of gold-rimmed sunglasses which he only removed in the aeroplane to inspect the mountainous land on the right-hand side. Farm dams glittered in steady morning sunshine. The peaks rose out of their green tunics of cultivated land. Then came a hundred kilometres of sugarcane fields and white wheat, as beautifully combed as a lady's hair, leading back to the coast.

King Midas put his shades back on, placed his hand on Sanjay's arm as he explained his plans for the weekend.

—For me the rugby is secondary. I want you and Ursula to stay with Lakshmi and myself in a proper luxurious hotel, to have that experience which we were never allowed to have.

—I'm not interested in hotels, uncle.

—Sometimes, my boy, you are the spitting image of your father. He had a certain holiness about his music. Some would say holier-than-thou although I took him for what he was. We are fortunate that your girlfriend does not also want to play the saint.

—Ursula is definitely not a saint.

They were sitting in separate rows. Ursula and Lakshmi, Sanjay's aunt, had the seats in front of them. Uncle Ashok kept leaning forward to explain some or other part of his plan to Ursula or to remind his wife about something they had already discussed. This King Midas, who had removed his rhinestone belt and looped it around the arm rest, had plans to turn everything into gold.

It was originally a pet name, as you understood, bestowed on the man by his wife and used behind his back by other members of the family. In recent years, they used it to his face. He would be pleased and taken aback at the same time and start into another explanation of his scheme to buy Land Rovers and second-hand Japanese cars in Botswana, drive them across the border, assign them new licence plates from a friend in the registration office, and, in this way, avoid import duties.

Sanjay understood his uncle's money-making charisma because he was also subject to it. He wanted to be close to the man because money, and therefore the units of life itself, multiplied in his presence. His father's old friends, like Logan and Satya, were no better off than they had been ten or twenty years ago, however much pride they took in the colour of their skins. Meanwhile Uncle Ashok, his father's brother-in-law who had never done him any good, was taking full advantage of the new dispensation. He had begun in the same place as his in-laws, after all, Aunt Lakshmi's brothers and sisters, who, on this same Saturday, were selling machine-cut suits to Africans on Grey Street. Between them, three brothers and two sisters, they had been held up at gunpoint a dozen times, a fact they blamed on the abolition of the death penalty.

Lakshmi's marriage had allowed her to escape from these conditions in which, as a woman, you were as likely to be insulted by a Tamil as by a cheeky young African. Having money was the only protection from insults. In the first year, Ashok turned a tailor's establishment belonging to his wife's brothers Nilesh and Uday into a profitable enterprise, taking out a loan for twenty used sewing machines and running them chattering twenty hours a day in the interior town of Newcastle. Then he turned around and sold the business lock, stock and barrel before the Chinese manufacturers put all the garment makers out of commission. With the proceeds he took over Mercedes dealerships up and down the South Coast.

Twice a week he drove with Sanjay from Pennington to Port St John's, taking the cash packed in a shopping bag to the bank in Shepstone, carrying a gun for protection. He was one of a dozen non-whites in the province, before 1994, who had a permit to hold a weapon. Today he had a collection of guns displayed on the racks in his carport.

Despite Uncle Ashok's explanations and his unwieldy way of talking, he was the individual you wanted to have on your side when there was a difficulty. You talked to him once and you would be sorted. He knew the right person to ask for a passport renewal or a notarised copy of a birth certificate, which office in the provincial administration could expedite the inspections on a building site, which doctor was the most qualified to examine a child with Down's syndrome. For Lakshmi he had organised a life filled with gold. The doorknobs in the house, which he bought from an emigrating Scotsman when Westville became a grey area, were made of gold. So was the Mercedes, gold inside and out, and the cushions on the long settee in the lounge area.

So was the figure of Lakshmi. You met her at a wedding or at a stick dance, fierce and fat and super-friendly, moving this way and that between the men, insisting that everybody join in, and saw that your aunt's corrupted eyelashes were laden with a pollen of gold. Sanjay imagined that one day her entire tawny-brown skin, her sagging lioness pelt, would turn to gold at her husband's touch in their king-sized bed.

When Lakshmi reached back to get his attention, he saw that her nails were painted in lacquered squares of gold nail polish. He wanted to hold her hands between his own for a minute and feel these painted shells, hard as lobster, on his palms.

—You're well back there with your uncle, Sanjay? You know how Ashok is only too happy to have you along with us. Now he can explain things to you until the cows have come home. He has given up on me, I'm afraid, because I am stupid. But he has such a high opinion of your abilities. He should love your father. Owing to that, he sees your father in everything that you do.

Uncle Ashok was impatient with his wife whenever he had to listen to her. So was Sanjay.

—He's sitting here, Lakshmi. He can tell me himself if he believes it.

—That lump in the corner? Do you know that to this day, although I am sure he loves me, he has never brought me flowers? He will bring me extra gold to make bangles, and Krugerrands to put under the bed, but he cannot bring himself to buy a birthday card or to take me out for dinner on Valentine's Day, like a modern man.

—Since I started to work with him, I could tell that he has his own way.

—You are very clever, Sanjay. As his nephew, you don't take sides.

—I do take sides, Lakshmi. People don't always notice.

Was it true? Did his uncle see his father in him? Why would he wait for this weekend, fifteen years later, to let him know? He hardly thought about his father nowadays. The air hostess had come along the aisle, distributing drinks to Lakshmi and Ursula. She had exacting brown hands, which Sanjay watched as she placed a cube of ice and then another in his aunt's cup. Her hair was tightly bundled at the back of her head.

Before she got to the next row, the plane tilted to the side and the seatbelt lights went on. The air hostess took the trolley back towards the bulkhead while Lakshmi settled in to the contents of her tray. After several minutes she turned back to him. He saw there were tiny shaved dots above her eyebrows.

—I want to tell you, Sanjay, that this one is absolutely exceptional.

—Which one are you talking about?

—This one to my left. She is young. She is modern. She is also beautiful. That I grant you. But she is also conscious of tradition. She speaks so clearly. I only wish my own sons, especially Vish, could have found someone like this to partner up with. Your uncle is already very impressed. You know how much attention he pays to someone's manners.

—Maybe we can talk about it later when they are not in earshot.

—She doesn't mind that I am talking. I won't let you get off so lightly. Otherwise your mother lets you get away with murder. It's time to make up your mind.

—I will do so. Don't worry. I like to decide quickly.

—We haven't had a wedding in the family for some time. You know what weddings are to us. They are the only chance for people to meet, apart from Diwali. It's a chance for the family to show off for a change.

—I don't need to make my decisions based on that.

—I am not saying you should. You must make your decisions based on your heart.

Sanjay had only recently started being short with his aunt. Lakshmi didn't object to his irritated manner because she was used to being treated that way by her husband. In any case, she was ridiculous. You had to be more than half-blind to look at the twenty-three-year-old woman in the adjoining business-class seat, with her bright red lipstick and her thighs thin in leopard-print stockings, and see a suitable match for your nephew. You had to have a heart that was made out of gold.

The drinks service resumed. The stewardess unloading cups and bottles onto the trays reminded Sanjay that, in the years after his father's death, once a week, Lakshmi had brought pots of food, as well as sacks of potatoes and tomatoes from Warwick Avenue market to their house and had never asked any return unless it was the freedom to advise her sister-in-law and to spread her gossip. She wasn't a bad woman. She was only vulgar and measured everything in terms of money. His father came to his mind. Sanjay had been there when his mother discovered the body. He could remember the purple flowers in his father's face. Yash had been even thinner in death. Lakshmi was fat in life.

It was difficult to think about that time. Sanjay and his mother had been subject to the never well-concealed scorn of the families, the other Naidoos and the Naickers. Apart from Lakshmi and Uncle Ashok, they began to treat Sanjay and his mother quite differently. They were more abrupt than they had been, laughed too much and too loudly when they came to visit, bared their teeth for too long, told jokes they wouldn't have told if his father had been under the same roof, and put cash notes ostentatiously under the plastic table mats when they were ready to make a move. They patronised Kastoori in front of Sanjay and seemed about to remember out loud the fact that she had found her husband hanging from the light fitting in the bedroom and that she continued to sleep in the same bed as before.

Kastoori had been freest during her marriage. She had been at the centre of her own household, collecting money in a biscuit tin for schoolbooks and uniforms, cutting Sanjay's hair while he stood over an unfolded newspaper, criticising Yash and his music.

Afterwards she had gone to work. Uncle Ashok had rescued her, giving her employment as his bookkeeper in town. He was unwilling to trust somebody outside the family with business information. In an airless room where Sanjay sometimes went to visit her after school, behind an electric fan which was never switched on even on the muggiest day in December, Kastoori did the accounts with the same exactness she observed in her twice-a-year ritual of baking, when she measured out baking soda and flour and chopped nuts to the milligram. She was as serious about money as her brother, although the one believed in spending money to make money and the other refused to spend anything more than the minimum. There were the rates and the municipality, books and uniforms for the government school, interest on the house loan, each of which she took as an insult.

Kastoori's relationship with money continued to be, Sanjay believed, the most intimate connection in her life. Money touched her more closely than he did. She had sold his father's records wholesale a fortnight after his death, along with his hi-fi equipment, to some of the same men who used to employ Yash, accepting a fraction of their original price. One of them had beat his father in front of him. Sanjay had recognised him when he went with his mother and one of his cousins to carry the boxes.

They got a terrible price for the lot. That, however, was the last bad deal she would accept in her life. Kastoori was the perfect treasurer for King Midas. She would take her brother's secrets to the grave.

In Johannesburg Ashok had booked in an international hotel in Westcliff. The four of them, Ashok and Lakshmi, Sanjay and Ursula, waited at the counter beside a hand truck loaded with the panelled suitcases.

The hotel had a palace's proportions, its driveway winding up the hillside to the entrance attended by a fountain rising from pink floodlights. Its turrets and battlements looked at the long apron of the lawn fanned by sprinklers and a parking area filled with Mercedes-Benzes and imported Jaguars. It put you in a stupor. Sanjay thought he could gladly stay with Ursula and live in the hotel forever when his uncle went back.

In the lobby were a number of deferential young white women. Some carried bottles of silver-lettered champagne and trays bearing flute-shaped glasses in the direction of the swimming pool. In one corner of the lobby was a man in a black dinner jacket and tight black trousers playing flights of Richard Clayderman on a grand piano. His feet, in a musician's narrow shoes, moved rapidly up and down on the pedals as if they had been greased. He reminded Sanjay of an old-fashioned movie actor.

Then there was the stern man behind the counter. He had already looked through several ledgers, taking the big books from a drawer and searching through them, his eyes square behind his spectacles. Finally he discovered their booking details, put the binder on the table, and picked out the lines with a curved hotel pen. You might have found something equally cruel and curved in his manner, but it was the kind of hidden cruelty that Uncle Ashok was good at defusing. He returned the man's glare from behind his sunglasses. They were chameleon lenses. Outside, in the unexpected Transvaal sunshine, they had been green panes. In the darkened hotel, they silvered and became almost transparent.

—Is there a problem, André?

—Mr Naidoo, maybe you can explain it to me. It says here, under the booking reference, that for these two rooms we extended you our highest client discount. And we did that because you reserved them in your professional capacity, as a travel agent.

—So far, so good.

—However, I cannot find the proof of your official registration. Usually I would find a copy of the fax attached to the booking. That has to be on the proper letterhead showing the name of your specific agency.

—I have my travel-agent card here.

—It will just be one minute, then. I will have to call for the confirmation.

—You can take your time, my friend. In the meanwhile I am going to show my nephew and his girlfriend out by the swimming pool. You can have our luggage taken up to the rooms so long. Is it a true fact that the wives and girlfriends of the New Zealand team are staying in this hotel?

—That information is strictly confidential.

—Well, that is what they are saying in the newspapers. Once you have the booking straightened out on your side, kindly send a boy to fetch us at the pool. I will inform you if we see any stray members of the New Zealand team.

—My thanks to you, Mr Naidoo.

You couldn't stop him when he was rampant. In fact you didn't want him to stop. Nor did Ursula. Nor did his wife. He was your champion. Uncle Ashok behaved in his own peculiar fashion when he was in a white space, much more madly than when he was in the bosom of the family. He played a part. He lived up to his surroundings and the in-eradicable sense of disapproval that the four of you felt to be standing in that hotel. You looked around the lobby on your way to the pool area and saw a hotel that could be anywhere. The wicker-armed settees, landscape watercol-ours, and plants in huge polished brass pots expressed the same neutrality as the uniformed staff standing behind the several desks and counters.

These things didn't discriminate on the basis of com-plexion, whether a hair on your head curled around the schoolmaster's ruler, nor in terms of accent and educa-tion. They wanted only to proclaim the colourlessness and inhuman fragrance of money, whether the medium of exchange happened to be dollars or rupees or electrons circulating in a computer terminal or the final days of the financial rand. They said that, denominated in money, all men were equal. They said that at last all men were equal. They knew nothing about your father and less about your mother. Money had been liberated since the previous year's elections, which made it possible to be rich and at the same time not guilty.

Nevertheless the hotel continued to be a white space. Your presence was noted. It was necessary to be on your best behaviour unless you sounded royal like Uncle Ashok. It wasn't that anybody said anything different to you. They were perfectly polite. Nobody even looked askance at Ashok or Lakshmi or Ursula when you went onto the deck and stood at the bar. Ashok ordered the drinks.

It was an unseasonably warm day in June, celebrating the rugby and the return of the Springbok team to international competition. The thought struck Sanjay that his father would have been impossibly daunted to enter a European hotel, run on European lines. He felt pain at the memory of how Yash always said the word as a compliment.

The sensation was cut short by Lakshmi, who leaned towards him although she only came up to his shoulder.

—I don't care what your uncle says, Sanjay, concerning how these hotels are open now and therefore we must use them. I can feel their eyes. They don't want us to be here whatever we are going to spend. Your uncle just doesn't pick up on it.

—He doesn't admit it. But he revels in it. Ursula is the same.

—Maybe you are right. I don't know.

There were men and women on the reclining chairs set out by the heated pool, two of whom were talking on big cellphones. Another man, with a circle of red hair around a big, red-freckled crown and nearly transparent grey eyes, stood on the steps of the teardrop pool. He paused half-way into the hot blue water, with a towel around his bullish shoulders. He put a swimming cap on, looked through Ashok and Ursula without seeming to notice them, put his towel on the side, and dove in. He was surprisingly loud amid the foam. You could see the muscles in his back as he chopped along the side of the pool. His arms were as powerful as a boxer's.

In this situation you had, for a certain amount of time, the power of telepathy. You had a superpower like nobody else had. You knew that the man, like the others around the bar, had counted four Indians on your arrival, felt your presence like a bone stuck in his throat, and vowed that the standards of the hotel, for which he was paying a considerable amount, should not be allowed to decline. You were only surprised when he got out at the other end, streaming with water, his red crest flat on his head when he took off the swimming cap, and spoke in a Polish accent to one of the men behind the bar.

In a white space Uncle Ashok had the virtue of skin like a rhinoceros hide. He had established himself at one of the outdoor tables beside the pool and had the women sit beside him. His sunglasses had become dark green again.

Ursula had her long arms out on the table. Her many bangles clattered on her wrists when she lit a cigarette. She was striking and ratlike in the face, thin in her white slacks and sandals, a woman out of an Indian cigarette advert. She liked having Uncle Ashok's attention. They had some chemistry which wasn't flirtatious. For there was nothing for Lakshmi to fear from a girl like Ursula. It was only in the constancy and admiration of Lakshmi, in her body's prosperity and the magical old light of her countenance, that her husband could work his alchemy in business.

In practice, one passion excluded the other. It was simpler to like a good-looking young woman across a table and to let it rest there. Sanjay sat down next to Ursula and borrowed her cigarette. The smoke was sour in his chest, as if a wire was burning somewhere.

—What was that about being a travel agent, uncle?

—No, for two hundred and ninety-nine rands a year, Sanjay, I maintain the certification. Then, around the world, we qualify for a reduced rate at the good hotels and lodges. I will put your name, and Ursula's name as well, on the same contract when you want to travel. We mustn't let this man ruin our day.

—I haven't, uncle. I was just curious about the travel-agent business.

Uncle Ashok looked at Sanjay as if he hadn't understood the point. The day was already ruined.

—The way this country works, someone is always going to look at you with doubt. We are here for the rugby. Nobody in this hotel can deny us the right to enjoy ourselves. And tonight, may the best team win.

—Have you placed a bet on the Springboks?

—You know better than anyone that I don't gamble, Sanjay. I don't find it enjoyable. Good company is what I enjoy. That is something you can't put a price on. Nobody can stop me enjoying. And here is the man with our keys. This hotel certainly takes its time.

Nobody would have thought of denying Ashok's right to enjoy himself. He enjoyed life to the last drop, from the expensive cars in his garage to the illegal fireworks he distributed at Diwali, the cubic-zirconium jewellery he bought his wife, and his favourite heavily muscled Tamil masseur. The only pleasures he had been denied were those relating to paternal power. His three sons, Sanjay's first cousins, were

213

unavailable day to day. The eldest and the middle son were working overseas as an insurance policy. One practised as an optician in Birmingham. The other had trained as a dentist in Australia. Then there was Vish, the youngest, who had dropped out of sight.

Without his sons Uncle Ashok had started taking Sanjay around. He took pleasure in his nephew's company, overflowing with disquisitions about the Johannesburg Stock Exchange. He had started to invest in shares for the first time rather than putting his money into buying insurances from the same Gujarati broker. Uncle Ashok was an inveterate shopper, a passion he indulged on every business trip to the full extent of his allowance for hard currency. In a locked cupboard in the Westville house he stored Burberry raincoats, golf clubs, pearl-buttoned shirts, and flowered Zegna ties, Harrods teas, bottles of Armenian brandy, and whiskies. Sanjay trusted his uncle because he was only after pleasure, a single goddess with uncountable faces. There was a kind of innocence in Uncle Ashok when he poured two cups of smoky whisky in the afternoon and lectured you about peat.

On the way up to the rooms Ashok and he waited for the next lift after the women and the valet occupied the entirety of the first one. They went up ten floors in a whoosh, and then walked some distance behind the others along the curving corridor. The place had been carpeted into silence. Up here the windows looked out over avenues lined with trees and the mortared walls of city estates.

Sanjay could tell that his uncle wanted to talk about something away from his wife. As much as possible Ashok kept Lakshmi out of the details of his businesses. He could be downright secretive when he thought you were trying to ferret out something. He didn't need your nose in his business until he invited you in.

—Sanjay, my boy, you remember I ordered a cellular telephone? I thought it might be the beginning of a business.

—I do remember. I got the cashier's cheque issued for it. You spent a fortune for something that will never catch on.

—Well, they have it ready. We can go to collect it. For this particular model, I will be one of the first to have it in the country. It weighs no more than five hundred grams. If it works out, Sanjay, I will get you one as well.

—I am telling you it's a gimmick. Just a gimmick.

—Wait until you have your own one. Then we can be in contact twenty-four hours out of the day.

Their rooms were next to each other. Ursula and Lakshmi stood in the doors, talking to each other, while the valet came back with the hand cart. Before they arrived Ashok stopped at the ice machine. It was a glowing bar in the dark corridor.

—You won't believe who contacted me last week.

—You can say to me, uncle. My lips are sealed.

—Vish. This impossible boy. Vish is back on the scene and living in Johannesburg.

—I can't believe it.

—When will I lie to you? I have not told his mother. For the moment, however, let it be a secret between us. I will break it to Lakshmi once I have had a chance to see him and size him up. We are going to meet with him before the rugby. After that, we have a consultation with my old chum Farhad, who was in London for so many years. Mandela has just put him on the National Executive Council. You've never met him?

—I've heard the stories.

—There is always another story to tell about Farhad but he will never tell a story about himself. Fortunately, my boy, I warned you that our holiday would be diluted with a small amount of business. Now go and enjoy your room. I will knock on your door at three sharp.

The door to his room stood open, although Ursula had pulled a disappearing act. There was music playing on the system in the lounge as you entered, a wash of harps and chimes and wind recordings emerging from a bar below the television and filling the room.

Ursula came out of the bedroom, already in her white underwear, the stain of her large nipples showing under the translucent material, and sprawled out on the couch. She looked like an antelope. You thought that she was more interesting than money.

—You settled Uncle Ashok down? Is he happy in his room and all? I had to make conversation with Lakshmi for four full hours today, on the flight, off the flight, in the car, in the hotel. The lady doesn't tire. You should have warned me.

—Flying makes her nervous. She talks when she's nervous. Around Uncle, you'd be surprised, you don't hear a peep out of her. And listen, Ursula, I didn't force you to come. You came of your own free will.

—It's true. I wanted to meet the great Uncle Ashok and Aunt Lakshmi. Now I can say that these rich Indians are exactly what I expected them to be. They are nothing special.

—How will you behave when you become rich? Just remember Ashok paid for us to come.

You and Ursula reacted strongly to each other. It was a part of the chemistry.

—When you are admitted to Ashok Uncle's company, nobody can forget he is the one who paid. Nobody mentions it out loud but nobody forgets either. If it wasn't for his money, you would notice he was standing there and watching your breasts. The mythology you have built around it is the worst aspect. I cannot bear the legend of Uncle Ashok and the legend of your father and of Logan the Black Consciousness activist who wants to say that Indians must be the same as Africans. I want you also, Sanjay, to liberate your mind. Like them, but in secret, you believe that money is the ultimate value. That is why you cannot accept yourself and love yourself.

—You just don't like sharing attention.

—Sit down here while I am doing my business. You can cause me such heartbreak, Sanjay.

He obeyed. Ursula began putting rollers in her red-brown hair, her fine big-knuckled hands reaching expertly around her head. The plastic cylinders hung above her head like ornaments on a Christmas tree. Sanjay noticed the apricot scent of her deodorant when she lifted her arms. Any reminder of her warm living body there underneath her clothes, her small breasts bound in her brassiere beneath her voice and her sarcastic manner, had the power to excite him.

He wanted to make her look directly at him and imagined putting his hands on her back, inside her mouth, sliding them along her neck, controlling her small, sharp-nosed head until he forced it to turn straight to him and never waver.

The girls at his school, consumed by boys and mothers and fathers and their cousins' children, had not dissimilar futures to Lakshmi and Kastoori already written in their stars. They didn't affect him.

Whereas Ursula, in each motion she made, in each syllable she uttered and then drew back with the top of her tongue as if she were stringing a bow and pointing it at you, exerted a decisive force on him. Sexual feeling saturated her body and her movements. He couldn't imagine what Lakshmi found to approve of in the girl. There should be a natural antagonism between aunts and Ursula, between the forces of restraint and modesty and the free energies of sexuality.

Sanjay put his hand at the top of her leg. Whatever Ursula said caused pleasure in him, as if her voice was tuned to the right frequency. It made you think that she wasn't in a bad temper at all. The most awful things could come out of her mouth yet they bore no connection to her feelings in that moment.

Ursula's parts worked independently. In her face, at this moment, you couldn't find the sense of an expression. Her zippered eyebrows pulled in, as if she registered the hot presence of his hand, while the clamshell of her mouth didn't even flicker. She brought her face close and kissed him so hard that he felt the side of her tongue. Her mouth was as cold as her hands.

—My uncle organised a vehicle and a driver. He told me to take you anywhere in Joburg you wanted. He wants you to experience luxury.

—Maybe he's in love with me.

—You should take advantage while it lasts.

—I am taking advantage. That is all I ever do. You know it too well. Let me go.

Ursula removed his hands. She took off her underwear and sat completely naked on the armchair. He was surprised again by her long dark body, with the top of the triangle of dark hair between her legs just visible, and wanted her complete attention. Ursula was a liquor, as dark and full as the ocean, which could never be drained, although you would try and drown.

She pushed his hands away again and went into the bedroom. He followed after a minute, remembering the stories she told about the many men in Durban, black and white and brown, young and old and middle-aged, sick and able-bodied, rich and poor, who approached her during her working hours, sent drinks to her if she was alone at a restaurant counter, called her at her parents' house when they found out her name and number from her medical records or insurance file or car registration.

Sanjay hadn't known whether to believe her, to credit the scale of such desire in the nondescript city. But he found her on the bedspread, inspecting herself, and decided that if there was an idle thought in an idle man anywhere in Zululand it would move in the direction of Ursula. He pitied the men who did without her. He burned with hotel joy. At the same time he saw that Ursula's dog-whistle appeal depended on the ever-present possibility of its turning sour in a single moment, putting you dead set against her stupid countenance and stupid red lips and the stupidity in each word that she uttered. It was exciting that she came so near to revolting your taste.

Sanjay went around the bed and put his hand on her open breasts. They were small but complete, dark brown on light brown as if someone with fine hands had stitched a cap on each one. There was a smell of mushrooms. It didn't come from anywhere specific. Sometimes it was so distinct he tried unsuccessfully to find it on Ursula's body, under her arms, which bore the clean stink of deodorant, in her navel, where he put his head to root it out, in the humid brown-black hair at the base of her thin body. The mushrooms were as invisible as money. He knew only that it was in Ursula and that, until her train of mushrooms ran out, he would never manage to leave her behind and he would find however much cash required to keep her. She was wrong. She was better than money.

He pulled her on top of him and felt the temperature of her chest and thighs. Her pulse was in them, faster than he expected. Using both hands she turned his head and put her mouth to his ear and began talking, although he couldn't understand what she was saying or if she was trying to say anything at all. The links of her watch pressed on his neck.

He turned round and saw, in the light sitting on the side of her face, the strokes of her foundation. She kissed him, harder this time, and fitted him between her legs. Her expression was crooked, tough as a policeman, the opposite of his friends' round-faced sugarcane romances, nodding and smiling by compulsion, whom they had known since standard five and never separated from for a day.

He had never been more aware that Ursula was nearly ugly. She was mere skin and bones. He placed his hands firmly on her hips and put her beneath him so that he covered her head with his neck. He could never reach Ursula and keep her attention until he was inside her. He wondered if there was anything at all within this bag of skin and bones and brown mushroom fragrance.

He pulled her into him with his arms and waited as she began to gasp, faster and faster, holding her nails in his back, until the moment snapped and she smiled so broadly, so suddenly, and so peacefully at him that he was dazzled. The cords in her neck and shoulders relaxed. He was broken by her smile, sizzled into the centre of her body, and then he clung to her neck.

He thought he was going to go off to sleep but then he found he was quite awake while Ursula shook slightly as she snored. She was innocent in her sleep and corrupted to the bone when she was awake.

Sanjay saw that he had lost his footing in his life. It had happened since he had gone to work for his uncle rather than continuing as a clerk at the bottling firm in Isipingo. He was still in the middle of his descent. He didn't know where he would land.

He lay next to Ursula and put his hand to her face. She was irritated, flicked it away, and refused to open her eyes when he put both his hands around her face. There was nothing inside this head of Ursula's. Everything was on the surface. Everything about her mind was as ugly and beautiful and as emphatic as her nose and long mouth.

—You can wake me up in an hour. Then I want to go shopping.

—I am going down to the bar in a minute. First, I wanted to tell you that I am going with Ashok to meet his son Vish, the one who vanished from the face of the earth. I didn't even think he was still alive.

—Vish is the moffie?

—I can't say for sure. They never talk about him. Sometimes you can't tell from how a man behaves. And, by the way, 'moffie' is not a good word.

—That's very good, Sanjay. Who is interested in good words and bad words? You can greet the moffie for me. Can you let me go so I can sleep for ten minutes?

Vish, who should have been the golden boy of the family,

was the principal cause of his golden father's unhappiness. Neither his uncle nor his aunt talked about the boy except in passing. Sanjay had known him quite well when they were growing up. Later on he realised that Vish had developed an entirely separate life from his family. At the age of seventeen, when he got his car, Vish went to nightclubs on the beachfront where they previously didn't allow Indians. He never looked back. The day he got his matric, he moved out to live with white roommates in a Berea commune and worked as a hairdresser, to the mortification of his mother and father. They heard reports from their friends about Vish operating a beehive hairdryer on old European ladies.

Only Ursula was crass enough to say it out loud, but his cousin was suspected of being a homosexual. Vish was the nearest thing his father could never turn into gold and thus he was the sorest point.

The shopping centre boasted an indoor fountain and a different population. You could see that the people had money, not more money and less money as in Durban, but real money. Where things mattered there was money. It was the year of money. It was the year of Ursula and Uncle Ashok and Auntie Lakshmi. Sanjay made the requisite allowances. He didn't mind standing outside the changing room in a boutique while Ursula tried on different outfits and complained that the owner of the shop had been studying her breasts. He didn't mind being enticed into jealous feeling.

At the jewellery store he watched as she put several pieces on her arm to compare them and he could hear the excitement in her breathing.

—You like these earrings?
—They're brilliant.

—Do they match my eyes?

—Your eyes are a different shade of green. They are much murkier. Let me see for real. When you're not in front of me I cannot say what is the true colour of your eyes.

—That doesn't sound like a compliment at all. I'm going to get you back for that.

She stood at the gilt-framed mirror, which was tall enough to contain her image from head to foot, and hung the earrings deftly in her ears. In its quieter and darker rectangle the mirror reminded Sanjay that Ursula's eyes were almost green, unusual for an Indian woman, flecked with gold as you might find in a polished stone, and that on account of them he might refuse to take his own warnings. Maybe money couldn't buy happiness, but it had brought him to Ursula. There were more interesting things than happiness. He might please his aunt and marry her.

—You're going to buy these for me, Sanjay?

—Ask him if I can write a cheque.

—I'll wear them tonight in honour of the rugby.

—The All Blacks won't be able to play if they catch a glimpse of you. That's our only shot, in my opinion. We're kidding ourselves if we think we can compete at that level after so many years of isolation.

—Give the Springboks a chance. They might surprise you. I forgot. You don't like surprises.

—I do like surprises. I just don't expect them to happen.

—Don't be clever.

He waited until she showed signs of passing to another shop.

—We need to get back to the hotel. I'm supposed to meet my uncle in twenty minutes. And then we only have another twenty minutes before our appointment with Vish.

On the way out Sanjay was surprised by the shopping centre, which was festooned with strings of overhead bulbs, vines of coloured lights along the escalators, chandeliers suspended above the big halls and skylights along the side of the building, streamers and banners overhead announcing the rugby, and giant advertisements in shop windows portraying women of unearthly beauty. In this M-Net world, Ursula was the down-to-earth one.

Sanjay wondered, if Yash had been around, whether he would have appreciated Ursula. She could have appeared on an album cover from the 1970s. His father would never have been able to afford her. The man had never managed to solve the problem of money for himself or for his family. Sanjay wished that Yash had taken out insurances. For three years until they increased her salary, Kastoori had to borrow money from her brother to pay for his school uniform. Sanjay still had the fear of falling into the same hole.

The day picked up pace. In the space of an hour he returned Ursula to the hotel and went with Uncle Ashok to another shopping centre in the vicinity, where it took twenty minutes to climb to the top of the spiral parkade and find a parking.

Uncle Ashok had something to say when he got out of the car.

—Listen, man, you can do me one big favour, Sanjay. Just save me from Vish after half an hour of conversation.

—You don't want to see him at all?

—No, I want to meet with my son face to face. I want to take down his address and be certain of how he is doing, if only for his mother's peace of mind. I want to be able to help him if I can provide any assistance. But I am not ready today to have a long conversation and to take the blame for everything that has gone wrong in his life. He knows exactly what to say to take all the enjoyment out of a day.

—Tap your watch when you want to go and I'll make an excuse.

Sanjay went into the mall before Uncle Ashok, who had something he wanted to do with his new telephone. He almost walked past his cousin, who was standing in front of the very tall cash register in the coffee shop. Half of the man was already gone, leaving the bare lineaments of his cousin, who was almost exactly the same age as Sanjay, almost the same height, but who now, judging by the looks of him, weighed exactly half as much.

—Vish-bhai, I didn't recognise you. How are you, my brother?

—I'm okay. Don't worry. Where is my father?

—Uncle will be here in a minute. He has some problem with his new telephone. You can trust me that he is really looking forward to seeing you. Now how many years, Vish, since I last saw you?

They embraced. Sanjay wanted to keep his arm around his prodigal cousin. Vish stepped back.

—It was that one Diwali, man, when your mother was staying by our house because the electricity was turned off during the boycotts. It must have been 1988. From the whole family, you know, Logan was the one who kept in touch. Since then you look exactly the same. Maybe I look different.

—You've gone thin, it's true.

—It went in the past three months. Can you believe it?

It was hard to adjust to his cousin's new figure. Vish had never been corpulent like his father and mother. Nor had he acquired, during his teenager period, the skinny, man-snake muscles of their other cousins, who had taken to weightlifting and rebuilding the engines of their Volkswagens and the pursuit of bigger hubcaps for their cars. Vish had developed an ordinary boy's figure. But today there was something unnaturally slender about him. His shirt and trousers were strung on the hanger of his body, barely disturbed by the living being within. His eyes were as big as saucers. The sharp ring of his collarbone was exposed in his neck.

Sanjay found a table and the waitress brought a pot of boiling water and a collection of tea bags. The lemon-scented water seemed to revive his cousin.

—You must get the proper attention, man, Vish. Your father knows every Indian doctor in Natal because, at some point, he has sold a Mercedes to each and every one of them. And who can you trust if not an Indian doctor?

—The minute I go into the clinic it is as good as a death sentence. I am not stupid, Sanjay. There is no treatment for whatever is wrong with me. You know I worked in a hair salon on Berea Road for two years after school? You won't believe, not one of the men I worked with is still alive. White men, black men, Indians, coloureds, the same. All gone.

—I am going to talk to uncle. This is something he can fix immediately.

—My father can't fix this. But I will give him a chance to help if he wants. There is a private clinic in Bryanston which is looking for patients for a new treatment. I don't know if he wants to help. You can convince him there. I thought it's worth a shot to ask him. I don't know what I have left to lose.

—I don't know what Uncle Ashok has done that you can doubt his willingness to help. He and your mother are the pillars of the family.

—I can't talk about that here. One day, when you are ready to accept the truth about my father, you will see for yourself. You will see that my father killed your father.

—Don't be melodramatic. He simply drew the line at some point and then refused to lend any more money. I don't blame him for that.

—One day you will find out the real story.

Uncle Ashok came in. He was carrying his new telephone, which he put on the table. He put his arms around his son and then sat down. He talked to Vish, this pile of skin and bones in the chair, as if they had seen each other the day before yesterday, nothing had changed between them, and Vish looked likely to live out the year rather than pegging in front of them. Sanjay wanted to stand up and leave. This father and son deserved each other.

Instead he kept quiet and listened and decided that he was better off without anyone like Yash to hamper him. He didn't bear grudges, but he suspected that his father's unhappiness would have hindered him as much as Uncle Ashok's prosperity counted against Vish. He studied the stacks of decorated cakes in an airless glass cabinet in the middle of the room. One was green and had pistachios embedded around the rim to make a crown.

—Vish, my boy, you will come to the rugby match today? I can have an extra ticket for nothing. You must just say the word and I will send a car to fetch you. Bring a friend.

—I have an appointment.

—Who has an appointment at the same time as the Rugby World Cup? Today this country has the opportunity to put the bad history behind it. Vish, when is the last time your mother saw your face? She never stops worrying about you. Come tonight and you can also put her mind at rest.

—We used to boycott rugby. We used to pray for the teams from other countries to win over the Springboks. In one year have they turned to gold in your eyes?

—Forget the Springboks for a minute. I have invited you, Vish. It is up to you to give us a chance. In the meantime, for both of you, I can show you the future. If you will permit me.

Uncle Ashok took his telephone out of the box and put it on the table. It was as heavy as a brick and had a long antenna. The display came on, showing a string of bright blue alphanumerics, and then went off again.

—It needs to be charged. Then I should be able to find some kind of a signal in the major city centres. You won't believe what I had to pay for this, Vish. One day this country will be like Europe and even the man in the street will carry a telephone. It will revolutionise the society more than all the Marx some of my friends used to read.

Sanjay picked up the telephone and tried to understand how it worked. He still couldn't understand the point of talking in the middle of the road.

—I can believe you, uncle. Two years ago I went with Ursula to Howick Falls. Vish, you must meet Ursula. The two of you are on the same wavelength. At Howick Falls we took our shots with an instant camera. It turned out the people there had never seen themselves in a photograph. That's what this country is, everything side by side. On the one side we have instant cameras. On the other side, there is total destitution.

—But they all love to talk here, whether they are below or above the poverty line. They love to talk. They live only to talk. Somebody is going to become a billionaire based on that fact. Vish, my boy, if you can come along this evening,

Sanjay and I are going to meet with some of the comrades and see if we can do a piece of business.

Uncle Ashok tapped his watch. Sanjay got the message.

—We have to make our way back to the hotel soon, I think, uncle.

—Vish, let me write you a cheque, my boy, in case you don't make it tonight. But I will see you very soon in any event. More and more of my business is centred in Pretoria. Only make sure to telephone your mother in the meantime.

Vish nodded and also got up from the table. Sanjay saw that he was trembling.

—Tell Lakshmi I will call her the first opportunity.

Uncle Ashok had been interested in technology since the beginning of the 1980s. He had imported cassette players from Hong Kong, copycat Redstone computers, ham radio sets, car-stereo conversion kits, eight-track players, and vacuum-tube amplifiers, which he sold by mail order.

Usually he made money. On occasion he lost it when a shipment contained nothing but defective circuit boards. Sanjay couldn't imagine that many people would need a mobile telephone on this continent of poverty and disease and civil disaster, but he recognised that his uncle's imagination exceeded his own. The man was a master of brands.

At the same time Uncle Ashok had been a fixer for the friends of the Natal Indian Congress. Through his bank account, money had been conveyed to the widows and orphans of township activists. It flowed to sympathetic lawyers and community organisations, supported the families of prisoners, rented cars to take people to the border when they needed to skip, and when the prisoners and exiles began to arrive back, arranged suits and pin money and accommodation and transportation. He gave money to Satya to write an African history book for children and to Logan to pay the school fees for the children of activists in detention. He had created a lot of goodwill.

In cooperation with his lawyer and doctor friends, for example, Uncle Ashok read contracts, made wedding arrangements for their sons and daughters, got scripts for their medications, and stood guarantee for the mortgages they took on houses sold by whites who were leaving. He could work in the dark, beavering away at his businesses and the needs of his connections despite the collapse in the economy.

In the stadium both these sides of Uncle Ashok's life were present. Sanjay and Ursula, Ashok and Lakshmi went through the VIP parking lot, where Mercedes-Benzes stood shoulder to shoulder, and up to the corporate boxes, where Ashok had rented a pavilion. To Sanjay's surprise his uncle went back to the subject of Vish while Ursula and Lakshmi were busy at the drinks counter.

—One consolation, Sanjay, is that we have his address. You can't imagine how it tormented my Lakshmi, not to be able to find her son. You will understand when you have a child of your own. You should have seen how your own father used to follow you around. He wouldn't let you out of his sight. Vish will never give us that simple satisfaction, to honour his mother and father.

—I'm sure he wants to, uncle. He must have a reason for how he behaves.

—Everybody has a reason. I can buy you a thousand reasons at zero cost. Vish has never cared about manners. Listen how he calls his mother by her first name.

—I admit, I was surprised by that.

—When he was still under our roof he should refuse to treat me like a father, only as a competitor for his mother's attention. He is making himself thin with this level of aggression. What can I do, Sanjay? I also have to protect his mother. After all, she has a heart of gold. But why are we quarrelling? Here is my good friend Farhad. The two of you have a few things in common. His wife, Parveen, and Lakshmi really hit it off when they came back into the country.

—Isn't Logan, the bodybuilder, close to Vish? Why don't you ask him to keep tabs on Vish?

—Logan is hardly a member of this family, Sanjay. What could he do for you when your father passed? How many times did he pick up the phone? Was he too busy with his driving school? Logan, and that Satya over there, do nothing for anybody's upliftment. That is because, at the bottom of all their black pride, is the fact that they are ashamed of the colour of their skin.

—They don't see it that way.

—By their fruits you shall know them all.

There was something bluff in Uncle Ashok's face which might have been terrifying, his gold-making blandness turned on his son and Logan and Satya. He was emotional when he turned to his new telephone and started to punch in a number.

Sanjay had been angry at Vish as well, but now his thoughts took a turn. His cousin's hand had trembled in the coffee shop. At times, when Sanjay looked across the table, he had found a look of the purest bewilderment among his features. Could he be angry at skin and bones? Could he stand in Uncle Ashok's rented pavilion and resent his son? The box in the stadium had three rows of benches and a table along the side on which stood red and white wines, prawn cocktail in tapering, amber-coloured glasses, and a bucket of ice guarded by a waitress with a pair of tongs. He went to find a drink and watched as she skilfully settled two ice cubes in it.

Ursula was watching the television sets tuned to the action although there was a good view of the field from the balcony. The Springboks were pacing themselves, stretching, tossing a ball casually as if nobody was in the stands, and running lengths between the try lines while the coach exercised his whistle. Television crews had installed their cameras along the side of the field while most of the stadium seats were already occupied. Men and women, boys and girls were filtering along the staircases to fill the remainder. They had to play catch-up, at rugby, cricket, and money-making, and cellphones, and computers, and television. Yesterday there had only been *MacGyver* and *Dallas* on television. Tomorrow there would be a hundred channels. They were in a country in a hurry, on their way to somewhere, and each of them was in a hurry, eager to become rich. Sanjay felt this excitement. Even the women had become more interesting. They wore tighter clothing.

Uncle Ashok was talking to his friend Farhad. Sanjay listened while he watched the match preparations. Farhad's other companion, Victor, stood beside him but didn't comment. Sanjay already knew his uncle's opinions. Uncle Ashok was on autopilot. He and Farhad were talking to be listened to.

—The machinery in our factories is thirty years out of date, Farhad. You come with your socialism and I tell you they are schooling Mandela there in Washington in the facts of life. Don't be fooled by what you might have read in books thirty years ago.

—Believe me, Ashok, the government understands that voting means nothing without getting the economic side right. That is first on the list.

—It must be first on your list. Without a strong economy you cannot accomplish anything.

—We understand that we have a mess. We used to believe they were so fearsomely efficient, that they knew what everybody was thinking, and recorded every telephone call. When we came in, it was amazing how haphazardly the ministries were running. They had looted the place. We can't rely on the recycled bureaucrats, and not just because of their loyalties. Nobody has any idea about computers. So we may be communists, in the long run, but, until the long run develops, we want to improve business.

—I'm glad to hear it.

—This economy is only a set of monopolies, monopolies and gangs. The whole thing is divided up already down to the level of the townships, by tea rooms and garages, who gets to run the Steers franchise in Benoni, who controls the water in the location. We can become another gang that happens to control parliament. You can help us break things down before it becomes a problem. You have a history with us therefore we can trust you and vice versa. Although I must be honest with you, equally, and tell you that I cannot see a big market for your telephones.

—I hear your guys are talking about buying submarines.

—I am telling you to think on a much larger scale than telephones. We are running a state for the first time. There are big contracts at stake, army, navy, atomic power stations. Who would have thought, ten years ago, that we would be standing here at Ellis Park, in our own private area, and talking about submarines?

Who would have guessed about submarines? Could Yash have imagined the return of an icon like Farhad and his wife, Parveen, dressed in a gold-trimmed tracksuit, who was loudly going around the benches demanding that somebody explain the rules of rugby? Farhad was employed by the Department of Foreign Affairs. Of the different advisors, he was rumoured to be the one the president telephoned late at night. Farhad was the most logical man when you listened to him, everything in plain sight, and yet it was a submarine country. His father's whole life had been underwater.

Sanjay went up to Ursula and ran his hand along her side. He was attracted to her and he pitied her at the same time. In Vish's face there had been no pity, only a lost dog in search of a bone. To his cousin everybody was a bone. To be at the bottom like that was a plight. And to be rich, at the top of the bottomless well of poverty, was a special sin, doubly so for a dark-skinned man.

The only person who managed to annoy you was Parveen. She had become increasingly flirtatious with age. She canoodled with every man, ignored every woman except the best friend at her side, and seemed to believe that her seductive spirit transcended her prodigal flesh. Sanjay tried to keep Ursula as a screen between himself and Parveen, knowing she would be daunted by Ursula, but eventually she got through. She was as gay as a fifteen-year-old girl.

—Sanjay, I don't believe I have seen you in donkey's years. Why don't you pay Farhad and me a visit? We are renting a large house owned by a former minister. There is a tennis court, everything. You don't even need to give us a warning. If Farhad is busy I will take care of your every need.

—That's very generous of you, Parveen.

—And don't be shy to come without your Uncle Ashok

either. Although if he wants to, of course he is welcome to stay. Farhad has a soft spot in his heart for your uncle. I don't know what they are busy talking about. The last time I heard it was something to do with submarines.

Men were streaming into the centre of the field. There were flashes to indicate the million cameras going off in the stands.

—I think the match is beginning, Parveen. I will tell my uncle that we should try and visit before we leave Joburg.

—You must do that, my dear. Come alone, or come with your girlfriend, and I will take you shopping to all the best places.

The match was indeed starting. Young white men had stripes painted on their faces, a parody of war paint, while others were blowing trumpets, carrying tape recorders and radios. Others were bare-chested, drinking beer furtively in the back rows. There was a vast sense of white power around them.

Everybody in the stadium was cheering. Ursula put her arms around him. The large television panel focused on Mandela in a green-and-gold jersey, number 6 like Francois Pienaar's. A jumbo jet came soaring over the field. The engines were deafening. The red lights on the undercarriage were each as distinct as a cherry. It seemed to stop in the air above tens of thousands of shouting fans, tons of metal about to fall out of the sky only a few hundred metres above them, to show off the good luck wishes written on the underside in huge letters.

For an instant, the giant aeroplane and its red lights passed over Ursula beside him. Nothing had ever been so loud. And then no place with sixty thousand people had ever seemed so silent.

—Are you planning to marry me, Sanjay?

—If the Boks win we can get married tonight.

—I am more pregnant than you realise.

The 747 turned around in the darkness above the city and reappeared above them.

Nobody could score a try. The lines were evenly matched. The Bok wing, James Small, had been sponsored by a radio station to tackle giant Jonah Lomu whenever he had the opportunity. Sanjay followed the two big men colliding and thought that he had never had anybody collide with him except for his father.

In the scrums the ball went back and forth, spun through the air on the throws of the fly halves, but was invariably intercepted and brought to a halt. The Springboks had convinced themselves that they were the best in the world but they weren't showing it. Some of their players were as big as boxers, as big as doorways that no opposing player could enter. They smashed into each other without regard for their necks and then passed the ball along the line with deftness, switching this way and that until the man in possession was brought down in front of the posts.

Then three minutes before time, Mehrtens missed a dropkick and left the All Blacks level with the Springboks. The referee gave twenty minutes of extra time. Mehrtens got a penalty for New Zealand. He was equalled by Joel Stransky. Stransky finished the game with a dropkick.

There were trumpets in the stadium. Confetti poured down. The rugby team had been boycotted and had rejoined the world to beat it. Mandela held the captain of the team in his long arms. In Johannesburg cars streamed by, honking their horns, and flashing their lights. Streamers and banners came down from office blocks and flats, and a double-decker bus with an open roof ran through the city showing the flash of cameras along the top. From outside, when Sanjay made it through the gates, he could see that Ellis Park was beaming with lights like an ocean liner. People were drinking with the police along the roads.

Ursula had taken ill during the match, perhaps disturbed that there was nobody to pay attention to her condition, and had taken a taxi back to the hotel. Sanjay had hardly noticed her disappearance, but when he wanted to talk to her, to find out if she was planning to hold him to his promise, she was nowhere to be found. He didn't want to escape from a wedding. The country was winning. He wanted to be kept to his commitment to Ursula. Behind his revulsion he loved her.

But there was nobody to tell. He had become separated from his uncle and Lakshmi in the queue for the exit. He found himself, instead, in the back of a long black car with a driver, heading towards Parktown. Parveen was in the front. Next to Sanjay were Farhad, Ashok's friend, and Victor Moloi. Victor wore a leather jacket, one sleeve hollow from the elbow down. He was reserved, seemed no older than thirty, and was intent on studying the watch on his wrist, which sported a fluorescent band around the rim.

Farhad was friendlier. Sanjay thought that he had the air of a mad scientist about him.

—You'll come with us, comrade. The driver will take you back to your hotel afterwards. This is not an evening to be missed.

—Where are we going, uncle?

—Sanjay, I'm not your uncle. We are headed to the house of the deputy president. He is hosting some of the players as well as the members of the rugby administration. It should be an interesting mix, people from the old structures next to the new people in charge. Rugby won't change unless it is pushed every inch of the way. But that is the brilliance of the deputy president. Even when he disagrees with you, you may never know. He will go out of his way to make you into his best friend. He has the capitalists eating out of his hand. He can even be friends with my wife.

—They're going to let me in here without an invitation?

—We don't work by the old rules, comrade. We have our own ways of doing things. We don't wear ties, although my beautiful wife would prefer it, and we don't insist on invitations from the high and mighty. And as you have seen tonight, we are the champions of the world.

Sanjay accepted the invitation but he didn't understand his new acquaintance. Why was he so friendly? Was it because he was also an Indian? Why did Farhad speak with such joy about everything? Why did he sound so young when there was nothing but a semi-circle of white hair around his head? The way Farhad referred to him as a comrade, and to everybody else as comrade and madam comrade, made it sound like he was making a joke at his own expense. Sanjay wondered if the older man wasn't drunk.

When they came to their destination the house was guarded by a boom gate and three policemen sporting rifles and white gloves. One came to the car window, recognised Farhad, and waved them along the driveway where they found parking places on a circle in front of the main entrance.

The celebrations were in full swing. They were greeted by Sparks, the chief of ceremonies, a quiet man who was one of the only people in a suit and waistcoat. You had heard that, apart from Farhad and the deputy president, he was the most powerful man in the country, but he didn't look like it. Farhad disappeared in the presence of his friend, the deputy president, whom Sanjay saw pressing tobacco into his pipe. He was, as the newspapers said, a handsome man, compact, confident, and aware of embodying the hopes of the country.

And in the same minute your hope, which was worn down day to day by what was reported in the newspapers, came back as strong as it had been five years ago, when Mandela stepped out of jail. You thought that your father had needed a greater father of his own and that each man, in fact, required a father to locate him in the world and to orient him towards the good, to insure him against evil. Mandela was your greater father, and the deputy president was his representative. In the middle of all the happiness and comfort in the house, from the lamps and paintings to the cheerful voices of men and women talking and the British drawl of the satellite-news presenter coming from a hidden television set in one of the rooms, you missed your father Yash with all your hot-and-cold, sweet-and-sour heart. You had never had the chance to be protected by him. He was supposed to be your insurance policy.

At this time you had wandered out the back and found yourself standing next to Victor. He didn't seem to want to interact with anybody at the party and had found his way to a window which looked out over a marble patio and a swimming pool with wickerwork chairs and umbrellas around it. He was limping, although not very strongly. You might have recognised him from the television and remembered that he had lost an arm in a Maseru bombing. He interested you more than anybody else at the party.

—Do you work with Farhad? I noticed you came in together to watch the rugby.

—Farhad works for the deputy president. Sometimes I work with him. Sometimes I work against him. I try to make sure the government stays on track from the point of view of the party.

—I don't understand what you do. Are you some kind of government agent?

Victor laughed. He took off his sandals, rolled up his trousers, and sat on the tiled circumference of the pool, where he could dredge his feet in the water. He was a tiny strong man. You could see the muscles were more developed in one part of his back. You thought you might be interested in Victor for the wrong reasons.

—What do you do, my friend? Why are you asking me all these questions? What do you have to tell me?

—I'm going to get married. I'm going to have a child. My life is over from today.

You both laughed. You sat down next to Victor and took off your shoes and socks. The water was as cold as Ursula's heart.

—To answer your question, I am not cut out to be a government agent. I work in the party headquarters for my sins. Originally I wanted to be an actor. Believe it or not, I began working in a production of Peter Polk's, one of the early ones before he became an international superstar. Nowadays, of course, he is in California. I believe he has his daughter there.

—I've never heard of him before. But you mustn't hold it against me. I have not read a single book since my matric setwork.

Victor put his hand on your shoulder. You saw you had lifted his spirits.

—Why should you force yourself? Today, if I had to start

over again, I would want to be in the movies. Even if I was to be an usher. Would you believe I have seen more than a thousand movies in my life? I began when I was in hospital for my arm. I have taken notes on each and every movie. Up until today I can spend the entire weekend sitting in the Ster-Kinekor in the shopping centre and watch one movie after another. The only reason I don't is that my wife would object.

—I told you that my life is over from today.

—You must make sure to choose the right woman. I happened to be lucky. But like tonight, she works very late in the hospital. They're seeing a lot of unusual cases in the wards.

1999

TRUTH AND RECONCILIATION

Everybody wished to confess, not to admit anything. The sins they remembered, before the end of the world, were general rather than particular. Nobody even knew how to tell the time. Banks of computers around the planet were predicted to crash when the end of the millennium arrived. All the machinery dependent on electronic calculation would go: jumbo jets and atomic power plants, satellites and radio stations, nuclear submarines beneath the ice caps and the stock exchange in New York. Each sin demanded to be told to its full extent before the day arrived. The culprits counted them out one after the other, arriving at a total just as if they were finding the sum of the cents in their hands. But there was no simple way to measure a sin.

Yesterday it had been Gert Rabie. Ann hadn't seen him in many years. In his surgeon's manner Gert had dissected what he had done wrong and what he couldn't have avoided doing, what he hadn't known and therefore for which he couldn't be held to account, and where he should atone.

Ann made her own calculations and used her own figures to make them. She had buried two husbands. She was bad luck for them. From the look of things she would out-last Gert as well. In three or six months or ten months' time, when the Pentium computers stopped counting, she would be called to his funeral and be a widow three times.

Whoever saw Gert and the chart of blue and red veins in his face knew the situation. When you heard his voice, quavering like an instrument he couldn't play, you could tell there wasn't much time remaining for Gert to say his piece. After all, she hadn't come to bury the man. She had come to listen to him before the end of the world when the computers ran out of numbers to count time.

—Can I order you a pot of tea?

—I don't drink black tea anymore.

Gert looked at her fiercely, blazing up like a log. His face was caught in the fire.

—So you've given it up. You are taking part in the modern mania to give things up, hoping for eternal life.

—You're wrong, Gert. I have no interest in living forever. Caffeine simply gives me a headache. Coffee. Tea. Chocolate.

Gert had become more old-fashioned. He cut his hair shorter than before. She wanted to move around the table and hold his stubbled head in her hands, gauge the weight of it. She used to like the bulk of him against her. You knew when he was in the house.

He began talking about former times.

—My memory is much clearer for those days, which may be why I like to talk about them. Tea was the centre of your day. You could spend twenty minutes, as a student, packing the tea leaves. Do you remember that? And you smoked the entire day. I could not understand how you wasted so much time.

—We didn't have to do anything, Gert. We were the arts students, compared to those of you in medical school.

Gert was laughing under his breath. Ann hadn't seen him as a human being in many years. She went on for his benefit.

—There was one bioscope, as people used to call it. When you were a houseman, the flat had no telephone. In an emergency the hospital had to send a messenger to our door. Finally they installed a private telephone, rather than the party line. The only time I used it was when my water broke.

—I was in theatre.

—Needless to say. According to your instructions the registrar gave me a general anaesthetic. When I recovered consciousness the nurse put a boy in my arms.

Memory wasn't enough. The years in which they hadn't spoken interposed. Whatever his charm Ann wasn't talking to the same man she had married and left. She had to look to find him, as she had to look with her sisters. Gert, freckled and jowled and waterlogged in the jaw, was blurred into his old, superfluous flesh.

She watched him place and replace the frosted-glass shakers of salt and pepper on the table, first beside him and then back in the middle, and saw that his surgeon's hands, once so precise that nobody could defeat him at pick-up-sticks, had been affected by Parkinson's. He was shaking as he shifted items around the table and called the waiter back. The verdict was clear.

—Last month I got lost walking to the Medical Association. I recognised the street I was on but the buildings had changed. The army office, the one which was bombed, had been converted into a bank. The hawkers sat on their blankets and sold cigarettes and batteries, red sausages on their charcoal grills, and those bags of hair the purpose of which I cannot fathom. I thought I was dreaming.

—What happened?

—I wasn't dreaming. Everything had changed. I called Carla from a telephone box to fetch me. She doesn't usually drive in the city centre. She believes that, if you so much as graze a pedestrian, the mob will pull you out of your car.

—That seems unlikely, Gert.

—I am not agreeing with Carla's opinion. I am trying to convey the fears we live with every hour of every day. Nobody is to blame.

Carla was Gert's second wife, a former teacher and government-school administrator. She had children of her own and drove a sports car thanks to the magic of maintenance. When she picked up the telephone Carla seemed to talk through a ring she didn't have in her nose.

Ann sat back in her chair, glad of the distance between their thoughts. Gert had been more talkative than she expected. Since his retirement, he had moved in with Carla. She owned a property in a security village. In her company Gert had hatched from the cocoon of his life to become a nearly hairless old man. He had shed his memories along with his hair. Yet the difference between herself and Gert was only in degree.

—And how is Carla? You usually have something to say about her.

—She is also considering taking a retirement package. We all tell her to do that. Take her experience and clear out.

—I didn't know.

—Your friends want us out of the government schools. They want to promote blacks. They put exclusively black history in the syllabus. Is there a difference between a black history of the world and a proper history? They say children must read black novels. Does a novel have a skin colour? Does a medicine care what complexion you have?

—Not as far as I know.

—That is my professional opinion also. A medical drug cannot discriminate.

There the conversation halted. Ann couldn't think how any exchange with Gert could go further. His mind had become more like a machine, operating according to certain rules. He had his speech about whites, and his speech about blacks, and his speech about himself, and he would give them as serenely as if he were sawing open the chest of another patient. She was different. She had lost her sense of proportion. Every pinprick and small tragedy moved her to tears and laughter. At forty, working for Defence and Aid, thanks to the influence of Sebastian and Farhad, she had been more level-headed.

Gert had his own agenda. He wanted Ann's help.

—Speak to Paul. Carla and I have suggested that he and Sabine go back to Canada. He is merely spinning his wheels over here. I have no understanding of the arts but I cannot see the point of this latest enthusiasm. Why does he want to retell the same stories that have been told in public already? The Truth Commission was in 1996. Here we are in 1999, after the fact. Must we go back and dredge up the past every three years?

—He wanted to work with Peter Polk. It may be Peter's last production.

—Polk will never retire. But you cannot explain to me the point of repeating, word for word, what has already been said. Who does it help to repeat and recycle? How is it art in the way that Rembrandt, for example, is art? I believe that Paul must establish himself properly in Canada. One day it will end here. The world's attention will be somewhere else. Then where will he be? What is his idea?

—He doesn't want to share in your resentments, particularly not Carla's.

There was almost no colour in Gert's eyes when Ann found him looking at her. She remembered the long-ago sensation of living entirely in the range of his gaze. Each of her feelings about this man, once as vivid as stained glass, had turned into useless memory. She wanted to brush them away.

—Can you say honestly that, on this piece of land, there is a place for us?

Ann had found joy and love, grief and mourning, and excessive memory and longing with age, but she still hadn't found patience. Instead she found abruptness in the place where her feelings should be. Gert remembered only those things that gave him pleasure. He didn't remember his own privileges. Ann wanted to throw seltzer water in his face. That was the reaction Gert's oblivion could bring out of a person.

—You have enjoyed a good life. It hasn't been taken away from you since the new government came in. At one point you had your own aeroplane. Didn't you fly with Christiaan Barnard to George?

—I am not denying the past. I am making a point about the future.

—Do either of us have a right to talk about the future?

—Do you know what? I promised to call Carla when we finished. I am going to ask at the counter if I can use their telephone. You can hardly find a telephone box nowadays.

He lurched across the room on his walking stick. Ann

had wondered how Gert explained the new dispensation, what formed the subject matter of discussions between him and Carla, where they placed themselves in the flux of things. She regretted having discovered the way he thought. The Rabies travelled in the capillaries of the old dispensation. Rabie had been the notary in court, the prison warden, the major in the old defence force, the warden in the Bantu reformatory. In her presence, in deference to her English allegiances, the family members hadn't defended the system. Neither had her own sisters. Gert had been supportive of Ann and Paul before the two of them left in 1979, but, when she thought back to it, none of the Rabies had expressed surprise at Neil's death.

The Rabies had enjoyed the benefit of the past. Now, like everybody else, they demanded a future as well. Who was she to put them down? Gert was downcast by her anger. She wanted to put a hand to his old face, as whorled as the bark of a tree, and tell him that human nature was there to be forgiven. But he was far away at the counter, talking on the telephone, where she would never be able to reach him.

—Can I help you, madam?

The waitress had found her. Ann looked at the young woman, who could scarcely look out from under her bob. She had a ring through her nose. One could hardly make contact with this new species.

—I'm waiting for my friend over there. You see the very tall gentleman by the counter?

—Madam, he has been standing by the telephone for five minutes. I don't think he remembers what number he wanted to call. The manager asked me to come and ask you if he needs some assistance, please.

—Tell him to call Carla. The number should be on a card he keeps in his wallet.

—I will do that.

Ann wanted to leave in any case. The Rabies would have to find a different confessor. Around Gert, even during the time they were married, her mind wandered to a different subject, then to another, then so far afield that she was often unable to recover the thread of a conversation. They never got to the subjects that interested her. She had wanted to hear what he had to tell her about Sabine, Paul's fiancée. Sabine was a case. Gert could be intelligent about individuals. Relying on his own eyes and ears, he was capable of making interesting judgements. He would have had a guess about how much was Canadian, how much was just Sabine.

Instead Ann was left alone. She couldn't help looking across the floor of the shopping centre and down through the railing, where the pedestrians on the lower level passed beneath neon panels and sales posters bearing images of paradise—such beautiful young women in their pearl-white, corpse-white skins, packaged by Tetra Pak. There were television sets the width of doorways, and tables of jumbled sales goods and other such sombre commodities presenting their ticketed faces.

Flowing around and between them had been fifteen- and sixteen-year-olds, some older men and women, who came face to face with such perfection only in the air-conditioned shopping centre. They were happy. For they were dreamers. Life was a dream of commodities. A good book, Sebastian said, was like a dream. So was every movie you saw in the cinema with the darkness around you. So had your life gone away like a dream.

She should have stayed in London. Instead she was here staring at Gert's hands, both holding onto the telephone on the other side of the restaurant. She couldn't decide whether they were shaking from the disease or from anger. After a certain point, anger was its own kind of disorder.

When he finally did come back, Gert didn't sit down again. He touched Ann's shoulder.

—I don't want to leave things between us on a bad note, Ann.

—Me neither.

Ann got up from the table.

—Can we walk and talk? I have something I would like to convey to you but it is the wrong setting. Apart from that, I have to collect some prescriptions from the chemist and visit the bank. I wouldn't ask you to stay if it wasn't important.

—I have half an hour to spare.

—Most of what I have to do is in this centre. First is the chemist.

They went along the top level of the shopping centre beneath the long skylight. There was a travel agency where several white women sat at telephones arranged along the sides of a bare table and gabbled into the receivers, a new method of doing business. A handwritten card in the window advertised the services of a migration consultant to arrange your move to Canada or New Zealand. Then there was a fabric store. It was closed, and the window was almost dark, with bolts of cloth hung on the backs of chairs, mannequins without arms, Singer sewing machines barely visible in the back.

Gert kept a list in his hands from which he wouldn't deviate. Ann looked at his list. It was composed in the neat strokes of Carla's fountain pen.

He looked further subdued when the pharmacist, a coloured man wearing short sleeves and a clip-on tie, didn't find his order already prepared.

—I called ahead for exactly this reason. I do it before the new month begins, every month, and they prepare the different drugs beforehand.

—I am sorry, Sir. I will collect your script now. Give me five minutes and I will sort you out.

—This could have been avoided.

—I know that, Sir. I wasn't on duty.

Gert wasn't as irritated as he sounded. He stood at the pharmacy counter, overly grateful as each of his medicines was produced and pushed over to him. Ann was reminded that he was the tallest man she had ever been close to. Six foot and three inches. That was an advantage which had carried over to Paul. She had loved him for it when she was twenty. Gert was so grateful for the white boxes pushed over by the pharmacist that her exasperation ended.

She was sorry for Gert. He could have been something better if he had risen out of the old system as Christiaan Barnard had. Instead he had served the provincial administration, making money in private practice on the side before retiring to Carla's gated community. His neighbours included former hospital superintendents and judges, mining engineers and colonels from the old defence force. Through a mixture of sweetheart deals and arms trading, they were steadily working their way into the new dispensation. Compared to his neighbours, acrimonious about every change, yes, Gert would be considered a liberal. He didn't need to keep her behind at the shopping centre to tell her that. Everyone was a liberal compared to somebody.

When they had gone into the bank, while they were waiting in line for the teller, he raised the subject on his own.

—And Ann, you know that I operated on Africans as well as Europeans, without discrimination. Whatever the rules of the province, whether there was a black body in front of me or a white body or a brown body, I treated it the same. Anatomy and physiology are the same. If I had been called, as one unimportant doctor in the greater scheme of things, I would have gone to your Bishop Tutu's commission and told them the same thing.

—The African patients couldn't walk down the same street as us. They had separate entrances, separate clinics. You didn't vaccinate them properly. Hundreds of thousands died unnecessarily. Is it so far away that you can't remember?

—I remember that the ones I operated on are better off because I was there. Paul understands that.

—I also understand, Gert. Don't worry. I am not your judge.

He signed the paper that the teller provided him, filling in his name letter by letter at the bottom, turning to check the calendar on the wall for the date, and relying on the walking stick. The skin was very tight on the cords in his neck. Ann thought that Carla was doing a valuable job. Clever men like Gert were careful not to be alone in old age.

—Now there you are wrong, Ann. You give out second chances but you are also a judge. Even when you were twenty years old you had the expression of a judge. My mother remarked on it before we were married.

Ann felt a flicker of contempt. She had never been so aware of Gert's woody complexion. She wanted to push the money back to the cashier as the woman counted the notes quickly between her fingers. She saw that Gert kept his nails as trim as before, scissored straight along the cuticle, the same as when he had to be in theatre at five in the morning.

—You should be careful withdrawing so much money at one time. Paul says they can follow you from the bank to your house. He read an article.

—Paul can talk nonsense sometimes, even if he is my son. He is imitating Polk, reading the newspapers to draw his stories out of them. In any case, I am taking this for Carla.

—Why does Carla want you to take money home?

—She is as bad as Paul. She believes it when the newspapers tell her that the computers are about to break. Supposedly we won't be able to withdraw from the account. I don't agree. When the world comes to an end, as I see it, we won't need any more money. And good riddance to it.

—The Romans believed you would need a coin. To pay the boatman who had to row you across the river Styx. When you died they put a coin on each eye.

To this Gert had no answer. He filed the notes into his wallet. They went down the escalator and outside the shopping centre. The trees in the pavement had unexpectedly bare branches, as if they were showing their naked arms. Gert was silent with his money, supporting himself on one side with the walking stick. Something had happened between them. He had come across the cruelty in her. She had spoken the answer to the riddle in the act of posing the riddle.

Ann felt the tension in her cheekbones. She knew she could seem terrible to other people. Still she wasn't a judge.

They came to the garage entrance. Gert produced his ticket. He read the time through his half-moon spectacles and calculated the fee. Cars came down the spiral ramp, paused for the attendant to lift the boom, and turned into the traffic leaving behind a cloud of leaden air.

Gert began to cough. She waited for him to go up the parkade steps so she could go back to her rented car. He leaned on the walking stick, holding it so tightly that it seemed his hands would become transparent and show their flickering snake-blue veins.

She realised he wouldn't let her go without saying his piece.

—One minute.

—Go ahead, Gert. Get it out.

—In case it comes out when I am not around to explain, I want you to understand the history and convey it to Paul. My family stood up for you at the inquest. They had to criticise the same people whom we had grown up with and mingled with, the people whose sons played on the same teams as our nephews and cousins. Behind the scenes we did whatever was necessary to protect you and Paul.

—I don't know what you intend to say.

—I am saying that today, twenty-five years on, I regret that I didn't do the same for Neil.

—You couldn't have known. They never admitted that the order came from the Minister. They were experts in turning a blind eye.

—No, they didn't publish what they were doing in the newspapers. But there were some indications. A certain man made a call to my cousin, who ran a section of Bantu Education at that time. This was when they had already placed Neil under house arrest. Neil continued to play with fire. World communism wasn't a fantasy of the government. The Soviet Union. Red China. They were arming the groups on the border. Many of our young men came back dead from the border. That was the inevitable context.

—If you had said something, Neil could have gone into hiding. He could be alive today.

—You are not hearing me. You were both under suspicion. I rang you to say he should tread lightly. Then you and Neil agreed to separate. I went back, for Paul's sake, and informed them that you were no longer connected to those activities. They promised to protect you on my behalf. They also gave Neil a chance to get out of the country. They kept up their end of the bargain.

Gert smiled again when he thought of the deal he had made between fortune and misfortune. His lips were as thin and firm, as properly handsome, as Paul's.

Ann couldn't tell how close this smiling old man was to being perfectly cold under the skin. She put her hands together and thought that they were equally cold, remembered the rings on them, and held on to the pylon on the side of the boom gate. Nothing happened in the right order. She was the fool of some fate that couldn't be read in a pack of Nadia's cards. It was a trick of this weird and unruly fate, which could never be believed in a book, that her relationship to Gert had outlasted her two better men.

—I would never have made a bargain to save my own life, Gert. At Neil's expense?

—It's not fair to put it like that. I am the last one to make excuses. I was surprised the Truth Commission didn't look into that case. It was seen as important at the time, the killing of a professor. But I didn't see the point of bringing it up myself, a case that was beyond redemption. There are times you must pursue it, other times when life simply has to go on. Even today, you can't put the blame entirely on one side. Look at Mandela.

—I have never heard you blame yourself, Gert.

He tried to put a hand on her shoulder. Ann stepped off the pavement.

—I can tell you, Ann, that I would have stayed with you, no matter what. On Paul's account. To be honest, you have a rather cold-blooded streak when it comes to men. That is what I believe.

Gert would have stayed and explained the situation in his terms for the rest of the day. He would never run out of sentences, old wine in new bottles, until the end of existence.

Ann turned back when she had reached the traffic light and saw Gert was bewildered again amid the rows of black pedestrians going past the entrance to the parking garage. She thought he had gone back into his dream. He stood with the ticket in one hand, walking stick in the other, the parcels at his feet, studying the ventilated garage as if he would find instructions on it. He didn't recognise the street he was on. You didn't need to be a doctor to arrive at a diagnosis. Gert had been overcome by a disease of forgetting, the most ordinary disorder that could afflict a man of his time and place.

She didn't go back and save him, or summon Carla to rescue her husband. For it was an impossible task. Gert had sealed himself inside his sentences as surely as if they were a structure of brick and mortar. More than the rand and the Krugerrand, these sentences created the country's false currency. You passed these moneybox sentences around like cents, taking them from one hand to place them in the ear of another. When there was an objection you only passed them around faster. You never looked at what they contained. She was the opposite of a judge who gave out an exact sentence. She wanted the Rabies to take their sentences back.

—

Ann overslept in Paul's rented flat in a four-storey yellow-brick block in Melville in Johannesburg, where washing lines ran along the balconies. Her body was sore as if she had exercised.

The telephone rang and gave up. It rang again and reminded her that there had been a telephone ringing when she had found Neil lying in the kitchen in an appalling circle of blood. On that day Ann didn't manage to answer in time, although she remembered the screeching note in the receiver of that heavy black telephone.

Ann got up. It was Sabine, Paul's fiancée, on the other end. Her voice was blurred, as if she were talking through a piece of cloth.

—I am at the shopping centre on the main road. In the Truworths, next to the Clicks pharmacy. Can you come here, Ann? The keys are on the sideboard.

—I'll be there just now.

—Don't say anything to Paul.

Ann drove carefully past the municipal library, then the electricity substation on the corner of the main road and a furniture store with heavy pieces in its barred windows. At a restaurant on the top floor of a building, at the end of a spiral staircase, there were white women sitting at outdoor tables. They were behind tall drinks, chipping their cigarettes against saucers, served by black waiters in bow-ties. These women were talking to each other with the intensity of squirrels.

Ann parked on the road. She entered the shopping centre on the bottom floor. The aerosol atmosphere came at her the moment she went inside. She went into the store, asked at the counter, and was directed through a door at the back.

She found herself in the manager's office. It was lit with fluorescent tubes, filled with furniture and filing cabinets, and contained Sabine, who was sitting on the couch with her hands folded in her lap. At the desk sat the dark-faced woman who was the manager. The woman was in her late forties, to go by appearances. Ann couldn't put an exact name to her. She had last seen this woman, with her big hoop earrings, at a party in the Soviet Embassy in London where a man had been preparing to defect, and then afterwards at the top of Farhad's enchanted house.

The manager got up from behind her desk and shook Ann's hand, her hand as plump and wet as a goldfish. Ann forced herself to smile. She wanted to take the woman by the hair and put her back into concealment behind the desk.

—I'm Mrs Lakhaney. I must thank you kindly for coming. As a policy we prefer to resolve in between family and friends and ourselves. Our only other recourse would have to be to call the police directly.

—I'm happy to try and resolve it privately. What is this about?

—Would you take a seat?

Ann sat next to Sabine. Sabine had her legs crossed, her earrings clipped neatly into her ears, her dark-brown hair pushed into a bun, and her face changed by the situation, too oblong today to be attractive. There was something unnerving in her diamond-grey eyes. Around Ann, Sabine was reserved to the point of rudeness. She was so composed, silent and untroubled, so blank, so disinterested in the secret history you carried in the heart, you felt the strong desire to prod her. With the proper instruments, you would have tormented her until she spoke freely.

The manager was a different story. Ann had such a clear

memory of finding this garish woman at the top of the house in Shepherd's Bush. She had been copying information from Farhad's notebooks. Ann had taken her journal away. The woman had been young at the time, as Ann remembered, only a few years out of matric. Her bosom was now stored away behind an old lady's tunic. She had been Parveen's best friend in the world until she ran away with the details of their operations.

Her name, she remembered after a minute, was Tanith. She didn't recognise Ann. Ann thought that she had been sent as a spy into the world.

—Sabine, do you want to explain what is happening?

—I can explain, if you don't mind. A woman at the till alerted us to suspicious activity on the part of this lady. I don't know Sabine's last name.

—I hope we can solve this without any need for names to be exchanged.

—Let's see. The guard followed her out of the store and found a number of items which hadn't been paid for in her possession. The sum exceeds a thousand rands. That is our usual cut-off for opening up a docket.

—What do you suggest, Mrs Lakhaney?

Ann had worked for a consultancy for some time when the Defence and Aid Fund closed down. But she had never seen Tanith again. London had been full of people avoiding trial. She had met the son of Edward Lavigne, a mining-company executive, at Tambo's memorial service. She had run across a card for Nadia's hypnosis practice, located in Wimbledon, which specialised in regressing clients to their previous lives. You couldn't predict the direction a life would take.

Suddenly Ann wasn't sure that Mrs Lakhaney was the former Tanith. The latter's young, gold-blush, gold-lidded face was difficult for her memory to hold on to, a plume of smoke vanishing into the room. It had been a strange evening, many years ago, when she had waited for Parveen's friend to get into a taxi before she explained the situation to Farhad. The party had ended at once and Farhad took her to check through any letters and documents the unwanted visitor might have inspected. He never mentioned it again.

When she had last seen her former boss he didn't look well. He laughed away her questions about his health, as if the condition of his body was also a government secret. Farhad had been planning for his new life at the United Nations, had Parveen's cousins staying in his house, and was steadily acquiring expertise in the field of agricultural tariffs. He continued to smile when you wondered how someone who smuggled Czech submachine guns was studying taxes on apples to benefit the farmers who had once been on the other side of those guns. Nothing surprised Farhad. She shouldn't be surprised either in how the twists and turns manifested.

Mrs Lakhaney jotted down her calculations, showed the figures to Sabine and Ann, and then sat back as pleased as if she had proved something. Ann counted the money in her purse. She liked to have her hand on the crisp notes.

—Mrs Lakhaney, I have more than a thousand rand in cash. I have two fifty-pound notes which I will give to you as well. What more can you ask for?

—I could call the Sunnyside police right now. Before they come, as I predicted, the private security will want to have a word. I warn you. They can be rough.

Ann stood up. She brought Sabine up as well. She thought, from the small pressure on her arms, that underneath her tartan skirt and blouse her future daughter-in-law amounted to nothing but a bucket of bones. She had wanted her son to find someone more substantial. In this arduous life the thinnest women were the least reliable.

—Mrs Lakhaney, in my opinion you would rather keep the money. Now answer some questions for me, Mrs Lakhaney. According to your office door T is your initial. Is it Tanith Lakhaney?

—It may be true.

—You changed your name when you got married, I assume. Tell me one thing. Did you ever visit London?

—I may have been there. During a certain period I travelled on behalf of my family's import–export business. Why, did you see me before?

—You don't recognise me?

—To the best of my knowledge, my dear, I have not laid eyes on you in my life. But I never had the best memory for faces, you understand.

On the way out Sabine returned to life. She opened her handbag on the escalator and went through it. Ann could see the girl's shoulders. She thought that, after all, she had lost her own courage since Sebastian's illness. She hadn't pursued the matter with Tanith nor did she want to explain the full facts to Sabine. She hadn't even reminded Tanith of the evening at Farhad's house when she had saved her from something more than embarrassment. Events came too close to the bone. The hospital, with Sebastian disappearing in the bed, had come too close. She had spent her life being cut to the bone.

She sat down heavily at a table at a café facing out on the ground level of the centre. Sabine sat beside her. There were umbrellas along the pavement and an iron fence which set the restaurant off from the street. Ann watched the trucks and buses clamber by, an iron stream burning in thin air, and thought that it was better they knew nothing about her case or her name or her history. She was out of breath. The altitude.

—I'll order a filter coffee. Do you want the same?

—A water is fine.

Ann went to the counter to give the order. When she came back Sabine was still silent. With her arms folded, she was quickly smoking a cigarette and pressing it into the ashtray after each puff. The bones in her arms were like matchsticks. Ann took the cigarette and tried it herself. The smoke filled her chest. Somehow she didn't need to cough. She could asphyxiate herself with no trouble. She handed the cigarette back.

—I didn't know you smoked, Sabine.

—That is my last one. I had the packet for six weeks without opening it.

—The only person who could make me smoke was my old boss Farhad. He got cigars from the Cuban Embassy in the name of revolutionary solidarity. They made my head spin. My late husband, Sebastian, would be egging on Farhad to get more from the Cubans.

—That's interesting.

—Tomorrow I am playing my part for Paul. I'm reading from the transcript of the inquest into Neil's death. I don't understand the reason to repeat things on stage that have already been heard in a public commission. When does it become an actual play? Does it make a difference that it's being recorded?

—It's Paul's experiment, Ann. You have to wait and see how it comes out. At the least it will be a record for people in the future.

Ann decided to hear this as encouragement. She put her hand on Sabine's arm.

—If you don't want to talk about what happened, that's fine.

—I don't mind. I just started to take things and put them in my bag. Usually I throw them away before I get home. Like a bug in my programming. I can't explain.

—I had a friend who took something very small, like a pencil sharpener or a lipstick, from anybody she thought had insulted her.

The waiter brought the coffee and the water and stood back while Ann poured the milk. Sabine put out the cigarette as if it had said something wrong. Ann wanted to put her hand on the younger woman's shoulder, and examine her earrings and her perfectly brushed hair and her shimmering ballgown-grey eyes, but she prevented herself. She couldn't be a judge inside her own family.

—Did you know something about that woman?

—I recognised her from a long time ago. But that was a different life. You wouldn't believe it if I told you the story. Anyway, I have too many stories to tell. Nobody is paid to listen.

—I don't mind listening.

—I'll tell you some other time.

There was a lot the girl didn't know but much more that she didn't want to know and would never pursue. Sabine had followed Paul to London and Dublin, where he performed in bars and provincial theatres. Now she was in Johannesburg, where she had no other reason to be than Paul. She spent hours each day writing letters to her family and friends in Montreal. She even read out to Ann portions of her letters to her family and friends, which she kept copies of. In them she described the dilapidated city and Paul and the production he was taking part in. She had made no attempt to start work again as a translator. She didn't create new connections in Johannesburg or try to have a life beyond Paul and his dramatic circle. In general, Ann thought, Sabine was placed at the very centre of her own web and unwilling to move. Some people had the luck.

For Ann it was strange to sit side by side with someone so oblivious, who couldn't see that she was burning from the encounter with Tanith. She wanted to tell somebody and relieve herself of the heat of the story. She might burn to ashes today from the history she contained, from the days at the public inquest and the years at Defence and Aid, and Sabine would have no conception of where she had vanished.

She couldn't blame anybody. She didn't go out of her way to show what was inside herself. Paul had needed three fathers, Gert, Neil, and Sebastian, to make up for what she hadn't shown him. She should have done more to improve him. Paul's taste in women could only be her fault. He had gone out with a beauty queen and managed not to mind that her voice was as high as a hummingbird, then with a long-legged Ethiopian girl whose parents lived in a compound in Addis and drove a Bentley with white leather seats during the famine. On the ladder of horrors Sabine wasn't so bad.

In any case, she couldn't give the girl any instructions. For Sabine was too self-contained, too beautifully brushed and polished like an heirloom, to accept the advice.

Ann changed the subject.

—I never thought Paul would stick to acting.

—He's different from his friends. It's true. He doesn't fill the room like other actors. But directing makes him happy. I think he gets it from his father. In any case, Ann, I have some news for you. What do you think it is?

Ann thought for a minute. Her mind was blocked.

—I have no idea.

—I am four months pregnant. That's the reason I stopped smoking.

—I had no idea. I'm flabbergasted.

Sabine took her hand and put it against her side.

—Sometimes there's a kick. You'll feel something in a minute. Paul can tell his father finally. Do you think it'll be good for him?

—For Paul or for Gert?

—Paul, I mean.

—Yes. He needs a reason to hurry. To get on with life.

—What do you mean by that?

Ann felt motion under her seasick hand. She withdrew it. She was surprised at how tight Sabine's belly was. It was already as hard as a drum.

—Paul never had a proper childhood, especially after he was expelled from school. He was caught with the bottle in his possession and he sacrificed himself for his friends, who were all as guilty as he was. But he had that kind of gentleness for everybody, for every animal. Then there was a chain of events which didn't allow us to recover our footing. Paul was sent overseas to school. He stayed overseas for university but he had plans to come back. Then there was Neil's death. Then the inquest. Then I was overseas but we were separated. I think, after 1990, Paul went on a long holiday from everything. He was trying to write his novel and work as a bartender in Dublin for three years. I never saw a word of that novel. So my son has had many excuses because of our circumstances. Whereas this puts an end to his pretending to be a child.

—That sounds ominous.

Ann put her hand back on Sabine's belly. She imagined that she could sense the furiously beating heart. It would be as fast as a hummingbird.

—Not ominous at all. Life is a very serious business. There comes a time to get on with it. Do you know the sex?

—The ultrasound is next week. Since it began, even before I suspected, I started putting things into my bag.

—Nobody can explain how the mind works. But why did you call me today?

—I like the fact that you don't judge.

Wanting to rest, Sabine stayed at home for the rest of the day. Ann brought her print-out of the transcript to the production. She was there early and waited at the back of the long room, where nobody paid her any attention. In front of her the stagehands' coats hung on the wall, smelling heavily of being boiled and starched in the laundry. They were turned to the wall and had the names of their owners sewn into the back of each collar in loops of grey cotton.

Suddenly there was noise again in the theatre. Two assistants ran past her. Some were adjusting the curtains. Polk came on the stage, dressed in his customary silver-buttoned denim shirt and trousers. He had been wearing the same outfit, along with an indestructible Casio digital watch, since 1970. Polk looked tired. Along with him were the other men and women who were taking part in the recording. They had given testimony in front of the Truth Commission and had agreed to read today what they had said three years before so it could be recorded. The idea of repeating something like that had sounded ridiculous to Ann at first. But she had come to see the wisdom in it.

Ann went up and sat with them on the stage. They didn't greet her but they made space. The women were mostly African, although there was also a coloured woman with a headscarf and a long red gypsy's dress down to her shoes, and a mouse-faced Indian woman wearing a green sari decorated with miniature stars. The Indian lady seemed unsettled in the formal high-heeled shoes she wore for the occasion. One man had brought a schoolboy's lunchbox, blue-lid Tupperware, and opened it to find the two halves of a red apple.

Ann wanted to drink in the spectacle of these different people. They were her mirror images. She should kneel before them. She should pray with them.

Janet Gilfillan found her on the stage.

—I heard you were here, Ann.

—Here I am.

Janet's red hair was up in a bun and her face and body were as perfectly composed as a geisha. Her intelligence seemed to live in her nose and eyes.

—How many years has it been since we met? I told Paul that we couldn't do this without your participation, of course. Neil's case was a turning point in our history. Not just because of his brilliance, and the absolutely brilliant book he published, but because of the open brutality. They were prepared to kill a man in full view. After that, nobody could claim to be unaware of the nature of the beast.

—They couldn't, but they did. They were aware, but they didn't know a thing. In a nutshell, that's our story.

Janet put her hands into Ann's. In them you could feel her bones. They were as solid as dice in the palm of your hand. She was taking a chance on you.

—Not intelligent people. Intelligent people always know. And therefore, for exactly that reason, this country can never show real respect for intelligence. Now where are you staying? I must come and collect you and have you to myself for a whole evening.

—For the moment, with Paul. And Sabine, of course.

—I'm impressed. My late father insisted I stay under the same roof when I visited Joburg. It put me under a lot of strain. Today I stay in a hotel and visit my mother. But you've always been an original, Ann. I admire you more than ever before.

Ann shook her head. She wanted to push Janet back.

—I am too old for compliments.

—I have to say the things I feel out loud. About Paul, I can see that someone has brought him up properly. Someone with a painter's hand. His voice is so good that he can get every word at the back of the room.

—You mean he knows how to project? He learned at boarding school. His teachers thought it was British to sound like a foghorn.

—And you know how to deflect, Ann. I have to leave you, however, to study my lines for this afternoon. I am going to kidnap you for myself some evening.

Ann had memorised her own lines. She was relieved when Janet went backstage. Half the things she said were unveri-fiable, neither true nor false. Was Paul, for example, so well brought up? Was Janet's admiration for Ann so strong? People spoke without bothering to mean it. Ann wasn't sure if the connection between them existed. They both carried too much experience. Janet had been born a witch, with a thousand years of recollections. Her first major role had been as Cleopatra at the Royal Shakespeare Company. She had been friends with Marlon Brando. Whereas Ann had been friends only with her three husbands, on and off, and with Farhad. She didn't have any heroism, or artistic talent, to boast of. She would never say she had done much with her own talents. She had buried them in the ground.

The other men and women who came to read started to sit around Ann, the men in brown and blue trousers, the women in shapeless dresses. You wouldn't take a second look at such a woman or man on the road, or through the window of a city bus, or behind the cash register. As witnesses, however, they were more than ordinary. They bore truth in their faces.

Did she bear the same truth? The others were here as tokens of what was absent. They stood for persons who had been subject to detention, torture, poison, murder, and disappearance.

She had her own absences. Very few of the facts concerning Neil's case had been uncovered. She wasn't sure what to make of Gert's memories and his mysterious caller. The most likely suspect in Neil's killing and a number of other crimes had emigrated to Adelaide, Australia, and was beyond the reach of amnesty. In cases that came before the commission there had been a lot of forgiveness and confession, a considerable output of tears and shame, and no practical consequence. There was no question of finding what had been lost. Subtraction, loss, disappearance were final. Once potent books could lose their uses. She and Neil had put so much trouble into keeping his books safe and yet today she couldn't say where a single one of those volumes was to be found. Sleepy Bukharin and Mao, Kropotkin and Sartre had vanished as convincingly as Chunu the vegetarian or her old neighbour Mackenzie.

—

Paul began the recital. The room went silent when he announced the order of the participants. He invited the first person to come to the table in the centre of the stage.

They sat down, one by one, when their name was called, and squinted to read the dot-matrix print in the folders they had been given. Their histories shimmered into the room. Ann liked listening to other people's stories, which seemed to come out of the same dream time in which she had passed her own life. Polk performed in the role of the Archbishop. He smiled and cried, read out documents, welcomed his witnesses, scolded his audience, and let his voice waver a note or two. He laughed and wept, admonished, welcomed, took the sins of the world on himself, and performed. You could close your eyes and believe the Archbishop sat there at the end of the table in his robes. But you also thought, from far inside your dream, that Polk showed off when he was acting.

One of the assistants, a shaven-headed man with a deep-brown face sporting a gold stud in his ear, played the role of the court reporter, conscientiously taking down notes about what had happened in each case and peering back over a pair of spectacles at his shorthand when the witness left the stage. Janet returned to read the testimony of the small number of policemen and commanders who saw fit to appear before the Truth Commission and earn amnesty.

Janet was no more than two handfuls of flesh, two cups of breathing and oozing flesh, her body sliding from the bone. Yet she occupied the auditorium with two clicks of her fingers. She was famous for her chameleonic talent, after all. She turned into a member of the Security Branch who had lost the talent for repentance. Her expression seized up when she was asked to elaborate on what orders she had given or had been given. She didn't feel any more remorse than was strictly necessary. She recited barebones stories, tales of suffocating children and burning bodies in acid, but only to make sure that the amnesty application would be complete and that nobody would be able to come back to them later.

Ann found her fellow witnesses more interesting. They were the hardest and the plainest to get hold of, people who had been rubbed clear of particularity until the stone inside was revealed. They talked about house arrests and midnight raids, young men who had disappeared, never to be heard from again, boys and girls who came out of prison with insults to the brain and could never come right again afterwards. The witnesses were confessing their suffering, reconciling to reality, far more than any guilty party. They were parting with their stories, admitting to their losses, admitting they were the kind of people who could be mistreated, exchanging stories and finding equivalents. Something was taking place before her eyes.

Ann was called to the table. Janet put on spectacles and her face was blind and cold as a mole. She read the questions and responses given by the Minister of Justice at the original inquest. It was strange for Ann to repeat her own answers from twenty years before. Neil had been placed under house arrest and named under an emergency proclamation. He had been living separately from her. He had remarried, converting to Islam to go through the religious formalities with Nadia. At the end he had been shot through the window and had bled to death in her arms.

The Minister of Justice claimed to have no foreknowledge of Neil's assassination. He denied giving any orders to eliminate activists aligned with world communism. He was a serious Christian, a lay preacher, and, at the time of the inquiry, had been ordained in the church. Ann remembered that he had spoken in the voice of a billy goat. Janet mimicked it perfectly. The Minister's recollection hadn't improved over time. In 1996, he had declined to attend the hearings of the Truth Commission and referred the commissioners to his 1979 testimony, which Janet was reading out across the table.

It astonished Ann to watch Janet impersonate the old Minister. She didn't act like Polk. She performed without thinking, a piece of blood and bone attached to the questions and answers, her eyes narrowing at every word. Janet lived out front, on her face, in the movements of her arms and hands. Ann was as inward as a clam. For this reason, despite the compliments, they would never be good friends. Neither needed any more friendship.

After the performance was over Paul took coffee in paper cups to the members of the crew, while Janet talked to somebody on the telephone mounted on the wall beside the ticket office, continuing to watch the witnesses and production assistants over the half-moon of her spectacles.

Polk had invited his friend Victor into the audience. Their relationship had spanned three decades and three countries, as they explained to Ann, and yet each still was delighted by the other man's thoughts. She watched them jealously, thinking that she had never enjoyed such a close relationship with another woman. She had never made those kinds of connections.

After Victor had left Polk, came to talk to Ann as if he knew that he had been the object of her thoughts. He had run out of energy. He had driven through the night from his second home in Sutherland, where he had been staying since an unannounced return from California. As a result, he looked more fragile and freckled than Ann recalled from their encounters at Farhad's house. He hardly came up to the shoulder of an ordinary man. It made you extra-conscious of his large eyes and forehead. Paul said Peter looked like an extraterrestrial. Together they were Mork and Mindy.

They stood in the entrance to the theatre from where one could make out the bulk of the mountain being submerged in rain clouds. People were moving around them.

—How's your friend Farhad? Wasn't he supposed to be the cleverest man in the government?

—They are sending him to the United Nations. But he is still close to people in the party. I don't believe he will retire even after that. He wants to go on forever.

—None of us will have the chance to retire. But there are other people who can do good work. Most of what you saw today was Paul's doing. You must understand where our originality comes from. For Shakespeare, an actor in Stratford will know the tradition of each speech. Each sentence he learns has a record going back four hundred years, which word to emphasise, where to breathe, when to take a break. But when Paul and I sat down, we had to think about each part of the production for the first time. We had to imagine how to tell this history for the first time. Now that's a privilege.

—Even if nobody cares?

—We don't judge a work of art according to the numbers. There are different ways of having an impact. There are different relationships of cause and effect. Who knows what will happen to somebody who happens to see a particular play? Who knows what it does to the playwright himself? Maybe it is enough if it changes his life or the lives of his actors. Maybe I can see something I couldn't see before. Maybe that will change another man's whole outlook.

Polk brought out two cups of hot water and lemon and shared them with Ann, dandling a tea bag, which he then squeezed out and put into a serviette. Polk saved the small things around him, from tea bags to old shoes and shirts. In everything he did, in the way he talked, he knew that he was the kind of old man other people couldn't help liking. Ann had never noticed before the pride Polk took in being what he was. She didn't dislike him for it.

Polk went back to his idea.

—In a real country, our families would have packed us up for the retirement facility. But here there is no one left to tell us to stop. Therefore the show will go on.

Who knew when the show would stop? There were rumours that this was his last production. Ann didn't want to ask. From the numerical point of view Polk had entered a golden age of productivity. He had been rehearsing new plays, or new productions of earlier scripts, once a year for the past decade, putting them on in New Haven and Nieu Bethesda. But there was a different quality to the work, as if he was conserving energy, and reducing the quantity of life expended in each piece. He wrote less and less from his own experience, more from reports in the newspapers, turning the few tragic lines that he read about truck drivers and mad mothers and burglars into full-length plays. The scripts were even sparer than before, two- or three-handers consisting of a few dozen lines of dialogue, or even a turn of phrase that you heard now in the one character's mouth, now in the other's, like a game of broken telephone.

—Why do you think the show should go on, Peter? When I put on the television nowadays, in my hotel room, I always prefer to see a comedy. I have had enough of tragedy.

Peter listened intently. It seemed that his mind was working for the first time today without the aid of machinery. You couldn't see the bones in his face, or the muscles working in his jaw.

—I have four answers for you, Ann. Do you want to hear them?

—Definitely.

—In the first place, we all have tragedies. We have plays to put them in common view. In real life, a tragedy is a waste, a cancellation, a third-degree burn. But to see such an event on stage, that is a different process. Afterwards, when you come out of the theatre, you have a sense that life cannot be brought to an end. Life, in general, is inexhaustible, endlessly creative in the forms it takes, and it cannot be defeated even when one part of it is destroyed, even when that one part is you yourself. It only comes back stronger in the next individual. This is the only hope we can have. Only a play can make you understand that, in my opinion, and certain pieces of music.

—Is this why the Broadway critics love you?

—I knew you weren't going to let me have four answers. I can tell you jokes instead of theories.

—Nobody has told jokes like that for donkey's years, Peter. The ones that come straight out of those books. It's gone out of fashion.

Had it been Peter at all? Had it been Gert who had liked to tell jokes? She remembered her first husband as humourless, thought of him as humourless, and yet he had loved to tell jokes. Gert memorised them out of joke books he bought in the airport. There were collections of Polish jokes and Russian jokes, jokes about Africans and Indians, Helen Keller and Gandhi, women and Jews, an old empire of jokes, populated by joke tellers, as forlorn and abandoned today as the Great Wall of China. How much had disappeared? Each day was a dark and darker glass obscuring the contents of life. Ann had assumed it would become clearer each day, as she got older, only to find the opposite was true. She didn't think on the same lines as Polk. He was too well adjusted for her.

—Do you know, Ann, I have read and enjoyed each one of Sebastian's novels? I found a complete set in the second-hand bookshop. For spy novels they have incredible psychological depth. Not everybody is happy, needless to say, as far as the story is concerned, but when you look back from the end, you can see that everything leads logically from one thing to the next.

—You object to that?

—Nobody here has the luxury of thinking that way. In a play or a novel we keep sight of each person and we demand to know what happens to him and to him and to him. In real life, we lose track of people all the time. They simply disappear and reappear without compunction. How many of the cases we heard today didn't have to do with someone vanishing? On the one hand, this place brings us very close together, explosively close. On the other hand, it manages to keep us apart so we disappear like that. Therefore we can't measure each other. Therefore, in my opinion, we can hardly know how to measure ourselves. We don't know how to put a price on good and bad.

—That's a strange piece of reasoning. It goes beyond me.

— It's the secret of my plays.

—

Back inside, Paul didn't see Ann at the other end of the stage. He had been intercepted by one of the assistants on the production and stood there talking to what looked like a schoolboy in a cloth cap. She still didn't understand why he had become an actor in the first place. He was nothing like Polk, or Janet. Paul had been busy all day directing the cameras, creating the film which would be seen around the country and the continent. When she had caught sight of him, he had reminded her of an architect on a building site.

Ann went along the stage, between the table and the steps, and stood next to Paul, although he didn't notice her there, and counted the golden-brown freckles on the top of her son's head. She had cured him of stooping. When he stood up straight he was a tower that she could place between herself and Sabine.

Paul was smiling. During the day he had been thin-lipped.

—I think it went well. I would have come to you after-wards, but they wanted to look at the footage right away in case they had to reshoot. In case the lighting or the sound went wrong. It must have been difficult for you to undergo.

—This is nothing, my dear. I remember listening to the Minister at the real inquest, in 1979, and wondering how he could look me in the eyes as he spoke. Only later I realised it was a sign of his power.

—It's the same man, believe it or not, who wanted to wash Mandela's feet last year.

Paul was the tower Ann had built and he was leaning in her direction. She wanted to put her hand against his side. She waited for the pain to start in her heart and was surprised when it didn't. She had lost him to Sabine and before that to history and boarding school. He was the final absence in her heart. In total he had caused her more invisible pain than any husband. By being around her, he caused her worry. Being away from her, he doubled her suffering. She arranged her travels to be around him as much as possible, and at other times around Sebastian's children, who as adults had become her close friends. Love was more mysterious than gravity. Children revolved around parents at first, making larger and larger revolutions, until finally the parents revolved around their children.

—I didn't know you were such friends with Janet. Usually she doesn't like women.

—I hardly know her, Paul. I know she married Peter twice, over the years, and divorced him twice. Like Elizabeth Taylor.

—They may be getting married again. Peter says he wants to settle down properly now that his main actor, Roland, is dead and finally there's nobody to spoil their relationship. Before this, according to him, he had to live in a triangle.

—That's why his marriages didn't work?

—Peter says a lot of things. He tries out ideas. I never know when he's being wise and when he's simply pulling my leg.

—I'm sure he doesn't know.

—He doesn't. He used to say that the Security Branch was his most attentive audience. Therefore our drama is the best in the world. The playwright's gospel, according to Polk. He says this is his last play, by the way.

—You are the one who did it, Paul.

—I didn't write it either. It comes straight out of old history. That's enough of this building though. I want to be outside. And Sabine must be lonely.

In the car, Paul rolled down the windows. They went through the city, past the three- and four-level commercial buildings, churches, mosques, furniture stores with garish leather pieces on display, bus stops where steadfast old ladies stood with their packets as if they were waiting to be teleported, then parking garages and corner cafés bearing Coca-Cola signs. Ann was confused. She wasn't sure what to tell her son. She shouldn't mention the department store or Tanith Lakhaney.

—I talked to Gert at length, Paul, as I promised you. I want to be on good terms with your father. I will be honest. I don't think he has, on his side, come to terms with the country as it is today and therefore he cannot even remember what happened the day before yesterday. He only has complaints about the country.

—He loves Mandela.

—Apart from Mandela, yes, who gave a licence to everyone to forget before they were forgiven. Even before they saw the need to be forgiven. I am a woman. I don't forget as easily. Sometimes I still believe Neil is there, in the same house. When I go to Durban I make my driver go past and look at that house. And what do I find? There's another family living there who have nothing to do with me.

They needed petrol. Paul drove into a garage. They waited in a line behind the other cars and a bakery truck with a loaf of bread stencilled on the back. In the confines of the car you were aware of how large he was. His eyes were shining. Paul also had a plan that he wanted to put into ears.

—I blamed myself for it. Do you remember that I borrowed Neil's car the day he was shot? I thought Margot was the woman I wanted to marry. Until we arrived at the hotel and found out. The two of you always had a plan

282

to get out when the time came. I was always impressed by that, the cloak-and-dagger aspect of your lives. You weren't like any other parents. At the last minute, after all that, because I took the car and he never thought of a back-up plan, the famous Neil couldn't get out in time.

—Neil wanted you to have the car.

—It was completely unreliable. It overheated twice on the way back. Margot never recovered. But we kept in touch. She has four children now, in London, and a husband who has some kind of seat on the stock exchange.

—And you're just starting now. We're only starting again now as a family.

—I guess Sabine must have told you?

—She told me under duress.

The attendant came to the car window. His blue overall was unbuttoned almost to the navel. His chest was strong and black beneath it. Paul took money out of the ashtray and settled it in the man's hands. You had always craved forgiveness from your son. Only Paul could give you absolution. But he wanted you to give it instead.

—You were too hard on Gert yesterday. You will have to cooperate as grandparents. He's not wrong about Mandela. What does Peter say? Mandela compels other people by forgiving them. He compels them to forgive others in turn.

—I can't forgive myself, Paul, whatever Peter has to say about it.

—Join the line, Mom.

2003

SPARKS

Where there was Sparks there was fire. In Zambia, in 1981, the chief had recruited him as an assistant. He used Sparks to carry his vinyl briefcase and stay close to his person. He was the last line of defence.

Each morning Sparks packed the briefcase with a satellite telephone, blinking on the top. Next to that went a Russian–English dictionary and a Makarov pistol. It came out at any possibility of danger. When there was a raid or a bombing he covered the scene while the chief stayed in the background. The stretcher-bearers brought out the bodies of men and women, boys and girls. Their forms were unfamiliar until he checked their faces and recognised them as friends and colleagues. Sometimes the fire brigade had to use a welding torch to take someone out from behind the wheel of a car.

Only when the ambulances left did the chief put his hand on that of his assistant and say, as seriously as if he were conducting the funeral, where there is Sparks there is fire. I expect fire.

At night, at home or away, Sparks slept on a mattress in the vestibule of his master's bedroom. For two decades he was the nearest and dearest person to the chief, much closer in a practical sense than Farhad. He was the emissary dispatched, in the first instance, to fix a problem or correct a misinterpretation. In 1998, back in Pretoria, when it became known up and down the Union Buildings that the Old Man was displeased with his second in command, Sparks brought the new crocodile-skin briefcase to the private balcony, separated by a curtain from the corridor.

Just inside the curtain the chief packed his pipe, red-brown strands of tobacco crammed under the rim. Sparks held the flame for him until smoke filtered shyly from the bowl. They went outside. The chief closed the buttons on his blazer and took a puff. The smoke filtered longingly from his neat lips and beard. He looked like a statue that was smoking. Not a sign of pleasure on his features.

The chief balanced the pipe on the ledge, shading it with one hand as it smouldered, and frowned at the pools and fountains in the prospect, the mounted cannon, the square kilometre of terraced gardens, and the police memorial. His eyes were as reflective as sunglasses.

—I told you before and I will tell you again, where there is Sparks there is indeed fire.

You weren't expected to reply to such statements. The chief stopped and returned the pipe to his mouth.

—Comrade Sparks, I wish that you still kept a gun in that briefcase. Some of the comrades could use the encouragement.

He pushed Sparks back through the curtain.

—Go and fix it now with the Old Man. He will take your word above mine. He trusts you above anyone except for Farhad. Remember this fact. He is the most famous old man in the world, but he is also the loneliest.

The chief never came at it directly. He maintained a sideways angle to any situation, making sure that he had room to manoeuvre. He was a master diplomat. He would be sideways even in the bedroom, although Sparks tried not to listen to his encounters with women.

In the hospital, however, in terms of management, the chief was uncharacteristically direct. He took a detailed interest in the case file, monitoring the daily list of injections and medications provided by the nursing sister. After inspecting the chart stored in a folder at the foot of the bed, he sat down and removed his narrow leather shoes in order to concentrate on the facts. From his briefcase he took out his notes, what he had learned from the internet as well as from an extensive correspondence with sympathetic scientists around the world, and engaged with the specialists as they arrived. Sparks was making his mark just by lying there, pointing the way to a different framework for science. No other patient in history had the president of the country as principal physician.

He was born Albert Mokoena to an assistant at a teachers' training college situated in a rural area. She had been romanced for two weeks by a Dutch administrator inspecting the facilities on behalf of his church charity. In thirty years Albert lived without anyone except clerks and ticket inspectors using his first name. In hospital he was so ill that he couldn't remember the six letters. He couldn't pin down where he might be positioned in the stream of time and space and how he had come to be in a bed under a blue-tinged neon bar. It made no sense that he should be on this bed. There was no sense in a life. There were only sensations.

The blood got heavy in his hips and refused to circulate. His body was as waterlogged as a riverbank. The air had stopped moving into it. While he watched, his chest stopped going up. He heard a lullaby of three notes, and then four notes, told in a woman's voice. She reminded him of his mother. The voice faded into the hum of the hospital machines and the neon light, came back as a sudden hiss in his ears, and ended in complete silence.

After that he was deaf. Some fabric dividing the different spheres had been torn and silence came in. Dots flashed in his eyelids, in a ravishing black and red evening, a semaphore that he was on the point of establishing as letters and numbers when the red light grew vaster until it occupied the vacancy in his head.

He died at 11.04 p.m. in the same minute he dreamed that the nursing sister had come in and was placing his feet in bowls made of blue-and-white china. He wouldn't have complained to her about that, or about the strawberry-red rash above his breast that had caused him many hours of irritation. At some point in hospital he had lost the power to summon the nurse. He had lost the right to complain. For a week, to all outward observers, he had been almost as calm as the dead. Yet this had been the most interesting period of his life.

The nurse didn't enter the room for twenty more minutes. The body was content underneath the sheet. It was patient and bided its time. It lay there half an hour later when the consulting physician signed the death certificate, listing the cause of death as acute malnutrition.

Dr Gerhard had been warned to alert the president's office before issuing a public statement. He went through the chart and whistled. Forty-nine kilograms. He hadn't expected it to be so low. In recent years the doctor had seen many such instances of severe weight loss. The wards were filled with wasted bodies, products of seven thin years. Why didn't people eat? They seemed to lose the will. Gerhard considered incorporating a vitamin into his treatment regimen to stimulate the appetite. In these cases nutrition was the key to long-term survival.

The nursing sister waited until the doctor continued on his round. She noticed how cold it got in the evening. She brought a heater from the supply room and plugged it into the socket behind the bed. She shivered, settled on the chair close to the element, spread her hands to catch the warmth, and calculated how long she could sit here until she needed to go back to the desk.

In the luxury wing of the hospital, where you put down a one-thousand-five-hundred-rand deposit to get a room, the nursing sister was the only living and breathing occupant. Professor Golden had passed away and was awaiting transfer to the morgue. They were saying kaddish for him in another place. The cardiologist had moved his remaining case to post-op. There were three suites lying empty, the doors of their bar refrigerators standing open and waiting to be stocked the next morning.

Sister Esther did a final check of the room. She counted the small bottles of whisky and seltzer and fruit juice made available in the refrigerator. She completed the forms concerning the recent patients, checking off the list for any expended medications and supplies so that it could be taken to the dispensary and the financial department. Esther was always surprised by how expensive it was to die on her floor. A death should shower the community with benefits. Mr Samuel Shabangu, her father's best friend, had died while trying to pack his trunks for Harare. They prepared to bury him in style, only for people to find, cached beneath the floor, many of the items that had disappeared from their houses. He had carefully labelled each item so it could be returned. As a result, people had forgiven the shadow of the man and even continued to remember him with pleasure.

Esther slept for ten minutes in the chair, getting hot by the heater. In her dreams she was waiting for the cleaner who took the night shift. She liked the feeling for the young man which was growing inside her. In her mind's eye she kept an icon of his friendly red-brown face, like the ones you saw in a Greek church. When she forced herself to get up, her attention turned to this image. She put the unused ampoules from the drug cabinet into her handbag. They could be resold to the dispensary. The cleaner was her go-between. He had the trust of the pharmacist and the hospital black market and knew who would give the best price.

Esther listened for the step of his thick black shoes on the staircase. She had a new message for him. She would take him by the lapels of his overalls and remind him that she was eight years older than him. There would be no more drugs from her side. She planned to give back the radio he had loaned her. At the same time, in another part of her mind, she hoped he would refuse to take it. Her reluctance might bring on some new intensity on his side, some declaration of his affection. For too long he had been taking her for granted.

There was still work to do, however. Esther stopped daydreaming, got to her feet, and rubbed her eyes. She unplugged the heater and took it into the hall. She turned the volume up on the radio and, when she came back, closed the door to Sparks's room. She pulled down the sheet so suddenly it gave you a shock.

In the bed a body lay calmly, making no demands, creating no complaints. One hand lay stiff across the stomach while the teeth were lengthening under thin lips. Under the sheet was a white-wine smell, as if the cork had been pulled under her nose, which made her lay the sheet back over the head once she had checked the pockets in the gown for anything loose. She noticed that her heart was beating fast. She had a fear of ghosts. She worried about Mr Shabangu coming back to his small house, which she and two of her sisters had moved into without a title. In the end, they had taken everything from him.

Esther went through the drawers in the room in rapid succession, then the cupboard. She had been watching as items arrived, keeping a mental list of what had come in and hadn't been taken out, making an educated guess about which of these things wouldn't be missed in the final accounting. Sparks's wife was unlikely to make a fuss. Like many family members, she might not even return to the room in which he had died. The woman didn't seem specially attached to her husband. Esther had seen her matter-of-fact dealings with the doctors, her brief appearances during visiting hours, and her irritated expression when she filled out the insurance forms. She had observed the handsome middle-aged man who accompanied the wife to the lift downstairs and who picked the threads off his double-breasted suit while he was waiting. He would be keeping her company tonight.

In the cupboard Esther found a set of silk sheets still in their plastic. She put three pairs of tartan socks and a scarf in the slouching bottom of her handbag. She considered taking the dressing gown, along with a battery-powered razor, but decided against it. It was too much of a risk. In the room remained a miniature colour television set and a microwave oven on loan from the office of the Presidency. They had been delivered the day after Sparks refused further anti-retroviral treatment. Esther was wary of them. It didn't pay to take a risk. Mr Shabangu had been careful never to take too much.

At her duty station, the telephone light was blinking. She ignored it for a minute. First she put her takings underneath the table. She decided to keep the scarf. She would present the cleaner with the socks, but not before she had washed them in the laundry room. Her father, the late Alfred Koroleng, who had passed away a month after his closest friend, would have appreciated the material. But they needed a proper scrubbing. They had been worn in bed. When she put the socks to her nose they reminded her of Sparks's tough feet.

You knew that Esther disliked handling your body. There had been no spark between you and the nurse. She had looked at you, when you were alive and too feverish to respond, with a certain hatred, not needing to stop dislike seizing her features. You had been surprised at how powerfully her repulsion affected you. You were in awe of the sister. You wanted to surrender to her tough pinches and the brusque way she rolled your body in the bed. She towered above you, holy and black and beautiful when she brought a basin and washed and combed your hair from the front.

You would have given her your cellphone if you had it in your possession. If possible you would have put your mouth on hers and kissed her with closed eyes and drawn her breath into your lungs. You would have made her see Sparks.

—

294

The clocks turned backwards on the most interesting day in the life of Albert Mokoena, during which he learned what counted in his history. At four in the afternoon his wife was the last person he saw and understood. He watched her through half-lowered eyelids, lying in this crematorium whose object was to burn his soul. He couldn't reply to his wife's questions. She cast her stone-faced pity upon him. Not even circumcision at sixteen had caused him such subtle pain as the appearance of pity in his wife's soul. It had been years since she had shown any real care. She had been as fierce to him as a robot.

Meanwhile his wife, Rose, had her own feelings and nobody to tell about them. She had such horror to see the thin body in the metal bed. It was nearly imperceptible under the sheets, yet it had recently lain beside her in her own bed and placed its arm around her shoulders. In the hospital it had tried to kiss her on the neck and even on the lips. It wanted to hang on her neck, clinging underneath her, when she made the mistake of coming too close. Rose washed away its touch in the basin. It felt as if there were ants moving underneath her skin.

Rose was relieved that her hospital visits would soon be at an end. She anticipated her life coming out of its cocoon. Her evenings had been unendurable during this last month of illness. While Sparks remained in crisis she stayed in the main bedroom of the house, locked on the top floor by an internal security gate. She couldn't invite her boyfriend to visit because some of her family members had moved in. The place was full to bursting. Honey, her sixteen-year-old daughter, sat in the next room along the passage, her big energetic feet bare on the deep white carpet that went throughout the house. It was Honey, above all, who had made her mother a prisoner. She sat cross-legged between a pair of earphones in the middle of the floor and kept an eye on the house. Nobody could have fun. Nobody could do what she wanted, see whom she wanted. They had made each other prisoners, mother and daughter.

To maintain her sanity Rose had been staying in bed with the electric blanket, gabbing to her family or her friend Parveen, Farhad's wife, on the speakerphone or taking her newly arrived cousins to the Italian restaurant in the shopping centre. She bought overseas magazines to read, when she escaped to shop, and a number of hats. On that floor of the hospital, it was not unusual to encounter a minister coming in for treatment or a private consultation. She might find herself in conversation with the president, who took a lively interest in her husband's condition and visited him several times a week. She couldn't afford to be dowdy. She had to dress the part.

She wore a different hat each time. Today Rose had on a gold-fabric hat making an oval broader than her shoulders, three bronze flowers tucked into the brim. She didn't remove it as she watched the nurse draw medicine into a syringe and exchange one pack for another on the drip. She remained sitting down while she gave the nurse, Esther, instructions on welcoming the president and where to display the bouquets to best advantage. Sparks watched. He couldn't dislike her. Rose had her reasons. Every woman he had ever met had her reasons.

Through half-shuttered eyes it was possible for Sparks to see the same woman who had worked in a secretarial capacity for a Zambian copper-mining company when they had been in exile. She kowtowed to the wives of the engineers, who bore the same types of hats on their sprayed heads, protecting their French and Italian complexions from the sun with broad brims. While Sparks guarded the chief, she earned enough money to support their household by retyping tables and sheets for the company bookkeeper and making carbon copies of executive memorandums. He wanted to remind her about the speed with which her hands had once flown along the Olivetti keyboard, ringing the bar like a cash register at the end of each line. He wanted to bring back her bare-headed beauty, to go back to the time when she took the straw hat from her lovely head and her shoulders ran in harmony with the typewriter ribbon, but his tongue stayed at the bottom of his mouth. It was like a cork trapped in a bottle.

The nurse left. His wife approached, after cleaning her hands with Dettol, and put her bag on the table. He goggled at her, breathing with a sick effort in his lungs, and saw, to his dismay, that she was smiling at him under her regal hat.

—Our troubles will be over soon, Sparks.

Rose's breath, so close, bore the scent of baking-soda toothpaste into his nostrils. It went down into the vacuum at the bone. He could have told his wife that he had always been in trouble. All the troubles of his boss had been his troubles. It also worked the other way round. The chief had brought him into the hospital and the chief would bring him out in the end. He trusted the man above everybody. The chief was the only physician he had ever required, sure to take him out of this forsaken private place in rudest health.

He wanted to tell his wife, in that case, that they should celebrate together. She should order a pizza from Coronations, six pies with six toppings of pineapple and pink ham, plus shawarmas from the Pakistani shop which arrived in a foil box on the back of a motorcycle. They could bring a crate containing those six-sided bottles of Fanta and green Sparletta. At the party he imagined, Sparks would laze at full length at the long outdoor table. The wicker chairs were shaded from the full sunshine by the gazebo, protected by a red line of unscented candles, where the chief once sat with a girlfriend, both in the same tracksuits, and argued with Farhad about economics before he sent his oldest friend overseas. Sparks would celebrate his own recovery while the pool cleaner glided along the sides of the basin, vacuuming the water, and Honey sat in the window of her room wearing earphones and checking for text messages from boys who would never send them. He would forgive himself for sending her to a white school in Pretoria. At that place it was impossible for her to make friends with a boy. He had mutilated her nature.

At the homecoming party, Rose would take off her hat. In her wig she would be as strong and insensible as a horse. They would rejoice in their prosperity together. To have come from the bush to this, and then to have returned from the very circumference of death, you had to be as lucky as a Chinaman. At his party Sparks would switch on each of the three television sets, glory in the soundtrack of three different channels, set the security gate clattering, and settle on the golf cart, which had its own place in the three-car garage. The music would be playing—Marvin Gaye, Four Tops, Donna Summer, Diana Ross. He would dance on the cement in the garage with Rose, both of them marvelling at its length and breadth. They had come through unscathed.

During the illness he had lost the freedom of the second and third dimension. The space in which he once lived had been as extensive as the continent across which their politico-military network extended. It had contracted to the capital

Pretoria, step by step down to the corridors and heavy-smoking meeting rooms of the Union Buildings. During his illness the space of his existence contracted to the halls of the hospital and cafeteria, from the whole of the hospital to this particular wing on the top floor, then to his room, then the bed, the length of his body, and now to the centimetre behind his forehead.

In the corridor his wife argued with the physician. In her voice he heard her sense of grievance. In a lady like Rose it was as implacable as diamond.

—No, we understand very well, doctor. This poor man is finished today. You must contact the president's office.

—We believe he has turned the corner. We have every hope of a full recovery.

—This man cannot say a word and I can see the fear in his eyes. Even my daughter, Honey, came back traumatised from her visit this morning. She thought she had seen the mere ghost of her father.

—We are busy adjusting the mixture of medicines. We are feeding him by intravenous drip.

—As you know, Dr Gerhard, we also have a good relationship with Her Excellency the Minister of Health. Let something go wrong and you will regret it. They will investigate you to the end of your days.

—I have been in regular consultation with the president, Mrs Mokoena. He has given his consent each step of the way. It was on his and your husband's own recommendation that we ended the anti-retroviral regimen. We hope your husband's system has the capacity to overcome the damage they caused. Bad nutrition can be devastating.

—I have given you a warning, doctor. I have done my duty.

There was no mixture of medicines nor drowsy syrups to save Sparks. He had come to a dead end. In the hyperbaric oxygen chamber he had screamed until they took him out after twenty minutes. Dr Gerhard, the president's personal physician, had supervised a transfusion, which left him with the horrible sensation that the blood running in his veins was not his own. Gerhard had arranged the administration of high doses of vitamin C to remedy the malnutrition and had tried to clean the thrush from his throat with his own hands. There had been ceaseless rounds of scans and painful biopsies, tests and blood assays in which the body of Sparks had been called to testify.

His health, after all, was a matter of state interest. Each fluctuation in temperature, any fall or rise in his total leukocyte count, was documented and publicised. Cabinet secretaries and panels of scientists followed his case history. Diplomats stood ready at the United Nations in New York to announce his return from the boundaries of the dead.

In defiance of this global attention Sparks concentrated on his wife's cockatoo hat. Rose displayed the flintiest dignity in public. She was like a stone that you had in your hand and couldn't compress by a millimetre. It was the best part of her character, he believed, the vantage point from which she was observing his extinction. She would wear a new hat to his funeral, where she would lead his coffin and attain her greatest dignity. By dying he was restoring her life.

If he could have reached her, he would have pushed her plaited hair back under her hat and reminded her that he had loved her shape. He had loved her hips with innocent affection. But he had misplaced the words.

Dr Gerhard pressed his stethoscope disc against Sparks's chest, square by square, moving the counters in an invisible game of checkers, until he heard something to please his ears. He hadn't asked permission, simply parted the robe in the process of his inspection. In the old days Sparks would have burned him for the presumption. Instead he passed out while Gerhard was counting beneath his breath. His feet had turned as cold as china dishes.

Like Terror Lekota, he had a lucky nickname. Lekota was a terror on the soccer field. In the corners of his eyes, Sparks had tiny flecks of black and gold. They were the electric sparks in his eyes.

In government it was his assignment to protect the chief by scorching his adversaries. He sent out ten thousand faxes and made telephone calls to journalists, composed position papers and editorials for the party gazette, delivered talking points to the parliamentary spokesman. The chief wasn't the friend of all the world like the Old Man. He was a born teacher. He couldn't let his disagreements rest. Since Farhad's departure, moreover, the chief had no natural friends of his own. He had to rely on politics instead. Working in the party structures, on behalf of his patron, Sparks counted the votes and sent all his rivals packing. He burned the liberals' fingers. He taught the ultra-leftists a lesson in tactics they wouldn't find in the Little Red Book.

When the chief became president, he and Sparks tackled the foreign pharmaceutical manufacturers. The foreign companies set exorbitant prices for drugs that could save hundreds of thousands of lives. They weren't the only culprits. Sparks attacked the medical associations wedded to old-fashioned models of disease. They couldn't measure it properly because they didn't account for poverty and, above all, malnutrition. When statisticians and pathologists calculated a thousand extra people were dying each day, he burned through their illusions. He dreamed of the flame rising to cleanse this crematorium country while oral thrush, in its rough white patches, descended upon his tongue. His mouth was drier than a bone.

He woke up when strong hands gripped him by the arms. They picked him up out of the bed and settled him in the wheelchair. The drips and monitors had been unclipped. He registered the invincible odour of vinegar in his hospital gown and hoped that the chief wouldn't notice it. He noticed that the pigment in his leader's eyes, on the rim of the iris, was turning the very palest shade of blue.

—Comrade Sparks. My sincere apologies. You were fast asleep. Comrade, can you answer a question?

He couldn't. Nor could he tell why the chief sounded as if he were playing a practical joke.

—I regret that I am not your new girlfriend, but we are going to take a tour of this section of the hospital. We will make an informal assessment of the privileges you can buy when you are rich and have to suffer from an illness. Even the rich have bodies to torment them. Comrade, do you still have the spirit of adventure?

Sparks held on to the wheelchair. The steel arms had blue inserts, like the first-class seats on an aeroplane, and rose at an angle from the back. He was too narrow to be safe on the wide seat. A strong instinct made him want to return to bed. He feared falling out of the wheelchair onto the floor. Someone would sweep him into a dustpan and under the door.

—The good news is that I am taking you off my own bat. These guards can stay here and scratch their backsides for ten minutes.

As he knew, the chief was stronger than he looked. Sparks was pushed abruptly out of the door and around the perfumed laundry cart in the hall. It flipped his stomach. He was not a Formula 1 racer. The wheelchair sped past the mineral-water dispenser and the entrance to the doctors' common room.

Soon Sparks was rolling at speed down the linoleum corridor. The sunshine made his skin tingle. In the empty suites in the luxury wing there were machines standing by. They were still plugged in, waveforms unspooling along their diving-helmet faces. He wondered if even the chief could roll him out of this place where they had decreed a death sentence against him. You went in with a headache and they gave you the death penalty.

On the third circuit around the floor, the chief pushed him into an alcove, next to a line of chairs that looked over the hospital premises, and sat down on the nearest one. He leaned over and examined the place in Sparks's neck where they had installed a valve. He put his hand on the patient's cheek, searching his face.

—You should be at my side, Comrade Sparks. Without you I am not properly protected. Farhad has never been a political fighter. My enemies are coming together. They are coming for me.

The chief gripped him at the wrists. Heat came into his face. He thought he would fall from the wheelchair into the arms of the chief.

—Look how you've improved since we stopped the anti-retrovirals. You are off the poison and you are coming back from the dead. The consultant faxed me the chart yesterday. It looks like your levels are finally coming right.

The chief stood up and went to the bay window, which revealed a multi-storey parking garage. At the other end of the alcove he had the small beauty and perfectly carved countenance of a chess piece.

—Now that you have the right vitamins in your system you can be out of here by month's end. Thanks to your bravery, we have exposed the lie of the infectious hypothesis. The only thing we must not allow is for the newspapers to twist the story. The information about your case must come through the Presidency, fully controlled. Otherwise Jimmy Carter will be on my head. What's that? Are you trying to say something? Speak up.

Sparks had started to urinate. The water gushed hotly into the bag on his lap, where he could feel the weight. Afterwards his penis lay back down dumb between his legs. It never stirred into action anymore, never relayed intelligence back, did nothing but cause him pain along the inner length of the tube when he managed to urinate, and produced a long sensation of discomfort when he was unsuccessful in passing water. A pair of scissors had cut the tapeworm of sexual feeling inside him. The only pleasure left in his thing was the uncomfortable pleasure of the hose that has emptied the bucket.

—Consequently I have taken your telephone, comrade. In future I will answer personally any telephone calls they make to you. I will leave a note for your wife because it is possible the liberal press will try to reach her also. They are always trying to ferret things out.

The chief came and stood behind the wheelchair. He put his hand on the patient's neck. Sparks could imagine the chief starting to stifle him with the pillow. He would refuse to struggle. He had turned out to be nothing but an inconvenience to both his wife and his employer. He wanted to help them.

—From here I go straight to the airport and directly to Addis. Five days there to engage with the Organisation of African Unity. Then I am inspecting the progress on the Timbuktu project. I left a good person in charge. Gerhard will fax me in the event of any change in your condition. On the day of my return, with any luck, I will arrange your discharge with full honours. Meanwhile, please, comrade, concentrate on recovering your strength.

In recent years, apart from boxing, Sparks had not paid enough attention to his own health. As bodyguard and chauffeur, factotum and go-between, his responsibility had always been to bury the chief or die alongside him in a car-bomb explosion or a burst of rifle fire. So he had neglected the cough that went on for two years. The consultant at the private clinic, a soft-spoken lady, Malika, tested him and prescribed a regimen of anti-retrovirals without explanation. The chief had subsequently obtained his records, concluded that his nutrition was poor, and had sent Sparks to Dr Gerhard, who started the first round of vitamin injections.

In the same period his girlfriend Thandie had been in and out of the hospital. Her sister, a Madam Mambaso of whose existence Sparks had previously been unaware, appropriated Thandie's cellphone. She answered it on her sister's behalf, promising to convey messages back and forth where possible. The madam had a loud voice, a countryside voice full of elbows. She wanted to borrow a substantial amount of money to pay for her sister's prescriptions while Sparks was trying to prepare for a parliamentary session. It was too difficult. Soon he stopped returning her text messages and lost touch with Thandie's situation.

Thandie never returned to her position at the ministry, a fact Sparks noted after a month when he walked past her desk and found another woman working there. He learned that Thandie had died from meningitis only when her sister messaged him to assist with the funeral expenses. His own condition was becoming poor. His cough had become so noticeable in cabinet meetings that he had to step into the corridor. Dr Gerhard, returning from running a marathon in Vienna and breathing good health into all and sundry, took blood samples with relish and filed the capsules of red-black liquid into an icebox while he outlined the principles of correct nutrition. Sparks admired his startlingly white hair. Yet there was something not entirely human in his complexion.

When did he begin to see Thandie? She entered the hospital room directly after Sparks's mother, who, despite the care he had taken to bury her, at significant expense in a flurry of flowers and lamb chops and in the added luxury of an American hearse, took him to task. The border post between life and death was open. He could still feel the sharpness of his deceased mother's nails where she held him by the neck, solid and dead as she was, and pinched him red.

Thandie, however, was gentle. She sat at the end of the bed, her wig perfectly brushed. She had very thin thighs in her trousers. Her composure reminded you of a Japanese lady.

Sparks tried to sit up. He wanted to catch her in his arms, snake his dried-out tongue into her blacked-out mouth. The two of them made a pretty pair. Who was the beauty? Thandie moved to the other corner and he gave up the attempt to embrace her. The sheet was too tight where the nurse had trussed him. Soon they would be together.

She had lost all the weight on her arms and legs. When she turned, Sparks saw that her expression was patchy, a doll with crosses of black thread at the eyes.

—Are you going, baby?

—I don't understand. I can't hear properly.

—Are you coming, baby?

—I can hear every word, Thandie, and put them together in one sentence. But why are you telling me this sentence? That I do not understand. For an entire month I have not been able to understand why each person comes into this room and gives this particular sentence to me. Why this sentence? Or why is it that sentence? It never makes sense. The Old Man said behind the most complicated sentence you can find something extremely simple. There is a need arising in the other person. But why not another sentence?

—Sparks, you are my fire. Burn me up, Sparks …

Then Thandie was an echo. Somewhere she had the remains of a body. She hadn't been cremated. At her funeral in Alexandria she had been a husk of herself in the open, purple-plated coffin which Sparks had bought. The occasion had been attended by her sister and five other members of her family, who came in a long-distance taxi from the rural areas. He paid their fares.

The master of the funeral parlour resembled a professor in his round glasses. He sat beside Sparks on the bench so long, waiting for the time to close the ceremony, constantly polishing the plastic flower in the lapel of his jacket with the spit on his forefinger. Sparks liked the other man's unclean character. The man eagerly wanted to talk business because he had found a man in the government with whom to discuss potential tenders. The parlour master was so unclean that he was proud of making big profits out of death.

When the elections had happened, people anticipated a flood of new investment from overseas, money from the car companies, new technologies, trade routes. Instead it had been the coffin-makers and traditional healers, funeral-parlour masters and graveyard priests, who did a roaring trade. Business was almost too good.

During Thandie's service Sparks had tried as hard as possible to stifle his coughing. It was impossible. He wasn't well. The master of the house looked at him thoughtfully whenever he coughed. Afterwards he gave Sparks his business card and fax-machine number.

At noon on the last day of Sparks's life, before the apparitions of Thandie and his mother, the medical technician had convinced him he was going to live to a ripe old age. The technician was the strongest man in the hospital. It scarcely taxed his light-brown arms to hoist his charge from the stretcher to the recliner.

—Let's get you comfortable and then we'll do the scans. You're a lucky man. Everybody wants to see what's going on inside you.

He untied the gown and rubbed cold ointment on Sparks's chest. It reeked of peppermint.

—There you are smiling, Mr Mokoena. Did you know that you were smiling?

Sparks hadn't known. He put a hand to his face. The technician went around the machine buckling him in.

—You should do it more often. You have the kind of face that's handsome when you're smiling. Never mind, I will show it to you on the computer screen. Do you know computers? I thought so. Men our age don't know computers.

The cylinder rotated and a bar of light flashed along

the body as if Sparks were inside a photocopying machine. He had time to reflect inside the scanner, unable to move his arms, and he saw that the technician was the only person who cared for his comfort. Not Rose. Not Esther. Not Thandie or his mother or the president of the country who had more important worries than the comfort of his personal assistant. The technician had an expression in his eyes which said that he expected Sparks to live through the day, to live and spread power, and that therefore he should be made comfortable. The technician wanted to please his patient and win his favour precisely because his goodwill had a certain concrete value and longevity. Here was the living proof that one day soon the fever in Sparks's head would subside and the spider web in his throat would vanish. Soon.

While the computer was working, green alphanumerics chattering on the screen, Sparks returned to the wheelchair. He saw the top of a colour photograph in the technician's pocket as he bent over the wheelchair. The technician noticed that Sparks was looking, took the photo out, and showed it to him. It was posed against a linen background. There were three children, mother and father behind them, and a dog with a copper bell on its collar. It had the name of a photographic studio franked along the bottom in purple ink. The technician took the photograph and tilted it towards himself. He pointed at the figures in turn.

—My family. On the right, Mr Mokoena, is my late son Grant. Now he passed away of an asthma attack three years ago. For some reason, on that particular night, I woke up and I went to his bed and he was already gone.

He put the photograph back in his patient's palm. Sparks held on to it for dear life.

—You can see he is a beautiful child. He was already smiling when you went to take him out of the crib, at six in the morning. He smiled up at you from the pillow. As if he had been waiting there patiently, preparing for you to come. He would continue smiling, throughout the day, until you put him in at night. This is something medical science cannot explain. You cannot put a number to it.

The technician pushed Sparks over to the operator's terminal, where he could see the bank of computer monitors beside the whirring cabinet of magnetic-tape storage. On one of the screens Sparks saw the outline of his own body in lurid colour. After a few minutes the technician arrived with the print-outs. He tore off the strips on either side and placed the sheets of computer paper in the pouch on the side of the wheelchair.

—Come over to my house when you are released. It will be a pleasure to celebrate with you. I have never had someone from the government in my house. And I am not interested in discussing contracts with you.

As usual they took the roundabout way back to the luxury wing. The technician pushed the wheelchair through the rubber doors, holding them open for a minute, and past the nurses' station. Sparks careened along the corridor, down a spiral ramp for three floors, and through the grand entrance hall to the hospital, where a pink-candle chandelier swung on a short neck of cord. He sped between a patrol of oncoming nurses and doctors and came to a halt in the large cafeteria that took up the bulk of the ground floor. Expensive cars were parked around the circumference of the fountain.

Sparks stood in front of a plastic table where the technician also took a seat. From the counter the sour smell of coffee sang to him. With a tablespoon of Cremora it would make him as giddy as a child. The attendant was pouring coffee into a dozen cups arranged on a tray. She didn't acknowledge their presence.

The technician sat back in his chair. He took out a sandwich and removed it methodically from plastic wrap, which he then folded into a square.

—You don't talk much anymore, Mr Mokoena. I have noticed the change. You mustn't stop talking. If you talk, you will thrive. When you came in, you were on that big telephone of yours every minute. I had no idea who you were. Since then I have done some research and I have every appreciation of your role in history. That is the advantage of working in a private hospital. We can get to know you and treat the individual at the heart of the disease.

Sparks was too young to die. The tears slipped out abruptly. He was the bearer of too many memories to be extinguished by a fever and malnutrition. Who else could testify to the president's secret hours? Who else had sat beside him on a folding chair in tough Angolan bush while he read outstanding correspondence and waited for the green light on the satellite telephone to signal an active connection? Who else had faced car bombs and bullets to protect the chief? Who had sat alongside him and Farhad in a fish-and-chips shop in Shepherd's Bush and planned how to smuggle Toshiba laptops with a built-in code into the country?

The technician rolled Sparks through the cafeteria doors into the sunshine between the buildings. He was grateful. It would have been terrible to die without coming back in contact with the air. His cheeks were wet in the wind and he wanted to dry them. He dreamed of stealing out of the hospital in the evening, taking a car on the highway, but he feared the obstacles.

The technician lit a cigarette, seemed to offer it to his patient, inserted it in his mouth, and smoked it rapidly.

—In fact today is the third anniversary of my son's death. I am sure he would already have been much better on the computer than I am. People of our generation can't really come to grips with the computer, even if they have the same training as I did. Grant would have been better if it hadn't been for the asthma. They say, our area, around Coronationville, has the worst air pollution in the world, owing to the factories and the mines. Anyway I cannot prove it.

His mouth was full of cemetery breath. Somehow Sparks had lost his balance on the seat of the wheelchair. He was tilting over, dizzy at the ears, which made him want to grip the wheelchair even tighter. He held on to the arm. The technician took his hand and returned it to his lap.

—I heard from the nursing sister that your daughter comes to see you. As a parent, there is a space belonging to that child. It doesn't go away because a child happens to pass away. The rest of life is nothing. I can roll over it like you in your wheelchair. But I still keep the old computer I was planning to teach him on. I do the budget for the whole family there, including my cousins and my brother-in-law who has a shop. For that it's fast enough. It has a Pentium chip.

Honey, Honey-Baloo, was Sparks's first visitor. She came out of the blue, taking a taxi. She would have spent her pocket money on it, but it was a government service.

His blood was being drawn when she entered the room. Despite the effort of the needle in his arm, he smiled to see how gawky she was, displayed in her school uniform trimmed in lace. Honey was the picture of health, as fat and lithe as a seal on a nature programme. At school she was taking dance lessons and would have pirouetted down the corridor, arching her back like a bow, if he had given her the slightest encouragement.

Honey ignored the nurse, who was putting the blood sample into a rubber-lined box, and opened the curtains. It was morning. The sky was beautiful. He wanted to drink in every litre of oxygen in the atmosphere and cure his rattling lungs. He was broken as a bottle.

Honey always spoke as if there was a secret between her father and herself.

—Dad, the taxi is waiting down there for me. Can you see it? I've never taken a taxi by myself before. There's a first time for everything. This is the one that the children of the diplomats are allowed to use.

Sparks was surprised to hear her voice again. He hadn't talked to her on the telephone and couldn't see her without turning his head. She didn't sound like either of her parents. Honey went to the leading school in Pretoria. She spoke like a white girl, sported a sharp-toned Model c accent, even moved like one of them when she tried out her dance steps. There was only something catching in her throat, as if you were turning a clasp, that made her sound any different. In the hospital, he had forgotten that his daughter sounded like the enemy.

—I gave him a tip out of my allowance, but the ministry is paying. Mother said it is a service they provide us with. So we might as well take advantage. I am going to come every day and visit you, except for the exam I have tomorrow. This morning we have first period off. The Japanese ambassador is coming to talk.

She sat in the armchair and checked her messages. Sparks watched her without trying to speak. His throat was fuller than before. It was her first independent adventure to the hospital to see the blood drilled from her father's bruised red-and-blue arm. She should have been going to a dance. He didn't want to find the same blankness as he had found in her mother's face, the product of some defect in the heart. It had taken twenty years to understand that there was nothing behind the stone wall of Rose's countenance.

Would he say the same about Honey? Before his illness had become severe she had already turned into half a stranger. She didn't try to make conversation. Instead she put on weight steadily in her room with boxes of Nando's chicken. That freshness and loveliness, the distinctness and transparency of the life in her, was hidden. Sparks opened the door and found she had no more to say to him than if he had been the armed response unit. She seemed to mix her face with concrete.

Around him and his daughter, around the rich in the cabinet and the ministries, were the multitudinous poor. They were arrayed against him in the house, his wife's relatives, two sisters and a brother, who prized their connection to the presidential spokesman. On the basis of the connection, they had some hopes for future employment which he was never going to fulfil. They mortified him, their pots of merry red beans steaming in the kitchen while they sat expecting something at the dining table, just as if someone had ordered them to their positions.

Rose pretended not to notice their behaviour. Sparks was embarrassed by the stain of their existence. If he'd had the courage, he would have slapped his wife for continuing on such comfortable terms with her siblings and poor relations.

She had brought both of them down. She put them both in the gutter. But he wasn't well enough to confront her.

For the first time, with the heavy fever, Sparks had become frightened of his wife. The day he had been too unwell to resist she had introduced her allies onto the property. Each day a cousin or a sister or an aunt arrived in Pretoria, as if to perform an exorcism. There were so many of them by now, they would never let him back in his own house. They would celebrate his funeral in the sunken lounge. Sparks could taste the sour beer they would drink. He could smell the charred, semi-sweet odour of the paper plates loaded with roast meat travelling along the corridors and balconies. When Rose married her boyfriend, these family members would come back to use up the insurance money. He looked around for Honey, only to find that she had already left for school. He had wanted to warn her against her mother.

In the evening, just before he heard the woman's song, Sparks thought about Honey again. He had wanted to remind her not to pick up the bad habits of her mother's relations. It was obvious that they had countryside manners.

He could hear Honey coming all the way from the house on her dancers' toes, as easy on her feet as a top. Her golden-syrup eyes would shine out. He worshipped her durability, the prosperity she had achieved in her mound of unwanted flesh, her capacity to make plans for the boys who would never look in her direction.

Love struck him like the gong beaten by the muscular man at the beginning of certain movies. Yet he couldn't recall the letters contained in the name of his daughter. His mouth was filled with marshy breath.

For a minute he knew he was about to lose consciousness and die. His blood pressure had fallen to zero. The skin had already started to shrink inside his lips, revealing his teeth, while the hospital machines chattered without taking alarm. For another minute he studied himself from the outside, looking down from the neon bar on the ceiling. Sparks had seen a sting ray in the modernised Durban aquarium, trailing silent tendrils through the tank. It had opened its vast white wings, it seemed to him, and was enclosing him in its long kiss.

Dr Ndlovu and Dr Gerhard, the specialists in charge of his treatment, met in the staff room at a quarter to six on the morning of the day he died. They had his charts on the table and the previous day's results from pathology.

Dr Gerhard held up the scans to the light, one after the other, and looked satisfied. He held them out to his companion.

—I believe we are making progress.

—I don't know what you mean by that, Dr Gerhard. I can also read a chart and to me this doesn't tell the same story.

—I am stating that we are making progress. You can see for yourself, Ingrid. When Mr Mokoena came to us, on request of the Presidency, he presented as a case of severe malnutrition. I took measures to correct that and they have succeeded. His weight loss has been arrested.

—So you think this man is on the road to recovery?

—Listen to my assessment, Ingrid. He is coming back from severe malnutrition. I am not saying our friend will celebrate his hundredth birthday.

Dr Ndlovu put the scans down. She buttoned her white coat to the collar and made sure she had the right documents on her. She was already angry at Gerhard, at his tanning-salon complexion and accent.

There was something in the pinkness of his face and in the starkness of his oblivion that provoked her. So what if he ran marathons? So what if he was from overseas? She didn't like the tone he took with her. For some reason, in the course of his life, he hadn't learned to behave with people and nobody had been in a position to teach him. Around anybody black, she thought, Gerhard exaggerated the crudeness of his manner and his corporal's way of speaking. She wanted to let her husband Victor teach him a lesson. But Victor would lose the fight. Gerhard had both of his arms. And in the system everybody stood behind everybody else.

—I am looking at the same charts and, in my opinion, he will be lucky to be alive tomorrow unless something drastic changes.

—Ingrid, I am not interested in politicising the science this early in the morning. We have our instructions to avoid poisoning him with anti-retrovirals. Within those parameters, within those conditions that have been set by the patient, let us try to be responsible physicians.

Ingrid wanted to laugh out loud. They were letting a man die in a room two floors above their heads because the politicians didn't believe in the existence of his disease. She and Dr Gerhard were pretending that it was a simple matter of professional dislike between them.

—I am going to see the patient now, Dr Gerhard. I have to be there anyway. My husband is there.

—Ah, what is Victor doing these days?

—He's all right.

—Tell him I miss the opportunity of seeing him. You promised to come to dinner in my humble abode. Don't think I have forgotten about it. Soon I will invite you again.

317

We have to find the right occasion for a proper veal. You know that I am a remarkable cook.

On the way over to the other wing it struck Ingrid that she didn't dislike Mathias Gerhard as much as she thought. He didn't let her get so far away. At a certain point, they had almost been friends. And she wanted easy dealings again. She wanted Gerhard on her side. She could have resigned from the case when it became clear that the Union Buildings were going to interfere in the day-to-day management. But it would have made more trouble. They had enough as it was. Victor had difficulties at the party headquarters. He thought if he could get to the top it would help. He had come to pass on a letter to the president, through Mokoena or one of the nurses, and was even hoping to run into the man at the top. Ingrid wasn't sure his hopes were well founded. You never knew who was behind your troubles.

She found him already in the room. The nurses knew him as her husband and gave him the run of the hospital. The shutters were still closed and the place was almost dark except for the light from the corridor. He watched the sleeping body as something fluttered beneath its eyelids. From how he held himself, Ingrid could see Victor had pain in the part of his arm he had lost. Phantom pain. Ghost pain. Absent pain. It flared up whenever something disheartened him. When it came on, he looked as if he were about to shrug.

She held him by the shoulder and steered him away from the bed. He was almost exactly the same height as she was. He was the most delicate man she had ever known. He had worked as an actor before he left the country. He had been blown up in a car, and had run an intelligence operation around Johannesburg in 1990.

—It's shocking. There's nothing left of Sparks over there.

—First of all, talk where he can't hear you.

—In Lusaka, you remember, Ingrid, Sparks was the first person to tell a joke.

—I can remember.

—He was carefree as long as he had a gun on his person. He was a terror in the boxing ring, the local Cassius Clay. Float like a butterfly and sting like a bee. Even though I don't agree with everything he has done recently, he was still a terror until last month. Big men on the National Executive Committee, those ones who had been in detention, those who were underground in the mines, they began to cry when they received a fax from Sparks. Now what does he weigh in that bed? I could pick him up in my one arm.

Ingrid didn't reply. She knew the stories about Sparks. She began to copy down the list of medications into her notebook. She liked to have her own records of the case.

—He can't hear me, Ingrid. You told me so yourself. It's not scientifically possible.

—Science doesn't know everything.

—It knows enough to say we shouldn't be keeping this body alive. We shouldn't be using science to keep it breathing. We ignore science when it's convenient. Whatever he did, Sparks is still the person who pulled me out of a burning car. I don't want you to keep him here like a mummy forever.

—I understand, Victor. It's not going to be forever. Did you find a place to put your letter?

—I gave it to the nurse. In case the president doesn't come while she's here she will give it to the other nurse. You remember the one who also knew my old friend Mr Samuel Shabangu?

—I remember. I think you can trust her to give it.

—She just needs the right opportunity to get it into his hands.

—Will you wait for me while I finish the examination? They have *Car and Driver* on the table outside.

Ingrid had opened Sparks's gown and was testing his breathing with a stethoscope. The rim of the disc was almost warm compared to the centre. She could tell that there was liquid in his lungs, as much of a nuisance as having a litre of milk sitting on his chest. She didn't like the implications. The antibiotics weren't reducing the temperature. The Presidency wanted pigs to fly. She made a note to the nurse to turn the patient over every hour. He was developing bed-sores. She wrote down her cellphone number under the note in case the current nurse didn't know it. They were always pretending not to know. She wanted to know immediately if anything unusual happened.

She went down to the parking lot with Victor. He was using her car because his own was being serviced. She held him for a minute against her cool doctor's coat. His face made a clean impression against her. She liked the fact that she could still subdue her husband. She had an idea of how to manage his unhappiness. She knew how to manage the case. She had become an old woman in his arms.

—I worry about something, Victor.

—What is it?

—You are expecting too much from your letter. The president may not be interested in the truth. Does he care that you have been falsely accused? Because they call you disloyal, he may treat you as a disloyal member of the party. He doesn't tolerate a lot of criticism. The man lying in that room is the one who made mincemeat of the critics. He is the same one who disparaged anti-retrovirals as the poison of the Western pharmaceutical companies. The president took him off the medication that had a chance of keeping him alive. When he is capable of doing such a thing, what makes you think he will treat you any better?

Victor had never seen his wife so beautiful. Her face was as sharply drawn as a portrait in pencil. In her collared blouse she looked like a movie star from the black-and-white movies they had watched in Lusaka. But she was more suspicious than him about people.

—You have your opinion, Ingrid. I think the president tries to keep an open mind. He has kept this country open for business in the last ten years.

—Everything can be out in the open because it's what happens behind the scenes that counts, my dear.

—Nevertheless, I have written my letter. Now that I have done everything I have no choice but to wait.

—You just can't expect miracles to happen.

—We had such a history together. Why can't we expect miracles?

In the age of technology, miracles were infrequent. They couldn't be recorded on a hard drive. The world for Victor was cockeyed. His comrades had turned against him, causing him considerable pain in his lost arm, and it would require a miracle, or an order from the president, to put it right. He forgot about it, most times, in the company of his wife. This unreachable pain went away when he talked to Polk, who looked at Victor as if he still had two arms, and sometimes when he was deep inside a book, or listening to a record, or lost in his seat under the spell of a movie.

Honey's taxi sped by him on the way out of the spiral parkade. She was excited to hear the Japanese ambassador, who had agreed to judge the debate team. She was captain of the team. Honey didn't notice Victor on the other side of the smoked-glass windows. Next time she would bring a recording of her piano lessons. Her father liked the idea of her being good at music.

On the highway Victor drove carefully, avoiding the fast lanes populated by trucks and Mercedes-Benzes. He had to clear up from his job at party headquarters. According to the fax, he had the right to retrieve his personal effects. He could save any personal files from his computer under the proper supervision. He was the final victim of Sparks Mokoena, who suspected Victor of leaking documents related to the purchase of advanced submarines and had burned him for it inside the party.

Victor found a parking spot near his destination. He walked a block through town. Central Johannesburg was filled with men speaking on cellphones, black Mercedes-Benzes bumping through the traffic, hawkers in front of their blankets, and scroungers pushing wheeled frames loaded with wire and glass to take to the scrapyard, where they would make ten cents per kilogram.

Inside Khotso House, where he had once been one of the few with an office, it was worse. He was met at the door by the human-resources manager and forced to move along the corridor, where he passed various officials and minor party men. There were many hostile pairs of eyes. People he had been friendly with turned away. His old secretary didn't offer a greeting. She had her head buried inside her cubicle. It was strange to have done something right and to be thrown into disgrace.

The human-resources guy was keen to make a good impression. He stood at the office door, a hand inside the waistcoat of his three-piece suit.

—We wanted to give you a chance, comrade. If there is anything on that computer that is yours, why, you are welcome to copy it and take it out of here.

—The computer will take five minutes to come on. I'll put everything in a box.

—You understand that I will have to look through those things and make sure you are not accidentally making away with the property of the party. The same goes for the information on that disk.

—What are you going to search for on the disk? Can you arrest ones and zeroes?

—There's no reason to be flippant, comrade. This is serious business.

The green cursor finally appeared on the computer and Victor showed each file to his supervisor before he copied it to the disk. When he was finished, the man copied all the files on his disk to another one, to keep a record of what had been taken. Then he checked through the carton. There were some photographs, playing cards Victor had used for solitaire when he had been in the hospital, and a miniature African mask he had taken from Mr Shabangu.

The office was flamboyantly locked behind him. He was free to walk in the company of the human-resources official through the endless corridors of Khotso House, past men who were suddenly talking very loudly on cellphones and shouting at each other about items on spreadsheets, until they came to the atrium. He was sent on his way after signing a receipt. He was getting a modest settlement.

The manager shook hands firmly.

—You'll find something very good, comrade. Very good. We will never work against you in the private sphere. In fact, when you think about it, the more outspoken you have been against us, the more likely it is business will find an extremely good place for you.

On the highway again Victor put the music loud and drove fast. It was Ingrid's music but his heart didn't mind. How had he allowed anybody to deduct his freedom? It had already been growing inside him when he'd slept among the dogs and horses in the cavalry yard alongside a father who had subsequently disappeared without a trace. The party had subtracted from his freedom. He had allowed it to take place. At home he would put his single arm around his wife, allow the light to reach him from the lamp in her soul, and be certain again, in the cockeyed condition, that miracles did happen.

2010
VUVUZELA

She was as light as a photon. She was fifteen. She was going to write her memoirs.

Correction. She was nearly fifteen. For her birthday Shanti had asked to take lessons from her dad's cousin Logan at the World Motorist Academy. Uncle Logan was a councilman and ran weightlifting classes, on the side, for poor children. She would be free when she could drive. Her memoirs, however, would begin when she was kissed for the first time. She had a tube of Lip Ice, piña colada flavour, in case the moment arrived. Any moment now. Joris was the approved candidate for the kiss. She had checked him out and decided in his favour despite the thinness of the evidence. She had tried to make it clear to Joris. But he was stretching things out.

—Where are you?

—Cherry, I didn't intend to be late. The traffic is hectic.

—My name is Shanti. I hate to remind you, the way you talk, you're not a gangster, Joris.

—There you are incorrect. I am a gangster. Give me ten minutes and don't be cross. Not my fault, Cherry.

Joris didn't take responsibility. Neither did he take offence when she questioned him. To Shanti he was supernaturally good-natured, like her father Sanjay since he had started taking pills and looking for every silver lining. Even without any pills, Joris was as merry as a cartoon, and refused to be drawn into an argument.

The truth was that he was hard to pin down. Six months in his company, being fetched and dropped and teased and telephoned, had revealed next to nothing to Shanti about what he did when he was out of her sight. She knew for sure only that he was tall, liked to stretch his long legs as if he were about to kick the ball, wore bright rayon shirts and tight trousers, and that, at some wavelength that she didn't understand, he seemed to like her back.

It was the first day of the World Cup. There was no reason to let the mystery of Joris ruin her day. The mood was buoyant. She would rather join in. Her legs were bare. Groups of men were blowing horns as they drifted towards the fenced-in parks where projectors were prepared to show the opening match from Johannesburg's Soccer City. She heard the chop-chop of a helicopter, and looked up to see it tilting in mid-air as if it were being held at the rotor. Everywhere you went there was good noise. She was listening to Mary J Blige on her earphones and turned the volume up. There was no sign that she was going deaf.

Shanti went down Long Street and turned off to the flea market on Greenmarket Square. The canvas stalls on the square, surrounded by international hotels and restaurants, sold ivory and soapstone statues, ink portraits and bead necklaces. She wanted another vuvuzela. The horns were blowing in streets and yards, on balconies, and from the roofs of inner-city apartment blocks. It took some time to find a stand that still had them.

The stall-keeper, his face hidden behind insectoid sunglasses, took them from a bucket and sounded each one. He had them in different colours, the seams showing on their fifty-centimetre bodies. Shanti took her earphones out for a minute, the music pouring an inch into the world, and came to an agreed price. Twenty rands. What could you get for twenty rands nowadays? She chose an orange one and put it at her feet.

She was trying to pay, her handbag open on her arm, when a man collided with her. He lifted the strap of her handbag above his arm, and bowed to her slightly to apologise. Shanti smiled back. She was happy, with or without Joris, in the surge of human beings. Her assailant was striking. She liked men. He must be about thirty, proud of his arms in a T-shirt. She noticed that he had a gold ring in his ear before he disappeared into the infinite sea of pedestrians. She should have introduced herself. She blew through the new horn to get his attention. It was too late.

At the same time she saw Joris sailing to the corner of the pavement. He had his arm balanced on the open window of his Toyota Conquest. She ran along the square and got in. He winked at her, looking like he had just won the lottery. He was triumphant to be Joris. Shanti forgave him for his stupidity. Correction. She appreciated the fact that he liked to win at anything and everything. Even his ride bore the name of victory.

She placed her new acquisition at an angle on her lap. It was too long to hold straight. Joris ran his hand inside the head width.

—I thought you had one at home already.

—I liked the colour. And I wanted one now.

—We have an hour left before the game begins. Shall

we check out the city? Most of the roads on this side here are open. There are Maseratis and Hollywood actors and famous politicians everywhere.

—Sure.

Joris turned the volume up. They shot around the corner onto Long Street, where there was a double line of cars. Shanti had been waiting for the World Cup since she turned twelve. The new stadiums and bus lines had gradually appeared, and the billion-rand terminals at the airport. It was like a dream to sit in the passenger's seat of the Conquest, with its graphic equaliser rippling red in eight bands, Joris's selection of heavy metal pressing heavy on her chest, and see the banners on the buildings and the hundreds of policemen positioned along the roads.

Joris drove with one hand. With the other he motioned to give him her handbag. She kept his cigarettes so he wouldn't over-smoke. He opened the clasp and reached in, put a cigarette in his mouth, let his sunglasses fall over his face, applied the hot tip of the car lighter to the end of his cancer stick, and adjusted his skull ring.

The mysteries of Joris. Joris came by funds in mysterious ways. He did mysterious jobs and received mysterious text messages in the middle of the night. He wouldn't share his telephone with Shanti. He had never taken her to his house and introduced her to his mysterious parents, although he was a regular at her place and had become fast friends with her family. It gave him the advantage. The only thing that was crucial for Joris, that she knew about, was never appearing to make an effort to win. Still, he made a contest out of everything.

Shanti rolled down her window and blew on her vuvuzela. The point was to be loud. She filled her lungs and blew again. Horns were blowing everywhere along the road and inside the bars. The country moved to a single soundtrack. Before, according to Uncle Logan, blacks and whites had different sports. The one had soccer. The other had cricket and rugby. Today, Logan said, they had different teams: Orlando Pirates and Kaizer Chiefs versus Barça and Man United. Uncle Logan was strange. He saw race in everything because he wanted to see it there and wouldn't be comfortable until he found it. He had published many pamphlets of his own on Black Consciousness and was working on his own autobiography of an African bodybuilder. She would ask him to read her memoirs when they were done. She didn't expect they would take long to do once she got started.

In the shops and bars on Long Street, Shanti saw the green rectangles of television screens trained on the pitch. She was happy she had managed to sneak out of the house wearing the shortest skirt in her cupboard. She had tricked her mother and father by wearing a long jacket over it. Her body felt that it would float away in the steady winter sunshine. Her heart went out of the window. But she still had her questions. She wouldn't let herself be kissed without obtaining some answers first.

—What are you doing with me, Joris?

—What do you mean?

—You are eighteen, right, if my calculations are correct? Nineteen? You would be out of school already if you didn't have to repeat a year. You can drive yourself where you like. You can go to most clubs. Nobody is holding you back. What are you doing with a fourteen-year-old? Even if I am almost fifteen? Even if I am mentally grown up?

—Oh my word. We are friends. You are my best friend, Shanti.

—Boys and girls can't be best friends. I am suspicious.

Before he replied, Joris took the time to work his way into the other lane, where there was a space, and then back into the same lane in front of a stopped truck. He was stupid. He would do the same thing on the highway at a hundred and forty kilometres per hour, the Toyota juddering like a washing machine. He needed to take every advantage as if it would kill him to arrive one minute later or to lose an argument against a girl. He would never let Shanti win any of their arguments although she, in fact, happened to be on the debating team and usually had the facts on her side.

—First of all, Shanti, in my opinion, okay, you are extremely narrow-minded for your age. So you have a narrow view of relationships. Because you grew up without having to worry about money. That sets you back. I have to keep an open mind all the time because nobody gave me any opportunities, you understand?

—I heard this already.

—Secondly, is there a better explanation than friendship? Whatever connections we can find, isn't it good to take advantage of them? More importantly, why are you asking such a strange question? Shouldn't you be asking yourself the same question?

—It's a fair question.

—Are you in love with me? I told you before not to fall in love with me.

—I think you have a much lower mental age than me.

—You're always correct, Cherry.

Joris took his arm back. Shanti wanted to tell him that there were other beautiful men in town. The Argentinians. The Spanish. The Brazilians. They were the most beautiful men in the history of the world. They had the right build, neither too thin nor too stocky. They weren't too clever for their boots like Joris. They weren't too stupid and too solid, like rugby players, but rather nimble and light. It wasn't called the beautiful game for nothing.

There was no point to arguing. If she opened her mouth and tried to make him jealous Joris would find a way to turn it back on her. He would lean in her direction, his lazy voice curling around his tongue like a snake, and talk directly in her ear. She would lose the argument. She would be lucky if she didn't lose consciousness.

Not that Shanti minded losing. She never got tired of listening when he was close to her. There was a reason she put up with the abuse. Joris had music in his body, a spring in his step, and the slim strong lines of a junior club player. Inevitably he was a forward. Despite his school results, he was good with his head. Frequently she was the only girl in attendance at the club practice. The team played under obsolete stadium lights smoking in the rain. Shanti sat, knees up, on the splintered old bleachers, trying not to get wet, while the players raised steam out of the wet ground with their togs. She laughed at Joris when he came to glug his carefully frozen bottles of concentrated orange juice.

She had told him she went to watch the practice games just to be able to look at his long legs. It was true. There was something perfect about them. She admired them stretched out in the car.

When the traffic stopped in the intersection, Joris looked at his telephone and frowned.

—Call Carlo, Cherry. My phone will be out of battery soon.

—What do you want me to tell him?

—Tell him we're going to be late. Tell him to make sure to bring the stuff. We'll pick it up at the same time as we watch the game.

—What stuff are you talking about?

—Stuff. Just stuff. I don't want you to write about every last detail of my life in your memoir. Call him, please, and relay the message.

Shanti looked in her handbag. Her phone wasn't there. She checked her pockets. She put her hand into Joris's coat. Nothing. She had been using it when she talked to Joris in Greenmarket Square before she paid. Where did she put it?

She leaned back, half into the rear of the Toyota, and began looking around with her hands on the vinyl seat. It wasn't on the floor underneath the passenger seat. Nor had it fallen between the seats. She opened the cubbyhole. Joris shut it impatiently, as if she had done something wrong, and pulled into a parking space. The car was standing outside a travel agency with old grey desktop computers hunched in three rows before their silent screens. There was a locked mesh door pulled over the front of the shop.

—What are you doing? I asked you to make a simple call.

—Don't play with me, Joris. Did you take my telephone? Is it in there in the cubbyhole?

—Nothing's in there that you have to worry about. When did you last check your phone?

—I had it when you called me. Obviously. After that I don't remember. Where could it go?

Joris looked worried. He wasn't joking with her.

—Did anything happen?

—This guy bumped into me while I was buying that vuvuzela. He had a gold earring. It could only be that one guy. This is just my luck. This is just my luck.

—Let's go back. I'll leave the car where it is. We won't make it if we try to drive back. Point him out to me if you see him. Sprint.

Joris locked the car. They ran down Long Street through lines of pedestrians. Loud music came out of the bars and restaurants. Shanti couldn't run fast enough. In a split second Joris was a long way in front.

There were Germans, Swedes, Australians in soccer jerseys who moved to block her as she ran by. She pushed them away and winced at the beer on their bodies. One of them put his hand on her shoulder. She hit him on the chest until he surrendered. She ran faster. She knew that her mother was only looking for an excuse to ground her during the World Cup.

For this reason she ran up and down Shortmarket Street trying to find the man who had collided with her. She looked out for a gold earring and followed every man who had one until she made sure it wasn't him. She wasn't sure how he looked anymore, only that at a glance he made an impression and that he had an earring and a necklace and a gold tooth and the muscles of a hero.

Nobody wanted to help. The expressions of the vendors in their stands, surrounded by their canvas walls, were forbidding. Their conversation was worse. They hadn't noticed anything. There had been no man with a gold earring working in Greenmarket Square. They didn't believe in pickpockets. The stall-keeper from whom she had bought the horn claimed to suffer from glaucoma. He opened one eye with his fingers and tried to show her the membrane.

She noticed a police booth, a Perspex cubicle on the other side of the square, and tried to push her way over. She ran into two men who were moving building materials in a supermarket trolley. She hit the trolley, fell down, and scraped her elbows.

When she got back up, the men offered to put her in the cart. She didn't acknowledge them. The sergeant in his short-sleeved blue shirt, his moustache shining, was no more helpful. He gave her a case number, for the sake of insurance, but refused to walk around the square and find the culprit. She told him she would report him. He told her she would have trouble finding another policeman to report him to. She memorised his badge number. He shouldn't trifle with her. Her family had connections.

Joris was standing in the entrance to one of the tourist hotels, talking on the telephone with one hand over his other ear. He motioned to her to wait and continued his conversation. She was annoyed with him for concentrating on his telephone at a time like this. Behind him the hotel doorman sat on the side of an empty gold-tubed luggage cart, brushing the lint from his trousers, and shining his shoes with a duster, placing them one and then the other on the side of the cart.

After a minute Joris took a pen out of her handbag. He copied something onto the side of his hand.

—So we are looking for Molteno Mansions, next to the Engen garage. It's a deal. Check you.

Joris snapped the lid shut and turned to her.

—I couldn't see him anywhere. But he could come back.

—I had a better idea, Cherry. I simply called your number and the guy answered on the other side.

—What deal did you make with him?

—Two hundred rands finder's fee and we're completely sorted. They give it back to you in the same condition it was in. That's where we are going right now. There's a cash machine on the way. I assume two hundred is worth it to you.

—But is it safe to meet them?

—Very safe. It's a business. Half the cellphones in this country are sold like this. How do you think I could afford such a good one?

—Next time I know where to go.

—Just don't think you can insult them the way you insult me. They sound like proper gangsters. We need to find Molteno Mansions as quickly as possible so we don't miss out on the game.

Joris led her by the hand. Shanti's irritation evaporated. The day was progressing, thanks to Joris. Thanks again to Joris. She didn't like to admit it, but in recent months Joris and his hatchback had saved more days than she could count. He was the perfect friend, willing to pick her up at home or accompany her to a friend's birthday party or listen to her complaints concerning Ursula, to meet her in Cavendish and watch movies from ten in the morning to ten at night or simply to drift up and down the escalators and through the food court, hand in hand, past the facades displaying blouses and shoes and carpets and stereo systems.

The opening of the World Cup was a day to enjoy. Not even the theft of her telephone was going to spoil it. Shanti was determined to get Joris to kiss her by the end of it. She kept her hand tightly in the crook of his elbow and wondered if she was smiling too brightly. She liked the idea that nobody could see her coming.

The queue at the cash machine snaked around the side of the building.

—How are we going to make it?

—Give me your card, angel.

She handed it over.

—You don't know the code.

—I watched you put it in a hundred times. It's not difficult to work out. When you don't go to a private school, you have to use your eyes. And your brain.

—I will be surprised if you come back with money.

—Cherry, relax. I will always come back with money.

Joris walked to the front of the line, making conversation with every young woman who was standing there in a football jersey, praising their choice of team, trying his repertoire of magic tricks. He did the same with her mother, producing a hard-boiled egg or a plastic flower from behind Ursula's ear when she stood still for a minute.

It didn't take long for his magic to work. He slipped between two tall blonde women who were next in line for the cash machine. Shanti was proud of Joris. He was up to any challenge she put to him. So he had a strange name. So he wasn't good at swotting. So what? He had told her that his ambition was to become a television magician, or a stand-up comedian, like the ones he studied on DVDs. On the other hand, she was never going to be married at all. She would put it on the first page of her memoirs. Her parents weren't a good advertisement for the institution. She could imagine hanging around with Joris for years, enjoying his larceny. The only black mark against him was that he wanted to hang around with her. So what did it say about her that she was grateful?

—I told you I knew your code. I took a hundred out. I had a hundred already.

—Why are you giving me half?

—You mustn't think I am hanging around with you for your money. I'm hanging around for your mother's money.

—Very funny, Joris.

—I am to blame somewhat. If I had been on time, the opportunity wouldn't have come up.

—It wasn't your fault.

—Still, it's my pleasure, Cherry.

They went through the narrow back streets behind parliament, past corner cafés and policemen and women riding on tall brown and black horses, cellphone shops doing brisk business selling SIM cards, glass bus shelters at which the tourists were lining up. Soon there were fewer people on the streets, many more inside the flaking pubs and restaurants and blocks of flats from which could be heard the same television announcer's voice. Shanti realised the opening ceremony was about to start.

Molteno Mansions turned out to be a narrow five-storey building rising between two shorter neighbours. The buzzers weren't working. The brick staircases were open to the elements, turns visible all the way to the roof behind a lattice of keyhole tiles. They were guarded by iron doors at the bottom. Joris rattled both of them without success. He called up to a man on a third-floor balcony who went inside, without questioning them, and buzzed them in.

They ran. Joris pulled Shanti up the staircase by the hand. She was half winded by the time they got to the top. The door to B7 was wide open. They entered a deserted room with a lounge suite wrapped in plastic and a computer lying on the floor with a pile of DVDs. On the wall were posters of Disney characters, Donald Duck and Goofy, in big yellow wooden frames. There were bean bags pushed against the wall. Next door you could hear the countdown to the opening ceremony.

In the next room they found two men sitting on chairs frowning at the television set. The occupants didn't seem surprised to see them. One continued to watch the screen. He had a gold earring and a buzz cut. It took Shanti a moment to recognise him as the man who had bumped into her on Greenmarket Square. He turned the volume down. He had the crossword page open on his lap. He didn't seem to notice her.

The other man got to his feet and shook their hands, balancing on one leg and then the other as if, like Joris, he was trying out the length of his trousers. He didn't introduce himself. Instead he pulled out the creaking middle drawer in the cabinet. There were more than a hundred cellphones inside.

—I think you should be able to find what you're looking for.

—You have a lot of cellphones.

—It's not easy, you know. It's a lot of work to answer so many of them, to keep them charged so that people can reach me, but it's something I take pride in. I get ninety per cent back to their original owners. Hurry, because the soccer is about to begin.

Shanti looked. Her cellphone was white with a hard cover, a metal ridge from top to bottom, and a scratch on the back corner. There were a few white ones in the drawer. She checked them, going down the rows, and picking them up when she wasn't sure. One was the same model as hers, but there was no scratch on the back when she turned it over. She shook her head.

—It's not here.

—You'll find something in there. I have the latest models.

—Mine isn't in here.

—You tell me what features you need, what type of functionality, and I will make you a good price. I can give you a Samsung. I can give you a Nokia. I can give you a Motorola.

340

—I'd prefer to have mine back. Joris, man, how's your battery? Can you call my number again?

Shanti's phone rang, as she suspected, in the other guy's pocket. He let it ring for a minute. Then he stood up, looked surprised that his pocket was ringing, worked the telephone out of his tight trousers and placed it smartly on the cabinet. He returned to his position in front of the television without saying a word. His friend picked it up and delivered it to Shanti. While the money was changing hands the other guy turned the volume back up. He tugged at his earring. Shanti saw that he had tattoos along the length of his arm. She still thought he was good-looking.

There were five messages from her mother. No stress. Shanti found the button and switched her phone off. She placed it in the bottom of her bag, which she closed and latched. There was no point being fooled twice.

—Now that you made us miss the beginning, we are officially your guests for the rest of the match. You should have thought of it when you took my phone in the first place. Joris, would you sit down please?

—Your girlfriend here has spirit. How old are you?

—I will be fifteen.

—In that case, Afzal, leave the bottle top where it is. We cannot corrupt a minor. You can bring out the Castles. My brother over there, what's your name? Joris? I never heard that name before. You come from which side now? Never mind. Help our Afzal bring the brews. You will find they are sitting under ice in the bath tub there. Then you two lovebirds can have the cushions from the bedroom.

Joris brought the cushions and sat next to Shanti. He put his arm around her again. The side of his face was rough where he hadn't been shaving. She put her arm around him.

It was as if there was some change in his attitude towards her. She couldn't have been safer. She wanted to call her father, who was so protective, and tell him where she was. Joris had come through for her again. She half turned to him and he half kissed her on the ear, as if he had made a mistake. The mysteries of Joris. The moods of Joris. He touched her on the chin.

—I think I may buy a second handset from these guys.

—Be quiet for the game.

The Mexicans were dangerous because they were patient, played Spanish-style, passing the ball sideways, back and forth. They waited for Bafana to make a mistake and then went forward. When there was a chance of losing possession, they stayed near the halfway line and let the other side exhaust themselves. Their discipline dissipated the unconcentrated attacks of the South Africans. Aguilar took a convincing shot at goal. He was disappointed by the Bafana goalkeeper. Dos Santos took the ball from Modise as if he were playing a kid's game. Joris snorted. He put his arm around Shanti's shoulder. She sat very close to him, aware of his breathing.

Siphiwe Tshabalala, the Bafana striker, put the entire match in peril. He sent the ball dangerously across the field, a long pass which still failed to meet the head of Mphela. It was a miracle Franco didn't intercept. The Mexican coach, Aguirre, looked confident. Soon, however, Tshabalala made up for his mistake. Bafana seized the ball, sent it spinning forward, starting from the centre circle with the foot of Dikgacoi and ending with Tshabalala, who flicked it past Óscar Pérez into the left-hand corner. The stadium rose in a roar. With his dreadlocks, on his powerful strikers' legs, the striker had a tremendous man's beauty. Shanti would have taken him over Joris.

Half-time came without a change. Bafana was hoping for Mexico to fail rather than making it difficult for them to score. The Mexicans came back strong, took charge of the game again, and crossed repeatedly to the other side of the field only to be frustrated.

Mexican discipline made its own good luck. Ten minutes before the end, Guardado moved the ball diagonally over the South African defence to the forwards. Rafael Márquez equalised for Mexico. 1–1. In the last minute before extra time, stealing a long shot, Mphela hit the Mexican goalpost. Extra time decided nothing. A draw for the home team. A blow for Mexican arrogance.

Pigs might fly, beggars might ride, and, with the permission of the Uruguayan fiends, Bafana might make it into the second round. It was all anyone had ever wanted for the unlucky country. The stadiums had risen. The airports had been refurbished. Tshabalala had scored the first goal of the competition. Even Joris, who made a point of never being surprised, was stunned. When the balloons went up he put both his arms round Shanti. He brushed her lips with his own, gladly concussed. Shanti would dress it up as a proper kiss in her memoirs. She would neglect to mention the fact that his breath tasted of beer.

Joris got a call and went to answer in the other room before his battery finally died. The handsome man held out his arm to her as if he wanted her to kiss his ring. She pushed him away.

—We let you watch on our television.

—So I should kiss your hand?

—Kiss me anywhere you want.

—Take pity on me and don't behave like a fool. I get enough of it from Joris.

—That's a pity. I'm more fun than I look. Let's go out and look from the roof. You can see parliament. There'll be fireworks. Your boyfriend will come when he's finished talking to his other woman.

The first guy was trying to find out which one of his cellphones was ringing. Shanti followed his good-looking leader through the window and onto a wrought-iron fire escape.

He went up four flights, only pausing to look rudely into the windows he passed. They wound up where the platform gave on to the roof. He leaned against the railing and lit a cigarette. When Shanti got near the top he helped her climb the last section.

—We haven't been formally introduced. I'm Sherman. What's your name, junior?

—Shanti.

—Shanti. See. We have almost the same name.

—Not quite. We only have two letters in common.

—You're a very tricky character. Did anyone ever tell it to you? Give me your phone for a minute, Shanti. I am going to call my phone so that you will always have my number. In case you want to get in touch. I have a friend who has his own taxi. He can pick you up from anywhere, day or night.

Shanti gave him her phone. She watched Sherman dial his own number. She took it back and put it into her handbag again.

—I don't want to pay twice for the same telephone.

—Look, I keep my promises. You can see half the city from here.

It was true. In the narrow roads people were streaming back to their hotels and cars in faraway parking lots, surrounding the buses and taxis, dancing with policemen, and, most of all, blowing their vuvuzelas. Up on the roof the sound was still deafening. The horns in the hands of the pedestrians were pointed up and down, left and right, out of cars and into their windows, and around the corner and into the sky, as if the largest jazz band in the world was running amuck.

Shanti loved it. The beautiful mayhem of the beautiful game. At the same time she tried to protect her ears. Bad mayhem. It had been a matter of months since people marched in Gugulethu and Langa, bearing rakes and tyres, and had burned Somalis and Shangaans to nothing but smoking bundles. Were they the same people blowing their trumpets?

Sherman, her new friend, looked as if he wanted to say something about it. Shanti wanted to tell him that he wasn't as good-looking when he was puzzled. For him in particular it was better to smile. Sherman laid his cigarette carefully on the ledge, trying to make sure it wouldn't be blown off, and tried to kiss her in the same motion. She moved out of the way. Sherman looked more puzzled. He tried again. She moved away again and then towards the fire escape. She didn't mind the attempt. Joris hardly made an effort in that direction. He seemed to be content to brush her on the lips.

Shanti wondered if she should go back down to the flat. Joris was already coming up the stairs. Sherman looked over the roof and saw him as well. He sulked, nudging his earring into his hand, where he examined it miserably. He produced a pouch and, holding it on his thigh, was rolling a joint, running his fingernail along the seam.

—Don't you have a girlfriend of your own? You must have lots of women.

—Okay, I have lots of women. In fact I have lots of children. It doesn't mean we can't kiss.

—It doesn't exactly encourage me.

—We should be able to have our fun. It's a free country.

Obviously not true. Everybody wanted to stop you having fun. When you cared about fun, it was remarkably difficult to find some. Shanti had been waiting six months for Joris to kiss her. Now he had, or might have done, depending on how you described it. In a span of fifteen minutes another man, someone who had many children and many mothers for them, had also tried to kiss her. That was just her luck. Seven lean years. Seven fat years had begun.

Joris arrived. He had brought vuvuzelas from downstairs. He kept one and gave the other to Shanti. They blew in unison, the horns screeching and flying in their hands, until they were out of breath. On the roof of the opposite buildings people were blowing back. Sherman smoked his joint. The smoke dissipated in the wind.

After a while Shanti became dizzy. She put the horn down in the corner and sat on the staircase. Joris kept blowing in reply to the neighbours while Sherman sat on the step above her. He was looking at her romantically, undeterred by the presence of Joris. He was sweating very lightly, his complexion shining like plastic, while he held the vuvuzela out in front of him. It was an effort to blow the long horns. He flicked the rest of his joint over the railing in disgust.

—They hate this, you understand.

—Who hates what?

—The corporations behind this World Cup. They fear the vuvuzela. If they had the choice, they would have outlawed them from the start. They have organised everything else to make money for them.

—My father would agree with you. He's also fixated on companies.

—In the end everybody makes money except ordinary people like me and you. We must also have the chance to make money. We also have the right to have our fun.

—Under the new constitution?

—What else is the point of a constitution?

There was an instant when Shanti thought Sherman was going to lean over and kiss her in front of Joris. It would start a fight. The idea appalled her although things like that happened at beach-house parties to older girls. She thought that her mother might find it interesting. There was a part of Ursula that was excited by the crookedness in people. Something else for Shanti to put in her memoirs. Sometimes it was as if her mother wanted to christen her in some skewed way.

Sherman didn't try a repeat performance. He waited until Joris sat down and slid his hand along the end of the vuvuzela.

—This is the AK-47 of sound.

—Considering your business, when there must be a lot of angry people, wouldn't it be useful to have a real gun?

—I am speaking metaphorically. And I am the one who never finished standard six back in the day.

On the way back to her house they stalled in traffic. Men were blowing their horns into their car. A motorcade came by, black Mercedes-Benzes driving in the side lane. The drivers wore sunglasses and suits and waved furiously to other cars to clear out of their path. Joris tried to follow behind them.

Joris didn't notice when Shanti took his telephone. She had figured out his password from watching his hands fly over the buttons. There was the usual endless set of blinking contacts and alarms. She would like to write her memoirs digitally, free of contradiction.

Shanti scrolled through the list of telephone calls while Joris was trying to make his way forward through the crowd and shout people out of the way of the car. They were forced to stop at a green light where the beggarmen and fools, schoolchildren and security guards, had moved their match into the street and were kicking the ball over the hoods of the cars. You waited uneasily for the ball to go through the glass.

—Joris?

—Yes, my Cherry?

—Who called you after the game?

—Why are you playing with my phone? Please put it back.

—Let me refresh your memory. My mother called you.

—Your phone was off. Ursula was worried so she called me to check. It's only natural.

Joris took the telephone and put it in his pocket. Soon they were on the highway overpass beneath Devil's Peak. It was a harsh day at sea. There were cruise liners berthed on the docks, stapled on their sides with portholes, and yachts riding the ocean, sliding into the waves, in the direction of Blouberg. But there was sunshine on the road. On the other side, the stone pines on the slope of the mountain were seething in a bed of light.

In Bishopscourt, where Joris turned off, it was almost silent. There were tennis courts behind the high wire cages around each property. Land Rovers glided on the parallel streets, tyres borne on their rear doors like backpacks. The houses were protected by armed response vans and venomous dogs. Cape Town, once a liberal city, had absorbed waves of right-wing immigration, including from Angola, Mozambique, Zimbabwe. They were tough white people intent on protecting their property.

At Shanti's house the gate opened. Joris spun the Conquest onto the brick circle by the entrance. Her mother would be watching the black-and-white screen attached to the closed-circuit cameras. On occasion Shanti found Ursula with her head down, completely asleep, lying before the monitor as if it were a household god. Her mother had come so far, from a poor household and a mother in the sewing union, only to worship a video screen. Ursula was still a beautiful woman in some ways and yet she didn't know what life was worth.

Shanti didn't want Joris to think he had won. This was one fight she had to win.

—Before I get out of this car, I want to know the real reason my mother is calling you. In the past week she called you ten times. Don't you think that's a little strange?

—Babe, I promised to keep an eye on you. You are forgetting how much I do for you. You're still too young to drive, after all. Who has to pick you up and drop you? Who promised to spend the first day of the World Cup with you?

Shanti undid her seatbelt and tried to control her breathing. She looked Joris so straight in the face he would turn to stone if he told her a lie.

—Are you having an affair with my mother?

—Are you really asking me that?

—I want a proper answer.

Shanti got out of the car and stood in the radius of the door. The Toyota Conquest had never seemed so ridiculous with its rusted wheels and tattered seats, the long sloping back and the perforated exhaust pipe which clanked like a castanet. It wasn't the chariot of a victor. It was the vehicle of a mere boy who could scarcely be forced into kissing her. She feared what Joris was going to say. She didn't want to lose him on the same day they had kissed.

Someone like Joris was her wild card. Her trump card against life. You couldn't put a price on him. During the past six months Joris and his mockery and his hatchback had been her own way out of the school labyrinth. There was room at her school for skateboarders and choir masters, field-hockey stars, speech-and-drama kids, but there was no obvious place for someone like Shanti, with her family and her history and her Uncle Ashok. She was too sharp for them.

Therefore Joris. She had held on to him for dear life. But he wouldn't even get out of the car and fall on his knees for forgiveness. He leaned across the gearbox to speak to her. Shanti held the vuvuzela tightly. She would swing it at Joris before she let her hands do what they wanted to do.

—I am not having an affair with your mother. Before we met, before the two of us met, she asked if I could take care of you. This was while the circus around your Uncle Ashok was going on and we were in the middle of his trial about those submarines. She simply covered my expenses so I was able to do that. Then when we actually met in person it turned out to be more of a pleasure than a job. And now I would say that you are fully my best friend in the world. Nobody has ever understood me so well.

Shanti could hardly get the words out. She thought she was spitting them out, seed by seed.

—When you tried to kiss me today were you also being paid?

—I didn't kiss you. Please don't tell your mother that. I meant it when I said we are the best of friends.

—Who do you think you are, Joris, James Bond? The spy who loved me? Forget it, man. You are just some type of gigolo.

Parliament-Funkadelic. Sun Ra. Public Enemy. Joris had given her music and insisted she listen to it and educate her ears. Her father listened to Motown like Logan. Ursula, however, controlled the hi-fi when it came to a party like tonight's. She put on Barry Manilow. Enrique Iglesias. Richard Clayderman.

The hits for grandparents kept coming while Ursula came and went from the master bedroom and fetched choice pieces of jewellery, laying her necklaces and brooches on her hand to display them to her guests, and then returned them to the safe. She had mild arthritis and, like someone on crutches, was reluctant to move quickly up and down the staircase.

Shanti stood at the bottom. She didn't offer to help her mother.

—Are you okay?

—I'm fine.

—Where is your friend Joris? We made it clear he was invited.

—He didn't hand in his report yet? He told me that you hired him to spy.

—Not a spy, Shanti, just a nice boy to keep an eye on you during a difficult period. In exchange you were free to come and go as you chose. But I simply can't play mental games with you in front of guests. Can we postpone them till tomorrow? Can you look for the good in the situation?

—I don't know what's good about it.

—There is always a silver lining. Go and greet your

uncles. I saw Logan already. And your Uncle Ashok may not have many days left on the outside. There may be a lot you can learn from his quarter.

There was nothing to learn. Shanti went outside and left her mother to die under the heap of her jewellery. At the back of the house the grills were already smoking. Beer bottles nestled in their tubs, disguised under the flurry of ice. Two waiters in black uniforms were moving chops in tubs onto the lawn. There were candles in paper triangles dotted across the grass, flickering in the wind and giving an affectionate touch to each person's face, even her uncle.

Uncle Ashok had been staying with them since being furloughed on compassionate grounds. His son Vish was around, looking so thin he disappeared if you looked at him from the side. Ashok's friends, Victor and his wife Ingrid, had been staying in a hotel and had arrived at four. There were many others. Parveen, her mother's uncanny double, and her husband Farhad, who was in a wheelchair. Paul Rabie, who was on television, and his Canadian wife. The cream of the crop. In short, there was nobody to talk to.

Shanti took her telephone out. She redialled the last number.

—Sherman? This is the girl whose phone you stole today. Tell me, are you doing anything? I mean right now. Do you have any good music? I don't mean typical pop.

It was the time for Barry Manilow at her house. Thanks to the left foot of Tshabalala it was the night of the vuvuzelas across the country. Shanti could hear them in her bedroom. They blew from the forest on the mountain as well as from parties in town at bistros and dance clubs, modelling agencies, backpackers' hostels, bed and breakfasts, in Portuguese restaurants and shisa nyama joints, on the beach in front of Atlantic Seaboard mansions, everywhere people were astonished that Bafana hadn't lost yet. The only silent places were the tin houses of Somalis and Mozambicans, Zimbabweans and Malawians, who had their own expectations of the World Cup, and what might happen to them, and preferred to stay out of earshot.

Shanti picked up her vuvuzela. She blew it from the window. Her chest was thrilled. Looking this way she enjoyed the warm black weight of the mountain with stars in her hair. She attracted the attention of a stray party-goer, who looked up from the back door. Amrita, Logan's daughter, came out and watched her. She was wearing a satin frock and a bow in her hair.

—Are you well, Shanti?

—I'm doing fine, Amrita.

—I'm also fine.

—Would you like to come up? The staircase is right there.

Amrita took her time labouring up the stairs. She opened the door and positioned herself uncomfortably on the carpet. Amrita suffered from a mild case of retardation. She was big and marvellous, serious and shy and doubtful in manner, and you had to be careful to put her at ease.

—Sit on the bed, Amrita. You can take your shoes off. Make yourself comfortable.

—When is Joris coming? If it is soon, I will keep my shoes on.

—You can suit yourself. But, regarding Joris, he isn't coming tonight.

It took Amrita some time to arrange her limbs on the bed. She lined up her shoes and crossed her legs. She was merely a second or a third cousin, a sketch of Shanti in crayon. In her frock and bow, with the new slope of her breasts and a faint moustache, Amrita was difficult not to enjoy. You wanted to smile at the sight of her. For one thing, you knew exactly where in her head you could find her. Shanti thought she could run her hand across her cousin's forehead and predict that Amrita was going to ask another question about Joris. She took a strong interest in Shanti's romantic life.

Amrita required another minute to produce her query.

—Have you broken up with Joris?

—Why do you ask?

—He's not here. He's usually right with you.

—According to Joris, we were never going out in the first place. Therefore it would be impossible for us to break up. But don't worry. I have another friend who is coming to visit tonight. He should liven up the party.

—You are so beautiful, Shanti. Anybody will come and visit you if you give them the invitation.

—Keep quiet, Amrita. You are much more beautiful in your way.

—How is that?

—Just to start, you are much more unusual. There are many other people exactly like me even if they don't look exactly the same. But I have never met anyone like you. What my father said about you is true. You take life at face value.

—You're joking me.

—On the contrary, I am not joking you, Amrita. You are one of a kind. There is nobody else on earth like you.

It was true. Amrita had an ideal heart, like Logan, her father, who continued to bodybuild well into old age and

354

who took his daughter everywhere he went, even placing her in the back seat of his modified car when he was taking driving lessons with one of his pupils. She sat in the office of the World Gym while he worked out. Amrita had her father's social conscience and was preoccupied by the idea of people losing their homes. In their garage she had prepared several hampers of tinned pineapple and cornmeal and tea bags and golden syrup, in case there were refugees in the days after the World Cup.

—Can we play some music?

—Amrita, you're welcome to stay here and play whatever you like on the stereo. I just saw my friend drive in. I want to go down and greet him before my mother intercepts him. You can see. He has the only car, apart from your dad's, that is not a Mercedes.

—What's his name again?

—He says his name is Sherman. When you come down later I can introduce you.

—I am going to try out some of your CDs first. Then I have to go and greet Uncle Ashok. After that I will come to see Sherman.

—That sounds like a plan.

On her way out the door, in fact, Shanti had to duck Uncle Ashok and his contingent. He had been her father's uncle and, by the law of transitive relationships, he was also her uncle. A great uncle. A grand uncle. Ashok was wearing his customary uniform of a blue tracksuit, decorated with a lightning stripe, and open sandals, his nude feet walnut brown. He was showing pictures on his cellphone to Logan and the others. They were images of his grandchildren who had been born and brought up, one batch in Leeds and the other in Nairobi, wherever his sons had found business opportunities. He couldn't visit them until his passport was restored, but he was reflective about his tribulations. Shanti had noticed the alteration in her uncle from deal-maker to saint. He had even taken his formerly outcast son Vish into his business. King Midas. He had turned his own heart to gold.

She couldn't help hearing his complaints as she tried to get through. She thought he sounded like James Earl Jones. You couldn't imagine that a voice like that was produced in a man like that. He was explaining his situation to a group of listeners.

—Somebody had to be the scapegoat before the World Cup. I even look like a scapegoat.

—It doesn't excuse it.

—At least they brought me out of jail, my dears, once the real submarines began to arrive and gave people something to believe in. Why would I invent a submarine? Sometimes I believe this country is more divided today than it was twenty years ago. Back then at least we had our hopes for the future. Did you see the Old Man on television? I hear he looks very frail in person.

Sherman had parked just inside the gate at the end of the driveway. His GTI, equipped with gold hubcaps and a tinted windshield, was slouching low, black as a packet of John Player Specials. It was, as she had told Amrita, conspicuous among the Benzes and Logan's dual-steering Honda.

The driver slouched as low as his Golf. She called to him to come inside but instead he waited. He was wearing a pair of long trousers and a dinner jacket over his T-shirt.

There was something romantic approaching a supernaturally good-looking man along a straight driveway panelled by lamps. The stars were flying over the mountain. Shanti could feel the evening on her legs. She had changed into a moderately short dress.

Sherman sat on the hood of his car and admired her. She admired him back.

—How old did you say you were again?

—I never told you. You didn't tell me your age either.

—It's more romantic, chicken. Where's your boyfriend?

—Joris is not my boyfriend. I broke up with him anyway. Come inside. I will introduce you to my family.

They went through the rockery where Ursula had turned on the floodlights. In their blue gaze the water tumbled over the stone parapet and into a maze of pebbles and plants. You could hear the music loud from the house. Shanti looked through the window into the lounge and saw her mother dancing on the carpet. Ursula must be drunk. She had her arms above her head and her blouse was singing with sequins. She patted hands with Parveen now and again.

—I'm glad you're such a believer in romance, Sherman. You can do me a favour. Don't take anybody's telephone.

—Someday you are going to be an amazing woman. Meantime I am prepared to babysit. I am prepared to be your man.

—You don't want to be exposed as a cradle robber. Everybody says I am very mature. That's my father there. He wants to be the best friend of every boy who likes me.

However, it was difficult to introduce Sherman to anybody, as if, at this instant, her family and her family's friends were too wrapped up in each other to acknowledge an outsider. She had brought them a present and they were refusing to accept it. Her father was involved in a complicated conversation with Uncle Ashok concerning the details of his legal case.

—Who is that man there, chicken? It can't be the person I think it is.

—That's my Uncle Ashok. Actually he is my dad's uncle.

—I have never seen anybody from the newspapers in real life. I would like to shake the hands of your uncle.

—I'm sure he'll be happy to talk.

There was wild speculation in the newspapers about the sale of German submarines to the navy, including bribes and secret transfers which implicated her uncle. But it was more accurate to say that Ashok had been implicated by a faction of the ruling party, playing pawn for pawn. He had been convicted and spent three months behind bars, confined to the sick bay, before his supporters had taken control of the government and secured his release on compassionate grounds. Uncle Ashok had become famous for his spaghetti-and-red-wine dinners in expensive restaurants on Sea Point promenade. The rich were on display in the windows of these restaurants, prosperous and permanent.

Uncle Ashok was the first to welcome Sherman. You had the sense that he was also on the lookout for new friends. Shanti was alarmed by how much he liked it. He was greedy for people.

—It's a pleasure to meet a gentleman. When you take such good care of my niece like this, then, Joris, you are also a friend of mine.

—My name is Sherman.

—You're Sherman, of course. What I was saying is that no matter how much we praise Bafana, the real winners of today are the people who built the stadiums and the airports. The real victory is already written into the contracts.

There was laughter in the other room where her mother was dancing among a group of women. After another

358

minute Logan went outside, as if he had heard enough. Shanti was dissatisfied. She looked around at the women in nice outfits and necklaces and rhinestone belts. There was black meat piled on platters on the long table in the dining room, candles on rubber boats in the swimming pool. Suddenly it revolted her taste. She wanted to buy nothing in her life, to become vegetarian and subsist on salads, to go out of the security gate, find the unfriendly poor, and let them pick the skin off her bones. She wanted to cross over to the other side, the side of Joris and Sherman, the side of Yolanda who cleaned their house and of Amrita who could do no harm. From this other side she would see the obvious wrongness of life inside the gate, jeer back at it, and be awakened into some new consciousness. Money, like life, like oxygen, corrupted you. It didn't know what counted.

She wanted to explain to someone. Sherman, on the other hand, wanted to keep talking to Uncle Ashok. Joris would have understood or said that he did and then said something to put her down. She went to the sliding door in front of the pool. Uncle Logan was sympathetic, but he was also stuck with Amrita, who was sitting with one foot in the water and telling him about the music she had been listening to in Shanti's room. Amrita gabbled to her father when she was excited. Father and daughter fitted together like two halves of a circle.

Uncle Logan had the bearing of a soldier, his hair trimmed to the scalp. There was a curious comparison between his very white hair and dark complexion. He was familiar to Shanti as a member of the family, not to say the father of the phenomenon Amrita, and yet they had never had more than a two-minute conversation. Shanti admired how self-contained Logan was. He had enough to interest him in his daughter and didn't need to show off.

While she watched them, Logan started to dance on the tiles. After a minute he took Amrita and showed her where to move her bare feet, teaching her very seriously and moving nimbly himself. He looked like somebody who knew how to dance. You took a look at Amrita, laughing her head off as she practised her steps, and saw that Logan knew how to bring joy out of his daughter. He played her into happiness just as confidently as the soloist played the violin.

There were certain incidental facts she needed to know to be able to write her memoirs. She turned on the lights in the pool, took the vuvuzela from behind the door, and went to join the pair outside. The pool sang in the middle of the lawn, an eerie blue jewel flickering in the evening beneath the mountain. In the blue light you could see where flowers had been kindled in the grass. The day had been dry but it was suddenly damp with cloud that had been flowing down from the heights. She felt the moisture in her shoes.

Shanti shivered and wondered if she should get a shawl. Amrita and Logan, however, had found her already and danced around her. Logan put out his hand and made Shanti spin once and again so that she was dizzy. The stars spun in their own circle. She broke away from her partners and sat in one of the canvas chairs by the pool. It was too cold to swim.

Amrita and her father continued to dance for another five minutes, beside themselves with glee, while Shanti watched the house for any sign of intelligent life. Her mother was standing on the balcony on the near side of the house, tracing a run in her stocking with her fingernail. Shanti made no sign that she had seen Ursula. She didn't understand how she could have been put into this family. Her father was the only individual she had something in common with.

After a while Amrita went inside and Logan sat in the chair next to her. He stretched his legs out.

—Did you have a good time at the party, Shanti?

—I invited Sherman and he came.

—In fact I enjoyed listening to your friend Sherman interacting with your uncle. He has some interesting perspectives. And did you see? He made an instant connection with Ashok. In fact Ashok needs the company of men. He used to have your father but now your father has the business to watch. Of course he has made up with Vish, after the boy almost died in his arms, but one son cannot be the whole of his life. I advise you to talk more to Vish, by the way, if you get the opportunity. He has been through more than most of us.

—So have you, Uncle Logan.

—I was never an uncle. Plain Logan to everybody. Even as a teacher I was known as Mr Logan, never by my last name. Today it is Logan the driving instructor. No change.

—You haven't changed at all?

Logan sat up. For some reason he was gripped by her question. She thought he would be a great teacher. He should be at her school.

—You know, Shanti, if I ask myself, have I been through much in the years between Mr Logan and Logan, including the accident with Amrita's mother, my answer is no. As far as I can tell I am completely unscathed. My experience has taught me nothing. I am the same as before it started. Is this philosophy too heavy for you?

—Not at all.

Two women came out of the house. They were wearing silver dresses to their knees and shoes laced up their legs.

One of them produced a packet of cigarettes. They lit up and continued to talk, the very thin cigarettes displayed in their hands. They didn't seem to notice anybody else. Logan hesitated when they appeared and then continued.

—Amrita and I have a tendency to be cooped up together. Then when I get the opportunity, I talk my head off to the first person who sits down. Yesterday you were just a child, Shanti. Today you have a different kind of confidence. I can see it. The first time I noticed was when you told Amrita that you were going to write your memoirs. She came back and asked me what they were. I told her it would be a book about you, the sum of your thoughts and feelings and impressions.

—I haven't started yet.

—I had a good laugh about that. But you must write it. Even if you have one day of adulthood to talk about.

Where would Shanti begin? It had been her own version of M Day. She had been kissed, or almost kissed, by two men. She had seen Nelson Mandela on television and something had begun to move in her. She had lost a telephone and bought it back and said goodbye to Joris and still planned to get even with her mother. But if she had to choose her own beginning it would be with Logan and Amrita.

Although Logan had paused as if he was about to say something else, he went to the side of the pool instead and, taking the net, dragged the surface for leaves and twigs, which he then tipped out onto the grass. The surface of the pool was soon spotless. When Logan had finished cleaning he looked in his jacket and then in his pockets. He looked worried.

—I had my telephone on me. I brought it with in case the gate wasn't working. And for the life of me I can't find it now. I may have put it on the table as you come in, but then somebody must have moved it.

—I know just how to fix your problem, Uncle Logan. Give me ten minutes.

—It's a cheap phone. Don't go to any trouble.

—It's no trouble at all.

Shanti went inside and found Sherman. The top of his shirt was unbuttoned. He and Ashok, Vish and her father were trimming cigars in the lounge. The box lay between them on the table. It had the name of a Cuban firm on the top. She called Sherman from his chair.

—Can I have a word?

—Sure.

—Let's go to my room.

Sherman smiled. It shone at you like the sunshine catching the gold tooth in his mouth.

—I was only waiting for you to ask, chicken.

Shanti pulled him up the stairs. He came more enthusiastically than she liked. Amrita had left the lights on in her room. One of her mother's Neil Diamond CDs had found its way into her stereo and was playing on endless loop, the music of office buildings and telephone answering systems. That was just her luck. She would record it in her memoirs as the day she gave up on romance. She didn't even have the consolation of living in a tragedy. The soundtrack to her life would be Neil Diamond.

—Is there something you want to tell me?

—There certainly is.

Sherman hesitated. He was smiling at her more brightly than Joris had ever done. He put his hand on her side. She saw the stars inside her room.

—I wanted to tell you that I am prepared to be your man.

—I meant, did you take my Uncle Logan's telephone?

—Yes, I did, chicken. I confess. But only to prove that I had the talent. It's waiting for him downstairs on the kitchen table.

—Am I going to find out that you took anything else?

—Nothing except your heart. Or do I have that already?

1976

THE POOL

The Olympic pool, at Howard College, dense with chlorine. Each time you turned your head to breathe you got the fresh sting of it in your lungs. Six in the morning.

On the next lap the attendant, a black man in a groundsman's uniform, asked you to wait while he laid out the blue-beaded ropes to make the lanes. Neil clung to the tiles on the deep end as the man settled all the dividers. The wind was sharp, raking him on the back, raising a spray around the big wooden beads. The attendant finished tying the ropes along the side of the pool. Neil went back in, counting out the laps, and liking the pressure of his thin strong legs on the water. It was the right time for the pool. In the afternoon it would be as warm as piss.

He had a second wind and swam freestyle in the still cool water for five laps until he was out of breath. Then he switched to breaststroke, coming out of the water at each stroke, and noticed that the students were filtering in. One stood on the high diving board, testing the spring before sliding efficiently from five metres to the bottom. Others were emerging from the changing huts in their costumes, several men and a woman in a one-piece outfit cut square on the thigh.

Neil had been coming to the pool for three months, the first regular exercise he had taken since cross country in high school. It was on doctor's orders. He had reduced his smoking to a packet a day. He was trying to gain weight by eating bags of peanuts.

Swimming in the morning, winter and summer alike, provided the most benefit for his health inside and out. He had an exemption from the conditions of his house arrest to use the athletic facilities at the university. Nadia was back in their double bed, her new gold-rimmed lady's spectacles folded into their case on the bedside table.

In the pool Neil didn't worry about Logan, the young teacher who had disappeared, nor about the money that had been transferred into his account to pay for the legal troubles of the Free University, courtesy of an unknown source in the United Kingdom. He forgot that the police could turn up at the door, any hour of the day or night, and arrest him and Nadia for transgressing the Mixed Marriages Act. Indeed he was free from any disturbance as he followed the lane and dreamed in the blue light. Neil dreamed of paradise. He had completed a short book outlining his conclusions about the ideal society. It couldn't be published until the banning order expired. But it was done.

In an ideal society: there would be no separation of types. No groundsman. No permanent professor. No student who wasn't at the same time a teacher and a researcher and a manual labourer, someone who worked with his hands and his heart. Spellings would be standard. Quantities would be decimal. In an ideal society: there would be no form of currency, frozen or stolen labour standing over succeeding generations, no inheritance, salaries, or dividends. There would be no form of competition. Every man and woman free to find a place in the sun.

Neil rinsed himself under the outdoor tap, opening the front of his costume an inch to wash off the chemicals. Thirty laps in total. The exercise produced a pleasant electricity in his legs. He didn't want to go home and deal with Nadia. The water in the pool sparkled in the arriving sun. It was furrowed in places by wind. He spread the towel out and sat on top of the concrete wall surrounding the pool area.

Paradise was at the pool. The grasshoppers had assembled, sparking here and there from the lawn as if to avoid some invisible hand. One of them settled on a corner of the towel, sharp red eyes as downcast as a Japanese maiden. It combed the material, bracing the armoured torpedo of its body behind it, and then sprang to the damp blue tiles along the side.

It was already becoming hot, the sky shining white and stern across to the harbour. Neil liked the temperature and humidity. He loved the climate and yearned for it when he was away from Durban. It made certain philosophies impossible to maintain, after all. Sartre and de Beauvoir, Claude Lévi-Strauss, and others from the Sorbonne wrote about the tropics, investigated their sad condition, proclaimed on their behalf, classified and determined the varieties of tropical consciousness. Yet they never could have prospered, burned through so many cigarettes and composed their endless volumes at one hundred per cent humidity. The hot form of life, the existence inside the body, precluded the other form.

In the sunshine Neil was jealous of his freedom. He swam by permission of the magistrate who had agreed to comply with a doctor's note. He went to work by permission. He was allowed to live by permission. In the ideal world he would be in Soweto. Sixteen-year-old boys and girls were marching against Bantu Education, boycotting their schools. They had murdered police dogs and had been shot from armoured cars. He should be marching with them. In his ideal world he would drive from the pool to a tan-brick building in Glenwood, five minutes from the Japanese Gardens, ring the bell, and be admitted to Ann's house. He would be relieved at the sight of her face. It was as dear to him, in the blank white sunshine, as his own hand.

The next young man who rose onto the ladder at the deep end recognised Neil and waved to him. The young man climbed out, found his possessions, and dried himself vigorously at the side of the pool. He used such fierce strokes he might have been trying to start a motor, his big bare shoulders flaking rooster-red from sunburn. Once he had wrapped himself in a towel, he came up to Neil, walking carefully, and shook his hand.

—Sir, I was in your Politics lecture this year. My name is Russell. I used to sit in the second row from the front.

—Good to meet you.

The young man's head was shaped like a box, yellow hair barbered flat on the top so that he had the look of a cartoon character. He seemed nervous. It should be the other way round, Neil thought. In 1976, the young held all the cards. To be over thirty was to undergo planned obsolescence.

—I tried to ask you a question once. About the fact that we are dealing with different levels of civilisation in the same country.

—Then I disagree with your premise. I don't believe the level of civilisation varies from person to person. What do kindness, generosity, justice have to do with the colour of your skin? And we have a responsibility to turn the question around and ask about the concept. The most civilised continent, Europe, has also caused the greatest amount of suffering, in terms of unnecessary death and destruction, in the past two centuries. So what is the upshot of that civilisation?

The young man tightened the towel at his waist. Neil wondered what was meant to be going on between them. He wasn't good with people. He knew that some game was going on, with this person or the other person, but he couldn't see where life ended and the board began. He couldn't see how to satisfy the other person.

—Dr Hunter, in class you talked about inventing a system to make English spelling more natural. Are you still working on that?

—Nothing so interesting right now. I'm trying to track down a man, a certain Logan Naicker, a trainee teacher. He happens to be a bodybuilder, and a Black Consciousness advocate, a huge influence on his students. The last time he was seen he was in the company of two policemen outside his mother's house. If we can find him in time we have a chance of saving his life.

—Yes, Sir.

—Not that I should be talking about this, given my own circumstances. The trouble is, under the new regulations, the police don't have to acknowledge their possession of the individual. They can make you disappear without a trace.

—Yes, Sir. Thank you, Sir. I also had a question about the material to expect on the exam. Do we have to study everything? Can we cover just the material for two out of the four questions?

On the way to the tennis-court parking, where he had

left the car, Neil decided he had mishandled the encounter with Russell. He had lived up to his own reputation for strangeness, for disturbing words and setting them against each other, for refusing to accept friendship, for turning on the conventions that made it possible to co-exist. On the one hand there was the sunshine world. This was the lawful domain, brilliant by the pool, predictable to the millimetre and millisecond by means of the scientific calculator and the quartz-crystal watch. In sunshine you could calculate your efforts to the last decimal. In sunshine the world was capable of measurement.

Then there was the twilight zone, like the television programme. The twilight descended in Durban and a trainee teacher like Logan vanished in a convertible Valiant. False accusations ruined Archie Msimang's existence and put him on the run from his former comrades until his accuser, Padayachee, had been revealed as a Security Branch plant. The forces in the twilight zone buried your illegal books, made informers of your friends, stole exam questions from the locked cabinet in the department office, burned the labourers' cottages your mother had borrowed money to build. These two domains sat side by side, so close the transition was seamless and instant, up and down the country. They required different schemes of measurement. He had disturbed his student by bringing the two together.

In Athens, Socrates had been murdered in the sunshine on account of his strangeness, for corrupting the youth and teaching them in the open air, for disrespecting the gods, for refusing to let words circulate, hand to hand, like obols. But, in the twilight zone, you could be executed out of the public eye, as he feared for Logan, and nobody would ever hear of you again.

—

When he got back to the house his son Paul was already at the gate. He had come to borrow Neil's car for the long weekend. He was driving down the two hours to Southbroom with his British girlfriend, Margot, planning to stay in a friend's beach house for four nights. He was already wearing flip-flops and beach shorts.

—You should have rung the bell, man. Nadia must be up and about.

—I like being outside. I can't soak up enough sunshine after the American winter. How was the pool?

—The water was perfect. You don't know where your body ends and the world begins. Why don't we go around the back?

They went through the garden. The bushes were bright with red and yellow flowers, lit by sudden butterflies, attended by convoys of bees moving heavily through the air. It struck Neil, out of nowhere, that it would be a shame to die. He should redouble his efforts for Logan. He could rescue the young man, hardly older than his son, if he found him in time.

—The place looks good. I don't remember it being in such good shape.

—I won't lie. Since the banning order came down, I have spent the bulk of my life out here. I never knew you could get such satisfaction out of a garden before. Nadia has, what do you say, green thumbs. Her grandfather, in fact, was a market gardener and has a lot to say about keeping plants. How is your mother?

—I can't tell. She seems fine. I used to worry about her a lot when I was overseas. She hasn't changed visibly from last time, two years ago. She gets on with Margot. They're both very matter-of-fact.

They stood there, unwilling to leave the sunshine and go inside. They wanted to breathe in more of the day. The window was open, and the radio on the kitchen table was playing Radio Port Natal. The announcer was a woman. She spoke in a clipped British accent, as if she were wearing a corset and a chastity belt. The British didn't repent.

—Both your parents strike me that way. Last time I heard about your father, Paul, he was the same as ever, travelling around the province to operate on his patients, and, if I understood correctly, learning to fly an aeroplane. So you don't have to worry about them. Your father is indestructible.

—It's difficult to tell from a trunk call. He's coming down to Southbroom. In fact he's flying down in his aeroplane.

—And do you have anything to say about Margot? Is there anything I need to know about?

—It's complicated, Neil. I fully expect to be uncomfortable if I follow my heart, if I study what I want to study, and try things I am not guaranteed to be good at. It's what I learned from you and Ann and my dad. That's how you can be fully alive, if you accept the risks. Margot's family are the opposite. They can't imagine leaving the United Kingdom. Her father just bought an expensive Mercedes that comes with air-conditioning. Her family are used to the environment always being at the same temperature. But then you miss out on a day like today.

Neil laughed. He didn't mind his stepson's idle chatter. It didn't obscure the content of life but brought it closer into view. He had already found Paul entertaining as a teenager when he managed to take the rules of his private school as seriously as religion. Paul had never found out about the details concerning Edward Lavigne. They had sent him to a boarding school in the United Kingdom. Paul, his red hair long over his ears, sounded more English than anything else. It was odd that someone so earnest would want to appear on the stage.

There was a warning he had neglected to give.

—You shouldn't make a definite plan to come back, Paul. Your mother asked me to tell you that, but I believe it for you as well. We have to be realists about the speed of change. At the best, what we will have here in ten years' time is an average African state. You cannot rely on this type of history. It may not be kind to someone like you, someone as sensitive as you.

—You've always said the opposite when it comes to yourself. You wanted to belong to something outside yourself. You wanted to count.

—Each person is a special case. I am merely suggesting you wait until you are in a position to make up your mind. In the meantime you can answer Nadia's questions. She's curious about Margot.

Nadia, in the kitchen, was resplendent in her cream silk dressing gown. She stayed in her chair, her legs crossed, when they sat on the far side of the table, and turned the radio low. Her long brown hair was tied at the back with a piece of elastic. Neil thought she had never looked more beautiful than at twenty-seven, her bearing and the bones in her face taking on the seriousness of a woman. She was pleased to see Paul and soon, as he predicted, was asking questions about Margot and laughing. She was even more beautiful when she was happy, her face shimmering to equal her dressing gown.

The reunion brought certain facts nearer to the surface. Since Neil had converted to Islam to marry Nadia in a brief ceremony, they had been more separate than before. Nadia, he believed, had made the greater mistake. She had married him and discovered that he was as true to himself as she was to herself. He had only himself to rely on when he made up his life. There was no valid public opinion in the country to which he might conform.

—Neil, by the way, I thought you could help me with the route. Do you have a map of the province to lend us?

—There's one in the cubbyhole of Nadia's car. I'll fetch it and bring you the licence disc and the certificate from the AA in case there's any trouble with the engine. I already called the weather service, the new one with the automatic announcements, and apparently you are in for good conditions.

Neil brought back the documents and a chamois cloth. He gave them to Paul. They planned a route together, placing dots on the spread-out map with a red ballpoint, while Nadia went to change. To be safe Neil wrote the directions down on a note card.

—From Port Shepstone, as you can see, it's a straight shot to the hotel. Are you in a hurry?

—I'm keen to be there. Margot's nervous about driving in the countryside. She doesn't like the idea of being in danger on holiday.

—I haven't heard of any trouble in the Natal schools. In any case, considering the role of the Zulu kingdom, this province has always had its own peculiar course.

—I'll tell Margot history is on our side.

—I wouldn't go so far as that.

They went outside to the car. Neil went over some of the finer points of its constitution. British engineering. You shouldn't flood the engine with the accelerator pedal if you wanted it to start again. The gearbox had a tendency to get stuck in third. The spare tyre, underneath a panel in the boot, had to be released with a wrench that was taped to the underside of the hood.

Neil waited until Paul turned the car on and off twice, showing that he understood the intricacies of the process, and then stood on the corner as the vehicle disappeared over the hill. He saw that the movers had cleared Mackenzie's house. The doors and gate were padlocked. The man had been his neighbour for a decade of thick and thin and yet they had never exchanged a word. Ann had gone to the funeral.

The pleasure he took from Paul's presence insinuated a note of dissatisfaction into today's dealings with Nadia. Her hair was sprayed in place. She suddenly looked like a young woman trying to be middle-aged.

—You think we'll meet Margot, Neil?

—Paul has been cagey about the whole thing. I'm afraid he's finally becoming an actor.

—Are you going to track down that teacher today?

—I still have some calls to make. We'll see.

When Nadia was ready to leave, she found him again in his study. He was sorting through the notes he had taken about Logan's disappearance. She was carrying the small suitcase she took to do readings. Inside were three decks of Tarot cards, healing stones, and charts and tables holding astrological data. Since their wedding Nadia had found an alternative path in occult pamphlets and Tarot cards, books which detailed extraterrestrial invasions and forgotten gods.

Neil stood up and put his arms around his wife. He wouldn't leave her. Their existence as a couple was a criticism of National Party doctrine. Her square cheekbones, her bright red-brown hair and eyes and skin, even her religion, which had come to him as a dowry, had travelled from the Indonesian islands on slave ships. He was whatever the Hunters had become. Maybe they were not a natural fit. There was, however, a certain way they fell in with each other when they were alone. They were accomplices in crime.

Nadia disengaged herself. When she got to the staircase she turned back.

—I could do a reading on you.

—I think I know my fortune for this afternoon. If by the time you come back you could have figured out the location of Logan Naicker, it would be much more useful than to know my own fortune.

—I'll see you, Neil.

He went back to Logan's case. The teacher in training had discovered Black Consciousness, the beauty of black and brown skin, and the supposed origins of science and mathematics in Benin and Egypt. Someone like Logan would never have the privilege, like Neil, of developing his own ideas at the Sorbonne. Instead he had made a mind for himself from second-hand photocopies and pamphlets and gone on from there. The trouble-causer and stirrer Logan.

It was a familiar type. It inspired the Security Branch's most rigorous efforts at suppression. According to the law, they didn't have to confirm or deny the name of a person in detention. It was difficult to get information out. However, Neil had a number to call, courtesy of Chunu the vegetarian. Chunu's distant cousin worked as a police clerk in the same enormous barred brown-brick building, a fact he didn't advertise to the world. According to what Chunu had told Neil, his cousin was interested in making connections on the other side, keen to protect his own future whatever happened in the country. Chunu had written down the number on the back of a religious calendar.

When Neil dialled, a confident young girl picked up. She was very formal, although she couldn't have been more than eight or nine to judge by her voice.

—Hello. Whom may I say is calling?

—I wanted to talk to your father. Could you put him on, my dear?

Someone in the background was reminding the girl to speak proper English. By the sound of her voice, Neil imagined she had pigtails.

—One minute. I will see if he is available.

Neil heard an exchange in the background. The girl was dispatched to turn off the radio. Her father came on the line.

—This is Neil. Chunu gave me your number. He told me I could call at this time.

—I don't know your name. What's your name again?

—It's Neil Hunter. From the university.

—I'm sorry. I can't help you. Please don't call again.

Neil tried Chunu's number without success. The vegetarian would most likely be at the beach, enjoying one of his elaborate picnics with his elaborate family. Neil realised that his legs were sore from swimming and went out to stretch them.

His dissatisfaction lingered in Paul's absence. The country placed him in the wrong. The Sunday papers reported, several times a month, on some mixed couple surprised in a hotel room by the police. Usually it was some hotel by the beach, the Blue Waters or the Elangeni, where you could

379

look out on the ocean and the splendours of Mini Town. One or both, man and woman, avoided the shame of the charge by plummeting out of the high windows into the sunshine. No matter how much you knew you were right, the police eventually made you wrong in your own mind.

In 1976, on January 5th, television began in South Africa with the broadcast of a circular test pattern and a computer clock. The African National Congress started to build training camps in Angola. In the same year, the French nuclear agency sold two reactors to the government, opening the way for the National Party to build atomic bombs, an insurance policy against a revolutionary takeover.

On June 16th, 1976, ten thousand schoolchildren walked to Orlando Stadium in Soweto. They demanded to be taught in English. Police dogs were unleashed, only to be stoned to death. Bantu Administration Board buildings, bottle stores, beer halls, and cars on the street were burned. The police fired volleys into the protestors' ranks. Hector Pieterson, thirteen years old, was photographed dying in an older boy's arms. The family name was originally Pitso but had been changed in the hope of the family passing as coloured. Later that day Dr Melville Edelstein, who ran workshops for the disabled, was stoned to death by the children and left with a sign around his neck.

On a Thursday afternoon in 1976, while Nadia was reading the fortunes of her acquaintances at a tea party in Glen Ashley and Paul was on the highway to Port Shepstone with his girlfriend in order to ask her to marry him, Dean Percival Lavigne came to Neil's door.

The dean was wearing a cravat, a linen jacket, and one of his many pairs of rectangular steel spectacles. Underneath them he was as fresh-faced as a spring lamb. His blue eyes were vast. Neil had never known a man before to own more than a single pair of glasses.

—Well, I am sure you're surprised to see me, Dr Hunter.

—I couldn't be more astonished, Percy.

—Indeed. That is often the effect. It is only one of my stratagems. When there is an outstanding problem to be fixed, and if an informal conversation will do the trick, I resort to an impromptu visit. When something really and truly counts, then you have to do it in person. In a great city like London, of course, it would be impossible. But in Durban I can get a fair quantity of business done simply by motoring along Ridge Road. Not to put too fine a point on it, knowing you are under house arrest, I also know how to find you.

—We can go through to the lounge.

The visitor took an interest in the house. He stopped to run his hand down the side of a Benin statuette, an elongated woman executed in green soapstone. Near the statue, high on the wall, was a framed photograph of Neil and Nadia, taken during their honeymoon in Seychelles. They were standing half out of an ocean that was like a dream, a seascape of silk-blue water. If you looked closely, you would see neither one of them was wearing a costume. The most advanced people were nudists.

—Is your wife here?

—She has an engagement.

—I would have liked to meet her at last. I hear she's beautiful. She was your student apparently?

—She translated a number of articles from French for me. She still does. Despite the years I spent over there my languages have never been good enough.

In the lounge Percy Lavigne didn't sit down. He roamed

around the room instead, keeping his hands together behind his back. Neil sat at the table.

—So, Dr Hunter. Your day of reckoning has come. For making a mockery out of my brother. I was made aware of that incident, you know, and your letter to the board of Curzon College. You may not have been informed that Edward parted ways with the school not long after that particular episode.

—I didn't know until you just told me. After we had to take Paul out, we didn't keep up the connection with the school.

—Edward is like a cat, nevertheless. He lands on his feet. I mention it for curiosity's sake. At present, he assists the chairman of the Anglo-American Corporation with scenario planning. They map out various alternatives for the country's future, the low road and the high road, and exert their influence for the high road. Thanks to business, a lot happens behind the scenes in this country.

—I agree with you there.

The dean stopped and unclasped his hands. He didn't like to be interrupted. In court he had testified for a fee about the treasonous leanings of people charged with being communists and was famous for his three-hour perorations on the evils of a socialised economy. Neil thought it was an advantage to have dispensed with shame.

—Business wants to know how to shape its future environment even when we are long dead. My brother Edward bears the crystal ball. He has always cared about the future of civilisation.

—How can I help you, Professor?

—I won't sit. I simply want to hear what's in store for us, Dr Hunter.

—What do you mean?

—Let the two of us look into a crystal ball. I have kept you on despite the conditions of your house arrest, so far, but what more can I expect in the coming year? When will I see an article fit to print in a journal? Will you try to restart your extramural education course? What do you call it, the Free University? Will there be another ruckus in the courts?

—It's not intended to interfere with anything else. It has nothing to do with Howard College.

—Speaking frankly, I cannot understand the logic. We ignore the project of world communism at our peril. Change will come in this country at its own deliberate speed, when we have educated the bulk of the population. To make that possible, I must protect the faculty from certain unwelcome associations. This has nothing to do with any domestic arrangements you choose to make. That, and whatever religion you follow or do not follow, I must leave up to your own discretion.

You weren't angry with Percy Lavigne on account of his speech. Instead, you burned with shame. You hated to resemble him. You thought you would blush in his face from white shame. You hated to speak the same language as him, to use the same corrupted syllables that came out of his mouth, to stand in the same sunshine when you went out of the house. And yet, as you could hear, a man like Percival Lavigne had his own reasons. He had his own fine web of reasons. In this web he had caught the entirety of life so that he could sting it and paralyse it. He too was working to make his own perfect world.

In the midst of your shame you wanted to explain to Lavigne and his brother that Nadia was the centre of your sinful arrangements. Even when you were dissatisfied with her, her body had no part in common with the sad and freckled human organism, the soiled and polluted, sagging and superfluous, over-used body inhabited, in fact, by you and every other woman besides Nadia. There was something perfect in the blankness of your wife's body. And only the sacrifice of Nadia would satisfy the dean.

—What do you want me to do?

—Since you ask, Dr Hunter, I will tell you. I want proper academic work. No more of these pamphlets on the dream of an ideal society. Drop this circus in the courts and work through the system.

—I don't mean it to be a circus. It just works out like that.

The dean clipped an ivory tip to his cigarette and lit it. It produced almost no smoke.

—Look, nobody doubts the sincerity of your passion for change. I have a proposal before the senate to admit a select group of students, well-prepared Bantus and Indians, and to educate them, in good separate facilities, to the same level as the European. You can help me. Failing that, I can recommend Australia as a suitable berth. There, politics is harmless. In Sydney you can find many of the same benefits that our lifestyle affords us here.

The first thing that came to Neil, when Percy Lavigne made his exit, was that the house had never held together without Ann's attention. She had known the sections under the stairs where the African ants took up residence and commenced their patrols across the property. She had learned to fumigate their nests, call in plumbers and electricians, and supervise the work of the boiler-maker. Neil had bought the place with money borrowed from his mother and so, given the financial arrangements, it stayed in his possession after the divorce. He often regretted it. At a party for Paul's graduation, when they last conversed in person, Ann had just had a tooth removed. Her cheek was swollen and yet he had felt a subterranean attraction to her flood his soul.

At the other side of the house the telephone rang. It rang and rang while Neil left it alone, unwilling to leave his notes on the Logan case, which, for some reason, wouldn't resolve into sentences before his eyes. The ringing stopped and then resumed. He went to get it.

—This is the professor I am talking to. Is that correct?

—If you want to split hairs, I'm only a senior lecturer.

Neil didn't immediately recognise the voice. He had the nagging sense that it had been familiar to him in another life. The caller was an older man without a clear accent. He could have been Australian or Irish, a Rhodesian or someone from a part of South West Africa. Over the scratchy telephone line there was no way to pin it down.

—Professor, I have some very bad news for you.

—You can't talk on this line.

—It doesn't matter who overhears. The time for that is past. They can prove you have been receiving payments from overseas. That is enough to convict. They can do more than convict.

—The most I did was arrange to look into certain cases.

—The facts according to you make no difference. After Soweto they are taking no chances. They don't want you trying to track down who is in prison and who is out of prison, always trying to find a way around the rules. You have to skip the country now. You can cross at the border post into Swaziland by tomorrow. I will meet you.

—I can't leave the country on the basis of an anonymous call.

—The time for questions is over, Professor. You can ask all the questions you want in Swaziland. Pack your bags.

The man hung up. Neil stood there with the dead tone. He couldn't imagine complying with his new instructions. He had taken people to the train station and bus station on occasions when having a white driver meant the difference between a successful escape, on the one hand, and being forced to produce one's pass and disappearing into detention, on the other. You bought the ticket and watched as the man or woman entered the line and went back to the department office, where you talked lightly to the secretary and looked through the airmail editions of the British and French newspapers and academic journals, uncertain of the stability of the daytime world. You remembered the scenes in classical poems where someone went down to the underworld, conversed with the people condemned there, and then returned to the surface.

The call could be a Special Branch trick. It wasn't unprecedented when they wanted to remove you from the scene. They might shoot you at the border post. They could discredit you in the newspapers. You had so many projects coming to fruition. Were you simply meant to cancel them and vanish with Nadia, head straight for the border, and hide by the side of the road when you saw a roadblock?

Nadia wasn't prepared to go. The two of you had a life to uphold. Yet you had no patience with people who wanted to be martyrs. You wished you had a number to call back.

Instead you found yourself dialling Ann's number. She would have good advice.

—It's Neil.

—Is there something with Paul?

—I just saw him. He took the Jaguar, which seemed to be in working condition for a change. I'll say this. Paul looks happy. I don't want to jinx him, as far as his happiness is concerned, but he does look jubilant.

—It's Margot. It's a chance for him to get away from the two of us. We can't be the simplest parents in the world. And Gert, of course, although he has never been close to Gert.

—No.

—But we aren't the worst either. Paul will be fine. And in many respects he is a happy young man. I would just like to know someone is there to look after him. So I am not opposed to Margot.

—I'm glad to hear it. It might be unwise to oppose his decisions.

—What's the reason for you calling, Neil? You haven't been in touch. I wondered what you would have to say about some of the recent events. It's still quiet here. The Transvaal seems like a world away.

—I wouldn't be surprised if we're coming to the end, Ann. I wouldn't be surprised if we are finally going to see a resolution before the end of the year. Things are heating up. In fact, I've just had one of these odd telephone calls. You remember we used to get them in the middle of the night.

—Did you recognise the voice?

—I've never heard this particular man before. There was something foreign about it, something I couldn't place. He told me to drop everything and leave today. I don't know how seriously to take it.

—Neil, that's extremely bad news. Is there anyone there to watch you? Can you come here?

—Nadia's out doing a reading. Paul has the other car of course. I should be fine. I'll lock the windows.

—I'm coming over right now, Neil. I'll drop you at one of your friends. You know what I'll do? I'll take you to Chunu's house. They won't think to look in an Indian area.

—I don't know if Chunu is prepared for an invasion. But I wouldn't mind seeing your face.

—Chunu would be honoured. He has always wanted to be your best friend. Neil, go and lock the door now.

You looked through the books. Which had to go with you? Which could be left behind? You had to destroy the telephone book. If you fled it was vital not to implicate anybody. You would remember to cross out Chunu's name in the volumes of dietary advice he had given you. You would retrieve each hidden book and destroy it in the same way the police burned books at the central depository. You couldn't predict what might be used as evidence under the Suppression of Communism Act.

The country was unhappy. It was corrupted in sunshine. You had summarised your thoughts about it in a book. But what was the worth of this book? Nobody could say. It was nothing more than a long pamphlet among ten million such productions. History had its own secret police who worked by the far more effective method of neglect.

In that faraway time you heard a car draw up on the road. The passenger doors closed, one and then the other. It happened a dozen times in a day on your cul-de-sac, but this silence was different and more perfect. The steps of two men moved along the driveway and towards the house. They moved confidently. You went to the half-door and before you closed the top you saw nothing but the endless beauty of the garden and the early stars. There was no mystery in the stars.

You came back inside quickly, remembering you were supposed to stay away from the window, when you saw a man warning you about the gun in his hand. He was making some gesture to you. He was Paul's age, khaki shirt buttoned to the collar, not the man you expected, lither and neater than you imagined. He looked at you as if he loved the thing he had found. The window had already splintered into the stars when you heard a gunshot and became aware of the overwhelming scent of gunpowder in your nose. First you were relieved that he had missed and then you were relieved that he had hit and you were reminding yourself that, in the ideal world, everything would count and nothing would be measured, everybody would be lover and beloved, and the secret to all things, on the sea and the sand, under the earth and over the sky, would be illimitable love.

ACKNOWLEDGEMENTS

Britta Rennkamp, Marina Penalva, Fourie Botha, Nasima Badsha, Trevor Sacks, Masande Ntshanga, Hannah Young, Alison Lowry, Jon Soske, Lynda Gilfillan, Daniel Herwitz, Rebecca Servadio, Gioia Guerzoni, Percy Zvomuya, William Dicey, Hoosen Coovadia, Omar Badsha.